THE Runaway EX

SHANI STRUTHERS

OMNIFIC PUBLISHING
LOS ANGELES

Omnific Publishing
1901 Avenue of the Stars, 2nd floor
Los Angeles, CA 90067
www.omnificpublishing.com

First Omnific eBook edition, December 2014
First Omnific trade paperback edition, December 2014

The characters and events in this book are fictitious.
Any similarity to real persons, living or dead,
is coincidental and not intended by the author.

Library of Congress Cataloguing-in-Publication Data

Struthers, Shani.
The Runaway Ex / Shani Struthers – 1st ed.
ISBN: 978-1-623421-45-8
1. England — Romance. 2. Relationships — Fiction.
3. Miscommunication — Romance. 4. Friendship — Fiction. I. Title

10 9 8 7 6 5 4 3 2 1

Cover Design by Micha Stone and Amy Brokaw
Interior Book Design by Coreen Montagna

Printed in the United States of America

*This book is dedicated
to the Runaways themselves—Layla, Joseph, Penny,
Richard, Hannah, and Jim—a great bunch of characters
that remain close to my heart.*

chapter one

"So, that's it, you're just going to walk away? After all we've been through."

"I'm not walking, I'm running—as far as I can get."

"But I thought we had something, something real."

"We did, until you took the 'real' and trampled all over it."

"But…"

"There's no 'but.' There's no anything anymore."

Turning on her heel, Layla Lewis strode across the floor of her studio flat. As she reached the door, intending to hurl herself through it, she burst out laughing. Thank God the angst being played out was purely in the realms of fiction—scenes being "rehearsed" from the book she was writing to check whether or not they worked.

From behind her, she heard a loud harrumph.

"And now you're laughing. I'm in pain here, serious pain, and you're laughing."

She whirled round to face her boyfriend. "Joseph, that's not part of the scene. We're done."

"But it could be," he said, quickly closing the gap between them. "It works."

Layla pushed at him playfully. "I've told you, no more words. She's too busy storming out of his life."

"Because of a misunderstanding?"

"Because of a misunderstanding," she confirmed.

Joseph shook his head ruefully.

"If people talked to each other more, misunderstandings wouldn't happen."

"If people talked to each other, I wouldn't have a book," Layla pointed out. "Besides which, it's not that black and white. Some things aren't."

Joseph looked at her again, a slight frown creasing his features. "I suppose." Eventually he shrugged his shoulders. "Anyway, it's a lucky escape, I reckon."

"For her? I know."

"I meant the poor bloke."

She shoved him a little bit harder.

"I'm joking, I'm joking," he said, holding his hands up in mock supplication. "I just wanted to see you all fired up again. You look bloody sexy when you're fired up."

"Stop it. You've got work to get to, and I've got a laptop to pound."

"Lucky laptop," he said, sighing long and low. "What chapter are you on?"

"Twenty-three. I'm over halfway through now."

"Fame and riches will soon be ours."

"Or a whole stack of rejection letters. It's hard to get a book published nowadays."

"Have faith, Layla. You're good, really good."

"Your trust in me is touching."

"My trust in you is absolute."

"I'm good at other things too, though, aren't I?" She couldn't help it; his close proximity was making her feel coquettish.

"Probably, but I can't think what else right now."

Before she could hit him for a third time, Joseph pulled her close for one last kiss — one last lingering kiss — a vivid reminder of what had transpired that morning.

"I suppose we could practice just a little bit more..." she said upon release.

"The reunion scene?" His voice was just as husky as hers.

"I'm not sure there's going to be a reunion yet."

Joseph reared back. "Whoa! So, it's a serious misunderstanding?"

"As serious as it gets."

Joseph looked almost sad at the prospect, sad and then mischievous. "Well, if I was him, I wouldn't let her go. I'd show her what I was made of."

Before she could even think of arguing further, she was back on the bed, what few clothes she had on rapidly discarded. His lips, his tongue, his hands ran the length and breadth of her body—patiently, impatiently, and then patiently again. What should she do? Reciprocate? Or just lie there, her arms above her head, in a state of wanton abandon? The wanton abandon option appealed—she had taken the lead earlier, pushing him back against the pillows, her inner dominatrix coming to the fore. It was his turn now, or her turn, depending on which way you looked at it. She'd revel instead in his touch, the hands that knew which buttons to press at exactly the right time; there was one button in particular that right now he seemed to be deliberately avoiding.

"Oh, Joseph," she murmured, the impatient one. *Press the damn button!*

"All in good time," he whispered back, reading her mind as well as her body.

So close, too close—she tried to hold off. Concentrated on other things instead—the sound of the city outside. Florence was coming to life around them, heat rising from the pavement as it was rising in her. Hustle and bustle, to and fro, car horns beeping, people yelling to one another, sometimes in greeting, more often in temper. The Italians, they were a passionate lot. Their love and lust for life was ingrained not only in them but also in the buildings that surrounded them, in the air itself. A passion that was all consuming; certainly it had consumed her. Correction, *was* consuming her.

"Ahh…"

But still his hands were nowhere near where she thought they should be. First it was her breasts being caressed, then her buttocks, and then it was featherlight fingers, trailing oh so slowly down to her stomach, lingering at her hip bone, reaching her thigh, her inner thigh. Now was when he'd get down to business. He'd start to move farther inward—she held her breath, feeling like she couldn't breathe at all. He stopped. Why the hell had he stopped? *Oh come on, come on*, she urged, but silently. At last his hands started moving again. *That's it. Good boy. Keep going, just a little bit farther. Just a… What? No! Not that way again.*

Layla's eyes popped open. She'd been so busy concentrating… savoring…anticipating…but now she stared accusingly at him. And that's what did it. His face was directly above hers; his blue eyes boring deep, deeper than he could ever go physically, touching a part of her that only he had the power to reach.

"Ahhhhhhhh."

It was over, without the need to press anything.

"Now *that's* something you should put in your book," he said, his smile as satisfied as her own.

"When my hands stop shaking, perhaps."

"Just your hands?"

"Not quite."

Detangling from her, Joseph sat up. Still reclining, she studied him. His blond hair had lightened in the almost incessant sunshine in Florence, their home for the last year. In Trecastle, a small village in North Cornwall, where they had both been living previously, it had been much darker. It was still long, though, still flopping over those azure eyes of his, obscuring them sometimes but tantalizingly so.

"What time will you be back tonight?"

Layla glanced at the clock on the bedside table. The entire morning was hers to write, but she would need to be at *La Pasticceria Barontini*, the bakery where she worked on a part-time basis, by three o'clock for the afternoon shift.

"Around seven, I think," she said eventually.

"That late?" He sounded disappointed. In the restoration workshop where he worked alongside master craftsman Paolo Rossi, honing and improving his already considerable carpentry skills, the preference was to start early and finish early.

"If you're home first, you can cook," she chanced.

"I cooked last night." His protest was immediate. "And the night before."

"Oh, all right, all right. I'll cook, but something quick and easy, though."

"Fine by me." He leaned in to steal another kiss. "I like quick and easy."

"Get to work," she replied, ignoring the double entendre.

"I will, but first I need to shower." Looking at her meaningfully, he added, "And so do you."

"Oh no." She was the one who could read minds now. "That shower, it's not built for two."

"So, two become one, simple."

"Joseph…"

"Get in there, *now*."

As much as he loved her fieriness, she loved it when he was masterful. Giggling, she rose from the bed and ran naked across the room, Joseph striding purposefully after her.

chapter two

The late March sun was just about perfect, bright but not blindingly so. There was a time when Tara had adored the hot caress of that big, bold ball of fire in the sky, but now she preferred cooler weather. Maybe in recent years she'd had too much of a good thing. Coming to a standstill, she spied a café with several empty tables outside it. Making her way over, she sat down. A waiter appeared immediately.

"What would you like, madam?"

He had an English accent, not Italian. Tara was disappointed. She hadn't come to Italy to hear English accents. She'd hear *those* soon enough.

Barely glancing at the menu, she answered, "Cappuccino please," not caring that in Italy, cappuccino was considered very much a breakfast coffee. She had decided that from now on, she could damn well have what she liked, when she liked.

As the waiter sauntered back to the kitchen, Tara relaxed, or relaxed as far as it was possible to do on an aluminum chair with no cushion to soften its hardness. Looking around her, she smiled. Florence. She was finally here, in a city she had always wanted to visit but had never made the time to. She had been in Rome too, just a couple of days before, and prior to that, Venice, both of which were also on her list of "cities I really *must* see." She enjoyed losing herself in culture, something that hadn't been in plentiful supply where she had just come from, and, in all honesty, just losing herself. Florence was her last port of call before heading home.

The waiter reappeared with her coffee and one of those dinky *amaretti* biscuits plonked on the side, small and round with an almond taste. She had developed quite a liking for them recently. Saying thank you, she noticed the waiter had dark, close-cropped hair, similar to Aiden's. His eyes were as dark as Aiden's too. Only his build was different. Aiden had a rugby player's build, solid and strong; the waiter was much slighter. Her hand shook as she picked up her coffee, but she quickly steadied it. She mustn't think of Aiden. He was the last person she should think of.

Unexpectedly, a tear tumbled over Tara's lower lashes and raced down her cheek, as though glad to have found escape. She immediately reached up and brushed it away. The café wasn't overly busy, just a few people sitting here and there. Couples of course; it was always couples in Italian cities, she'd noticed, each respective pair looking longingly into each other's eyes. If she'd thought she'd gotten away with her show of emotion, however, she was wrong. The waiter was hovering again.

"Sorry, miss," he said, looking slightly awkward.

Tara glanced up. He looked young, around mid-twenties, younger than she had first thought. Previously, she had put him around the same age as her, thirty.

"I couldn't help noticing. Are you okay?"

"I'm fine," she replied, hoping her eyes weren't shining too brightly, betraying the words she had forced from her mouth. "I've got a slight cold, that's all." As an afterthought, she added, "Thanks for asking, though."

It was nice to know he cared, that *someone* in this big, anonymous city cared.

Instead of leaving, however, he pulled up a chair.

"Hope you don't mind me resting my feet for a bit. We're not busy, and the manager, Franco, he's away on an errand at the moment. Or at least that's what he calls it, an errand, but he's not fooling me. What he's doing is drinking *Aperol* at someone else's café, leaving me to run his. The Italians, they love café society."

Taken aback by his actions and his words, Tara couldn't quite decide if she did mind him sitting down and talking to her. He hadn't exactly given her time to mind. Looking at his friendly face, she relented. It wasn't so bad talking to someone; she hadn't done so properly since leaving Australia three weeks ago.

"So, you're from England," the young man was talking again. "Whereabouts?"

"Erm, er, Cornwall. I'm from North Cornwall, from a small village you've probably never heard of. Most people haven't. It's called Port Levine."

The waiter shook his head. "No, I can't say I have. I'm from the other side of the country, from Whitstable in Kent. What brings you to Florence?"

"Apart from the art and culture, you mean?" she replied, unable to keep a note of sarcasm from creeping into her voice. Softening her answer, she added, "I'm just passing through. I've been in Australia for a while now. It's time to go home."

"On your own?" the waiter probed.

"On my own," Tara confirmed.

Holding out his hand, the waiter introduced himself. "My name's Lucas. I'm a student at The Florence Academy of Art and, as you can see, a part-time waiter too. Glad to meet you."

"Hi, Lucas. I'm Tara. Glad to meet you as well."

"Hey, you're smiling. That's better. Nobody should be sad in Florence."

Another couple came in and sat down at the table beside her, and Lucas gestured to Tara with a nod of his head that he had them to attend to. As she watched him take their order, she mulled over his last words to her. He was right. Nobody should be sad in Florence; it was a beautiful city, one of the most beautiful cities she had ever seen, a city that made you feel glad to be alive.

Refusing to allow any more tears free rein, she immersed herself in the scene before her: people rushing to and fro, lights shining from other cafés, from shops and bars too, holding back the dusk. Mentally, she reeled off the sights she'd seen: the Coliseum in Rome, the Doge's Palace in Venice, the attributes of a certain famous sculpture residing proudly just a few streets away. She'd seen all these things, but she had seen them alone—not quite what she'd envisaged.

She had finished her coffee. Quick to notice, Lucas was by her side again.

"Another one?" he said hopefully.

She had meant to have only the one coffee and then move on, go back to her hotel room and have a sleep before dinner. Perhaps even blow off dinner altogether; her appetite wasn't up to much lately, and she was tired. She'd been walking all day, just wandering through back streets, soaking up the atmosphere, the history of ages long gone. But it was pleasant at this café, in this square, and Lucas looked as though he'd genuinely like her to stay, so she acquiesced; another coffee would be fine.

When he returned to her table, he'd included two biscuits this time, not one. His obvious gesture made her laugh.

Sitting back down, he said, "You know, I've always wanted to visit Cornwall. Never managed to, though. I've been just about everywhere else in the world, but never there. Spent a summer in Australia too, near Sydney. Loved it. Great surf."

"There's great surf in Cornwall too," Tara offered.

"I'm sure. But the weather's not usually conducive to a dip in the ocean. That's what I don't miss about home — arctic temperatures, even in May."

Tara couldn't agree. Yes, it rained a lot in England, and okay, temperatures sometimes never got up to speed, but where she came from, it was so beautiful, few places could compete. She remembered lush green countryside, interspersed every now and then with granite rocks and boulders, rolling down to dark, dramatic cliffs that fringed endless stretches of golden, glittering sand. When the sky was blue, it contrasted magnificently against such jeweled tones, a natural work of art no artist could ever hope to capture fully on canvas, no matter how great their talent. When skies were stormy, there was an incredible intensity to them, dark and brooding like the hero in a Brontë novel. As a child, she had loved to watch clouds race across such a sky from the comfort of her parents' cottage, staring out of the living room window, a log fire burning in the grate, feeling warm and safe inside. That's what called to her now: that warmth and safety, a need to be protected again, nurtured. And the only place she could feel that was at home.

"Your coffee's getting cold," Lucas pointed out.

"Oh, right, yes. Thanks." Tara took a sip.

"So, you're swapping Australia for Cornwall. Briefly or permanently?"

Making a deliberate effort to keep her voice steady, Tara replied, "Permanently."

As much as her roots called her, she wouldn't have swapped the two if she'd had a choice. She would have stayed, put down new roots, got married on the beach, bought a house in the 'burbs, had kids, dozens of them. She imagined her children speaking with an Ozzie twang—it would have given her such a kick to hear.

She noticed Lucas looking expectantly at her, clearly wanting her to elaborate. He seemed mystified by this sad girl sitting in front of him. For her part, she longed to confide in him, to tell him why she was going home. She had confided in no one, not yet. Would a total stranger be ideal? She could offload, and then she could leave, never see him again. But as tempted as she was, something deep inside told her to hold back. What she had to tell him would only bring him down, and she didn't want that. She wanted him to remain as he was, happy and carefree. As all people had the right to be, every day of their lives.

"I used to work in a café too," she said at last. "Right on the beach. In fact, that's what it was called: 'Right on the Beach.'"

"In Australia?"

Tara nodded.

"Where in Australia?"

"Lyons Bay. Two and a half hours from Sydney. It was stunning, that beach. I've never seen sands so white, like tiny grains of caster sugar. We ran a café, open for breakfast and lunch, but often, in the summer months, we'd continue well into the evening, ramp the music up, get the barbecue going, that sort of thing. People would hang around. We'd crack open the beer. Just hang out, just *be*."

"We?" Lucas raised an eyebrow.

He didn't miss a trick.

"Yes, we," Tara conceded. "But like I said, there is no *we* now; it's just me."

"Is that why you're upset?"

"I'm not upset. I'm tired."

Lucas seemed to consider this. Leaning forward, he said, "How long are you here for?"

"In Florence?"

"In Florence."

"Only a few more days. I haven't been to the Uffizi Gallery yet. That's going to take at least two days to get around, I think."

Lucas nodded again, as though agreeing with her estimation. "Look, if you want a tour guide, if you want…I don't know…someone just to *hang* with, let me know. I'd be happy to do both."

The kindness of strangers, it threatened to make her cry again. But regarding talking, she'd made up her mind. He was not the one.

She reached into her bag and located her purse. Delving into it, she brought out ten Euros.

"Does that cover my bill?"

"Yes. I'll get you change."

"No," she insisted. "No change."

As she rose to go, he looked disappointed.

"Thank you," she said, meaning it on several levels.

"The pleasure was all mine," he replied, understanding her perfectly.

She scurried away, clutching her brown leather tote to her chest.

Dusk had not been held back after all. But the streets, busy earlier, were even busier now: men and women in sharp suits rushing home from work, students, not the scruffy kind so often found in Britain but elegant, in designer wear, hurrying to meet friends, perhaps. In amongst the crowds, she had never felt so alone.

Trying to move farther forward, she found she couldn't. It was as if the air around her had solidified. She stood where she was, in another of Florence's piazzas, a different one than the one she'd had coffee in a few minutes earlier, she was sure. The café she had sat in was gone and so was Lucas, with his kind, smiling eyes, urging her to share. She so wanted to share. She couldn't do this alone. She needed a shoulder to cry on, but whose? There was no one. Once tethered so tightly to the world and all that was in it, she was now cast adrift, floating out to sea, toward a boiling center which threatened to suck her into it, to engulf her forever in darkness.

How the hell was she going to face her parents? How would they react to her news? Perhaps it was better not to tell them—to just cut and run. Run farther than she already had. Rush toward that boiling center.

Her mother's face appeared before her. A little tired round the edges but enlivened with love for her and her younger sister, Leondra—Leo for short. Her father's face too, pride evident in his eyes whenever he beheld his two girls. She didn't want to wipe those looks away. She wanted them to remain forever. Not be…she struggled to find the right word…*contaminated.*

The tears she had tried to stem earlier in the café could be caged no more. They fell, and she let them, powerless to stop their flow. Some part of her, the Tara that was hitching a lift in the back seat of her mind, an impartial observer looking on, honed in to what was happening around her. People were staring at the young woman crying so openly in the piazza, worried frowns upon their faces. She was not so anonymous now, not just another girl walking home or meeting a lover.

Her parents would be so surprised to see her. Apart from a visit three years ago, she hadn't been home since. Why she had left it so long, she couldn't fathom. Even the visit she had made back then had been brief, spending less than a week in Cornwall, the rest in London, revisiting old friends, whooping it up with them instead. She should have spent more time at home; she should have made more of an effort to see them. She should have realized how precious they were.

"You've got wings. Now fly." It was one of her father's favorite sayings. And she had flown, as far away as it was possible to get.

And now she had to fly back. Now she wanted them more than anything else in the world—well, almost anything. But would they be able to cope with her return?

Dropping her bag, she clutched at her stomach as though pain were slicing her in two. The Tara inside saw concerned looks turn into alarm, but like the Tara on the outside, she ignored them too. She couldn't return home. She wouldn't! She'd head deeper into Europe instead; she'd disappear. People did that all the time, but she'd never understood why before. She did now—some problems were hard to face.

Quite a crowd had gathered now. People whispering to each other, wondering what to do about the lone woman gone to pieces in a city where no one should be sad—whether to approach her, whether she was mad, perhaps.

If only she could fade away, evaporate. She tried to, hunching over, becoming smaller just as a hand reached out and touched her gently. Another kind stranger.

"Tara?" he said—a gentle voice but one with wonder in it too.

It took a few moments to register that this "stranger" knew her name.

"Tara," he said again, more insistent now.

She straightened up, expecting to see Lucas, the dark-haired waiter, again, to witness the same concern on his face he had shown earlier.

What she saw, however, took her breath away. At first she refused to believe it; she *couldn't* believe it. There was no way, absolutely no way.

"Tara," he said a third time, and then she had no doubt.

He had barely changed in all the time they had been apart. Beautiful still, his hair a bit lighter, his eyes the shade of cornflower she remembered. A face she had loved to distraction in another lifetime. A face she had let go when adventure had called.

As her hands lowered, the crowd started to disperse, the relief that someone had taken it upon themselves to care for her, that they didn't have to, palpable.

"Joseph?"

He smiled at her then, a smile as soft as the memories she had of him.

It was. It was Joseph Scott standing before her, like a gift from the gods.

chapter three

The phone. Where was the bloody phone?

"Hi, Penny. Did you lose the phone again?"

Penny couldn't help but laugh. "Hi, Layla! Yep, I lost the phone—*again*. Damn those cordless inventions."

"Is it okay to talk? Is Scarlett asleep?"

"She's cat-napping. There's a difference, a big one, unfortunately."

Immediately Layla was sympathetic. "Is she still not settling?"

"Put it this way… I reckon world peace will be settled before she is."

"I don't know how you do it." Layla sounded truly impressed. "Looking after a baby, I mean. It must make you feel, I don't know, so grown up."

"It makes me feel like an extra in *The Walking Dead*. And not a live extra either."

Layla giggled.

Penny raised an eyebrow. What was so funny? She was serious.

"Penny, we're coming to England," Layla continued. "Next week. I've just booked tickets."

"To Brighton?" Penny could hardly believe her ears.

"Erm, no. Cornwall, actually."

"Oh, of course. It's Hannah's turn."

Penny couldn't help it; she was disappointed. But it *was* Hannah's turn. Layla had come to Brighton when Scarlett was born, had stayed two weeks in fact, relishing being back in her hometown. But Trecastle was where her other best friend lived.

"But I was thinking you could come down and visit? You and Scarlett? Just for two or three days. It would be so great to see you. For us all to be together again."

"I'm not sure, Layla. It's a long drive—and on zero sleep, a dangerous one."

"Perhaps Richard could drive?"

"Richard?" Penny almost spat the word. "Willingly take time off from work, you mean? Do you seriously not know the man by now?"

"Oh, Pen, I'm sorry. I feel awful coming to the UK and not visiting."

"Don't apologize. It's fine. I miss you, that's all."

"I miss you too. I love it here, but…"

"But what?" Penny prompted when Layla faltered.

"It's not the same. It's great." Layla rushed to reassure her. "It's just not the same."

"No, it's warmer for a start. The weather right now, it sucks." Never one to harp on about the vagaries of the British weather system, Penny changed the subject. "And how come you're talking to me, not ravaging that man of yours?"

"Believe me, I would be if he were home, but he's not. He's gone AWOL."

"Richard's late too," Penny said with a sigh. "Despite promising he wouldn't be."

"Men…" Layla began.

"Can't live with 'em, *can* live without them," Penny completed their one-time mantra. It seemed a lifetime ago since they were two single girls about town.

"I'll phone him soon. I just don't want to appear too eager."

"Eager for what?"

"We've got scenes to practice."

For a moment, Penny was nonplussed. "Oh, you mean for that book of yours?"

"The saucy ones, yeah."

Penny pretended shock. "Layla, you're not writing porno, are you?"

"I wasn't, but I could be persuaded."

"You two, you're incorrigible."

Layla was gigging again, like a schoolgirl who'd just noticed the head boy finally noticing her. Before Penny could comment further, a familiar sound started up.

"Listen, can you hear that?" She held the phone up.

"Er…I think the entire neighborhood can hear that, Penny."

"Yep, the kraken awakes. Look, I'd better go and see to her. Speak soon, though. Call me as soon as you get here."

"I will, Pen. I promise."

"And I hope they don't keep you waiting too long."

"They?"

"Joseph and his tool bag."

Relishing the sound of Layla's laughter, Penny prepared to deal with its antithesis. She tackled the stairs two at a time and entered Scarlett's bedroom. In the crib, a less-than-angelic creature writhed, her tiny face screwed up and an alarming shade of puce, fists punching the air like some pro boxer in the making. What was her problem? She'd been fed, she'd been bathed, and she had the freshest of nappies on. There was nothing to cry about. *Nothing.* For the umpteenth time, Penny wondered where this child of hers got her fierce personality from and for the umpteenth time decided not to pursue that particular avenue of thought. If she'd asked Richard that question, she knew damn well what his answer would be — her. Instead, she picked the baby up and started to rock her gently.

"It's okay. Don't cry. Everything's okay."

Her attempt at soothing fell woefully short.

Leaving the bedroom, the ranting, raging bundle still hard at it, Penny went downstairs and into the kitchen. Perhaps another bottle of milk might do the trick. Scarlett couldn't get enough of the white stuff; she had as much of a penchant for it as Penny had for gin — or rather, *used* to have for gin. The days of consuming alcohol with anything approaching wanton abandon were over. Nowadays, one glass, no matter how diluted it was with tonic, and it was game over. Just another way in which her life had changed, changed so much she barely recognized herself on the rare occasions she was brave enough to look in the mirror. Instead of the funky blond chick with a zest for life, she saw an utter wreck: dishwater hair in need of highlights, black bags under her eyes you could fit a week's worth of shopping into, and skin the color of Richard's socks—the white ones that had been washed too often with the coloreds and had turned a murky shade of gray. If she stepped farther back from the mirror to view her entire body, it got worse. Chubby instead of curvaceous, she found that none of the clothes she used to wear fit her now. She'd had to invest in a whole new wardrobe. A bonus, you might think? Not when kaftans hadn't made a fashion comeback.

She freed one hand to grab a chocolate digestive and rammed it into her mouth. It was gone before she'd even had a chance to taste it. Next, she filled a bottle with some pre-made formula and gave it several seconds in the microwave. Testing it for temperature first, she then plugged it into Scarlett's ever-complaining mouth.

Oh, glory be! Silence at last.

Well, silence punctuated with greedy guzzling, but it was a definite improvement.

Standing in the kitchen, the baby in her arms but feeling somehow lonelier than ever, Penny missed how fun life used to be when Layla was living in Brighton. But she was glad one of them was having fun still. She didn't know a happier couple than Layla and Joseph, but not sickeningly happy, *deservedly* so. There'd been a time—just over a year ago—when she thought her friend might miss the boat completely regarding the gorgeous Mr. Scott, might return to her ex instead, the dastardly Alex Kline, and set sail with him into a slimy sunset. But thankfully she'd realized—in the nick of time—that what lay beneath his flash veneer was anything but glittering. And now she was writing about it—her "runaway year" in Trecastle—the place where she had "woken up," found the man of her dreams, and laid the nightmare to rest.

Briefly Penny glanced at the clock; it was edging its way past seven. If Joseph was late, Richard was too. She cursed those meetings of his, his demanding clients, and Richard, too, for trying to appease them. A solicitor in an up-and-coming law company, his workaholic ways had come between them before—sans-baby days.

Not as worried as Layla about appearing eager, Penny went in search of the phone. Where was it? Despite recently speaking on it, she was damned if she could find it. That was sleep deprivation for you. It corroded the mind. To add insult to injury, Scarlett expunged the teat from her mouth and started screaming again.

Oh great, here we go. Richard, where are you?

"There, there." Penny started bouncing from one foot to the other. "What is it? Wind?"

Why she bothered asking, she didn't know. It wasn't as if Scarlett could reply, although the thought that she might temporarily cut through the fog in Penny's brain.

"Yes, Mum, I've got wind—chronic, bend-you-over-double, gut-wrenching wind."

She even managed a smile as she pictured the cheeky response.

And it wasn't true Scarlett couldn't talk. At seven months old, she could say "dada"—despite the fact that Penny had spent hours and hours teaching her "mama." But no, "dada" had been her first word. Richard had been delighted.

"My perfect girl," he'd cooed, holding her close. Penny had watched his awe-struck reaction, feeling like she'd been kicked in the teeth.

Penny knew something was wrong with the way she was feeling. She wasn't *joyous* enough. The few mothers she had met at prenatal classes seemed to be joyous, feverishly so, which is exactly why she had stopped seeing them. She had nothing in common with them at all—zero, nada—certainly not their willingness to ride each and every wave of pain during childbirth and their determination that "breast was best." Scarlett drank so much milk, if Penny had gone along with that theory, she'd be constantly on tap—nothing would get done. Looking around her, she realized nothing got done anyway. The kitchen was a mess, bowls, plates and cutlery from the day before still waited to be crammed into the dishwasher, and the floor tiles—they were white once, weren't they?

The phone rang. Not lost at all, it was on the table, right in front of her.

"How's my tiny angel?" Richard enquired.

"I'm fine, thanks. How are you?"

Richard ignored her sarcasm. "Before you start shouting, I'm leaving the office now. I'll be home in ten."

Shouting? Why was he so sure she'd start shouting?

"You'd better be," she replied, feeling very much like shouting—if only so she could be heard over Scarlett's incessant bawling.

"Poor thing, she sounds upset. Is it wind again?"

He was as obsessed with wind as she was.

"You should take her for a stroll," he continued, "up and down the road. The night air might calm her."

It might, but she didn't want to go for a "stroll." She wanted to stay at home, as she had done all day, and hide. What if one of the neighbors was out strolling too? She'd been so smug when pregnant; would they notice she wasn't so smug now? Motherhood was far from the easy ride she'd thought it would be. A funds manager for Charity Now!, she'd been delighted at the prospect of a year's sabbatical. Maternity leave? Eternity leave more like. She'd never missed work so much.

"Penny," Richard prompted. "Are you still there?"

"Yes." That monotonous tone was back.

"Put Scarlett on, would you? Tell her it's Daddy."

Sighing, Penny did as she was told, her only consolation that Scarlett looked as unimpressed as she did with Richard's inane ramblings.

Listening in for twenty seconds, she could bear no more.

"Richard, I think me and Scarlett will go out after all."

"Oh good, good." Richard sounded delighted. "She needs regular doses of fresh air. It might help her to sleep better, you know."

Not this baby. Not even alternative medicine had helped, and Penny should know. She'd exhausted many of them: cranial osteopathy, homeopathy, and acupuncture. None had offered the miracle results they so earnestly promised.

"Ten minutes, you said?"

"Well, give or take a minute."

"Look." Exasperation lifted Penny's voice slightly. "I'm not going to shoot you if you happen to be eleven minutes instead of ten."

"Are you sure?"

No, she wasn't.

"Enjoy your walk," Richard said at last. "Tell Scarlett I love her."

And me? Do you love me too?

That remained a mystery as Richard rang off.

Slamming down the phone, she tried to stop her fury at Richard's failure to impart any loving sentiment to her—again—from overwhelming her. Depressed and in charge of a baby was bad enough, but depressed and furious? Making her way to the pram that was stowed neatly in the second of their two living rooms, Penny stopped abruptly. Depressed? Was that what was wrong with her? Surely not! She had never been depressed in her life. But something rang true about her self-diagnosis. Certainly this was not the way she remembered herself. Had she been okay in the hospital? She remembered smiling a lot despite the stifling heat of the ward — heaters full-blast even in August — but perhaps that had been the heady aftereffects of all the drugs she'd insisted on having. She also remembered just staring at the tiny bundle beside her, marveling at every one of her fingers and toes, unable to believe she and Richard had created something so beautiful, so...so *perfect*. Fast-forward to today, and the only thing she couldn't believe was how much her ears ached from the aforementioned perfect bundle's wailing and whining.

Doing her utmost to wrestle a resistant Scarlett into her pink all-in-one romper suit, fleece-lined to combat the chilly weather, she felt even more depressed that she could be depressed. No, she couldn't be, not her, Penny Hughes, party girl of the year, an accolade she had awarded herself several years running. Depression was such a taboo subject — something that happened to other people. If Layla were here — if *only* Layla were here, someone who understood her, who never judged her, who was always on her side, an ally — she'd laugh too at such a suggestion.

Giving up on the romper suit — Scarlett was clearly not going to comply — Penny stuffed the baby into the pram, layering blankets over her instead, which, of course, she immediately proceeded to kick off. Breathless from the effort of going several rounds with the tiny tyrant, she felt hot, angry tears burst from her eyes too.

You know what, babe? It was her last coherent thought before she, like Scarlett, tumbled toward a glorious meltdown. *Two can play at that game!*

chapter four

"*Joseph and his tool bag.*" Layla loved it. Penny could always make her laugh. How she missed her. It was such a shame the distance was so great between Brighton and Cornwall. A week didn't allow for a visit to both destinations, not without spending two of those days on the road, anyway. And she and Joseph wanted to celebrate with Hannah and Jim, their respective best friends, the launch of new album for Jim's band, 96 Tears, an album that was garnering quite a bit of attention in the music world. They were on their way, those two, Jim with his music and Hannah with her art. Recently a London gallery had contacted her, showing an interest in exhibiting her paintings. She was busting out, going nationwide!

Layla was looking forward to Trecastle too — the rugged coastline, the wildness of the ocean, miles and miles of golden beaches, and Gull Rock. Her Gull Rock, a granite monolith set about a mile out to sea and the backdrop to so many poignant memories. Florence was beautiful, people the world over beat a path to it, but it was that tiny village on the North Atlantic Cornish coast that held her heart captive.

Putting her mobile on charge, she padded over to the fridge, retrieved a bottle of Pinot Grigio, and poured herself a large one. Joseph was probably doing the same but with bottles of Peroni in a bar with Paolo, an after-work jolly. He'd be home soon.

Savoring for a moment the coldness of the wine, she checked cupboards next, wondering what to make for dinner. *Aglio e olio*—spaghetti with fresh herbs and garlic. She had all the ingredients for that. She'd accompany it with a green salad, scattered liberally with black olives from the Tuscan hills that surrounded them. For music, she put on Rhianna, her hips swaying as the singer's rich voice filled the air.

She was on the fourth song and her second glass of wine when she noticed an entire hour had passed since talking to Penny; it was ten past eight. Where the hell was her errant boyfriend? Checking her phone, she saw that there were no alerts at all.

What should she do? The dish she had chosen would take only minutes to cook. The work was in the prep; there was no point in putting pasta on to boil before he arrived home. She'd phone him. She didn't want to nag—he was entitled to a drink with friends—but she was hungry, and not just in the culinary sense.

Joseph's number went straight to answer phone—twice. It wasn't like him not to pick up. Paolo was next on the hit list; hopefully, she'd have more success with him. She didn't. Annoyance began to gnaw away at her. Annoyance laced with something else—fear?

The music was beginning to grate.

"Sorry, Rhianna, no offense," said Layla, pressing the off button.

The silence that ensued was almost worse. It felt ominous somehow, false. Shaking her head to dismiss such thoughts, Layla started pacing instead. There were several others at the workshop—Marco, Vincenzo, and Pietro—but she didn't have their numbers to phone them. She suddenly felt alone, a stranger in a strange city. What if something had happened to Joseph—something bad?

Usually thankful for her writer's imagination—short stories had proven a useful source of income in the past—Layla now cursed it. Once the idea of something bad happening to Joseph had crept into her mind, it took hold.

Accidents happened; they happened all the time. Big accidents, small accidents, and those of catastrophic, life-changing proportions. Perhaps one had happened tonight. At the workshop, they had saws—miter saws, reciprocating saws, chain saws, every type of saw you could think of. It would be so easy for an accident to happen. All it would take was a slip of concentration, a momentary lapse. She'd kept him up late last night too, too late in hindsight. He'd be tired today, not firing on all cylinders.

Images poured into her head—blood-spattered images, most of them, like scenes from a horror film. Paolo could be with Joseph right now in an emergency room somewhere, unable to leave his side, willing him to hold on, to fight for his life.

She needed to get to the hospital now, or at least *a* hospital. Pray God that the city didn't have half a dozen to choose from. And that she could find a taxi to flag down…And that she had money in her purse to pay the taxi man…And…and *stop!*

It's only eight thirty. There is no need to panic!

No, it wasn't late, but considering he should have been home three hours ago, it was late enough. She forced herself to stand still, to control the panic that had kicked annoyance well and truly out of the ring. His phone had probably run out of battery. That was feasible, far more so than him lying bloodied on a gurney somewhere, a vision she wished would stop presenting itself to her with such force.

She needed more wine. As she reached for the bottle, memories of someone else she had tried to phone but got zero response from surfaced—Alex, her boyfriend before Joseph. The reason she couldn't get through to him was because he had left her, traded her in for a younger model with no warning whatsoever. If there had been any warning signs, she hadn't seen them, not with Alex. On the contrary, she'd thought he was preparing to ask her to marry him. What a fool she had been back then, simple and naïve. She'd never allow herself to be fooled in that way again. Never.

On the landing outside her door, she heard movement. Her hand round the bottle's neck, she paused. Yes, there was definite movement. The bottle and her thoughts forgotten, she sprinted to the door and almost yanked it off its hinges.

"Joseph," she breathed upon sight of him. "Thank goodness you're all right! Joseph?" She peered closer. "You are all right, aren't you?"

If he'd been in a bar for the last three hours, she'd expect him to look merry, but that wasn't the first description that came to mind. Or sheepish for not phoning home. He didn't look that either. His skin, normally the color of West Country honey, was ashen; his eyes were dull instead of glowing. Shell-shocked is what he looked. As if he'd seen a ghost. The reason he was late, she sensed, might shock her too.

"What's the matter?"

"I…Look, Layla, can you let me in?"

"In? Oh, yes, of course." Hurriedly, Layla stepped aside. Once he was over the threshold, she closed the door behind him.

"Joe…" she tried again.

"Sit down. We need to talk."

"Is it Paolo?" she asked, crossing over to the kitchen table, an image of him on the gurney instead of Joseph vivid in her mind as she did so.

He sat down opposite her. "No. Everything's fine with Paolo."

"And you're not hurt at all?"

"I'm not hurt, no."

"And your job, you've still got one?"

He looked confused. "I've still got my job, Layla. Why wouldn't I?"

"Thank goodness!"

Her shoulders, so tense before, slumped in relief. Whatever had happened, it couldn't be that much of a crisis. No one was hurt. He still had his job; she had hers. Their perfect life — the bubble they lived in — could continue. And it really was perfect; she had never known life to be so good, so fulfilling. Then her thoughts darkened. Joseph and Paolo might be okay, but what if someone wasn't? A member of Paolo's family, perhaps? That would be dreadful. Joseph and Paolo had become close many years ago when Joseph had spent six months in Florence, learning the art of restoration. They'd never lost touch, so when an opportunity came up to return to the workshop on a full-time basis, he had jumped at it, taking Layla with him. During the time they had been here, she had grown close to Paolo and his kin also. Often they would eat with him, his wife, Luisa, and their five children, all of them enjoying big, noisy mealtimes together at his rambling farmhouse on the edge of the city. She loved watching Joseph play with the kids. He got right down to their level, laughing and joking with them as though he were a kid himself. And the little ones loved him for it. If she and Joseph were lucky enough to have children one day, he'd make a great dad. But right now, it was Paolo and Luisa's children she was concerned with. Tentatively, she asked if they were okay.

"They're okay, Paolo's okay, and Luisa's okay. It's got nothing to do with them or my job. It's…it's to do with Tara."

Tara who? Layla thought for a moment. The friends they had made in Florence had typical Italian names — Gabriella, Kristina,

Isabella. Tara sounded English, or perhaps it was Irish in origin. She couldn't remember a Tara. And then she did.

"Do you mean the Tara you used to know?"

"Yes. The Tara I used to know."

"The Tara you used to go out with?"

"A long time ago, yes."

"The one you lived with in London?"

"The very same."

"Tara, the reason *why* you left London?"

"Well, one of the reasons." Joseph had clearly had enough of her quick-fire questioning. "Look, Layla, I think we've established which Tara I'm talking about."

"Your ex-girlfriend Tara?"

"My ex-girlfriend Tara," he confirmed.

"Well, what about her? She's in Australia, isn't she?"

"No, she's not. She's here, in Florence. I bumped into her today."

Tara was *not* in Australia? She was here, in Florence? And Joseph had *bumped* into her? She'd been right. He had seen a ghost—a ghost from the past.

"That's why I'm late home," he continued. "We had some catching up to do."

A catch-up that had put the fear of God into her. And still might do, if the look on his face was anything to go by. He looked more serious than she had ever seen him. What was Tara doing here? What was the catch-up about? And why hadn't he taken time out to phone home, to let her know where he was? What had Tara had to say that was so scintillating he couldn't bear to tear himself away, not even for a minute?

"Why didn't you phone me? I was worried." *Worried?* That was the understatement of the year.

"I didn't expect to be so long. I lost track of time."

"Didn't you hear your phone ring? I called you."

"I'd switched it off," he confessed.

Switched it off? It was equivalent to shutting her out. Now that she knew he was safe, she could feel the first stirrings of anger. But with Herculean effort, she strove to keep her voice normal, enthusiastic even.

"Wow! So, Tara's in Florence. That's a coincidence."

There was no fooling him.

"But that's all it is, a coincidence."

"And how is she? What's her news? Is she on holiday here?"

"A holiday of sorts," Joseph replied, ignoring her first two questions.

"A holiday of sorts?" she repeated. What was that supposed to mean? "Is it a working holiday, perhaps?"

Joseph shook his head.

"Is she with friends or family?"

"She's on her own."

"Sightseeing?"

"Sightseeing," he confirmed but dully so.

Christ! Why was he making this so difficult? He was the one who had said they needed to talk.

"Joseph," she demanded, all brightness gone, "what is she doing here?"

"I've just told you."

"Actually," she said, "you really haven't."

When no more words were immediately forthcoming, no more *explanations*, she couldn't suppress her anger any longer. Tara aside, he'd been insensitive, bloody insensitive. If he hadn't come home at the time he did, she'd be out there now, paying some poor driver a small fortune to trawl her from hospital to hospital. He'd not only been insensitive, he'd been disrespectful. He'd been...and the thought was formed before she could stop it, *Alex-like*. Grabbing the edge of the table with both hands, she pushed back her chair, the screeching sound of wooden legs against ceramic tiles making Joseph wince as she stood abruptly.

"You should have phoned."

Joseph rose rapidly to his feet too. "It wasn't that simple," he declared.

"Why? Did you have brain freeze or something?"

"No, of course not."

The need to pace again was also overwhelming.

"You switched your phone off. I can't believe it." She was talking to herself as much as to him. "You meet your ex, and you switch your damn phone off, for *hours*."

"Layla." His hand reached out to grab her. "It's not like that."

"What is it like, then?"

"I'll tell you. Just bloody stand still, will you, and stop firing questions at me. This is difficult enough as it is!"

His raised voice shocked her. Rarely did the man shout. Mostly they spent their time together laughing and loving. That's what she'd envisaged them doing more of tonight, not arguing like this, the walls of the bubble they lived in quivering perilously. Quickly he filled the ensuing silence.

"We went to a café to talk, and the reason we went to a café, that we talked for as long as we did, is because she had a lot to say. She's not in a good way, Layla. She's distraught. When I found her, she was crying, standing in the middle of the *Piazza Santa Croce* and crying. It took some coaxing, but I managed to get out of her what was wrong, which is why I didn't call. I didn't want to interrupt her, in case she clammed up again. I'm sorry for that. I should have found the time, but that is my only crime here. Don't try and lay others at my door."

"What other crimes? What do you mean?"

"You know full well what I mean. That meeting Tara was engineered."

Engineered? As much as she was surprised at what a coincidence their meeting was, she hadn't actually gone as far as to think it was engineered. Not until he had just said so. Before her mind could run with that idea, he was speaking again.

"Layla, you should know I wouldn't do such a thing. I'm not Alex."

His insight startled her. He was right. He wasn't Alex. She shouldn't be comparing the two. Pushing thoughts of *her* ex far away, she asked why Tara had been crying.

"She's in trouble."

"What sort of trouble?"

"I can't say." Now he did look sheepish.

"Of course you can. We tell each other everything."

"No, Layla, I can't."

The resolve in his voice was a new shock.

"Why?" she asked simply.

"Because it's not my secret to tell."

A secret? She was stunned.

"But you know what it is?"

"I do," he admitted, "but only by default."

"Because you happened to be there?"

"Exactly."

"Joseph…"

"What?" He seemed to ask the question with baited breath.

"That sounds bloody engineered to me."

The hand he had on her, she threw off.

"Layla…"

"I…Just wait. I don't want you to touch me. I need to make sense of this. You come home over three hours late, not having bothered to phone or text, and you tell me you've bumped into your ex—and not just any ex, but a significant ex. That she just happens to be in Florence, in the same city as you, and that she has a secret, a secret that's upset her, and you too by the looks of it, a secret that you have no intention of sharing with me." Trying to breathe instead of snort, she added, "And wasn't it you who said this morning that people need to talk to each other more so misunderstandings wouldn't occur?"

"And wasn't it you who said that sometimes things aren't that black and white?"

Damn! He had called her bluff. Nonetheless, she demanded to know if he was deliberately trying to be facetious.

"No!" Briefly he looked offended. "Look, it's not a secret; that's the wrong way to describe it. It's a…a situation."

"A situation you can tell me about?"

"No…"

"So, it's a secret, whichever way you dress it up."

Joseph sighed, a long and protracted sound, his frustration as evident as hers. "Layla, I *am* talking to you. I'm trying to tell you as much as I can. This secret, it's not something silly; it's as serious as it gets. I have to honor Tara's wishes."

"Honor her wishes, not mine?" Layla challenged.

Joseph remained unmoved. "It's her parents who need to know next—who have the *right* to know—who can help her."

"Next after you, you mean?"

"Yes, after me. But I'll tell you one thing. I wish I didn't know. I wish I'd never left the flat this morning. I wish I'd stayed at home, with you."

If there was one thing she believed, it was that. He looked *wounded* by whatever news Tara had imparted.

In a bid to fight her way out of confusion, Layla concentrated on practicalities instead. "Her parents? Do they live in Florence? Is that why she's here?"

"No, they live in Port Levine, where she's from."

"Port Levine? Where's that?"

"It's in Cornwall, not far from Trecastle, about a twenty-minute drive."

That's right; she had heard of it before. It was the same village that Jim was from. She had never visited it when she lived in Trecastle, had had no reason to.

"Joseph, tell me the truth this time. What's she doing in Florence?"

"Hedging is what she's doing, trying to put off going home."

"Going home to Cornwall, you mean? Australia's over and done with?"

"Yes, she's en route to Cornwall."

A light pinged on inside Layla's head. She started backing away from him as though he were suddenly contagious.

"She's going back the same time that we are, isn't she?"

"She wasn't going back at all," Joseph re-emphasized. "She wanted to disappear, take her secret and run. But she can't. She *has* to go back." His expression grew more nervous as he added, "I said she could travel with us."

Layla tried to reply but couldn't. He had quite literally rendered her mute.

Seizing the opportunity to further his cause, Joseph continued, "All I want to do is make sure she reaches home. After that, it's up to her parents. But if I can get her home, I'd feel as though I'd done my bit, and if you knew why, you'd understand."

Her voice returned with a vengeance. "If I knew why, I probably would, but I'm not allowed to, remember?"

She shoved her way past him, going over to the window by their bed. Opening it, she leaned out; she needed some air, some fresh, clean air or as clean as it could get in a busy, polluted city. Nonetheless, it was preferable to the air inside the flat, which seemed stale all of a sudden. It was choking her. After a moment, she swung back around. Joseph was standing in the same spot, staring almost beseechingly at her.

"There are probably no more seats left on the plane."

"There are. I've checked."

"You've checked?" She was incredulous. "Already?"

"*We* checked, earlier on Tara's iPhone. Layla, don't look like that. We weren't going to book anything, not without running it by you first."

We? As though they were a unit—Joseph and Tara, her place by his side usurped.

"Joseph, I…I can't do this."

Her words, the look on her face, perhaps, spurred him into action. He came rushing over. Trapped between the bed and the window, she had nowhere to go. His hands shot out, grabbed her by the shoulders, and held her in a grip she knew she wouldn't be able to throw off, not this time.

"Look at me." Green eyes locked on to blue. "I know this is a shock. It is to me as well as you. But this secret…this situation, whatever you want to call it, I *will* be able to tell you and soon. It's not the kind of secret you can keep. *Everyone* will know soon enough. And before you ask, no, it has nothing to do with me, nothing at all. But Tara's a friend, Layla, and she needs help. I *have* to help her."

"It does have something to do with you, and it has something to do with me too."

"What do you mean?" His brow furrowed as he asked.

"Because it's affected us. It's caused me to doubt."

"You have no reason to doubt me, I swear."

Didn't she? She'd thought she had no reason to doubt Alex, but look at what had happened there. Did anyone really ever know anyone? Truly know them? What lay in their heart of hearts? Although she'd met Joseph two years ago, they'd only been together for just over a year. Was that time enough to know someone or no time at all?

"So, you haven't been in touch with Tara before now? You had no idea she was going to be in Florence? You're not having an affair?"

"An affair? Are you joking? Layla, when would I have time to have an affair? You keep me busy enough. Who do you think I am? Superman?"

She had to concede, he had a point.

"She's a friend, nothing more," he reiterated.

"But she used to be so much more."

"A long time ago, *years* ago, but a friend is all she is now."

"I know she left you, Joe. I know how much she hurt you." Not because he had said so. He hadn't. She knew because Hannah had told her—Hannah, another one of his exes. The world seemed littered with them suddenly. "Do you still have feelings for her?"

"No."

It was only one word, but perhaps all the more effective because of it. In desperation, she searched his eyes, supposedly the gateway to the soul, scanning them for some evidence of guile of deceit. But there was none. Was she surprised or not? She couldn't tell. As if in a haze, she realized he was speaking again.

"Layla, what Tara and I had, it can't hold a candle to what we've got. You're the one I love, the *only* one."

"You promise?" She was tired suddenly of arguing. He was going to help Tara with or without her consent. That was one thing she knew with absolute clarity.

"I promise."

"And you'll tell me soon? It will come between us if you don't."

"I'll tell you everything, and you'll understand."

She had to say it; she had to be honest. "It feels like you don't trust me."

"I do trust you. Do you trust me?"

When she faltered, he had to prompt her.

"Yes," she finally answered.

As he reached out to tuck her hair behind her ear, she braced herself for the question she knew he was going to ask.

"I just want her to know she's not alone."

"I know."

"So, is it okay? Can she come back with us?"

For the first time, Layla had an inkling of the impossible situation he was in, that *they* were in. The ex had shown up in need of help. Joseph was a nice guy. That's what she loved about him, his kindness, his compassion—qualities Alex had lacked. Joseph would do anything for anyone, even Tara. She should trust him. She *should*.

"Yes." She wished she could feel more certain about her answer. But even if she wasn't, she had convinced him. He looked visibly relieved, color returning to his cheeks. "As long as it's not *Australia's Most Wanted* we're accompanying back."

"That's not it, I promise."

Although she had meant that as a joke, neither of them laughed.

"When we're home, in Cornwall, what then?"

"When we're home, she'll be taken care of."

"By her parents?"

"That's the plan."

As though sensing that something had shifted in her, Joseph grew bolder. He pulled her to him, and she allowed it, needing to feel him close, solid proof that he was still hers. She tilted her face upward, and immediately his lips sought hers. She hesitated at first but then kissed him back, purposefully. When Alex had cheated on her, she had run, swapped Brighton for Trecastle. She hadn't stayed and fought. As it turned out, it had been the right thing to do; he hadn't been worth fighting for. But Joseph was. Maybe Tara didn't want him, but if she did, let the battle begin.

"Layla," she heard him murmur, felt him growing hard. In contrast, she softened. "Layla," he said again, and this time she realized he was trying to get her attention.

"What?" she said, drawing back, slightly resentful she'd been made to.

"I thought it would be nice for you to meet Tara before we fly back. You know, get to know her a little."

"Sorry?" She was sure she hadn't heard right. "You want Tara and me to meet beforehand?"

"I think you'll like her."

Pulling away farther, she asked, "What did you have in mind exactly?"

"Dinner, round here, tomorrow night."

"Tomorrow night?"

"Yeah." He smiled then, that smoldering, intense smile she loved so much. The one he kept just for her. At least, she hoped so. "I did sort of mention it to her."

Clearly the word "mention" was Joseph-speak for invited already. Well, let her come along. Their first meeting would be on home turf.

It would give Layla the upper hand at least. Looking into his eyes, she still saw no guile there, but in Tara's she might see something different. A pre-flight meeting could prove very useful indeed.

"Okay. I'm fine with that. But I'll tell you something."

"What's that?" he said, his smile widening.

"You can bloody cook!"

chapter five

Joseph had offered to meet Tara outside the *Duomo*, a Florence
landmark, and walk with her back to the flat he shared with
his girlfriend, but she had refused. He was doing quite enough for
her already; she didn't want to push it. Still, looking at the piece of
paper on which she had written his address and directions, she had
to admit she was lost. Taking shelter in a doorway, she wondered
if she should just forget this whole crazy idea. Surely his girlfriend,
Layla, would not be as amenable as he had said she would be about
Tara accompanying them back to Cornwall. If she was, she was extraordinary. Tara wasn't sure she'd be as accommodating in similar
circumstances. But Joseph had insisted—in fact, he'd used that very
word to describe Layla: extraordinary.

She thought back to their meeting the day before. What were
the chances of it—in Florence of all places? The odds must have
been a million to one, at least. Without words, he had taken her by
the waist and steered her away from the thankfully departing crowds,
stopping finally at a café so they could sit and talk. And they had
talked. Or rather she had talked. A huge outpouring of words, words
she had been tempted to tell Lucas earlier but had refrained. With
Joseph, there was no holding back. Afterward, she didn't know if she
had done the right thing. The look on his face, she'd never forget it.

"I'm so sorry," she had said. "I should never…" but he had stopped her.

"Tara," he'd said, reaching across the table to hold her hand, "I'm here, and I will help."

When he had told her about Layla, the woman he lived with, she knew she had to relieve him of his promise.

"It's not fair, on you or her."

"If I could tell her…" he had started.

"No!" She hadn't meant to shout, but she didn't want anyone else knowing, not yet. "My parents," she had said by way of explanation.

She had tried to leave then. The last thing she wanted to do was cause trouble, to be a burden, but there was no way he would let her go.

"You can tell her," she had said at last, "just not yet. Please."

If he was worried, he didn't let it show, and that had reassured her. That's when he had said Layla would understand, when he had called her "extraordinary." And maybe he was right. She should trust him. She always had in the past. Implicitly.

A young woman passed by, dark haired, shades still in place despite the late hour. Stepping forward, Tara seized her chance.

"*Excusi*," she said. "*Parlez-vous Anglais?*"

She was well aware she had asked her question in French, but Italian flummoxed her. French did too, but at least she remembered a smattering of it from her school days.

"Yes," the woman replied, her accent heavy. "I speak English. Can I help?"

Tara thrust the piece of paper at her. "Do you know where this is?"

"This?" the woman said, staring at the paper. She then looked at Tara in abject disbelief. "This is here. You are standing outside it."

Tara swung round and stared at the bells, stacked neatly above each other and, sure enough, over the top of one, in big, bold letters were the words Scott-Lewis — Lewis must be Layla's surname.

"*Grazie*," she said, turning back, but the woman was already hurrying away, muttering under her breath, no doubt something about the idiot English.

Taking a deep breath, Tara clutched the bottle of wine she had brought with her to her chest, the tissue paper it was wrapped in rustling. She had stumbled upon their address inadvertently. It must be a sign. A sign that she was meant to do this, to let Joseph help her, to lean on him, even if she felt she didn't deserve to lean on him, not really, not after the way she had left him when she knew he still wanted her—when nothing had filled her mind but what waited for her.

Water under the bridge. That's what he'd said when she had brought up the past. And he looked as if he meant it. Although her news had winded him, fundamentally he was happy. She could see that. Layla Lewis was obviously good for him. And living in Florence, they had embarked on *their* adventure together at least. Long may their adventures continue, she thought, biting down on her lip.

It's now or never. Taking a deep breath, she forced her hand upward and pressed the small, round button with her index finger. Seconds passed—seconds that seemed eternal. Perhaps Joseph had changed his mind, seen sense, didn't want to get involved after all. And if that was the case, she wouldn't blame him. Not at all. She'd do what she had tried to do earlier; she would walk away. Unburden him.

But, oh, when she had first seen him, looked again into those impossibly blue eyes—if she were honest, she was still reeling from it…He was standing there right when she needed him, someone she had loved and who had loved her, who would not hesitate to take her in his arms and hold her. Ease the pain inside. Maybe heaven was still on her side after all, to throw a lifeline to her like that. He had been so gentle, so understanding, and, ultimately, so supportive. Part of her couldn't help but berate herself that she had ever let a man like him go. Despite Aiden.

"Tara, is that you?"

Joseph's voice over the intercom broke her reverie.

"Er…hi…yes, it's me."

Her voice sounded so small, like a mouse when once it had been a lion's roar.

"Hold on. I'm coming down."

Just a few seconds later, he was there, in front of her again, pulling her to him, enfolding her in his arms. He looked gorgeous, even better than he had yesterday, in a dark blue linen shirt this time and black jeans, casual but stylish too. Joseph always did have style. She had been proud to have him by her side.

"I'm so glad you came."

"Thanks." Whether he heard her reply or not, she didn't know. She wasn't even sure she had said the word out loud.

Releasing her, he grabbed her hand and pulled her inside. "Come on up. Layla's dying to meet you."

Tara wasn't sure about that, but she followed him anyway, hoping—no, praying—it was the case. At the top of three flights of stairs, he opened the door and stood aside. She would much rather he went ahead. Then she could walk in behind him, hide in his shadow. But, no, he was as gentlemanly as ever. She was to go first.

Stepping over the threshold, she entered the compact but cozy room. Cooking aromas immediately filled her lungs—tomatoes and herbs predominantly. Joseph loved cooking. She did too. They'd had some great times in the kitchen together, not all of them cooking related, she couldn't help but recall.

"Tara, this is Layla. Layla, meet Tara."

A woman stepped forward, about her own age, quite a bit taller than her and very pretty despite the heavy makeup—battle armor, perhaps? Brown hair, naturally highlighted, fell softly about her face. Eyeliner and mascara gave an almost feline quality to her green eyes. Her lips were red, full, and smiling, but not naturally so; it was more forced than that. Happy to meet her? She didn't think so.

"Hello, Tara. I'm glad you could make it."

Her words were as disingenuous as her smile. Tara suddenly felt hot all over. On her forehead, she was sure big beads of sweat had broken out. One hand flailed behind her for a chair to hold on to but found nothing. She was going to hit the ground, she thought, face first. She shouldn't have come. What a ridiculous idea. And then Joseph had hold of her arm. Her knight in shining armor—again.

"Take a seat. I'll get some wine."

"Oh, er, here, I brought a bottle," Tara managed, thrusting it at him.

Joseph took it from her while Layla continued to scrutinize her opponent. What did she see, Tara wondered? What kind of first impression was she making? They were very different in looks. Tara had short, bleached-blond hair, a style that suited her elfin-like face. Over the years she had cultivated an edgy look—a stud in her nose, lots of rings on her fingers, even a lip ring at one time, but she'd since had that removed. Mainly she wore skinny jeans, tank tops, and flip-flops.

She'd done so in Cornwall as well as Australia; although in Oz, tiny skirts had replaced the jeans. Tonight she had scoured her rucksack for something a little more formal, deciding on a black knee-length pencil skirt, black-and-white-striped top, and ballet pumps.

"Oh, Barolo. I love this," Joseph said, looking studiously at the label on the wine bottle. A little too studiously, perhaps? The atmosphere was thick like treacle in the studio apartment and just as sticky. Unless Joseph was totally thick-skinned, which she knew from past experience he was not, he couldn't have failed to notice it.

Pouring all three of them a large glass, he completely emptied the bottle. She took her glass and gulped at it. Layla and Joseph followed suit. Perhaps it would be better once the alcohol had kicked in. The atmosphere would ease.

Joseph turned his attention to more culinary matters, no doubt grateful that he could. Layla sat down opposite her, smoothing a tight T-shirt over equally tight jeans—an outfit chosen to highlight her perfect figure, no doubt. Her shoes had quite a heel on them, Tara noticed. Layla wasn't that much taller than her after all.

"So, what brings you to these shores?" Layla asked, that smile still in place.

"To Florence? It's a city I've always wanted to see."

"On your bucket list, then?"

Tara started. "Er, something like that."

"And Australia? It's history, is it?"

Tara nodded. "Yes, it's time to go home."

Layla appeared to consider this for a moment. "No one special who could tempt you to stay?"

"No one."

"Oh, well, no place like home…or so they say."

Was that sarcasm in her voice? Tara didn't know her well enough to tell. Gleaning courage from the hastily imbibed red wine, she leaned forward.

"Layla, Joseph, I want to thank you so much for flying back with me."

Before Joseph had a chance to reply, Layla cut in. "The pleasure's all ours."

That was definite sarcasm. She should tell her the reason why. It was only fair. Tara formed a sentence in her brain and then tried to verbalize it, but it was no use; her mouth wouldn't comply. Joseph knew, but if she hadn't been in such a state yesterday, she wouldn't have told him either. It was her parents who needed to know, who had needed to know first really. If there was a natural order to things, that was it.

Tara could sense the air around her grow heavy with expectation—Layla's expectation. Joseph caught her eye, an apology in it. Tara didn't acknowledge him; instead, she looked back at Layla and spoke her next words slowly and deliberately.

"You don't know how grateful I am."

Layla's face colored. She looked away. "Need any help in the kitchen?" she called across to Joseph.

"No, no," he replied, returning to the table, hastily refilling their wine glasses from a second bottle of red wine. "Everything's under control."

He pulled up a seat between them and downed his second glass as swiftly as his first—if it was his second, that is, and he hadn't been at the cooking sherry as well to steady his nerves. She wouldn't blame him if he had. For a short while, they talked about general subjects: artwork, sculptures, the weather here compared to England.

Everything was beginning to blur around the edges, which was good. It was what was needed. Layla too looked slightly more relaxed; she wasn't sitting as rigidly upright as before. Her lipstick had worn off; her lips were pink now, their natural color, much prettier, less formidable than the red. Hopefully it would be okay. They'd get through this meal, through the plane journey home, and then, when she was where she needed to be, she could say good-bye. Let them enjoy their holiday.

Joseph looked at his watch.

"Dishing up time," he said, smiling at her, smiling at them both in equal measures, she noticed. She was right; he was just as nervous as she was.

The food looked delicious. His cooking really had come along in the time they'd been apart. She scanned the kitchen area for cookbooks and wasn't surprised to note there weren't any. Joseph had always scorned them, used to like to make it up as he went along—an inventive cook. Before them was placed a salad, resplendent with artichokes, mozzarella, and tomatoes, a dish of crusty bread, and the *pièce de la resistance,* chicken cacciatore, red sauce bubbling, smelling divine.

They all helped themselves, but meagerly so. It seemed that they, like her, didn't have much appetite. Both she and Layla remarked on how good the dish was, but both of them seemed to be just pushing it around their plates rather than into their mouths. Joseph at least seemed to be making some headway, valiantly helping himself to the virtually ignored salad and bread and just as valiantly chomping his way through it, although she could see it was with effort. That he was willing to put himself through this for her, for the times they had shared, touched her.

"Music," Joseph said suddenly. "I was telling you about Jim's CD. I'll put it on."

He looked grateful to have something to do other than eat.

The first track of *Jagged Shore* filled the room—a soft, soulful tune, haunting almost. Jim's gravelly voice was perfectly suited to the Celtic-influenced guitar and drum accompaniment. Tara smiled fondly as she continued to listen. Jim had always shown a talent for music, right from their primary school days.

Layla was speaking to her again. "So, you and Jim grew up together in the same village. Is that right?"

"Yes. There was a group of us that all hung out."

"That's how I got to know Jim," Joseph elaborated. "Tara and I used to go to Port Levine regularly to visit her parents. Whenever we happened to be in the pub—The Admiral, it was called—Jim would be there too, entertaining everyone with his guitar and some song he'd just written. We all sort of hung out together."

"I know. You've told me before," Layla replied somewhat pointedly. Turning her attention back to Tara, she asked, "Do you know Hannah?"

"Jim's girlfriend?"

"And my best friend."

Tara cringed. Layla was letting her know she had allies too.

"Er, no, I don't know Hannah. He met her when he moved to Trecastle, didn't he? Joseph's told me a bit about her, though."

Layla looked across at Joseph, her head to one side and one eyebrow raised as if questioning just what Tara had been told. For his part, Joseph was staring at the wine bottle again, a third one, the label on it clearly as fascinating as the first and second.

Tara sensed it was time to divert the conversation.

"This CD, it's brilliant. Is the band doing well?"

"Very well." Joseph looked relieved—and proud. "They're gigging all over the place now, getting themselves quite a following."

"That's fantastic. Just in the UK or abroad too?"

"In the UK mainly, but they've got some European gigs lined up too."

She was about to ask more, but Layla clearly wanted to divert the conversation further.

"So, your parents," she said. "They must be over the moon you're coming back."

"They don't know yet," Tara admitted.

"They don't know?"

"Not yet," Tara repeated.

"Wow! Another surprise."

Joseph intervened. "There was no problem booking you onto the flight, Tara. I even managed to get you a seat just across the aisle from us." Looking at Layla, he added, "We're both really looking forward to getting back to Cornwall, to seeing the gang again."

"Have you been back at all?" Tara asked.

"I haven't, not since we arrived in January last year. Layla has, but not to Cornwall—to visit her friend in Brighton, which is where she's from. It's about time we both paid a visit, though. It's not as if it's on the other side of the world, is it?"

"No," Layla muttered. "Tara's the one from the other side of the world."

"Anyway," Joseph continued doggedly, "we're leaving on the Monday flight from Pisa and should arrive back in the UK just after noon. Jim's coming to meet us at Bristol Airport, and he'll drive us the rest of the way. You'll be home in no time."

Home. The thought of it both terrified and cheered her.

"Are you going to tell your parents or just turn up on their doorstep?" Layla asked.

Like I turned up on yours? The barb was clear.

"I...I don't know," Tara replied. "To be honest, I hadn't thought that far."

"Perhaps you should. Think that far, I mean."

Layla jolted suddenly. Had Joseph just kicked her under the table? Certainly Layla was glaring at him. Tara should really wrap this up, get out of here, fly back on her own—except wait; he'd already booked her ticket. The damage was done.

Coffee was just as strained. Tara quickly drained her cup and then pleaded tiredness as a reason to leave early. It was not actually a lie; she felt drained both mentally and physically. Layla looked tired too all of a sudden, she noted.

"I'll walk you downstairs." Joseph got up just as she did.

"No, there's no need…" Tara began, not wanting to cause more trouble than she had.

"It's fine. Layla doesn't mind, do you, Layla?"

A direct challenge, perhaps?

"No." Layla smiled sweetly—too sweetly. "Of course not."

Standing, she too came over to Tara and held out her hand. Such a formal gesture, considering they'd shared a meal together.

Noting the coolness of Layla's grip, Tara held her gaze. "Thank you, Layla. I mean it."

Layla faltered for a moment, softened almost, her expression merely curious rather than defensive as it had been all evening. But then she extracted her hand and turned back toward the table, starting to clear up the mess.

Tara and Joseph walked to the front door in silence. At the bottom of the stairwell, they stood for a few moments more.

"I'm sorry about—"

"Layla will come round—"

They looked at each other and burst out laughing. They used to do this a lot when they were together, speak simultaneously.

"You go first," he said.

"No, you. I insist."

He motioned upward with his eyes.

"Layla will come round. She's…she's just a little nonplussed at the moment. But she's fine really. She's a lot like you—feisty. I think you'll get on, eventually."

Feisty? Tara supposed she could have been described that way once, but now all that fire that used to burn inside her seemed spent.

"I'm sorry you can't be honest with her. It's just…"

"Tara, we've discussed this. It's fine. I understand the reason why, and Layla will too when I can tell her."

"My parents…"

"I know, and I agree."

"And it won't be long. Just a few more days, that's all I need."

Before he could reply, the light clicked off, and the hallway was plummeted into darkness. Not total darkness: the moon was bright in the sky, and it seeped in through the glass window over the top of the front door. Neither hurried to turn the light back on. They just stood there, drinking each other in. At least she was drinking in Joseph, the shadow of his face transporting her back to happier, more carefree times. Her early twenties were wrapped up in this man.

They had met in a pub in Hammersmith. Each was a friend of a friend—a setup, although it had been strenuously denied. No matter. As soon as she saw him, his dark-blond hair, his broad shoulders, his shy smile, she knew her friend's instincts had been right—she was going to like him. And he liked her. They had hit it off straightaway, had moved in together within six months of knowing each other, had loved living London life—working hard all week, him as a carpenter, she in public relations, but spending weekends browsing round shops and markets. Camden Town in particular, hanging out in coffee shops, laughing with friends in pubs and bars. They would also walk through Hyde Park on Sunday afternoons, stopping only to feed squirrels and birds—so tame they'd come right up to you as you held out tidbits for them. It had been a simple life, a life she thought would continue, until wanderlust had set in.

One of Tara's all-time favorite movies was *Point Break* starring Patrick Swayze and Keanu Reeves. She loved the surfing scenes, that whole "life's a beach" attitude, and particularly the last scene, with Swayze's character, Bodhi, standing on Bells Beach in Victoria, Australia, watching the Fifty-Year Storm approaching, determined to be at one with the elements when it did. Coming from Cornwall, surf was in her blood, but she wanted more—vaster oceans, paler sands, and endless sunshine. Australia called and wouldn't stop calling. Joseph loved his job, loved London, loved them more than her in the end. And her? She had her dreams to follow. Saying good-bye to him had been hard, though. The entire plane journey, she had wondered what the heck she was doing. As soon as she touched down in Sydney, she knew: the right thing. It was like coming home, better than anything she'd seen in the movies. Quickly she settled in, had started meeting people. Joseph was not forgotten, but he was consigned to the back of her mind as her new life took over, the odd postcard exchanged soon becoming no postcards at all. All contact lost. Until now. Now, some incredible twist of fate had thrown him back into her life.

Reaching up a hand, she touched his face, running her fingers along the familiar contours of his jaw.

"Thank you," she said. Would he notice her eyes glistening?

Joseph covered her hand with his and held it there for a few seconds.

"Anytime," he whispered.

With great effort she removed her hand. She wanted to hold it there forever. Stay with him in the dark, removed from reality. But she couldn't. Reality was waiting. *Layla* was waiting. Opening the door, she journeyed onward.

"See you Monday," she heard him call after her.

chapter six

Despite Scarlett screaming blue murder in her motorized swing—the same swing that promised to soothe baby into the land of sweet dreams, the swing she was considering taking back to *Yummy Mummy* and demanding her money back, this very afternoon in fact and with menace—Penny managed to focus entirely on Layla.

"So, you're flying back with her?" She had heard the first time, despite the crackling on the line between them, but she couldn't help but double check.

"Yep. Joseph even managed to get her a seat in the some row, if you can believe it."

Believe it? Only just.

"And she's got a secret, a secret you're not allowed to know?"

"That's about the gist of it."

"Even though Joseph knows."

"Oh, yeah, he knows all right."

"Wow! That's put the cat amongst the pigeons."

"The what?" There was that crackle again.

"It's something my Gran used to say. It means the situation you're in, it sucks."

"It's certainly different." Layla sighed, a heavy sound.

"What does Hannah think? Have you told her yet?"

"Yeah, I've told her. Joe's been in touch with Jim too. He's coming to meet us at Bristol Airport. I spoke to Hannah early this morning. We're crashing at theirs."

"What?" Penny almost choked. "Tara too?"

"No, not Tara," Layla quickly corrected. "She's going to stay at her parents'. They live in a village along the coast a bit, Port Levine."

"Port where? Have we been there?" Penny asked.

"No, it's not really a tourist village."

"Oh, it's a proper village, then."

"Yeah." A mock derisory laugh from Layla—that was good. "One of *those*."

"So, what does Hannah think?"

"She thinks it's odd, like me."

"And me," Penny insisted. "It's *very* odd. If Joseph is in on this secret, then you should be too. He's your boyfriend, not hers." Another thought occurred to Penny. "Hey, you don't think she's on the run, do you? From the police, I mean?"

"It had crossed my mind."

"Wanted for fraud, robbery, or…"—Penny gasped, getting quite carried away—"even murder." On another intake of breath, she added, "Layla, you could be in danger."

"I've thought about that too. I've even tried to check her out on the Internet. She lived in a seaside town not far from Sydney—Lyons Bay, apparently—but there's nothing anywhere about any murderous single white female currently on the loose."

Penny's shoulders slumped. "Oh, well, in that case, I think you should tell her to get lost."

"I can't. He won't…" Layla's voice sounded small all of a sudden. "He…he's asked me to trust him. He said he'd tell me why she has to come back soon."

"How soon?"

"As soon as he can."

"Not good enough. I'd tell him to get lost too."

"Penny," Layla admonished.

"Oh, all right, all right, but do you, Layla? Trust him, I mean?"

"Why shouldn't I?" She was defensive now.

"You tell me."

"I do," Layla replied, but far too quickly. "The secret, it's got nothing to do with him…apparently."

"You don't sound convinced." Penny decided to be honest with her.

"No. I am. They haven't seen each other in years. Why would it have anything to do with him? It's just…"

"It's just what?"

"It's just when they split up, she was the one who left him, not the other way round. Although Joseph and I haven't spoken about it much—you know what he's like; he hates making a big deal of things—I know from Hannah that he was really cut up about it when he first moved to Trecastle. It was the main reason he moved there."

"Like you did because of Alex?"

"Yes. And like me, it took him a while to get over it. Perhaps he still isn't."

"Are you over Alex?"

"God, yes."

No doubt in her voice there, Penny was glad to note. Alex had been a rotten, two-timing—no, make that three-, even four-timing bastard, far too flashy for his own good and far too old for Layla. Forty-three he had claimed to be to Layla's then twenty-eight. Yeah, right. Believe that, and you'll believe anything. What she had seen in him was a mystery, the arrogant arse. Working as a marketing executive in his company, Easy Travel in Brighton, where Penny had also worked for a while, Layla had spent years mooning over him before he had deigned to ask her out, and only then after he had worked his way through most of his other staff members—the ones who happened to be at least ten years younger than him, that is.

He and Layla had lasted a year before he reverted to type and ran off with the latest girl on the block, leaving Layla not only heartbroken but bewildered too. The only thing he'd left in his wake was a Post-it note telling her to carry on with business in his absence. It was the marketing manager, a witch of a woman called Hazel, who had filled Layla in on the rest—in front of the entire workforce, humiliating her further. That Post-it note, it had killed Layla, made her feel like dirt, probably not even as grand.

When an opportunity had come up to move hundreds of miles away, she had taken it, desperate to escape Alex and memories of him.

She'd said that in Brighton, they were everywhere. Although Penny had been against the move to Trecastle at first—she had wanted her best friend to stay close—it had been good for Layla. It was where she had met Joseph. And Joseph loved Layla; it was obvious.

With that in mind, she decided to give Joseph the benefit of the doubt—so easy to do on someone else's behalf. "Then maybe it's the same for him. Maybe there is a valid reason why he has to keep quiet. Maybe you should do as he asks. Trust him."

"Yeah." She could practically see Layla's head bobbing up and down like that dog on the telly, the annoying plastic one that advertised insurance. "Yeah, I know."

"Look, I have to go. The baby…"

"Of course."

"Call me when you're on British soil."

"I will," Layla promised.

Ending the call, Penny didn't go to Scarlett straightaway. Instead, she managed to zone her out for a few moments as she pondered the conversation she'd just had.

She didn't envy what Layla was going through. That age-old issue of trust, she had to concede, was a tough one. Would she trust Joseph if she were in Layla's Converse boots? She didn't know. Mind you, that was probably because of her personal track record. In the past, she hadn't always played fair with Richard. She had never overstepped the mark, mind, never slept with anyone else while married to him, but flirting, she had certainly done that, until one of her flirtations had turned sour. Dylan had turned from a seemingly harmless admirer into a stalking maniac, texting her constantly, begging her to meet him before turning up on her doorstep, accusing her of leading him up, well, quite aptly, considering where he was standing, the garden path.

Hot on Layla's heels, she had fled to Trecastle too, to escape not only him but Richard's wrath. He knew about Dylan; she had told him. What Richard didn't know was that she had continued to see Dylan long after saying she had cut all ties. In her defense, it was only as friends, something she thought she had made crystal clear to Dylan. Obviously not. But initially his cheeky, bad-boy ways had made her laugh at a time when she had needed laughter—when things were rotten with Richard, thanks to the hours he worked, and when her best friend had upped and left. She had felt alone and unwanted, as though she had suddenly stopped mattering to everyone who mattered to her. Her liaison with Dylan was innocent. Okay, she begrudgingly admitted, semi-innocent. But, for a while, she had liked the way he had made her feel, the way he had looked at her, as though she were desirable, at least.

She was sure Richard would leave her after Dylan-gate. But, to her surprise, he hadn't. He had followed her down to that funny little village in Cornwall instead — that village Layla loved so much, that she always insisted was drenched in magic — not to divorce her but to tell her Dylan wouldn't be bothering her again. He'd made sure of it. And to tell her he loved her too, she mustn't forget that bit, that he worshipped the ground she walked on. Perhaps Layla was right, after all, about the magic. She had fallen into his arms then, told him she was pregnant — she'd only just found out herself — and all had been right with the world again. During her pregnancy, they'd been as close as they were before her flirting and his workaholic ways had come between them. But now something had come between them again — spectacularly so — in the shape of little Miss Scarlett. Whoever said having a child brought a couple closer had obviously never road-tested that theory.

Penny looked down at her tracksuit bottoms. Correction: her baby-food-splattered tracksuit bottoms. Just as well she was no longer interested in flirting. Who'd want to flirt with her now anyway? She was a mess. A harassed, neurotic, and depressed mess — oh, and frumpy too, she mustn't forget that. How Richard could bear to look at her, she didn't know, let alone make a move on her. Although to be fair, he hadn't for months now. Not that she minded. She was never in the mood anyway.

Harassed, neurotic, and depressed…Those three little words would not stop haunting her. They were all the things Richard had implied she was when he had come home to find her in the same state of meltdown as Scarlett — both of them consumed with anger and, in her case, despair too. A mum-and-baby combo.

"What the hell?" he had said, going to Scarlett first, she noticed, picking her up and cradling her to him. And wouldn't you know it? The baby had quieted at his touch, making Penny cry even harder. All day she had tried to soothe Scarlett, and all day she had failed. Actually, she hadn't cried. That was putting it too politely. She had *howled*, like a wolf might howl at a full moon. What a sight she must have looked.

Even Richard couldn't ignore her howling. It was deafening. After a few startled moments, he had actually come over to her, baby still in arms, and acknowledged her.

"What is it, Penny? What's the matter?"

I need a hug too! A hug and a truckload of Valium.

Those were the words she should have said, but she was too busy howling. Some part of her was wondering—the part of her that was just holding on to the edge of sanity—if there was a full moon outside, and if so, what did it know that she didn't?

As predicted, Richard did not put the baby down, not until Scarlett fell into an exhausted sleep—a sleep Penny knew wouldn't last. She'd be up through the night, two o'clock, four o'clock, and then from six she'd be awake for good, all while Richard slumbered peacefully in the spare room, his ear plugs and eye mask firmly in place.

When at last he had carefully laid the baby in her crib, spending ages upstairs doing so, either enraptured by Scarlett's—temporary—peaceful repose or trying to summon up the courage to come downstairs and face his increasingly deranged wife, she had opened a bottle of wine, determined to down it in one. Trouble was it had made her retch. In a fit of pique, she had downed some water instead. All that howling made a girl thirsty.

Eventually Richard had returned to the kitchen, sauntered casually over to the fridge, grabbed himself a beer, turned to her, and said, "Penny, you really need to sort yourself out, you know. The way you're acting, it's not good for Scarlett."

And that was it; she was off again—howling. *Everything* was about the baby; *nothing* was about her. It was as though she'd ceased to be a woman in Richard's eyes. She had become something else entirely; something she didn't know how to be: a mother—despite reading manual after manual on the subject.

An argument had ensued, a vicious, snarling argument—and yes, he had snarled at her as much as she had snarled at him—and that's when the words "harassed, neurotic, and depressed" had been alluded to. No, not alluded to, thrown slap bang in her face. "Neurotic" in particular a favorite among the trio.

Look, I'm trying here. I'm trying to be Mother of the Year. I'm doing everything I can, but she hates me. Yes, that's right, hates me. She screams when she sees me at night, in the morning, through the day. Nothing I do is right. I can't seem to make her happy, to make her gurgle, to make her coo. None of the things that those bloody textbooks I devour tell you babies should do. But I try, Richard, I really, really try.

If only she had said those words in that order, but she hadn't. They had come out stuttering, disjointed, and mixed up instead. Even she had thought she was an idiot.

"Penny," he had said, rolling his eyes at her, deep-brown eyes she used to drown in once upon a time. "You're making something out of nothing here."

"But Richard," she had protested, "I'm not…"

And then he had come out with the clincher.

"Yeah, you are. Looking after a baby, it's not rocket science, you know. It's easy."

That was *not* what she had wanted to hear. Escape beckoned—the front room. She had stormed toward it, slamming the door behind her, the subsequent shaking of the doorframe impressive. Next, she had pushed the sofa up against it, thrown herself on the rug in front of the telly, and damn well howled some more.

She had refused to come out, either—not for him, for Scarlett, or for Armageddon. He and the baby, they were welcome to each other. She only interrupted the love fest between them anyway. Instead, she had relished being alone—something of a novelty lately—finally grabbing a cushion off the sofa, propping it under her head, and falling promptly asleep, the darkness that ensued a comfort.

Richard had left bleary-eyed and bad-tempered the next morning, clearly unable to cope with even one broken night when she had endured countless. He had handed the baby to her once she had un-barricaded herself, mumbled, "God knows what today's going to be like. I'm exhausted, and I've got an important meeting, too," and then slammed his way out of the house, the doorframes quaking some more.

She had looked down at the bundle in her arms and, for a moment, not even a moment really, had thought Scarlett was going to smile at her. Certainly something was going on. Sadly, it had been wind—wind followed by a massive follow-through that squirted right out of her nappy and soaked them both in a brown and fetid mess. And then, as though the baby was affronted by what had just happened, as though it were Penny's doing, not hers, she had started screaming again. Quashing down bitter disappointment, her own tears threatened again as she headed upstairs to the bathroom, but this time she had managed to keep them at bay.

Layla had been the first adult she had talked to properly since her meltdown. It was such a shame it was only on the telephone. If Layla were here, in the flesh, Penny might feel more able to cope.

The baby's cries became too loud to ignore.

"Don't worry. Mummy's coming."

As usual, her reassuring words had no reassuring effect at all. Forcing herself up from the sofa, Penny walked over to the gently swaying swing, more determined than ever to take the ruddy thing back. It seemed to be ticking Scarlett off even more. Richard had assembled it. Hopefully she wouldn't have too much trouble taking it apart. She'd need a screwdriver, though, if she could find one. Richard never put stuff back in the right place. But first she had better feed the baby, and then she'd need to wait awhile for the food to go down. Scarlett tended to suffer from wind otherwise, by which time she'd probably need changing again and then…Crikey, would she ever get out?

In the kitchen, Penny opened a jar of something organic—something orange in color and smelling like Play-Doh. Both she and Scarlett wrinkled their noses at it, united in their distaste at least. Perhaps she'd mash up some banana instead and then look forward to having it thrown back at her in big slimy lumps. Placing Scarlett in her bouncy chair so she could free her arms, she wondered whether to run upstairs and get Richard's earplugs. If there was one thing the baby hated more than the swing, it was her bouncy chair, despite jolly pictures of circus animals emblazed in bright colors upon it. As Scarlett carried on doing what she did best—bursting her mother's eardrums—Penny thought again about trust. Yep, it was a precarious subject, littered with pot holes so deep, if you fell into them, you ran the risk of never seeing daylight again. Layla didn't know whether to trust Joseph. Richard probably didn't know whether he could trust his neurotic wife with his precious baby. And worst of all, Penny didn't know if she could trust herself.

chapter seven

W ell, that was a journey Layla never wanted to repeat. The tur-
bulence outside was nothing compared to what was happening
inside the aircraft. The atmosphere was so fragile it could shatter at
any moment, send them all plummeting to the ground.

Breathe, just breathe, she told herself for the umpteenth time as
they waited on the tarmac outside Bristol Airport for Jim to come
and pick them up in Joe's old Land Rover Defender, the car he had
given to Jim on permanent loan when they had left for Florence. As
he had sat between them on the plane, he was standing between them
now, refereeing Layla's behavior — or at least that was the way it felt
to her. Behavior he had challenged her about after the two girls had
met for the first time.

"You know what, Layla?" he had said upon re-entering their
apartment the evening Tara had come for dinner — was it really only
four days ago? It seemed one heck of a lot longer than that. "Sarcasm
really doesn't suit you."

"Oh dear," she had replied — sarcastically. "And there's me thinking I looked so damn good in it." Rounding on him, she had continued, "And how come it took you so long to say good-bye to her?
It's just one little word. It takes, hang on, let me practice it in my
head. Yep, around two seconds, I'd say, at a stretch three. What were
you up to?"

"We were planning what battle armor to wear on Monday, if you must know. She's going for chainmail, whereas I'm opting for a full-on Teflon suit. And even then, I'm not sure it's going to be effective in repelling what comes out of your mouth."

Sarcasm was obviously catching.

Furious, she had been about to throw the tea towel at him when she had seen a smile play around the edges of his mouth. Beyond furious, she had thrown it anyway.

"There's chemistry between you," she had declared.

"There's not."

"There is. There's a sizzle."

"A sizzle?" he had pondered. "Is that even a word?"

"Oh, shut up, Joseph. You know what I mean."

"I don't, actually. I don't read or write romance novels like you do. I tend to live in the real world, a world where the only *sizzle*, as you put it, is between you and me."

God, she hated it when he got smart—something he must have noticed.

"Layla, Layla," he had tried to appease, coming up behind her and catching her round the waist, refusing to let her go even when she had slapped hard at his hands. "Look, I'm not serious. Come on, chill out. I thought we had an understanding."

"*You* have an understanding, you mean. You and Tara." She had accidentally-on-purpose stood on his foot then, his hands springing open in surprised reaction.

The playful smile had gone from his face.

"Layla, we had this sorted. I thought you were cool about it."

Men! They were such simple creatures sometimes.

"I don't know what I think, okay? Be careful how far you push me."

"Layla," he had said again, and there had been something in his voice. Was it a note of pleading or just sheer exasperation?

"Just don't," was all she'd been able to come up with in reply before going into the shower room, the only place in this tiny studio she could seek sanctuary.

Grabbing her cleanser and some cotton wool from the wicker basket she kept beside the sink, she had scrubbed furiously at her makeup. She had troweled it on in layers before Tara's arrival: concealer, foundation, powder, blusher, highlighter, mascara, eye powder, lipstick, lip liner—the whole damn lot, wanting to look the best she could. After all, who knew what was going to walk through the door to greet her? She must be impressive if she could ensnare her ex again so easily with some conveniently drummed-up sob story. Impressive? In a way she was, diminutive but with a sass about her. She was pretty, definitely, her blue eyes a match for Joseph's, her features petite like she was. She'd stand out in a crowd, Layla would give her that. But there was something canny about her, something… well, secretive was the best description. Why, oh, why was she in their lives again—*his* life?

Relations had been strained between Layla and Joseph following the dinner date. Both of them had been glad to have respective jobs to escape to on Friday, coming home in the evening and tiptoeing around each other. Being polite, agonizingly so at times. Even at the weekend, they had offered to work. Paolo as well as Stefania, who ran *La Pasticceria Barontini*, had been surprised but delighted. At night, Layla kept strictly to her side of the bed instead of lying in his arms like she usually did. Last night, he had whispered her name when he had come to bed, only a few minutes after she had. But she had ignored him, pretended to be asleep—even made a show of snoring gently to prove it. She couldn't help herself. The more time she had to think about it, the more addled her mind became.

And now they were back in the UK—all three of them. Layla had scoured every inch of the in-flight magazine on the way over, pretending to find articles on global warming and the art of Spanish cuisine utterly scintillating. Fooling no one.

"Good to be back, huh?" Joseph attempted to put his arm around her.

Layla stepped briskly forward, just out of reach.

"Oh, there's Jim. Over there," she said by way of excuse.

Jim jumped from the car to greet them. Tall and rugged, his hair shaggy above his shoulders, he looked every inch the musician he was.

"Joe!" he said, walking toward them. No, that wasn't right. He *swaggered* toward them, not in a "hey, look at me" kind of way, more in a "hey, don't sweat it" manner. It wasn't possible to get more laid-back than Jim. In loose jeans and his brown leather jacket, just as battered as the Defender, he oozed every kind of appeal, although, knowing Jim, it was by accident. Not by design. Going to Joseph first, he grabbed him and enfolded him in a bear hug. Within seconds, he had done the same to Layla, whispering a "Hello, gorgeous" in her ear as he did so. And then he stood and looked at Tara.

"You haven't changed a bit. You look fantastic."

Tara smiled at him, a smile that made her look like a kid, not the thirty-year-old woman she was. It was the first real smile Layla had seen on her face.

"Jim," she said, closing the gap between them. "It's good to see you too."

Jim threw his arms around her, and they hugged—and hugged and hugged. Good thing Hannah was back in Trecastle, thought Layla. She might have something to say about the length of time they were spending hugging. Then again, they were old friends. They shared history together—Tara and Jim, Tara and Joseph. Layla felt even more of an outsider.

After piling their luggage into the back, they climbed into the car.

"You sit up front," Joseph had urged Tara, one thing Layla was grateful for.

In the back seat, Joseph's hand reached across to hold hers. Briefly, Layla considered snatching her hand back but decided against it. The situation was tense enough. She really didn't want to inflame it further.

Jim chatted happily while he drove, either oblivious to any atmosphere in the car or choosing to ignore it—probably the latter. He told them all about his band's next round of gigs in a fortnight, kick-starting in Exeter and ending in Edinburgh. He talked about Hannah too, telling Tara how much she'd like her—that everybody liked her. Layla zoned out, staring out of the window instead. This route to Cornwall was a meaningful one for her, one she had taken many times with her mother as a child and then again when she had bolted down just over two years ago—on the run from Alex. And here she was again, accompanying a runaway this time.

Still, it was a journey she loved, the green hills on either side of the road as rugged as the men in the car, strewn with rocks and boulders, reminding her of just how wild this part of Cornwall was. Not like the south, where it was more pretty than rugged—"Champagne Cornwall," as Joseph dubbed it. This was the real thing. It was natural up here, unkempt almost, and all the more beautiful because of it.

Leaving the dual carriageway, they traveled tiny, twisting roads instead. Jim handled them expertly, still laughing up front with Tara. What was it that had drawn Tara back here? Layla was dying to know. And what was so important she needed Joseph with her—his strength to strengthen her? Was there really no significant other in Australia? She had been there for years. Five, she had said, or was it six? Had she formed no significant attachments in that time? Australia was history; she didn't intend going back. Yet all she had with her was a rucksack. It wasn't much to show for a life lived elsewhere.

This part of the journey always passed quickly, and before long, Layla could see signposts to Trecastle. Any minute now, the sea would come into view. It would look beautiful on a day like today, almost exactly the same shade as the sky, the dividing line between them barely if at all distinguishable. And in among gentle waves would be Gull Rock, her rock. One day she would reach it—or perhaps it was better to let it always remain out of reach. Up close it might not look so impressive; it might look ugly and scarred instead. She shifted uncomfortably at the thought.

"You okay?" asked Joseph, noticing.

"Fine." She smiled, trying to mean it this time.

Soon they were entering the village itself, bypassing the spot where she had first met Joseph—*crashed* into him more accurately, knocking him off his trail bike on her first wet and windy day in Trecastle while executing a three-point turn in her beloved red Mazda. It was some introduction, she thought, her face softening at the memory.

Joseph squeezed her hand. Was he remembering too?

The main road that ran through the village—the high street, the locals called it, although it was actually called Castle Street, named for the twelfth-century ruins that dominated the cliff top—was quiet on this March afternoon. It wouldn't liven up until the next holiday season, Easter. Then the tourists would swarm in, the owners of pubs, restaurants, and shops eagerly anticipating their influx. Although a tiny village, it was the castle, steeped in myth and legend, that drew the visitors here—the castle as well as the glorious beach it overlooked, one of the finest in Cornwall. Enclosed by granite cliffs, Trecastle Strand was a gorgeous swathe of golden sand, as good as any Mediterranean beach. Better, in fact, because the caves in the cliffs made it more interesting. They were dark and mysterious, hiding secrets of their own.

Conveniently, the beach was only a ten-minute walk from the village, down to the end of Castle Street, then down again via a steep hill, green hills rising up either side of it, yellow gorse adding a glorious dash of color. You could either drive down to it, although parking was limited at the beach, or leave your car in the village and hop aboard the Land Rover service that ran during the summer. It surprised her how many perfectly fit young people made use of the Land Rover and how many older people chose to get the exercise instead.

They drew up outside Hannah and Jim's flat, the bottom half of a Victorian terrace, the only row of Victorian houses in Trecastle. Most of the buildings were later than that, although some were older, an eclectic mix. Immediately, the front door opened.

"Layla," Hannah yelled. Her golden-brown hair, shoulder-length like Jim's and almost exactly the same color, flew behind her as she sprinted up the pathway.

She grabbed the door handle, yanked it open, and virtually pulled Layla out of the car. "I've missed you so much."

Layla smiled. As her hand had clung to Joseph's in the car, she now clung to her best friend — her *other* best friend — glad that Hannah, like her, didn't know Tara either.

The two boys and Tara came around to stand on the pavement beside them. Flanked by their breadth and height, Layla noticed how fragile Tara looked.

Breaking away, Hannah approached Joseph next. "Hi," she said, briefly hugging him too.

Layla wondered if it was going to be okay crashing at Hannah and Jim's flat, or whether it might be painful for Hannah. Although it had been a long time since Hannah and Joseph had split up, it had taken her even longer to get over him. Would his close proximity dredge up old feelings? Despite being with the delectable Jim — and he really was delectable, with his smoky green eyes and lazy smile — Hannah had pined for Joseph. Jim knew that but was prepared to accept it, not because he was weak but because he'd take Hannah any way he could get her.

The turning point for Hannah had come just before Layla and Joseph had left for Florence. That's when Jim had played his trump card. Unbeknown to Hannah, to everyone, he had written her a song — *Angel's Heart* — and had played it in front of everyone at their friend Mick's thirtieth birthday party in the Trecastle Inn. That song had touched everyone in the house, not just Hannah, and was now one of the songs featured on *Jagged Shore*. It had made Hannah realize what she had in Jim—an absolute gem—and to lay feelings outgrown to rest. At least Layla hoped so.

"Come on." Jim's cheery voice filtered through her thoughts. "Let's go in, get a drink."

All went to follow him, all except Tara.

"Erm…" she began rather sheepishly. "Do you mind if I don't? I'm really very tired. I just want to…to get home, see my parents."

Jim was about to say something, to protest, perhaps, but Joseph spoke first.

"We don't mind at all, Tara. It's not a problem."

"But how will you get home?" Hannah looked genuinely puzzled. "You live in Port Levine, don't you?"

Joseph was quick to offer. "I'll drive her there. Can I take the car, Jim?"

Immediately Jim threw him the car keys. "It's your car, mate. I'm just looking after it for you."

Layla swallowed—hard.

Of course he was going to drive her home. She should have expected that.

Joseph turned to her. "Is that okay, Layla? I won't be long."

With four pairs of eyes staring at her, what could she say? *No, it isn't okay. None of this is okay. There's something about it that actually feels very un-okay.*

Instead she replied, "Sure. There's no rush."

Joseph reached across and kissed her on the cheek. He looked—how did he look? *Proud* of her? Yes, that was it, definitely. She'd never felt such a fraud.

Tara said good-bye to them all and hopped back into the car. Again she looked fragile, lost almost. Layla started to feel the first stirrings of sympathy. And then she stopped. *Don't be taken in by her. Not yet. Not until you know the full story.*

The full story? That was something she didn't think she'd ever know.

chapter eight

It was a few minutes into their journey before Tara spoke.

"This isn't easy for you, is it? I mean with Layla."

"Hey." He reached across to cover her hand with his, only momentarily taking his eyes off the road so he could look at her too. "It's not easy for you either." After a moment, he added, "That's why I'm here."

"But I don't want to cause trouble."

"You won't. You haven't. Look, don't worry about it. Please."

But she did worry. Layla didn't like her; it was obvious. And Tara didn't blame her—who would? Layla probably thought she had designs on Joseph, wanted to inveigle her way into his affections again. How wrong she was. It was Aiden she longed for, his dark smoldering eyes, the way he looked at her so intently, as though he couldn't bear to tear his gaze from her, not even for a moment, that satisfied half-smile on his face after they'd made love. This longing for him was worse than she had anticipated. She ached—every inch of her. She loved this man, too, sitting beside her. Of course she did. A part of her had never stopped loving him, but it was in a different way entirely. She had never felt about anyone the way she felt about Aiden, lost to her forever now, a million miles away, or as good as.

When she had first arrived in Australia, she had spent a lot of time backpacking, living on savings and money her parents had given her for the trip—insisting she take it while they had it to give. They'd rather live to see her and her sister enjoy their inheritance than leave it to them in their will. She had met a lot of people backpacking, had quickly forged friendships with them, hanging out on the beach, in bars, traveling in cars and on coaches across great tracts of land under skies that seemed so much bigger than the skies in England, though how that was possible no one seemed to know. Weeks turned into months turned into years as time flew by. And then she had met Aiden, after coming full circle to Sydney—or close to Sydney. Lyons Bay, to be precise, his hometown. Why she had chosen to stop there, she didn't know. She'd intended to find work as a waitress in the big city itself, but en route, the fabulous stretch of golden sand and lively vibe of the small seaside town had grabbed her attention, maybe because it reminded her so much of Cornwall. It was funny, she remembered thinking, you come all this way to find things not so different after all.

Aiden had been on the beach, enjoying the blistering day, chatting with a group of friends, splashing in the surf, riding the waves, brilliant at it as all Ozzies seemed to be. She had noticed him straightaway, had been studying him furtively from her vantage point higher up on the sands, grateful that her Ray-Bans covered her prying eyes. When he had finally noticed her, she had pretended to be surprised.

"Hey," he had said, wandering up to where she was sitting with a group of friends she'd only just met—their English heritage the common bond. "How you doing?"

Gina, one of the group, had started giggling.

"Who does he think he is?" she had stage-whispered to Tara. "Joey from *Friends*?"

Tara had smiled too and then told him she was doing fine.

"Mind if I sit beside you for a while? I just spent an age out in the ocean, and my legs feel like they're about to give way."

"Oh, really, have you?" she had replied, well aware she was fooling no one. He had spied her watching him, and she'd known it. Thankfully, he hadn't seemed to mind.

As he had introduced himself, she had relished the twang of his accent and the smile not only on his face but also in his velvet eyes. She had also loved the broadness of his shoulders, his washboard stomach, his sun-kissed skin, a whole catalog of things.

As they had sat there, the pair of them, smiling goofily at each other, the group had gradually broken up, some heading toward the sea, others in search of a drink.

"Do you want a drink too?" he had asked her, motioning to Right on the Beach, the café directly behind them. "It's on the house if you do."

"Oh?" She had cocked her head to one side. "How come?"

"Because I own it, and for you, gorgeous, everything's on the house."

Eventually, they had wandered over together, grabbed two bottles of ice-cold beer from the fridge inside, and found themselves a shaded spot to drink them in. One bottle of beer had turned into two, the day began to fade, and night had fallen. Still they had talked—couldn't stop talking. There was nothing more interesting to her in the world that night than the man sitting opposite her. Everything about him had fascinated her, from the way he laughed to the way his face grew serious when she was the one doing the talking. As the sun rose the next day, they were still on the beach but this time sitting side by side, his arm wrapped round her, her head on his shoulder. As morning bloomed, she had sensed the world around her was set to change yet again; the adventure she had embarked on was ramping itself up a notch.

Aiden had helped her find some digs near the café—just a room, nothing fancy—and offered her a job as a waitress at his café if she wanted it. She had. They started to spend every day and night together. She needn't have rented a room, really, since she had stayed over at his apartment most nights—nights they had spent in contented bliss, exploring each other to the full, minds as well as bodies. Soon, she had given the room up and moved in with him.

"Don't worry about traveling," he had assured her. "We can still do that. The café will be okay with Caro and Den running it. We can take off wherever you want. Have you seen Ayers Rock yet?"

She had, but she had wanted to see it with him, to marvel together at the grandeur of the sandstone monolith. To witness the different personalities it took on during sunrise and sunset, the many different hues. At first subtle, then blindingly bright. She had wanted to feel the romance of it. Having seen it before with a bunch of near strangers, it had missed that particular quality for her. With him, it had been intense.

She had already known love with Joseph. She didn't dare think she'd strike gold twice, not so soon after him, but that's exactly what she had done. Two perfect years she had spent with Aiden, on that beach, in the café, traveling whenever they could, living the life she had dreamed of before the dream had grown teeth.

"Tara, we're here."

What? So soon?

He was right. They were outside her parents' cottage. There it was in front of them, picture-postcard pretty, whitewashed walls gleaming in the sun, wide instead of tall, and with a slate roof her father was forever mending. A large, equally pretty garden surrounded the detached house, and a winding path led to the front door, painted a bold shade of purple, her mum's favorite color.

"Oh God," she breathed.

Joseph killed the engine and turned to her.

"Tara, you can do this."

She was glad of his faith in her, because she wasn't so sure.

"Tara—"

"I know," she interrupted. "Just give me a minute. Please."

A moment of silence passed, then two, then three. Moments that seemed endless.

Roger and Lily Mills were in that house, just a few feet away. Her dad she imagined in his favorite armchair by the hearth in the living room, wading through some broadsheet he walked down to fetch every morning from the village store. Her mother would be in the kitchen—she loved baking—or indulging in her second favorite hobby, knitting. She was forever knitting items for local fêtes; her brightly colored cashmere socks were in hot demand. As much as Tara longed to see them, she hated to break the idyll of their lives. And she would; there was no doubt about it. She would tear it apart, destroy it. No, no, she couldn't do this. She should never have come back. But where else could she have gone? Who else would have her if not her parents? She couldn't wander forever, despite what she had thought.

Home, it's where the heart is, where you return when the going gets tough, if you're lucky enough to have a home. And she was. Roger and Lily had brought her and Leo up in the most loving of family environments. Strange, then, that she had been so desperate to leave, heading to London when she was eighteen and then to Australia some years later. And now she had returned. The prodigal daughter.

"Okay, I'm ready."

"Sure?"

He looked so concerned. Yes, she had been incredibly lucky in life; she couldn't deny it. Perhaps that's why luck had run out on her; you were only ever dealt so much.

"I'm sure."

"Do you want me to come in with you?"

"You mean shock them even more by turning up out of the blue after all these years and with my ex-boyfriend in tow? They'll think we've got hitched or something."

Joseph raised an eyebrow. "I see your point," he conceded before adding, "It would be nice to see your parents again, though. They're good people."

"They liked you too, Joe. They were so disappointed when we split up."

"They weren't the only ones," Joseph replied, but lightheartedly. His next words were more serious. "Don't keep them in the dark too long, will you, Tara?"

"I won't." Her voice was barely above a whisper.

"Despite what you think, they'll want to know."

"I'll tell them soon," Tara promised. "Perhaps not straightaway, as soon as I've clapped eyes on them, but once I'm…I'm settled. In a day or two."

"Of course."

Reaching for the door handle, she stopped. "Thanks for bringing me home, Joseph."

His smile was so gentle. "The pleasure's mine."

"I really don't know if I could have done it without you."

He held her gaze. "You know where I am —"

"— If I need you," she finished for him. "Yeah, I do."

"Phone me tonight. Let me know how it went. And maybe to-morrow night, or soon after, come to Trecastle. Get to know Layla a bit more, and Hannah. Have some fun."

Fun? She didn't think she'd ever have fun again.

"Yeah, that would be nice," she said, her feet once again touching home ground.

chapter nine

"Hey, you back in Trecastle yet?"

"Oh, hi, Penny. Yeah, we're at Hannah's, actually. Well, I am. Joseph has driven Tara back to her parents' house at Port Levine."

Penny frowned. Was that a slight catch in Layla's voice?

"How is Hannah? And Jim of course?" At the mention of Jim, she became all swoony. Ever since Jim had played that song for Hannah in the Trecastle Inn, the one he wrote especially for her, the one he surprised her with so spectacularly, the one he had sung with so much feeling in his voice, she'd had a bit of a crush on him. It was just such a romantic thing to do. If she had been Hannah, she would have jumped on Jim there and then, in front of the crowds, smothered him in kisses, dragged him back home, swung from the chandeliers with him, and generally lost herself in the throes of passion. Yeah, right, chance would be a fine thing.

Returning hastily to the subject of Joseph, Penny asked, "Has he been gone long?"

"Long enough," was Layla's terse reply.

Layla then told her about the flight over, the atmosphere you could cut with a knife, the strangeness of being back in Trecastle under such mysterious circumstances, how it took the shine off their holiday—which was a shame, because nothing should take the shine off Trecastle for Layla. It was too special a place for her. Penny felt for her, wished she could be with her, but she was chained to the house, to the baby, to her life in Brighton. At least that's what it felt like — chained. Gone were the days she only had herself to worry about. Now she was part of a family, a grown-up. It was a feeling that didn't quite fit right but should. At nearly thirty-two, she was certainly grown up, so why did she feel like a teenager inside? Still.

Then again, would she be able to help Layla make sense of the situation she was in? It didn't make sense to her either. They would need the full story for that.

Brightening, she said, "Richard's coming home early this evening. We're going out to Donatello's for a family meal, our first in a public place. I think it's called 'making an effort.' On his part, I mean."

Penny quickly filled her in on what had been happening in her life over the last few days — a breakdown, basically.

"Oh, Penny, I'm so sorry to hear that. I hope today goes well. I miss our drunken nights at Donatello's. You know, the house wine followed by copious amounts of Limoncello. That stuff, it's as lethal as Grappa. Is Alejandro still working there?"

"Last time I checked. Shall I say hi to him from you?"

"Yes, please, and tell him there's not a risotto marinara in the whole of Florence that can match his. It truly is the best."

"I will, Layla," Penny promised, laughing. Wistfully she added, "I can't believe you're in the UK and we're not going to see each other."

"You know I'd come and see you if I could, especially now I know how down you've been feeling, but there's even more of a reason to stay local now."

"To keep an eye on things, you mean?"

"Exactly."

"I totally understand, but let's speak every day. We can try to keep each other sane. Oh, here's Richard now. I can hear him at the door. Speak tomorrow."

"Sure, speak tomorrow. Bye, hun."

Penny glanced at herself in the mirror. It was still not the reflection she'd like to see, but makeup had at least toned down the black rings around her eyes. Her hair was newly washed, and she'd spent five minutes curling it. She would have spent ten, but Scarlett had kicked up a fuss, and she'd had to pick her up and walk around the house with her instead. Still, she had an array of curls at least, even if they were a bit haphazard.

As for Scarlett, she was in a red velvet dress, red tights, satin red shoes, and a red hairband. Unfortunately, she had grabbed furiously at the headband and pulled it round her neck. Terrified it might strangle her, Penny had removed it—biting down on her disappointment that Richard wouldn't enjoy his baby's outfit in its entirety. After all, if she couldn't look good, she damn well wanted the baby to.

If she thought Richard might be impressed with the way she had dressed Scarlett, however, she was wrong.

"Blimey," he said, somewhat taken aback. "She looks like Mrs. Christmas."

Penny bit down hard to stifle the retort that wanted desperately to tear from her lips. Mrs. Christmas indeed! How dare he? Choosing clothes for the baby was something she enjoyed. It reminded her of dressing her Barbie as a child. She had loved to do that too, had spent hours mixing and matching outfits for her: shopping attire, beach wear, cute pajamas with matching fluffy slippers, and—her favorite—glitzy evening dresses of which her mother had bought her almost obscene amounts. "Anything to keep Penny quiet," she had heard her mum say once to the next-door neighbor. Not that she'd been a difficult child, not at all. It was just her mother was a bit like her, lacking in any obvious maternal instinct, which wasn't great when you had a child to consider. Although Penny was determined to do better than her mother, she had a sneaking feeling she might do even worse.

The evening ahead, though, was going to be a success. Plastering a smile on her face, she said sweetly to Richard, "Shall we go?"

Richard looked slightly disgruntled. "Haven't I got time for a beer first?" he asked. "I've only just stepped through the door."

"Tough," Penny replied, this time through gritted teeth. She and Scarlett had been ready since lunchtime; they were not going to wait a minute longer.

It was good to be out as a threesome. Penny felt bolstered by it, more confident. Quickly, she put the Qashqai into gear and headed into the Brighton town center, heavy traffic unfortunately causing a ten-minute journey to take twenty. Not the flying start she had envisaged.

After she had squeezed into a space in one of the multi-story car parks, Richard climbed out of the passenger seat and made his way round to the boot of the car. Retrieving Scarlett's Bugaboo, he expertly assembled it in seconds, much to Penny's complete and utter annoyance. It never clicked so easily into place for her. He then took the baby out of the car seat and walked off with her still in his arms.

Oh, great, I'll just push an empty pram, shall I? she thought waspishly.

Donatello's was heaving— modest prices and great food an effective marketing match. They managed to bag a table after waiting just a few minutes in the bar area, Penny eyeing a cocktail the girl next to her was drinking, thinking how long it had been since she'd downed one. Margaritas used to be her favorite, served with a sea salt rim. Valentino's, a cocktail bar in New Road, next door to Brighton's famous Theatre Royal, served a mean margarita. She and Layla, who was more of a creamy cocktail type of girl, had had some riotous nights in there as well.

Richard perused the menu whilst Penny secured Scarlett in the high chair Alejandro had fetched for her. Scarlett went in without protest, so preoccupied by the hubbub around her, she'd forgotten to scream. While the baby was quiet, Penny delved into the baby bag, a big multi-colored padded affair— gone were the days of heading out with just a tiny handbag— and retrieved a jar of baby food.

Richard immediately looked up. "Don't give her that." He looked distinctly disapproving. "She's got a couple of teeth now; she can chew something."

Chew on this, Penny wanted to respond while shaking her fist at him. Reminding herself that this was supposed to be a pleasant outing, she replied instead, "The baby doesn't like chunks. She just spits them out. She gets on better with this stuff."

"That stuff's rubbish. If you must give her mush, mush it yourself."

She was about to tell him to mush off when he started speaking again.

"Besides which, I've been reading about this new approach. It's called 'baby-led weaning.' You give them exactly what you're having, no exceptions— steak, pork chops, broccoli, carrots, the lot. You just cut the food up into bite-sized pieces for them, and they pick and choose what they want."

Baby-led what? Penny was incredulous. When had he looked this up? At work, when he was supposed to be oh-so-busy on his oh-so-VIP cases?

"And what if a piece of steak gets stuck in her throat? What if she gags?"

Richard seemed almost pleased she had asked him this question. "Ah, you don't want to worry about gagging. Apparently, that's a perfectly normal response to dealing with large bits of food. Keep an eye on them, for sure, offer water if needed, but generally, babies have the wherewithal to sort it out for themselves."

"And you want to try this baby-led nonsense now? In a packed restaurant?"

"What harm can it do? I'll get the spaghetti bolognaise, and she can have some of mine."

"But she'll make a mess," Penny declared. That red velvet dress was from Boden. It had cost a bomb, and she didn't want it ruined.

"She won't." Richard was adamant. Leaning forward to tickle Scarlett under the chin, he continued, "Will you, my tweedle-pop?"

Tweedle-pop? Had he completely lost the plot?

If she hadn't been so tired, she would have protested further. Instead, she took a sip of lemonade and told Richard to do what he wanted, hating the smug look on his face. The way he looked dapper in his Gresham Blake suit, the way having a baby hadn't ruined his physique. He still looked the same—good. Better than good. *He* was the one who was glowing.

When the food came, Richard, true to his word, popped some of his spaghetti and sauce on a plate and placed it in front of the baby. Penny had opted for Layla's favorite, risotto marinara, not least because she wouldn't have to share hers with Scarlett if she did.

"Richard, not so much," Penny warned. "Start with just a little bit. I've told you, the baby isn't used to solids."

"Her name is Scarlett," Richard replied.

"Yes, I know that."

"So, how come you never say it?" Richard sounded pissed off. "It's…it's weird."

"Weird?" Penny couldn't believe it. "You're the one who's weird, Richard."

Unable to look at him any longer, Penny stabbed viciously at a prawn with her fork instead. It was delicious, but she recognized this only subconsciously. She was too tired to care about food, either. Last night had been another horrendous wake-fest. Instead, she chewed on it mechanically, just going through the motions, gazing out the floor-to-ceiling windows at the people hurrying by.

It was a while before she realized Richard was in a state of panic.

"For God's sake, Penny, stop daydreaming and help me."

Help him? Why?

Looking at where Richard was staring, Penny's mouth dropped open. Scarlett was flinging spaghetti and sauce everywhere. It was all over the floor, over Richard, over the female half of the couple sitting at the table next to them, and on Scarlett's expensive red dress.

"Oh, no," she began, just as the aforementioned lady, unfortunately clad in something expensive-looking too, stood with a look of thunder on her face.

"Bloody hell," said the woman, not caring at all she was swearing in front of a minor. "Can't you keep that baby of yours under control? My top is ruined."

"I'm…I'm…" Penny was all set to apologize—the cream blouse the lady had on did indeed look as though she was going to have a hard time removing those stains. Just then, Scarlett started screaming. Obviously the spaghetti-hurling game had worn thin. Instead, she began a new game, rocking her highchair back and forth, her feet catching at the table, their purchase lending her strength, hurling her all the way back into the woman's legs—who caught her just before she crashed to the ground.

Galvanized into action, Penny grabbed the highchair from her and tried to disentangle Scarlett from it, her hands working furiously at the clips that had her trapped. Just as she managed to bust her out, Scarlett vomited. Huge amounts of lumpy red sickness with spaghetti strands in it spilled all over the floor, splattering everywhere, but worse still, all over the woman's shoes. Pray God they weren't designer—Kurt Geiger or something—but Penny had a sneaking suspicion they were.

It was like she had been caught in some sort of living nightmare. Surely this couldn't be happening? All around her, she heard groans of disgust. Quickly, she looked to Richard for support, but he was just sitting there, his body rigid, the same aghast look on his face as was evident on the faces of the other diners.

"That does it," said the woman, her fury almost tangible. "I knew we shouldn't have come here. It's too down-at-heel for us, and the clientele prove it. Come on, Derek, we're going. They can pay our bill."

As Derek and the spaghetti-and-vomit-splashed woman pushed indignantly past her, Penny heard her say, "Incompetence, that's what it is. Sheer bloody incompetence."

The old Penny would have retaliated immediately. She would have turned on the woman in a flash, told her to go and take a running jump off the end of Brighton Pier, preferably in a raging storm so there'd be no chance she'd surface again. The new Penny, however, just ran out onto the streets, babe still in her arms, desperate to escape the dozens of faces that seemed to swim before her, all of them silently agreeing with what the woman had said. She was a bloody incompetent mother.

Blinded by tears, she rushed headlong into Brighton's Lanes, a warren of tiny cobbled streets lined mainly with antique and jewelry shops. Only vaguely was she aware of Scarlett struggling in her arms, of people staring in horror as she rushed past them, wondering who the heck this kidnapper was in their midst and whether or not to tackle her, to bring her down, to extract the protesting bundle from her. She only barely realized too that someone had hold of her arm, was spinning her round and shouting her name out, over and over again, trying to get through to her.

"Richard," she said at last.

"Of course it's me," he said, as furious as the woman had been. "Thanks, Penny. Thanks a lot. Leave me to deal with the aftermath, why don't you? God knows how much the bill was. I just slammed down a whole wodge of cash and legged it too."

"Leave you…?" It had been his bloody idea to feed the baby solid foods. She had tried to tell him not to do so on this occasion, to wait until they were at home, when it would be much easier to gauge her reaction, to deal, as he put it, with the aftermath. She had tried to tell him, but as usual, he hadn't listened. Richard Hughes would never win any awards for listening, that's for sure.

"Honestly," Richard was still babbling on. "I don't know what's wrong with you at the moment. Really, I don't. It's like *Invasion of the Body Snatchers* or something."

And in truth, Penny didn't know what was wrong with her either. Still, his observation of that fact did nothing to temper her mood. Quite the opposite. She handed Scarlett over to him and, without further ado, continued to run.

chapter ten

"Another cup of tea, Layla? Or shall we crack open the wine?"
There was a twinkle in Hannah's eye as she posed the question. Wine, of course, Layla thought. After the day she'd just had, she could do with a bucketful of the stuff.

Jim had popped down to May's, the mini mart, to get some provisions for tonight. Earlier, both he and Hannah had shown Layla to the spare room, a room he usually kept his music equipment in: guitars, an old drum kit, scores and scores of notebooks, all filled with songs he'd written over the years. It had all been cleared out, put in a friend's garage apparently, in honor of their overseas visitors. Now, a double bed, chest of drawers, and a Lloyd Loom chair graced the room—home for the next week. On the walls, Hannah had hung a couple of her pictures, one depicting The Lizard on Cornwall's south peninsula and the other Bedruthan Steps, back in the north. The huge canvases brightened the room considerably.

"Thanks for making room for us," she called to Hannah as her friend set about grabbing two glasses from the cupboard and a bottle of red from the wine rack.

"Not a problem. It was brilliant to have the excuse to do it. You know what Jim's like. I've asked him a hundred times to clear out his stuff, that we could use the extra space so we can have guests to stay, but it takes a rocket with him sometimes."

Layla smiled as Hannah poured them a glass each.

"And how's it going with Jim? Good?"

"Oh, yeah." An almost beatific smile lit up Hannah's face. "Really good. We just…I don't know…We click. We always have done. It just took me a while to realize it."

Layla knew what she was referring to. "And us staying here—Joseph staying here—it's all right?"

"Of course it is." Hannah seemed resolute. "It's great to have you here, to have you *both* here. So, come on, give me the lowdown on Tara. I want to know every last detail. I have to say, though, she's quite striking, isn't she?" As though she had put her foot in it, Hannah quickly added, "Although nowhere near as pretty as you."

Layla rolled her eyes. She didn't care who was the prettiest. It was how a person made you feel that counted. Looks faded; feelings tended to stick around.

As she had confided in Penny, she now confided in Hannah, the wine in the bottle before them reducing drastically while she did so. Hannah was just about to pour out the last dregs when Jim walked in.

"Just in time," he said, eyeing the wine as he walked up to Hannah. Snaking an arm around her shoulder, he bent to kiss her lightly on the lips.

There was a knock on the door. Jim went to answer it.

"I'll have to dig out that spare key whilst you're here," Layla heard Jim saying to Joseph. He had returned, then, an hour later, she noted. Not unreasonable at all.

"Hey, babe." Joseph came over to her and bent down to kiss her as Jim had kissed Hannah. As he stood back up, he touched one hand to her mouth, as though wanting to keep the impression his lips had made on hers intact.

Hannah quickly found a second bottle of red and another two glasses, filling them alongside her own and Layla's. Handing one to everybody, she lifted her glass and said, "To no-longer-absent friends. It's great to have you both back."

"It's good to be back," Joseph returned. "And, Jim, congratulations on the new CD. We play it all the time, don't we, Layla?"

Clinking glasses, Layla had to admit she was feeling happier. It was great to see Hannah and Jim and hopefully the rest of the crowd—Mick, Curtis, and Ryan—as well as other familiar faces from the village at the pub a bit later on. She was home.

After they'd drained their glasses and Layla had freshened up—travel always made her feel grubby—all four made their way to the Trecastle Inn, the pub where Layla had worked with Hannah during her year here. Hannah still worked at the inn, but not so much nowadays, thanks to her art taking off, and not tonight, either, or for the next few days. She had taken time off while Layla and Joseph were visiting.

"I see May's is still going strong," Layla remarked to Hannah as they walked down the high street arm in arm, the boys trailing behind them, deep in conversation.

"Yep, and Harvest Moon too. Martha's weird and wonderful bath concoctions fly off the shelves. She does mail order now too."

"I'll have to pop in," replied Layla. "Get something divine to wallow in. I'm on holiday, after all."

The Trecastle Inn looked as resplendent as ever—if resplendent was a word that could ever be applied to the slightly run-down red brick building that stood in front of her. Probably not, but beauty was in the eye of the beholder, and resplendent was how she would describe it. She had loved working there, with its laid-back atmosphere and the people who frequented it, had enjoyed the sociability of bar work—such a contrast to working in an office. There were other pubs in the village, but this was the one the slightly younger crowd favored, a crowd she had bonded with straightaway, had become a part of. The other two—Pilgrim's Rest and The Cornish Man—were more restaurants than pubs. They didn't have the rustic charm, unintentional rather than stylized, that the Trecastle Inn had.

Inside, tables were scattered liberally across the wooden floor, some round, others rectangle. Around them was an eclectic assortment of chairs and benches. On the left-hand wall, a big chalkboard artfully detailed the local beers on offer—Doom Bar and Tribute the most popular—while the jukebox, standing against a central pillar, was thankfully silent. Layla remembered that the sound that came out of it was less musical than whiney. The bar itself was set toward the back of the pub, and Tom, a casual worker when she had worked there, was manning it.

"Joe, Layla!" It was Mick, coming toward them, his ruddy, open countenance a welcome sight. A local fisherman, he was also a very popular village resident, the life and soul of any party. Layla returned his beaming smile. With or without Martha's potions, she could feel herself relaxing.

As Jim had embraced Joe in a bear hug at the airport, Mick did too, patting him heartily on the back upon release.

"My main man," he declared. "It's good to see you."

Turning swiftly to Layla, he held her first at arm's length.

"You lovely little minx, you," he said fondly before bear-hugging her too, depriving her of oxygen in the process.

Layla couldn't help it; she giggled as he let her go. She noticed Joseph smiling at her reaction to Mick, clearly glad that her mood had lightened.

Mick had made no secret upon first meeting Layla that he found her attractive. But when he realized his feelings weren't reciprocated, he had backed off, turning his attentions elsewhere. There had been many times Layla had thought it a shame she couldn't reciprocate. Mick was a simple and straightforward bloke; life with him might have been simple and straightforward too. But you couldn't help who you had feelings for or the depth of those feelings either. When they hit, they hit hard.

Curtis and Ryan came forward next. Jim's band mates — Curtis played guitar, Ryan played drums — they occupied another planet most of the time, Layla often thought, a planet where they were both permanently lost in the rhythm of life. She was fond of them, though. Slightly younger than the rest of the crowd, just past their mid-twenties as opposed to thirty onward, they, like Jim, looked every inch the musicians they were, despite or because of the rather dubious hoodies they were currently sporting.

As drinks were passed round and banter exchanged, Layla could feel her tension dissolving. If she tried very hard, she might even be able to expunge Tara from her mind completely. Maybe the girl wouldn't impact much on their stay here. Maybe Joseph really had fulfilled his role. Maybe she wouldn't want him for anything more.

"But if she does," she remembered Joseph saying, "I'd like to think I can be supportive without you losing your cool about it."

Cool was exactly what she'd been. Perhaps it was time to warm up. Moving closer to Joseph, she smiled as his arm wrapped round her shoulders, despite the fact he was deep in conversation with

Mick. As her arm went around his waist and she snuggled up to him, relishing his closeness, she looked over at Hannah, laughing with Jim, Curtis, and Ryan. She felt part of one big, happy family here—a family she'd never really had growing up as an only child, estranged from her mother most of the time—although happily, they were closer now—and her father lost to her at seven. Hannah, like Penny, was a sister to her. Although with Hannah, she never fell out like sisters sometimes do. With Penny, however, there had been one or two arguments in the past. But always they made up, their bond strengthened further, if anything.

They stayed in the pub much longer than they'd intended. Eventually, though, Hannah managed to tempt them away.

"Come on, I'm starving. Let's go home, get dinner on the go."

Saying their good-byes, various promises exchanged between them all to meet again the next day, same place, same time, all four left the pub behind them.

"Hang on," said Joseph, holding Layla back. "We'll catch up with you guys in a minute. I want to take a trip down memory lane." Winking at her, he added, "Literally."

Layla knew where he wanted to go—to his workshop, a little farther down the high street. Coming to a standstill outside it, she thought he seemed a bit misty-eyed. Having ended his rental contract on the building shortly before they moved, the building had subsequently been brought and transformed into a quaint little shop with living quarters upstairs. The shop, called Honey Bee, specialized in local honey, all types and flavors, and a wealth of honey-related products: honeycomb, honey fudge, salad dressings, even face, body and hand creams. Looking at the products neatly displayed in the window, Layla made a mental note to pop in there the next day, as well as Harvest Moon. The honeycomb looked delicious.

Immediately she felt guilty for loving the new shop. This had been Joseph's premises once, where he had forged his career as a carpenter, built a reputation for himself—and a good reputation, too. He had never been short of work. A mental image of him leaning over his workbench, engrossed in his latest project, came to mind. How anyone could look so good with so much sawdust on them she didn't know.

"There's no turning back, is there?" He sounded almost regretful.

"I don't suppose so," she replied, a wistfulness in her voice too.

He turned to look at her then. In the silver glow of the moonlight, he was mesmerizing—the magic of Trecastle at work?

"Do you like it in Florence?"

Like it? Yes, she *liked* it and said so. "Don't you?" she asked.

"Of course I do." He didn't sound convinced.

Had Tara returning home made the idea of following suit more attractive? She promptly chased away the frown that accompanied such a cynical thought.

"I don't think our time's come to an end in Florence quite yet," she ventured.

"Maybe," Joseph complied. "It just feels so right being here, though, doesn't it? As though we're part of a jigsaw. We *fit*."

She couldn't help it. She had to ask. "Does Tara intend staying put?"

Joseph looked genuinely nonplussed. "I don't know what Tara intends to do." Then he seemed to realize her suspicions. "Whether she does or not has nothing to do with what I've just said."

"I know," she replied, perhaps a little too quickly to be entirely convincing. After a moment, she added, "And your services, has Tara dispensed with them?"

"My services?"

"Your help," she corrected begrudgingly.

"I don't know that either." Was there a slight warning in his voice, or was she imagining it? Still on the defensive, he added, "I said I'd be here for her if she needs me, just like you would be for one of your friends. All I'm trying to be is supportive."

"I'm not saying anything to the contrary."

"You're implying it."

"No, I'm not," Layla lied.

Turning on her heel, she started walking up the high street, back past the pub, the village store, more gift shops, this time selling New Age and Celtic memorabilia. Shops cashing in on the region's Dark Age history, when the castle on the cliff had been a formidable stronghold, full of life and courtly goings-on. A time when soldiers had been forced to defend their homes, their ladies, and their families. Right now, she felt a surprising affinity with those soldiers. She too had to find some way to fight off the enemy that had suddenly invaded. Striking from nowhere and so effectively too.

Joseph quickly fell into step beside her.

"Before you say it—" she couldn't keep her voice from sounding waspish "—yes, I do trust you. You're the one that's paranoid, not me."

"I'm not paranoid," Joseph immediately retaliated. "I just get the feeling you're not being honest with me, that's all. You say you trust me, but I'm not sure you do."

Oh, and you blame me for that, do you? she thought, but she refrained from saying it. Acting the harridan every time Tara's name was mentioned wasn't going to endear her to anyone. Still, there was no way she was not going to stand up for herself.

"Joseph," she said, coming to a standstill outside Uncle Davy's Cabin, fine purveyors of fish and chips, or so the sign above the black-painted door would have you believe. "Just cut me a bit of slack, okay? Tara turns up out of the blue, the one place in the world where you happen to be, and you just happen to bump into her."

Briefly, she paused. It reminded her of a line from that film—what was it? *Casablanca* with Humphrey Bogart and Ingrid Bergman. He'd mused about how, of all the bars around the world, she'd wandered into his. The fact it was a romantic film, a romantic sentiment, irked her even more, but she bit down on that for now.

"You then tell me you want her to accompany us back to Trecastle," she continued, "because she's in trouble, because she has a secret, and not just any secret, but a big secret. Because of it, she can't face coming home alone; she needs a chaperone. I accept all this. And that you can't tell me what this so-called secret is until the time is right. I also accept that you want me to trust you, and I'm willing to trust you because I love you. I've never loved anyone the way I love you, and I never will. But every now and then, I get a bit antsy about it. Don't worry, though, because I remind myself who I'm doing this for—you, not her." She cocked her head to one side. "And you know what? In some ways, I admire you. What you're prepared to do for a...*friend.* But, whatever way you want to look at it, it's a strange situation. The kind you find in books and think, *yeah, right, as if.* So, forgive me if my enthusiasm wanes every now and then. Like I said, cut me some slack. Because you know what? That's exactly what I'm doing for you."

Layla would bet a pound to a penny the look of surprise on his face reflected her own. The pent-up feelings in her since finding out about Tara had obviously needed release—more so than even she had realized. Holding his gaze, she refused to look away. Nonetheless, her breath caught in her throat as she waited for his reaction.

Incredibly, he laughed.

"Joseph!" she admonished.

"I'm not laughing at you, I promise."

"What then?" She was absolutely flummoxed.

"It's your eyes. I swear they fire sparks when you're all riled up…"

Just as she was about to stomp off, he grabbed her by the waist and pulled her back, straight into his arms.

"I love you too, you know."

She could believe it, the way he was looking at her.

Repeating the words she had used earlier, he added, "I've never loved anyone the way I love you. I never will."

Swept away in the moment, she could only nod in reply.

"*You* are the only woman I want."

"Oh, Joseph…" she murmured.

"Despite the fact you're a complete pain in the arse at times."

With a thud, she came crashing back to earth. "Hey, you are too, you know," she protested.

"I don't doubt it," he replied, laughing again.

Swiping at him, she pretended offense.

A couple of moments later, she was laughing too.

"Come on," she said. "Let's get back. Hannah and Jim will be sending out a search party at this rate."

She threaded her arm through his, and they walked the rest of the distance in comfortable silence, a gentle breeze blowing in off the Atlantic and wrapping them in its embrace.

At Hannah's front door, Joseph fished around in his jeans pocket for the key, first one and then the other. Finding it eventually, he let them into the flat.

Inside, Layla could hear voices from the kitchen. Hannah's and Jim's and…someone else's.

The warm glow she had felt from the look on his face when Joseph had told her he loved her, a look she hoped he'd very much emulate when they were alone together later, grew cold. Yes, there was definitely a third voice—a female third voice—tones concerned rather than jovial. What was going on? Was that Tara in there with them? In need of more support?

Layla looked at Joseph. Even he looked confused. If Tara was in the kitchen with Hannah and Jim, he clearly hadn't known beforehand she would be. Bracing herself, Layla picked up her pace. If Tara was in need of more support, fair enough. But she couldn't expect Joseph to give up his holiday entirely for her, nor could she expect Layla to remain in un-blissful ignorance for much longer. Neither of them could. Not when it affected her too. They'd have to come clean, the pair of them. They'd have to.

Steaming into the kitchen, she stopped short.

"Penny," she breathed. "What are you doing here?"

chapter eleven

When Joseph had driven away, Tara had stood at her parents' front door for what seemed like an eternity, doing her best to breathe evenly, to remain calm and collected. In reality, however, it could only have been minutes. But not just one or two minutes, she was sure. A fair few of them had stacked up.

She was back. She was home, in Port Levine, the small Cornish village where she had been born, where she had spent her childhood and the majority of her teenage years, among green hills and whitewashed cottages, a place of simple beauty. A place unparalleled because of its simplicity, she hadn't found its match, no matter how far she traveled. And perhaps she never would. It seemed unlikely now.

At last she found the courage to announce her arrival, rapping on the cast iron doorknocker. She knew the doorbell didn't work; it hadn't in years. Her parents were cool about it, though. They didn't sweat the small stuff. The big stuff, she couldn't vouch for.

It took another couple of minutes before the door opened, retreating slowly inward, revealing inch by inch the hazy interior and then the shape of her mother, a small woman too, smaller than Tara, a little over five feet.

"My goodness…What are you doing here?"

"Hello, Mum." Tara smiled at her, for a few moments savoring the emotions running riot across her mother's face—surprise, confusion, and then utter delight.

"Tara, darling," Lily breathed, and then, not so much calling but shrieking, "Roger, Roger, come and see who's at the door."

Immediately she started fussing. "Oh my, what am I doing, leaving you standing on the doorstep? How very remiss of me. Come in. Come in, darling girl. Oh, it's so good to see you."

Tara didn't need asking twice. She flew into the circle of her mother's arms, loving the perfumed smell of her, a mixture of roses and baking, such a familiar scent, so clean, so…so pure somehow. Behind her, another voice.

"Good heavens above, I don't believe it. Tara."

Tara flew to him too, to her dad. His smell was different than her mum's; it was more musk and tobacco but just as comforting. She adored her mum, had grown closer to her as an adolescent, but when she was small, she had been a daddy's girl through and through, the bond between them incredible. It was good to be back, so bloody good. She should never have left for so long. It was unforgivable. *Unforgivable.* The word brought her up short. They looked different than the picture of them she carried around in her head. They looked older. Of course, she had kept in regular touch via phone and e-mail, but she hadn't actually seen them, not in the flesh, for three years. Both of them refused to use Skype. "Bah, I'm not getting into all that," her father would say whenever she had asked him to consider it. Perhaps if he had, her surprise today at least wouldn't have been so bad. Time had marked them. Her father's once broad shoulders now had a slight sag to them, and her mother's hair was more gray than black. The opposite had been true when she had left.

"Your bags, where are they? Daddy will get them." Her mother was fussing again.

"It's okay," Tara insisted. "I haven't got any bags, just a rucksack. I can manage."

"Let's get you inside, then," her mother conceded. "I'll put the kettle on."

Ah, yes, English tea. Now *that* she'd love.

Tara followed her mother through to the kitchen. The woman was at sixes and sevens, reaching for the kettle, then the biscuit tin, then wondering where the "special" tea bags where, the posh ones she had got from the supermarket in Bodmin as opposed to the generic ones the village store sold. Tara had to urge her to calm down.

"But how long are you staying?" her mother couldn't resist asking. "Say it's more than one or two days. I…It's just so lovely to see you."

One or two days? It would be longer than that. But telling her she'd come home for good would only excite her more. She would reveal all—in time.

"Definitely more than one or two days, Mum. If you'll have me, that is."

"Don't be silly." Lily batted lightly at her daughter's arm. "This is your home. It always has been, and it always will be. Stay for as long as you like."

Tara smiled her thanks. Her father came into the kitchen, and after staring at each other for a few moments, the three of them hugged some more.

"Oh," said Lily, finally breaking away. "If only Leo was here. Wouldn't it be perfect, Roger? Our two girls back home, all of us together again."

"How is Leo?" Tara asked as her mother busied herself with the tea making and her father pulled up a chair.

"She's doing very well, darling. Loves living in Penzance. She's made a lot of friends there. Likes her job too."

"Good, I'm glad."

"When was the last time you spoke to her?" enquired Roger.

Tara thought for a moment. "About a month or two ago, maybe more."

Again, she'd left it too long. But then, she'd had a lot on her mind recently.

"I know," her mother said, her face beaming. "We'll give Leo a call later, let her know you're here. She might be able to get a few days off. I'm sure Driftwood can spare her for a short while, although they're such a busy shop. She says it's heaving most days."

"Mum." Tara hoped she didn't sound too uncharitable. "Can we just leave it at us for a short while? It's been years since I've had you all to myself. I know I sound selfish, and we'll call Leo soon, but just for a while, can it be the three of us, please?"

"Yes, dear, whatever you want," Lily said, returning to the table. Her mother stared at her before asking, "Is everything okay?"

How was she going to answer that? Tell them straightaway? That everything was not okay—far from it. She supposed now would be as good a time as any. Get it over and done with; reveal the truth, a truth that was starting to get the better of her. Looking at their faces, she couldn't do it. Let their happiness last a little longer.

"Everything's fine, Mum. I've done a lot of traveling recently, and I'm jaded, that's all."

"Of course, of course." Her mother looked relieved. "After we've all had tea, I'll get your room ready for you. Until then, tell us everything you've been up to."

Tara smiled, glad to talk of her travels in Italy, of what she'd seen. She omitted the part about meeting Joseph again in Florence. Telling them would raise suspicions when she wanted to keep their first hours together again simple. That too could wait.

After her second cup of tea and several biscuits, a mixture of custard creams, and homemade shortbread, Tara and Lily made their way upstairs to her bedroom. It was just the same as when she'd left it at age eighteen to move to London. White wallpaper with tiny pink roses on it, a single bed with a pink quilt cover, and a pine side table with a lamp on it. The table was where she used to pile all her books, unable to fall asleep without reading at least one or two chapters of the latest blockbuster—Stephen King, Dean Koontz, Anne Rice. She'd had a taste for horror.

There was also a pine wardrobe. She knew if she opened it, there would just be hangers rattling in the emptiness within. On the cream carpet was the fading evidence of the hot chocolate she'd knocked over as a teen, scrubbing desperately at it with water, just making it worse. She remembered her mother taking over, telling her not to worry, they could always get a small rug to cover up the stain. She was lovely like that, her mother, always so kind. As was her father. They didn't deserve what she was going to do to them.

"All okay for you?" Lily asked.

"It's perfect," Tara replied. And then, unable to stem the flow of tears, her voice caught on a sob as she said, "It's so good to be home, Mum. You've no idea."

Lily's arms went round her straightaway. For a while, her mother just held her, but then she pushed her away slightly, although continuing to hold on to her shoulders.

"*Why* are you home?" she asked, her eyes a faded denim rather than the bright blue they had once been.

"Because…because I missed you. You and Dad. I needed to see you."

"But you never phoned to say you were coming."

"I thought it would be nice to surprise you."

Although the first part of that exchange was true, the second wasn't. She hadn't told them she was coming home in case she changed her mind at the last minute. And she might have, had it not been for Joseph.

"It is a surprise, a wonderful surprise. But, Tara…" Her mother hesitated. Around her eyes, the lines and wrinkles deepened. "If there's a problem, if something's happened to you whilst you've been away, something…well, something not so good, don't be afraid to tell us."

"Nothing's happened, honest. Everything's fine." *For now.*

Her mother sat down on the edge of the bed, smoothing her skirt as she did so.

"What about this boyfriend of yours? Aiden? Why hasn't he come over with you?"

"Oh, Mum, we're not joined at the hip, you know. Aiden and me, we can spend time apart."

"So, you're still together?"

"We're…We still get on, yes."

"But are you still together? You know what I mean."

"Erm…no. No, we're not."

She could have lied, but it would have been one lie too many.

"Is that why you're here? Why you're so upset?"

"Yes."

Not strictly a lie, it was *one* of the reasons.

Lily shook her head. "What a shame. He sounded like such a nice young man."

"He was. He is. These things happen, though. You know that."

"They do indeed." Lily sighed. "And you're young. You'll find love again."

No, I won't. Instead of voicing that thought, she simply replied, "I know."

"Ooh, help me up," said Lily, stretching out her hand, which Tara took in hers, relishing the softness of it. "I shouldn't rush you. You'll tell me everything in your own time; I know you will. You just need to find the right moment, that's all. You were like that as a child—you liked to pick your moment. Not like Leo at all. Leo would just blurt out whatever was on her mind, sometimes in the most inappropriate of situations. Now, why don't you freshen up whilst I go and make dinner? I think I know what you'd like—stargazy pie," she said, referring to one of Tara's favorite supper dishes, a mackerel pie with a pastry crust, a typical Cornish dish that was as spectacular as it was comforting. "Then you can regale us about all things Australian. You know, it's a place I've always wanted to visit, but it seems so far away."

Tara laughed now, genuinely amused. "Mum, it *is* far away."

"I know, I know." Lily laughed along with her. "A world away from here, that's for sure." Reaching out to touch her daughter's hair, she added, "But I'm glad you're not a world away anymore. It doesn't matter the reason; I'm glad you've come back."

Wrapping a towel round her—a fluffy pink towel that her mother had neatly folded and left in the bathroom for her—Tara tiptoed with wet feet across the landing to her bedroom. Standing in front of a gilt-framed oval mirror hung to the right side of the wardrobe, she rubbed at her hair with a second towel. Being short and spiky, it wouldn't take long to dry.

Aiden would have loved her mum and dad. He had often said how much he was looking forward to meeting them.

"We'll have to go back soon and visit them," he'd said. "I've never been to England."

"Yes, definitely," she would reply, but time had slipped away from them. The café was always very busy, even in winter, and when they did have time off, there was always somewhere in Australia for them to fly to, some new sight to see.

Lying in bed together one night, another night too hot to sleep, they had passed the hours talking instead, neither of them minding they'd be tired the next day, loving their nocturnal world, a world that felt like it belonged to them exclusively.

"So, come on, tell me more about Cornwall," he had told her, "about where you lived, what you used to get up to."

Aiden had loved hearing about the great surfing beaches of North Cornwall. As she spoke, he would lie back against the pillow, his arms above his head, soaking up every word. Trecastle was definitely one of the best beaches, she had told him, along with Polzeath, Crackington Haven, and Widemouth Bay. Surfers were out constantly, no matter what the weather, eager to pit their wits against the might of the ocean. The south had great beaches too, with some of the best breaks around. Occasionally she had traveled to Porthcurno and Porthleven with friends, even Praa Sands, just outside of Helstone, where she had once seen dolphins chase the last rays of sunlight. But it was World's End that held her heart, which she found herself describing to him most often, a tiny but breathtaking bay not far from Port Levine, set off the main road and down a narrow single track. That was the beach she had grown up on, shunning the bigger bays with their shops selling ice cream, donuts, and brightly colored floats for a golden stretch of sand left largely untouched. She had hoped her descriptions would bring Port Levine and World's End alive for him, but how successful she was, she didn't know. Words couldn't do justice to where she came from. It wasn't just the way it looked; it was how it *felt* too, different from anywhere else in the UK, from the rest of the world, unique.

"I can't wait to go," he had sighed. "Let's go the next chance we get."

"Okay," she had agreed, as excited as him at the prospect. It would be so much fun to show him her country as he had shown her his. But the "next chance" never came.

She could feel her eyes water.

No, don't cry again. It's over. Accept it.

Try as she might to push memories of him away, they refused to lie low. As her mother had done earlier, she sat on the edge of her bed, hugging the towel to her.

He hadn't asked her to marry him that night when it had been just the two of them, content in the afterglow of coming together. No, that wasn't Aiden's way. He had asked her in front of everyone, in a packed café, going down on one knee, both hands clutched dramatically to his heart. He was like that, Aiden was, full of drama. That's why his café was so popular. Like some light source in the night, his zest and drive attracted people, people who wanted to hang around him, who used the café as an excuse to stay close. She had found his light dazzling.

"Everyone, can I have your attention?"

She had been busy handing a customer his order of tuna baguette with fresh salad when Aiden had shouted those words out. Ensuring the plate was set safely on the table before whirling round, she had wondered what the heck he was up to.

Aiden had stood less than a few feet from her, a beaming smile on his face.

"You may not know this—" he had continued to address the crowds with great flourish "—*she* may not know this, but this beautiful lady standing right in front of me is the love of my life. The minute I saw her sitting on the beach out front in a bikini so skimpy I swear it was illegal—and if it's not, it should have been—I knew I wanted to marry her."

"Aiden!" she had gasped. Her bikini had not been *that* skimpy, she was sure.

Winking at her, he had turned to his café assistant, Den, next. "Music, Maestro, if you please."

Beaming too, Den had hit the play button on the CD machine, and "Truly, Madly, Deeply" by Savage Garden—one of their favorite songs—had blasted into being.

Immediately, Aiden had fallen to one knee.

"Ouch," he had joked, pretending to wince in pain, "this position, it doesn't get any easier." When the laughter had died down, he had continued, "Seriously, folks, the reason I'm down here today—the *first* time I've ever been on bended knee, I promise—is not for the good of my health, although in a roundabout way, I suppose it is. It's to ask my lovely lady if she will bestow on me a great honor."

Looking straight at her then, his brown eyes full of merriment but so much more as well, he had asked her *that* question. "Tara Mills, will you marry me?"

Everyone in the café had held their breath. She had held her breath. For his part, Aiden hadn't appeared to be breathing either. Her silence had continued far longer than she had intended it to. She had seen worry flicker across several faces, but not Aiden's. Despite the fact his breath had caught, he had known he had no need to worry.

"Yes," she had said at last, her voice barely audible.

"Sorry?" he had teased her. "I didn't quite catch that."

"Yes." She had said it much louder the second time, louder than the music even, which continued to play, and then she hadn't been able to stop saying it. "Yes, yes, yes."

Jumping to his feet, Aiden had grabbed a Coke can off a nearby table, pulled the ring off it and held it out to her. Obviously he hadn't second-guessed his actions either. To cries of delight, he had placed it almost reverentially on her finger.

Holding her to him, he had whispered, "I'll get you a proper ring soon, I promise."

And he had—a platinum band with diamonds all around it, even though she had protested, had said they couldn't possibly afford such an extravagance. He had insisted, had said she was worth every penny spent and more. But she had treasured the Coke-can ring equally. She had kept it. It was in the bottom of her rucksack now, in the same box as the diamond ring, nestled side by side. All she had taken of their life together. Except for memories. And those she kept safe in her heart.

chapter twelve

The look on Layla's face when she had seen Penny at the dinner table last night had been a picture. Then again, what must she have looked like? Not the Penny from days of old, that was for sure. She hadn't even looked in the mirror since running off in the Lanes like that, heading for home, throwing stuff, any stuff, into a suitcase, her only intention to escape—from Richard and, she felt terrible to admit, the baby too.

Richard and Scarlett had come in after her. Realizing she wasn't downstairs, he had gone upstairs looking for her. In the bedroom, Richard gently placed a struggling Scarlett in her crib while attempting to calm Penny. Sadly, he hadn't done a good job.

"Thanks for taking the car; I had to get a taxi home. Scarlett's filled her nappy, and it's a real humdinger too. I was going to catch the bus, but I honestly don't think we'd have been let on. As it was, the taxi driver insisted we keep all the windows open."

"If her nappy's dirty, change it," Penny had snarled, grabbing her favorite skull T-shirt out of the built-in wardrobe and throwing it in the suitcase. Why, she didn't know. It was tight-fitting; she'd look hideous in it now with her ever-pregnant tummy.

Richard had grimaced at the prospect. Nappies were something he generally left to her. Realizing he had bigger fish to fry than the state of Scarlett's behind, he had said, "Why are you packing? Where do you think you're going? You've got a baby to look after, you know."

"You can look after her," she had shouted, actually hating his chiseled good looks at that moment, hating them just as much as she used to love and admire them.

"Look after her? I can't. I've got to go to work. *Someone* has to pay the bills."

The red mist had descended, as it seemed to do so with alarming rapidity nowadays.

Trumping Scarlett's wailing, she had screeched, "And what do you think I do all day? Lie down on a bloody chaise lounge, feeding myself peeled grapes and sipping champers whilst the baby slumbers sweetly beside me? What I do is work, Richard. It's bloody hard work. The hardest work I've ever done, and I don't get paid for it. None of us mums do. Or feel appreciated, it seems. We're just bloody taken for granted."

Richard had made a show of tutting. He hated it when his wife swore. He thought it unnecessary. Which, of course, made Penny want to swear even more.

"And I've got a job too, remember?" she continued, far from done. "But I had to take maternity leave. In fact, you insisted I take extended maternity leave, which means statutory pay after a while, which means very little pay at all, so don't whine on about having to pay the bills by yourself." She was sure she'd been foaming at the mouth by this point. "Why you couldn't take paternity leave is beyond me. One week you had off when the baby was born, one pitiful, lousy week. You could have had more, but no, not you. You couldn't wait to get back to the office, could you, to escape? If you think it's so easy looking after a baby—and don't deny it, you use the word 'easy' all the time to describe what I do—then do it. I'm looking forward to finding out just how easy you think it is when you're doing it on your own."

Richard had paled visibly at her words. "On my own?"

"Yes, Richard, on your own," she had repeated. "I'm off. I'm going to Trecastle. Layla's over from Florence, and I'm damned if I'm going to miss out on seeing her."

As she slammed shut her suitcase, he had grabbed her by the arm.

"Penny, you can't…"

He really had looked quite ill at the prospect.

"I can, and I will."

"But you're her mother," he had declared, as though it were some sort of astounding revelation.

"Yes, Richard, and you're her father. And this —" she had swept her arms wide "— is the twenty-first century. Dads tend to pitch in as much as mums now." With great contempt, she had added, "Well, some of them do. Good luck, Richard. I'll see you in a week."

As she had stormed downstairs and out of the house, her suitcase in one hand, the car keys in the other, she had called back, "If you're lucky…"

"And he didn't rush after you?"

It was Tuesday. She and Layla were at the Trecastle Inn, sitting at a table outside as the weather was so nice. Penny was relating a more detailed version of what had happened in Brighton as opposed to the potted one she had managed last night.

"How could he? I took the car."

"Oh, yeah, you said. Has he called you?"

Penny took a sip from her wine glass before replying. They had opted for the pub's un-oaked Chardonnay, a better choice than the Pinot Grigio, according to Hannah.

"He hasn't stopped calling. And in between calls, he's bombarded me with text messages, sent regularly through the night too. The baby must have kept him up." A smile crept over her face at the thought. If she had, it served him right.

"And are you okay, being apart from Scarlett, I mean? It must feel strange."

Yes, it did feel strange, as though she was missing a limb. But it also felt something else. *Good* would be too strong a word to describe it. She didn't feel good. But perhaps it was relieved. Relieved to have some time where she didn't have to think constantly about the welfare of another human being; she only had herself to worry about. Pregnancy included, that hadn't happened in a long while.

Layla must have guessed what she was thinking, because she reached out a hand and covered Penny's with it.

"Everybody needs a break sometimes, Penny. Even mums."

"Especially mums," Penny replied heatedly. "Anyway," she continued, not wanting to dwell on the subject any longer, "never mind me. Me is boring. What about you? All this stuff with Tara, it must have knocked you for six."

Layla looked fed up suddenly.

"Yeah, you could say that. The more I think about it, the more strange it seems."

"I know Joseph drove her back home, but has he seen Tara since?"

"He's texted her, they've spoken once on the phone, but no, he hasn't seen her."

"That's something, at least."

"It's only Tuesday, Penny," Layla said wryly. "There's plenty of time."

"Well, I think you've been very understanding about everything. I'm not sure I would have been."

"Penny." Layla looked at her squarely. "I *know* you wouldn't have been."

Penny pretended offense. "Are you calling me unreasonable?" she questioned.

"No, I'm calling you bloody unreasonable."

Penny laughed along with Layla, but a part of her did wonder. Was she bloody unreasonable? To leave her baby like that and her husband too? It was only for a few days, but even so…Richard had to work, she knew that. His firm wouldn't be impressed he'd had to take emergency leave. Perhaps sleep deprivation and ear-bashing over a prolonged period had actually driven her closer to the edge than even she had realized. If she hadn't left on a voluntary basis, the men in white coats might have been called in and forcibly ejected her—not to Cornwall but to a local asylum instead. There was no doubt about it; she was losing the plot, *really* losing it. She needed the break. Unreasonable or not, Richard would just have to cope.

"Hey, look who it is," Layla said, spying Hannah.

The third cog in the wheel, Hannah drew up a chair beside Layla. Tom seemed to appear from nowhere.

"And what would madam care to drink?" he asked Hannah, assuming a waiter's stance.

"A glass of white wine, my good man," she replied in suitably clipped tones.

"At your service," Tom continued, tugging at his forelock as he backed away.

Turning her attention back to them, Hannah smiled widely. "So, here we are, together again."

Penny raised her glass as well as an eyebrow. "Surprisingly so," she said. "What is it about this place that brings us running, huh? First Layla, then me, then…Tara."

"We should give it a nickname, shouldn't we? 'The sanctuary for lost souls' or something," Hannah mused, taking her glass from Tom, who had swiftly returned.

"And do you?" Layla's green eyes grew serious. "Think Tara's a lost soul?"

Both girls contemplated.

"Don't know…"

"Couldn't say…"

"I know you don't really know her," Layla persisted, "either of you, but you know what I know, at least. And it is all a bit bizarre, isn't it—this secret of hers? How Joseph's the only one allowed to know, for now anyway."

"Bizarre?" Penny scoffed. "That's one way of putting it."

"I wonder what the secret is, though," Layla continued to agitate. She looked at Penny. "We've ruled out mass murder, haven't we?"

"Mass murder?" Hannah's mouth fell open.

Quickly Layla explained their *Australia's Most Wanted* theory.

"Oh, right. I see," replied Hannah. "I think."

All three fell silent as they pondered.

"Hang on," said Hannah, straightening. "*Point Break* was Tara's favorite film."

"*Point Break?*" Penny didn't get it.

"It's a film with Patrick Swayze and Keanu Reeves in it," Hannah explained. "It's a cult film, actually. I'm surprised you haven't heard of it."

Penny shrugged her shoulders. She hadn't.

"How do you know it's Tara's favorite film?" Layla inquired.

Hannah leaned forward. "When I was going out with Joseph, I remember I fancied watching it one night, and he was like *no way.*

When I asked why, he explained it was because of Tara. She used to play it almost on a continual loop. He was sick to death of it."

"I still don't see what it's got to do with anything," Penny interjected.

"Well," said Hannah, "what if Tara was not only watching the film but studying it? You know what I mean, gleaning ideas from it. I watched it anyway that night. Joseph worked late or something, or he may have gone to the pub with Jim and Mick." She paused for a moment, trying to remember. "Anyway, the movie centers round a group of cool dude surfers who perform a series of bank robberies, and Keanu Reeves, who's majorly hot in the film, is the cop intent on busting them. It was the film that started Tara's obsession with moving to sunnier climes, apparently. What if she wanted to live the film in its entirety and got involved in a similar sort of group in Oz? What if she's been busted too, is on the run, and has come home to hide?"

"If Keanu was trying to catch me," Penny said with a sigh, "I'd let him."

"You know what I mean," insisted Hannah.

"I do, yeah, but it's a bit farfetched, isn't it?"

"Oh, and your mass murder theory isn't?"

Penny had to admit neither scenario sounded likely. "So, if it's not about murder or grand larceny," she said, "perhaps it concerns an affair of the heart?"

Layla shook her head. "No, that can't be it. I asked her outright if she'd been involved with anyone special in Australia. She said no."

"So, just an affair, then."

"Penny," Hannah hissed.

Penny noticed fresh anxiety darken Layla's face. "Sorry, I didn't mean she was having an affair with Joseph or anything." Aware that she should stop right now, before the hole she was digging got any bigger, she apologized again. "I didn't think."

"Do you ever?" Hannah mumbled.

Penny was about to bite when Joseph and Jim appeared, effectively diffusing the situation. Penny was quickly distracted by Jim. She had to admit, he had gotten seriously hunky since the time she last saw him. That whole rock-star thing, it lifted him somehow. His hair was also longer and slightly wilder too. He seemed so confident, so at ease with himself. Must be all that touring Layla said he was doing with his band, 96 Tears. Life on the road had given him an edge.

"What are you girls talking about?" Joseph asked, pulling up a chair beside Layla.

"Oh, nothing much," Layla replied with a brightness Penny could tell wasn't entirely genuine. "We're just catching up."

"Refills?" said Jim, spying their empty glasses.

As he took their orders, Penny checked him out once again. Hmm, Team Joseph or Team Jim? It was a hard choice to make. If she were single, who would she go for? Joseph, with his cool, blond demeanor, or the music man? She'd have them both if she could, the thought of which made her giggle.

"Are you okay?" Layla looked bemused.

"It must be the wine," Penny said, forcing herself to behave. "It's gone straight to my head." To Hannah and Joseph, she explained, "I'm not used to drinking anymore, you know, since the baby."

Jim returned to the table with a tray of drinks. He sat down beside Hannah. Penny felt like the odd one out. Or maybe she was just odd. She certainly felt it — very odd, as in "about to keel over" odd. It was no good; she'd have to go back to Hannah's and rest up. That sofa bed they insisted she stay on while she was down here was surprisingly comfortable. She couldn't wait to get back to it, if she were honest, but before she left them all to it, an idea formed. There was no point speculating about the mysterious Tara; they needed to find out for sure why she was here. An old saying popped into her head: "Keep your friends close but your enemies closer," a saying that suddenly made a lot of sense. Instead of avoiding Tara, they should be getting to know her, gaining her trust so she'd confide in them too this secret of hers, sooner rather than later, ending Layla's torture.

Hiccupping slightly, Penny said, "Why don't we have a gathering, tonight or tomorrow night, at yours, Hannah's, or at the pub, and invite Tara?" Looking at Joseph intently, she continued, "I've heard so much about her from Layla; it would be lovely to meet her." At this point, Penny winked at Layla.

"Oh, right, yeah." Joseph looked slightly taken aback she had asked such a thing. "She'd love to meet you too, I'm sure. I'll run it by her."

"Fantastic," Penny enthused.

Quickly she looked at Layla for approval. What she saw, however, surprised her. Instead of a conspiratorial look on her friend's face and an *I know what you're doing* wink, she saw unbridled horror. Confused, she looked at Hannah instead. She was busy staring into her wine glass, avoiding eye contact with anyone.

Having to hold on to the table to keep herself steady, Penny got up. Her legs felt wobbly beneath her, like they were made out of some sort of spongy cake mixture, not solid bone. How on earth, she wondered, would they support a dignified exit? But exit she must. Layla was still giving her the evils.

"Erm, I'll see you all later," she muttered. "I'm off for a nap. Hope you don't mind."

And with that, she staggered away, eager to avoid the fallout from her suggestion.

chapter thirteen

What the hell had Penny done? Invite Tara to the pub with them so that they could get to *know* her? Layla didn't want to get to know her. She'd be more than happy never to see her again, to be honest. But, no, that wasn't good enough for Penny. Penny, in spectacular Penny-style, had instead insisted they all cozy up together at the pub or, worse still, at Hannah and Jim's flat. There was no way she wanted Tara in Hannah and Jim's flat, stamping all over her territory, even if it wasn't her territory, strictly speaking. But hopefully Hannah would see her point.

While Jim was speaking to Hannah, Joseph leaned into her. "That's a good idea, isn't it? What Penny suggested?"

"Meeting up with Tara? Wonderful."

"It's thoughtful."

"Very."

"Shall we make it tonight?"

"Tonight?" she said too loudly.

Inwardly, Layla cursed herself for screeching. Despite her inner turmoil, she reminded herself to remain cool, calm, and collected at all times. The trouble was, Penny's mention of an affair between Tara and Joseph had upset her. There was no way she felt up to seeing Tara tonight. She'd stall for as long as possible.

Noting the look on Joseph's face, she hurried to explain. "It's just people will probably need more notice than that. A day or two, perhaps, rather than a few hours."

"Good point," Joseph conceded. "I'll give her a call later, see when's convenient."

"A call? Why do you have to call her? Can't you just text?"

Joseph shrugged his shoulders. "Yeah, I suppose. I just thought—"

"A text will be fine, I'm sure."

It was hard to sound nonchalant through gritted teeth.

"I'll do it now," he said, sighing slightly.

As he punched the invitation into his mobile, Layla tried to un-grit her teeth. It could all be innocent, perfectly innocent. She clung to that thought like a barnacle to a ship's keel. Even so, Penny and her bright ideas about a cozy get-together. She could slaughter her.

Draining her third glass of wine, she was beginning to feel blurred around the edges. Lunchtime drinking rarely agreed with her. In this instance, however, the blurring of the lines felt good. Blur might just get her through the next few days, through the cozy meet with Tara. She couldn't help it. She might trust Joseph, but Tara? Why should she trust her? There was something about her. Actually, there was nothing about her. Despite thinking her canny and furtive when she had first met her, subsequently she hadn't seemed that way at all. She seemed nice, a regular down-to-earth ordinary girl, which just made it all a thousand times worse.

"And who are you texting?" Hannah addressed Jim, who was also on his phone.

"Oh, just a few mates, part of the old Port Levine crowd. I thought it'd be good to round them up too, give Tara a proper homecoming. She was popular in the village, was Tara."

Joseph immediately caught on to the idea. "Hey, what about Murray? Is he still around?"

"Murray?" replied Jim. "Yeah, yeah, he lives down near Newquay now. He runs a surf shop there. He might come up, though, seeing as it's Tara. I'll add him to the list."

"Be great to see him and Del. He was a laugh, wasn't he? Do you remember he used to accompany you on harmonica every time you played in The Admiral?"

Jim rolled his eyes. "Yeah, and I wouldn't have minded if he could play the bloody thing, but he couldn't. He kept putting me off my stride. I'll see if he's around too."

"And Graham, or Gray, as he suddenly insisted we all call him. He used to get really cross if we forgot. He used to think we were doing it deliberately."

"Usually because we were."

As Jim and Joseph laughed, Layla had to bite down on a wave of emotion. Graham wasn't the only one they had pissed off. She tried to examine exactly what it was she was feeling. Anger? Yes, there was a certain amount of that. And jealousy? She hated to admit it, but it was in the mix too. Who were Murray, Del, and Gray? What was this world they were talking of? A world that included Tara and Joseph but excluded her? Tara had been popular in the village? You could say that again.

"Well, that's the men sorted," she said, determined to contribute to the conversation in some way. "What about the women? Tara must have had some female friends surely?" Or was she one of *them*? A man's woman? Incredibly, both Joseph and Jim had to think for a minute. So, her instincts on that were right, at least.

"What about Nico? She and Tara knocked around quite a bit together, didn't they?" Jim replied at last.

Joseph nodded. "Have you got her number?"

"No, I lost touch with her a while ago, but maybe Murray or Del will have it. I'll check with them."

"And Alice, they were good friends."

"Yeah, we'll need to check her whereabouts too."

"Wow, it's going to be some reunion," Layla interjected once more.

"Yeah, it will be," Jim said quite happily, infuriating her more.

Just what made Tara so bloody popular anyway? What did she have that could make a man drop everything that was going on his life to accompany her back home, just because she wanted him to? That got Jim rounding up their old cronies — cronies who no doubt would drop everything too once they knew who was back in town? Such was the effect of golden girl Tara Mills, a superstar around these parts, it seemed. It was too much. Layla needed to get away from talk of Tara's adoring fan base, go down to the beach, and let the salt air cleanse her. But she didn't want to look obvious. When Jim inadvertently offered an escape route, she was grateful.

To Joseph, he said, "I've got band practice in a while, up at Ryan's house. Do you fancy tagging along?"

"Yeah, that would be great." Joseph looked genuinely enthusiastic. Then he turned to Layla. "Unless you want to do something together, that is?"

"No." Layla ensured she sounded just the right side of disappointed. "I'll miss you, of course, but we need to make the most of our friends whilst we're here. Hannah and I had talked about going for a walk over the headland anyway."

Hannah looked up. She also looked startled. "Had we?" she said in surprise.

"We had," Layla insisted. "In fact, let's go, right now, this very minute."

Thankfully in an obedient mood, Hannah rose to her feet. As Penny had, she needed the support of the table to do so. Once her friend was standing, Layla started marching toward the beach, setting quite a pace for Hannah to match.

"Hey, hold on," said Hannah, puffing slightly. "Wait up a bit. Are you okay, Layla?"

Layla didn't reply. She just kept on walking, not stopping until the hard pavement beneath her feet gave way to soft sand. She hadn't visited the beach yet—she hadn't had time—but now she felt a desperate need to see Gull Rock again and the ocean that lapped against it. Quickly it came into sight, timeless and enduring—comforting. Turning to Hannah, noting the concern on her face, she finally answered.

"No, I'm not okay. I'm far from it. I can't pretend I'm cool with what's happening."

"Hang on," said Hannah, slightly confused. "What is happening exactly?"

Layla rolled her eyes. "You know, this whole Tara thing, everyone meeting at the pub to welcome her home. The whole world, or so it seems, looking forward to seeing her. Who *is* this girl, Hannah? I mean really? What does she want with Joe?"

"Calm down, Layla." Hannah took hold of her hands. "I'm as baffled as you are about who she is and what she wants. I don't know her either, remember? But we mustn't jump to conclusions. We mustn't presume she wants anything from Joe."

"But she made him come back with her to Trecastle, emotionally blackmailed him, or as good as." On a sob, she added, "And he let her, Hannah. So easily he let her."

"But her reason for coming back, it might be what he says, a perfectly valid one."

"And it might not be. It might be because Australia isn't quite the El Dorado she thought it was. It might be Australia sucks and she wants back what she threw away."

"After so many years?"

Layla glanced again at Gull Rock.

"If it's love, what does time matter?"

God, she was getting deep. She blamed the lunchtime drinking.

Hannah pulled her close, stroking her hair, comforting her.

"Look, let's not get carried away, not until we know the real reasons behind Tara's reappearance—which hopefully won't be too long, from what you've said. What we were doing in the pub—me, you, and Penny—it was stupid. It's got you all fired up, and no wonder. We need to stop speculating and deal with facts only, not make-believe."

"Easy for you to say," Layla replied, pulling away slightly and wiping roughly at her eyes. "It's not your boyfriend who was once in love with her."

"Not to my knowledge. But who knows what went on back in Port Levine?"

"Really?"

"Like we've just found out, Tara was popular—certainly with Jim. He couldn't stop talking about her yesterday. How well she looked, how nice it was to see her again, what a laugh she was, the good old days. I had to tell him to shut up in the end."

Layla attempted a smile. "Looks like we've got a lot to live up to."

"Not at all. Just be yourself, Layla. That's who Joseph loves. Not Tara, not me, but you. And he has done from the minute you met. Nothing can come between you."

Layla soaked up Hannah's words, willing herself to believe them.

"And don't go in all guns blazing with Penny, either. What she's suggested does make sense. It's in our interests to get to know Tara too."

"You're right. Perhaps I shouldn't be so resistant."

"Perhaps you shouldn't," Hannah agreed. "But it's not too late. Offer Tara an olive branch. Maybe suggest meeting up, just the two of you, get an insight into her personality. Don't be so ready to condemn her without good reason."

Layla balked slightly at the accusation. "And you don't think sharing a secret with my boyfriend—a secret that's upset him—and then telling him he's not allowed to share it with me is good enough reason to condemn her? I can't wait for this holiday to be over, to get away from here."

Hannah stood firm. "No, I don't. There's no good reason, not yet." She also looked hurt. "And don't wish the holiday over. I've been looking forward to seeing you for ages."

Layla slumped. "I'm sorry, Hannah, I didn't mean that. I love being here again, you know that. It's just Tara…She's changed everything somehow."

"She's changed nothing," Hannah said. "Not yet. And don't think you're alone, either. I've got your back. Whatever happens, I'm here."

Layla forced herself to calm down. She didn't want to argue further with Hannah, a voice of reason in the wilderness. A lone voice, it seemed. But she was wrong; Tara *had* changed everything. She had taken her bubble and burst it. Nothing was ever going to be the same again. Deep down, Layla knew that.

chapter fourteen

All Tara wanted was a quiet night to sit with her parents as she had done since her arrival, peacefully, contentedly, reveling in their silent nearness. Sweetly they had lit the fire for her, even though the clement evenings hadn't warranted it, knowing how much she and Leo had loved to sit by the fireside when they were kids, toasting marshmallows or just staring as orange and yellow flames danced around each other. It was obvious, however, that Joe and Jim had gone to quite a bit of effort for her. A fair few people were coming to welcome her back. It was sweet, but it was also nerve-racking. She wasn't the party girl of old. She was different now.

As for Layla, she doubted Joseph's girlfriend would want to see her again. The coolness emanating from her on the plane journey from Florence to Exeter was enough to give an Eskimo chill blains. She'd just have to avoid her tonight, that's all. Or maybe she shouldn't. Maybe she should try to get to know her better, show her she had nothing to worry about. That she wasn't here to tread on anyone's toes.

The other blight on the horizon was that she was tired—bone tired. All she wanted to do lately was sit and doze. But this Tara did rail against. Tiredness was not going to get the better of her. Joe had suggested they meet in The Admiral, Port Levine's only pub, but Tara had said no. Although the Trecastle Inn wasn't a pub she was familiar with, she knew it was one hell of a lot livelier than her local.

Bill and Grace, who ran The Admiral, would probably keel over with shock if the cozy, quiet confines of their pub were suddenly invaded by the marauding hordes. She smiled as she imagined the looks on their faces at such an assault. They'd be horrified. No, she couldn't do that to them. The Trecastle Inn it was.

"I'll come and get you," Joseph had offered.

"No, it's okay. Dad will do the honors."

And so he had, leaning across to kiss her on the cheek just before she got out of his Vauxhall, alighting not right outside the pub but a little farther up the high street. She needed to steel herself before coming face to face with everyone, before becoming the center of attention, when all she wanted to do was hide. But she'd hide soon enough; maybe she should just relax, give herself a night off.

She could tell the pub was heaving. Music rang out, some old rock tune she recognized but couldn't quite put a name to, over which was layered the lively sound of chatter and laughter. Were they all here for her? Surely not. Her mouth felt dry. She couldn't go in. She just couldn't. Anxiety flared in her stomach, sent a pain shooting from one side to the other. This was all wrong. She shouldn't be here with the intent of enjoying herself. Not without Aiden. Not after what she'd done to him.

"Tara? Is that you?" She heard a voice behind her. "Tara! It *is* you!"

She was swung round. A man stood before her with shaggy blond hair, stubble on his chin, and a gleaming white grin.

"Murray?" Tara said, squinting. "Murray, I can't believe it. How are you?"

"All the better for seeing you." He held her at arm's length before enfolding her in a big, friendly hug. "You look fantastic. Still a babe."

Still a babe? She didn't think so. She felt older than the landscape that surrounded them.

"How did you know...?"

"Jim texted me. He said you were back. There was no way I was going to miss out on a get-together with you." He motioned to the door. "Come on, let's get inside. Quite a few of the old crowd are in there. What are you drinking?"

Tara breathed deeply. There was to be no escape.

"Tara! How are you?"

"Tara. Great to see you."

"Tara, you look amazing."

"Tara, you've come back to us."

So many people had come to see her, to welcome her home, the one that had gotten away. Familiar faces lit up before her. Murray, Del, Gray, Crazy-Boy AKA Dean—who wasn't crazy at all, just full of mischief—Nico and Alice, to name just a few. She had to hand it to them; Joe and Jim had really pulled it out of the bag. Despite her earlier misgivings, a little flicker of excitement caught alight inside her. It was great to see them, all these people she hadn't seen for so long. Friends she had grown up with, had made regular visits back from London to party with, two weeks in the summer usually, a week in the autumn, and most Christmases. The one exception had been the holiday she'd shared with Joseph three months after they'd met, wanting to be alone with him at such a special time of year, wanting to be alone with him full stop, if she remembered correctly. But her mum had been so disappointed she hadn't come home that Christmas, although she had tried hard not to show it. Nonetheless, Tara hadn't done it again. The following Christmas, she'd taken Joseph back with her.

Thinking of Joseph, where was he? As lovely as it was to be among her oldest friends, she needed an anchor, someone to lean on, a bit of reassurance.

Her eyes leaving the crowd before her, all eager to hear tales of Oz—what the surf was like in that part of the world, had she ridden any killer waves, how the beaches compared with the beaches around here—she scanned the room for Joseph. It took a while to see through the throng of people, some standing shoulder to shoulder in places, blocking her view, but then she saw him. Leaning up against the bar, talking to someone she didn't know, a redheaded man, quite ruddy in appearance. Immediately he met her gaze. And smiled, a lovely smile—a smile that used to make her melt once upon a time, that still made her tingle, even now. It was a slow, deep smile, different than Aiden's often-cheeky grin, a smile that made you feel special, like you were the only person in the world who mattered to him, which was nonsense. It wasn't her who mattered to him. She didn't matter at all, not really, not anymore. It was Layla who mattered.

Having located Joe, she looked for Layla too. She was just a few feet away from him, engrossed in conversation with her friends,

Hannah and a blond woman, the latter with her hair piled rather haphazardly on top of her head while Hannah's fell loosely around her shoulders. They stood on either side of Layla, as though forming a shield around her. Protecting her from whom? The stranger in their midst? Tara shook her head. She mustn't get paranoid…or flatter herself.

Suddenly, Joseph was by her side. "Hey," he whispered into her ear, smiling too at the crowds around them. "You okay?"

"Fine," she mouthed back, but actually, she was starting to feel a little uncomfortable. The heat coming off so many bodies was like a furnace.

"Do you want another drink?" he asked, eyeing her nearly empty glass.

"No, not yet," she answered, preferring to keep him by her side.

Together they chatted to those nearest them. Joseph had visited Port Levine frequently with her; there weren't many of her friends he didn't know.

Crazy-Boy regaled them all with memories of a party they'd had on the beach one night, back in pre-Joseph days. They had all been around seventeen at the time, or on the edge of. A group of them had taken food, what few bottles of beer they had been able to smuggle from their parents' houses, and a portable barbecue to their favorite beach, World's End—a bay they had nicknamed as such because it really did seem, as the sun slowly sunk into the ocean and enfolded it in moonlight instead, that nothing else existed beyond what the eye could see. And perhaps nothing did, despite what geographers and atlases would have you believe.

The tide had been out, receding farther and farther, tipping itself into the void. As the sun sank into that same void too, Crazy-Boy had thrown down the gauntlet.

"Who's up for a swim?" he had asked.

"A swim?" one of them had protested—Nico, she thought. "The water's freezing."

"Yeah," another protester had shouted, "and it's getting dark, Crazy-Boy. I'm not going in now."

A bit more cajoling, a few dares thrown in for good measure, and they had all, without exception, stripped down to their underwear and run into the sea, running for ages, it seemed, before they were deep enough to swim. As Nico had predicted, the water had been freezing, but it had also enlivened them. Cue much hollering and whooping, frightening off the seabirds that hovered curiously above them.

Quickly, she had found her own space, had lain there, on her back, bobbing gently in the surf, loving the way she felt connected to nature, the night sky above her. After a while, Crazy-Boy had swum up beside her.

"Everyone should swim by moonlight at least once in their lives," he had said.

And he'd been right. It was magical. Something she had never forgotten, nor had the rest of the crowd, it seemed. Everyone looked dewy-eyed at the memory.

Eventually, they had clambered back to shore, dried off as best they could with what towels anyone had thought to bring, and the party had begun. Music booming from the ghetto blaster, more hollering and whooping—everyone in high spirits, everyone except the old couple who had lived in the house on the cliff-top overlooking World's End. Incensed, they had rung the police.

Crazy-Boy was laughing now. "God knows what Mr. Earnshaw must have said, but they sent practically the entire Cornish constabulary out. We had to run for our lives, remember? Scatter every which way. And where did I end up? Back in the bloody ocean. Out there for an age I was before it was safe to come back in."

"Yeah," groaned Del, who had also been listening intently. "And I ran straight into the arms of PC Plod, grounded for a month after that. Especially when my parents realized that beer was involved. I tried telling them I'd barely had a sip, but it was no use. The old don't listen to the young." Looking at the pint in his hands, he held it aloft and added, "Cheers, everyone! At least we can drink what we want now."

Tara too held up her glass, even though it was empty. She had managed to hide with Nico that night, behind a rock, the two of them walking home when the coast was clear, relieved they'd escaped but sorry for those who hadn't. But it was the swim by moonlight that characterized that night for her, that had given her a hankering to do it again. Only once with Joseph, who wasn't a keen swimmer. Mostly with Aiden, the pair of them desperate to find temporary respite from the heat that even the night couldn't dissipate, immersing themselves in the waters of the Pacific, lying side by side under a white moon, giggling. After a while, they'd swim to shore, lie down at the water's edge. They'd stop giggling and become more intent. His mouth would find hers; she'd respond in kind. They'd come together, the water lapping at them all the while, sand on her body, on his, the tang of sea salt on skin, on lips, on tongues, her cries rising to match the seabirds, his too.

Before she could stop it, her face crumpled. She lowered her head, trying to suppress the despair that such memories provoked.

Don't, Tara, a voice inside her urged. *Not here.*

A hand was on her arm, but whose? Momentarily she was confused. She found herself being steered away.

"Joseph, I—"

"Need some fresh air, yeah, I know. Come on."

She allowed herself to be guided toward the door, relieved that he had intervened, that he had stopped her from making a fool of herself.

Outside, Joseph looked around him, as if deciding which way to go. "Over here," he said, nodding farther down the road.

They stopped outside a shop that looked as though it specialized in honey.

"This used to be my workshop," he explained to her. "An alley runs down the side of it. No one will see us here."

In their hidey-hole, Tara let the tension that had built up prior to this evening flow from her. Like a Cornish tide, it was ferocious in its intensity. Joseph's strong arms held her while she sobbed. He hugged her close, some small part of her relishing how familiar he felt, despite her despair. Even after the sobs subsided, she stayed that way, as did he, not moving at all. How many minutes passed, she didn't know and didn't care, either. She needed this hug. Eventually, she stepped away; she couldn't commandeer him all night. It wasn't fair on Layla. It wasn't fair on him.

She said as much to Joseph.

"Layla's fine," he reassured her. "Honestly, don't worry about her. And certainly don't worry about me. I'm here because I want to be, because you're my friend."

"Friend." She repeated the word slowly, as though she were testing it. "We were so much more than that once, weren't we?"

"We were. You were the love of my life, until…"

Where he trailed off, she picked up. "…And you were mine, until…"

Joseph laughed, but then his face grew serious. "I'm so sorry, Tara. About Aiden."

"Me too." Her reply was heartfelt.

"You don't think you should have stayed?"

"How could I?" Tara was unyielding. "Joseph, we've talked about this, back in Florence. There was no way."

"There's always a way."

"Not in this case. I'm where I should be, where I *have* to be."

"Your parents, have you told them yet?"

Tara hung her head, a part of her ashamed she hadn't been able to do so. "It's hard, you know? Every time I resolve to say something, I fail. I…I just want everything to be normal. Just for another day or so."

"I understand."

She knew he was telling the truth. He did understand. He always had understood her. Perhaps that's why he'd been able to let her go so easily—he understood her dreams. Suddenly she felt like the luckiest girl alive. She had loved two good men in her lifetime. And they had loved her right back. Some people never experienced that.

"We'd better go," she said at last, still worried about Layla. If they were gone for any length of time, she'd notice.

"Yeah, sure," he replied.

They walked only a few steps before she stopped again. Slowly, she turned her body round to face him.

"Thanks for being here for me, Joseph."

He was silent, his eyes holding her this time, not his arms. She hesitated before speaking again, but she had to tell him.

"I never stopped loving you, despite leaving you. I…I still love you."

"I love you too, Tara."

As she turned away from him, he caught her arm.

"You can do this, you know. *We* can do this."

"I know."

"If you want me, I'm here for you, every step of the way."

Caught between bittersweet emotions, she turned to face the world again.

chapter fifteen

"You can do this, you know. WE can do this."

"I know."

"If you want me, I'm here for you, every step of the way."

Oh. My. God! Penny's hand flew up toward her mouth. Had her ears deceived her, or had she really just heard Joseph utter those words? And not to Layla, either—Layla was back in the pub, deep in conversation with one of Tara's friends. It must be Tara deposited down that dark alleyway with him. He was saying those words to his ex. What did they mean? They could do what together? Elope? Back into the wilds of Australia, somewhere the world would never find them? She must be dreaming. Quickly she pinched herself, readily affirming she was definitely not dreaming. She knew Joseph and Tara had once been a couple, but that was all over, had been for several years. Joseph had Layla now. He was loved up to the hilt. *They* were loved up. You only had to look at them to see they were smitten. Well, Layla was smitten, certainly. And Joseph had been. Wasn't he still? Or had Tara come back and eclipsed her?

Penny sensed movement—oh no, they were getting closer. She looked wildly around her. *Hide, quick.* But where? They were on one side of the honey shop—surely Joseph's workshop once upon a time? She'd go around to the other side. Propelling herself forward, she threw herself into the gap, nearly knocking herself out in the process. It was so small she had to turn sideways to fit, something she wished she'd known pre-hurl. They were still talking as they walked away, their voices low, conspiratorial, in the thick of devising some cunning plan, perhaps? Working out how they were going to break the news to Layla that she was now superfluous to requirements. A cold sweat broke out on her forehead at the thought.

A vibration coming from her hip distracted her. Damn, it was her phone! Quickly, Penny reached into her pocket to retrieve it. As she answered, she poked her head round the wall to see whether the deadly duo were still beating a hasty retreat or had been alerted to her presence. With great relief, it was the backs of them she saw, rather than startled, angry faces stomping toward her, demanding an explanation as to why she was stalking them.

"Richard, what do you want?" she practically hissed.

"Charming. It's nice to speak to you too, Penny. I've been trying to get in touch with you all night. Why haven't you picked up?"

Because she had wanted a break from his incessant questioning, that's why. She was fed up with being asked, "How many scoops of formula do I add to the water again? Six or seven?" and "She really doesn't like that so-called 'scrumptious lasagna.' and I don't blame her. It smells rank and looks even worse. I wouldn't feed it to my dog if we had one. Does she like fruit?" If he'd bothered to help out a bit more at home, he would have known the answers to these questions and more.

"I'm picking up now, aren't I?" she replied almost begrudgingly.

Earlier, she had crept out of the party to buy cigarettes. How she wished she hadn't. And why she was craving them again, she didn't know. She hadn't smoked for years, had given up the habit in her mid-twenties. But some cravings, she was learning, never go away. Having purchased them from the mini-mart, she'd headed over to where she remembered Joseph's old workshop to be to have a sneaky puff. Again, she wished she'd steered clear. What she'd just heard, she didn't want to know.

"Do you think it's teething that's giving her the bad nappies? I can't believe how many times I've had to change her today."

"What? Er, yeah, maybe. Give her some of those teething drops, the ones I got from that new ethical supermarket in town. *Teethease,* I think the drops are called."

"Oh, right. Where can I find it?"

Where can I find it? He defied belief.

"You'll find it where we keep all our medicines, Richard. In the cupboard above the washing machine."

Richard sighed. "Penny, you seem distracted. What's the matter?"

Of course she was bloody distracted; her best friend appeared to be in the process of being dumped—again. Poor Layla. Joseph had asked her to trust him. And, to her detriment, she had. First Alex, now him. This second betrayal would be enough, she was sure, to send her friend running to the nearest nunnery.

"It's nothing, Richard. I…I…" *I what?* she wondered. She didn't know.

Richard went back to his favorite topic. "So, it is teething upsetting her poor tum?" Worry entered his voice. "It's not…You don't think she's ill, do you?"

A cold trickle of fear ran through Penny at this thought too. "How is she otherwise?"

"She's fine. No temperature or anything. Just red cheeks."

"You say she won't eat the food I've left. What is she eating then?"

The phone went silent.

"Richard," Penny persisted. "What is she eating?"

"Well—" and it was a sheepish *well*, Penny noted "—I was tired last night, too tired to cook, so I got us a curry."

"A curry?" What the…

"It was only a korma," Richard rushed to his own defense. "It's mild."

"It's still a bloody curry. It has all sorts of things in it—nuts for one thing. Babies under a year old aren't allowed to go anywhere near nuts. It can lead to anaphylactic shock." Blind panic seized her. "Oh, no, she's not having trouble breathing, is she?"

"Her breathing's fine," Richard assured her.

Penny sighed in relief. "But spices, cream, not to mention copious amounts of saturated fat—it's not good for her. How much did she eat?"

Again a pause before replying. "Quite a bit, actually. Practically all of it, to be honest. I was only left with the rice and a few bits of chicken."

Penny rolled her eyes. Above her, she couldn't help noticing the stars had dimmed, as though they too had joined Joseph and Tara in hiding.

"And that's why you've got the disastrous nappies. Stick to food suitable for a baby. She needs to be built up to new tastes, not assaulted with them."

"Perhaps you need to be more adventurous about what you give her, then," Richard retaliated. "Not just food out of jars."

Penny could feel her nostrils flaring. That cigarette, she needed it now more than ever.

"It's *organic* food, Richard, meant for babies. There's time enough for chicken bloody korma in the future."

"I don't remember my mum ever feeding me or my brothers out of jars," he continued imperiously. "She made everything from scratch, she did. Everything."

"No wonder she didn't last long." The words were out of her mouth before she could stop them. She immediately tried to make amends. "Richard, I'm sorry. I didn't mean…"

"No, it's fine." The indignation in Richard's voice grew stronger still. "You've made yourself quite clear. You're not the type of mother my mother was, I know that. My mother would never have left her child, for a start."

"I haven't *left* the baby, Richard. I've just come to stay with friends for a few days. I'll be back soon."

"Her name is Scarlett," Richard suddenly yelled down the phone. "Why can't you bloody well say it?"

Penny was too startled to speak.

In the ensuing silence, Richard ended the call.

Whoa! What a night this was turning out to be. Once again, she and Layla were on the brink of losing everything. By rights, she should go home, this very night. Rush back to Hannah's, pack her stuff, and get in the car. Resume her motherly and wifely duties. But she couldn't. Not tonight, anyway. She'd drunk too much.

Frustration and despair fighting for supremacy, Penny slumped against the honey shop's newly whitewashed wall. Almost mechanically, she went through the process of lighting up a cigarette. Taking a puff from it, she choked. It tasted disgusting. She tried the same thing again, hoping for a different result—the definition of madness, some would say—but she was disappointed when the next drag provoked the same reaction. She threw it to the ground and stamped on it, grinding it with her foot for much longer than was strictly necessary.

Into her mind popped a picture of Richard, standing there in their kitchen, possibly feeling as distraught as she was right now, or maybe just plain angry. Questions reeled through her mind, one tumbling after the other. Why did she say that about his mother? Why *did* she always refer to Scarlett as *the baby?* What was wrong with her? Should she go and see Doctor Walker and get herself checked into the local asylum after all? Amazingly, she giggled at the thought of her in an asylum, Layla in a nunnery. An insight into the future, perhaps? And not the dim and distant future either; the likelihood seemed more immediate than that.

The giggling turned into slight hysteria—she certainly sounded insane. Is this what motherhood had done to her? Was the responsibility of another life more than she could cope with? Reaching up one hand to her mouth, Penny tried to stifle the giggling. Her upper body was literally shaking with laughter, but it was not a joyous laughter; it was anything but. Eventually and with considerable effort, she managed to gain a semblance of control over herself, only to find she'd given herself a nasty case of hiccups.

Like most men, Richard had adored his mother. The eldest of three sons, he was probably very special to her too. She had been a devoted mother, from what Penny could make out. Richard didn't talk much about his childhood.

"Don't see the point," he had said once by way of explanation. "It's over and done with. It's now that matters."

His mother had died when he was in his early twenties, before Penny had met him. His two younger brothers had been late teens and coming up to twenty respectively. Her death had hit them all hard. Their surviving parent, Bill, hadn't handled things well at all, depending on alcohol to deal with life. His dependency on it had been what pushed Richard's mother, Peggy, into an early grave, Richard was sure of it. But despite his resentment toward his father, he still did his duty by him. Especially since his father had landed in the hospital a couple of years back with a suspected heart attack. That had made them both see sense. Richard visited when he could, made sure the man was comfortable financially, but there was still that resentment there, she knew—resentment that his mother had tried so hard to give her children a "normal" upbringing and in doing so had worn herself out. Penny wished she had met Peggy, wished she was still alive. She could have picked up some great mothering tips from her. Her own mother lived in Slough, and although they got on well enough, she was unfortunately too much like Penny for Penny's liking—no mothering tips there, then.

Brushing away a rebellious tear, Penny tried with the cigarettes again. She was determined to have at least a few puffs from the white stick. But it was no use. As she had rejected smoking all those years ago, it now rejected her. Admitting defeat, she leaned against the wall and closed her eyes instead, waiting for the worst of the hiccups to subside. Eventually, she felt composed enough to return to the pub.

As soon as she entered, Layla spotted her and came hurrying over.

"Hey, where have you been? I've been looking for you."

Good job you didn't find me, then, thought Penny wryly. *Or rather, us.*

Instead she answered, "I needed some fresh air and to speak to Richard."

"Oh, how is he?" Layla looked cheery enough, cheerier than she had when she had torn her off a strip for suggesting this get-together with Tara in the first place. "How's Scarlett?"

"They're fine," Penny lied. "Look, tomorrow I think I—"

Layla interrupted her before she could get any further. "Tomorrow I'm going to meet Tara. I've decided. I think you and Hannah are right; I should make an effort to be friendlier toward her." She hung her head slightly, as though in shame. "I've been a bit of a bitch, actually. I've let my insecurities get the better of me."

"Layla, everyone has insecurities," Penny countered.

"I know, but the way I've behaved lately, I'm not proud of myself. I don't want to be that sort of person."

You're a better person than Tara, Penny wanted to shout. *She's a scheming, manipulative bitch.* As for Joseph, well, what a disappointment he turned out to be.

She turned her head from side to side. Where were they, anyway, the low-down, conniving pair of schemers? She should go right up to them, confront them, tell them in front of everyone that they were rumbled, that she had heard them and their sickening pledge. But wait a minute…Could what was said really be considered a pledge? Or was she blowing it out of proportion? She had to admit, she had a tendency to do that—quite often, when she thought about it. Were they merely words of support? She didn't know. That was the trouble. She just didn't bloody know!

It took a minute or so to realize Layla was speaking again.

"I've just spoken to Tara, actually. She was by the door. I grabbed her as she came in. Like you, she'd popped out for a bit of fresh air."

She'd popped out for a lot more than that, Penny wanted to tell her, but then confusion got the better of her.

"Did she come in alone?"

"Alone? Yes, she was alone. Why?"

The sneakiness of it! They had crept out and then crept back in separately. That was it, evidence of their wrongdoing. She was going to expose them—now.

"Penny, I'm so glad you're here." Layla once again broke into her vengeful thoughts. "Tara was lovely. She said she'd like it if we met, just the two of us. But to be honest, I'm a bit nervous about it. This whole situation, it's still so…so strange."

"You can say that again," mumbled Penny.

"Sorry, what was that?" Layla leaned closer.

"Oh, nothing, nothing," responded Penny airily.

"Oh, okay." Layla unknitted her eyebrows. "I don't think I could do any of this without you by my side, listening to my ramblings. I know it must be hard for Richard and Scarlett to spare you, but I'm grateful they can, if just for a few days. Without you and Hannah to talk to, I think I might have gone to pieces."

Drat! That would make going home tomorrow harder. It would make it downright impossible. Perhaps it would be better if she stayed, just for another day or two, give Richard time to cool off. She knew he'd booked the entire week off work anyway—a miracle for him. It was difficult getting him to book time off even at Christmas.

No, she'd have to stay. The baby had Richard; she'd be okay. Layla needed her. The thing is, she might need her a heck of a lot more if what Penny suspected was true, that Joseph was in the midst of changing allegiance. As much as she wanted to shout from the rooftops what was going on, she reminded herself that right now it was only a suspicion. What she'd heard had been damning, but not quite damning enough. She'd do better to watch and wait. Things seemed to be moving fast. If something was going on between them, they'd trip themselves up soon enough. And if they did, she'd be here for the fallout—and to give Joseph and Tara what for.

chapter sixteen

After the party at the Trecastle Inn, Layla, Joseph, Hannah, Penny, and Jim made their way back to the flat. Despite her earlier reservations, Layla was pleased; it had been a good night, really enjoyable. The atmosphere had been electric, and Tara and Jim's old crowd was certainly a friendly one. She'd been absolutely engrossed talking to Nico — she was someone Tara had grown up with, had been good friends with, although they had lost touch when Tara moved to Australia.

"Missed her, though," Nico had said, another sun-kissed babe, as diminutive as Tara. "But it happens; people go their separate ways all the time."

Layla was about to agree when Nico had started speaking again.

"Tara and Joseph, though, I never thought they'd go their separate ways. They seemed as though they were made for each other. It was a shock to everyone."

Layla had balked at this.

"Are you okay?" Nico had asked innocently.

Layla hadn't let on she was Joseph's current girlfriend.

"Fine," Layla had replied, her voice slightly strangled, she knew.

Eager to know more about her nemesis, Layla had continued to quiz Nico in an oh-so-interested way. How had the girls spent their days during the summer? What kind of things did Tara like to do, besides what everyone did around here, surfing? Was travel always something that had interested her?

From the picture Nico painted, Tara seemed like the sort of girl Layla herself would have liked to hang out with—fun. She came across as sweet too, a staunch friend. The words *sly, sneaky, manipulative,* and *mean* were never even hinted at.

In a way, Layla was glad. The girl whom Joseph had loved before her seemed like a truly lovely girl. Her nemesis? Perhaps she had overreacted.

Bearing that in mind, Layla had eventually torn herself away from Nico in search of Tara. She had spotted her coming in the main entrance of the pub and headed over to her straightaway.

"Hey, Tara, nipped out for a bit of fresh air?"

"Er, yeah, I just needed a quick breather. You know how it is. I'm fine now, though. Ready to start working the room again."

Layla had laughed. "Before you do, though," she had tentatively started, "can I have a quick word?"

"Yeah, sure, what about?" Tara had replied amenably.

"I wondered what you were doing tomorrow. Whether we could meet for lunch?"

"Lunch?" She had seemed startled by such an invitation.

Layla had rushed to reassure her. "Don't worry. It's not because I want to have a go at you or anything, I promise. I've been unfriendly, I know. I'm sorry. Perhaps we could get to know each other a bit. We do have quite a bit in common, after all."

"Joseph, you mean?"

"Exactly. It would be good to talk."

Tara had grinned back at her then. "That would be lovely. Yes, thanks, I'd love to. Where do you want to meet?"

"I'll borrow Joseph's car and come to Port Levine, if that's okay. Does the pub there serve lunch?"

"Yes, yes, they do."

After committing to memory Tara's parents' address and setting a meeting time for half past noon, Layla had disappeared back into the crowd, feeling quite proud of being so grown up about the situation. When she had told Joseph about it later in bed, she had hoped he'd feel the same way. He had, drawing her closer to him in the darkness. She hadn't resisted him this time. She couldn't resist him, in truth. With Penny in the front room, though, and Hannah and Jim close by, she knew they had to be quiet. Sadly, a fit of giggles got the better of her, causing not just her body but also the bed to shake violently. God knows what the other occupants must have thought. Eventually the giggling had subsided, and in the stillness of the night, they had found their rhythm, moving together silently and faultlessly, his eyes holding hers as they reached their climax together. In the morning, when she had woken, his arms were still round her, as though he'd never let her go. Hopefully, he wouldn't. He and Tara might have been the perfect couple once, but now she and Joseph were.

Later that morning, Joseph and Jim announced plans to check out a music venue in Exeter that 96 Tears was playing a gig at soon. A bit of a lengthy drive, they'd use Hannah's car, as Layla was commandeering the Defender and would be gone for most of the afternoon. When Penny had eventually surfaced, her hair very bed-head, her eyes still rimmed with kohl, she and Hannah had quickly decided to go shopping in Bude. There weren't many good shops around these parts. You had to go into Exeter if you seriously wanted to add to your wardrobe, but Bude had a better selection than most Cornish towns. A little farther up the coast, the drive was a treat in itself too, past the beaches of Crackington Haven and Widemouth Bay, huge expanses of sand and ocean, viewed majestically from the road that ran beside them.

Layla almost wished she could join them, but she'd made plans with Tara, and she couldn't break them. Watching Hannah and Penny get ready for their outing—the boys had already left—she felt a little wistful, however. She didn't have long to spend in their company, and she wanted to make the most of every minute. But it might be nice for them to spend some time together too, Hannah and Penny. Although her best friends were so different—Penny was feisty, Hannah was dreamy—they actually got on very well. They were laughing now about something to do with surf wear and diamond jewelry. Another chalk and cheese match. Smiling at the pair of them chatting away, Layla glanced at her watch. It was a few minutes after noon. She'd better leave now if she was going to make it to Port Levine by twelve thirty.

"Okay, girls, I'm off. Wish me luck, won't you?"

"You won't need it," declared Hannah.

Penny, Layla noticed, didn't look so sure.

"Penny, what's wrong? Are you okay?"

"Er, yeah." Penny smiled back at her. "Just be careful, though, huh?"

Layla laughed. "On the road, you mean? Don't worry. I can handle the Defender."

Penny's eyes clouded over. "No, I'm not talking about the bloody car. I'm talking about Tara. Just be careful of her, okay? Stay on your guard. Remember why you're going to see her — to gauge her, to see what she's all about. To find out what she's up to."

Layla was taken aback. Penny didn't like Tara, she could tell.

"She does actually seem very nice," Layla started.

"I thought so too," Hannah chimed in. "Really friendly."

Penny looked exasperated. "I'm just saying, that's all. Just…take care, Layla."

Layla held her gaze. Did Penny know something she didn't? She'd been a bit funny last night too, on the walk home. Not funny toward her, but a little off with Joseph, ignoring him almost. Perhaps she was being over-protective, motherhood bringing that streak in her to the fore. Layla decided that was it. It made sense. Penny couldn't possibly know anything she didn't.

"I will," she reassured her. "You go off and have a good time. I'll see you all later."

The drive to Port Levine took twenty minutes, the Defender's clunky handling indeed proving something of a challenge to Layla. She fondly remembered her red Mazda, the car she had first driven down here in. It was a much easier car to drive, much smaller. She'd had to sell it when she and Joseph moved to Florence, though. Not that it was worth much, but every penny counted at the time. Joseph hadn't bothered to sell the Defender. He had given it to Jim instead to look after, along with the trail bike he used to whizz along country lanes in. Good job Hannah and Jim's flat had plenty of parking at the back, not just a carport but roadside parking too.

Before long, she had pulled up outside Tara's parents' house. Turning off the engine, she sat in the car for a few moments, admiring the chocolate-box scene before her. Port Levine was small but perfectly formed, with a charming selection of dwellings, most of them detached or semi-detached, a post office that doubled as the village shop, and one pub, a communal meeting place. There was a Methodist church too — another communal meeting place, no doubt. Tara's house, the one she grew up in, was gorgeous, white with a thatched roof and a purple door. Someone in the family had a quirky sense of humor. The garden in front was pristine, a garden path dividing two perfectly manicured lawns with plenty of plants in sharp-edged borders promising a riot of color to come.

Taking a deep breath, she also checked her face, smoothing down her hair and applying a fresh layer of lipstick, a plum shade, perfect for daylight hours. Satisfied she looked okay, she made her way up the paved path to knock on the purple door. It opened so quickly, she wondered if Tara had been hovering behind it — either that or she'd been looking out the window at Layla preening herself in the vanity mirror.

"Hi, Layla. It's good to see you. Come in."

Layla stepped tentatively inside. The interior was just as lovely as the exterior, with low ceilings and oak beams. It was homey, traditional-looking, a lovely place to grow up in.

An older woman in a faded pink apron came toward them. "Hello," she said, extending her hand. "I'm Lily, Tara's mother. Pleased to meet you."

"Pleased to meet you too." Layla smiled, noting the warmth of her grip.

From the direction of what must be the living room came her father. "Hello, dear. Layla, isn't it? I hear you girls are off to lunch."

"Yes, yes, we are. The Admiral, isn't it, Tara?" Layla asked.

Tara nodded. "Is that okay? They do a mean lasagna in there."

"Sounds fabulous." Layla smiled at her.

"Off you go, then, girls. Have a lovely time." Lily's mother walked with them to the door, waving as they walked down the path.

"They seem lovely, your parents," Layla remarked. They also hadn't made any comment regarding her status as Joseph's current girlfriend. They knew Joseph, had known him well. She had expected some comment to be made.

"They're the best. Me and my sister, we're fortunate to have them."

"And the door. Who chose such a fun color?"

"My mum. Purple is her favorite color."

"It's one of mine too," Layla replied.

The walk to the pub took a few minutes. A coaching inn dating back to seventeen sixty, it was an imposing building built of granite and slate. Inside were more beams, painted black, not natural and gnarled as they had been left in Tara's house. In the fireplace stood a huge cast-iron grate, bereft of a fire as the day was far from cold. It was beautiful, more like May or June than early April. Tara was greeted like a long-lost friend.

"Tara! How lovely to see you again," said the man standing behind the bar. "Grace, look who's come to see us," he called behind him.

Grace emerged from a small doorway just behind the bar. "Tara!" she said upon sight of her. "Your mother said you were back when I met her in the village store a couple of days ago. What a wonderful surprise it was for them, and not only them, but for us too. We're thrilled to see you."

As the three hugged and caught up, Layla took a step back. A few moments later, Tara was introducing her to them. Sweetly, they fussed over her too.

After choosing their drinks and what they'd like to eat, the two girls took a seat beside the fireplace, Layla thinking how romantic it would be to be here on a winter's night. She stopped short. Was this the exact place Tara and Joseph had sat on those aforementioned winter nights, thinking just the same, how romantic it all was, basking in the glow of the fire? How pretty Tara would look in such demure lighting. Was she having a laugh at Layla's expense by sitting with her in the same place? A dig of sorts? Layla shook such thoughts from her head. This jealous streak, where had it come from? She'd never been particularly jealous before, but then, she'd never been in love before, not real love. It seemed to be a double-edged sword.

The bartender brought over their drinks—a healthy tomato juice for Tara, a not-so-healthy Coke for her.

Taking a sip of her drink, Layla decided to dispense with any more small talk.

"Look, Tara. I'm sorry I've been a bit off with you—"

Tara cut in. "Please don't apologize. There's no need. If anything, I should be the one saying sorry. I've burst into your life, disrupted it. But I promise it's only temporary. And I didn't mean to. It wasn't premeditated or anything. I swear."

Layla was taken aback. It was as though such words had been eager to escape Tara for ages, and she was now seizing the opportunity to let them. Quickly, she studied Tara's face—was she protesting too much or being genuine? According to Joseph, they had met purely by accident in Florence. Maybe it was true.

"It's fine," she tried to reassure her. "Joseph's told me everything." She immediately corrected herself. "Not everything. I mean, as much as he can tell me. And I hope whatever it is that's drawn you back here is sorted very soon."

Tara looked away, her big blue eyes shiny.

Tentatively, Layla laid a hand on her arm. "And if I can help, in any way, I will."

Tara looked back at her. Yes, she was definitely holding back tears. "I can see why Joseph adores you."

Layla blushed. "Can you?"

"Yeah." Tara smiled. "We…we were great together for the years we were together, but I think we both knew we weren't each other's 'forever' partners. You two, you can see you're in it for the long haul."

Layla smiled too. Regarding the long haul, she knew she certainly was. They might have only been together for just over a year as opposed to the "years" he'd been with Tara, but her "forever" partner was exactly how she thought of him. Her mind returning to Tara, she asked if there had been anyone special for her in Oz—a question she had asked her the first time they had met, at the apartment in Florence.

Tara took a moment to answer. "I met guys, a few of them. But, no, there was no one special."

Although Tara had hesitated, Layla saw no reason not to believe her this time. Finding that special someone, it was hard. To that, the members of a thousand dating sites would testify.

"And what about the future?" she pressed on. "Are you home for good? Or do you plan to travel again sometime soon?"

"I haven't made any plans for the future. I'm just taking each day as it comes. There's plenty of time to decide what I'm going to do."

"Yes, of course. Maybe you might even go back to London?"

"Maybe…" Tara was noncommittal.

"Oh, look, here's the food," Layla said, looking up.

Both of them, on Tara's recommendation, had ordered the lasagna. Layla was starving, and immediately she started digging into it. The grilled cheese on top was delightfully gooey.

"This is so good," she said in between mouthfuls. Then, noticing Tara playing with her food rather than eating it, she asked, "Aren't you hungry?"

"Oh, yeah, I am," Tara replied, quickly lifting her fork. "Mum cooked a big breakfast, that's all. You know what mums are like, insist on cooking the full works."

She didn't, actually. Growing up, Layla had mainly had to get her own breakfast. Her mum, Angelica, hated cooking with a passion. Cocoa Pops or some such delight had been her breakfast staple. But still, it was a valid excuse. Tara was tiny; she didn't look as if she ate much at the best of times.

Conversation turned to more mundane matters as they ate. Layla was unable to concentrate on too much but the food in front of her. It really was delicious.

Finishing, she sat back in her chair and wiped her mouth with her napkin.

"Fancy some dessert?" Tara said, amused.

"Ooh, yeah," Layla began and then burst out laughing. "Sorry, I troughed that, didn't I?"

"You did a bit." Tara was laughing too. "But it's good to see my recommendation passed muster."

"It certainly did." Eyeing Tara's plate again, she said, "Your mum's breakfast must have been mega."

"It was—egg, bacon, tomatoes, mushrooms, the works. That as well as French toast."

"Sounds lovely," Layla said. If she had to guess, she'd say only two or three forkfuls of lasagna had passed Tara's lips. In contrast, her own plate was scraped clean.

"Oh, do you want it?" Tara said, starting to push her plate toward her.

"No, no," Layla replied, making a show of clutching at her stomach. "I'm bulging as it is. I think I'll leave dessert too. Another time, maybe."

If there was going to be another time, thought Layla wryly. As much as she was enjoying Tara's company, she couldn't deny wanting the mystery surrounding her resolved. Until it was, she was stuck in a limbo of sorts, unable to move on.

After a second round of drinks, they talked more, Layla about life in Florence, Tara about her travels in Australia, each of them genuinely enjoying hearing about the other's experiences. Another hour quickly passed. Layla noticed Tara looked tired; she had also started wincing slightly. Layla wondered why.

"Are you okay?" she asked, concerned.

"Yeah." Tara seemed to attempt to smile in reply but instead screwed her face up slightly. "Actually, I've got a headache coming on. I have had since this morning."

"Poor you," commented Layla. Tara actually did look like she was in pain.

"Sorry. Do you mind if I go home? I think I need to lie down in a darkened room."

"No, not at all. Come on, let's go. I'll walk with you."

Tara was quiet on the walk back, one hand spread wide, massaging her temples. As they passed the Methodist church, she stopped suddenly.

"I think I'm going to be sick."

No sooner had the words left her mouth, she turned to the grass verge and bent double. Layla watched in horror as she retched violently.

"Tara, are you okay?" Immediately, she berated herself. Why did people ask such stupid questions in situations like this? "Here, let me help you." Layla started rubbing her back. Whether that was helping or just irritating her, she didn't know.

Promptly, Tara was sick again.

"I'll run and get your parents," Layla said, mentally calculating the distance between the church and Tara's house. It wasn't far, just a few meters. She'd be minutes.

"No." Tara's raised voice startled her. "I'll be fine. Please…have you got any tissues on you?"

Layla scrabbled about in her pockets. She found one that was thankfully still pristine. She quickly offered it to Tara, who took it gratefully, wiping at her mouth with it as best she could.

"I'm sorry, Layla. I'm so sorry."

"Not at all. You're unwell. You can't help it."

"Can you please help me home?"

"Of course."

When they reached the pathway to the cottage, Tara stopped. "I'm feeling much better now," she insisted, although to Layla she looked worse than ever, her face whiter than fresh snowfall.

"Are you sure?"

"Yes, I'm sure." Rushing on, she added, "Don't tell my parents, will you? They'll only worry."

"But surely they'd want to know if you're unwell?"

"Layla," Tara persisted. "Please. I just need to lie down, that's all. I'll be fine."

"Okay, no, I won't tell them. Not if you don't want me to."

"And don't tell Joseph either?"

Layla started. Why ever not? What a strange thing to ask.

"Erm...okay, I won't say a word."

Tara looked at her then, held her gaze.

"Thanks for looking after me, for sticking with me. Vomit—it's never pleasant to be around."

Layla smiled. "I won't say it's my pleasure," she joked, "but I'd never leave you in such a state."

Tara looked at her front door, as though trying to measure the distance between it and the garden gate. "Actually, I think I can make it from here, thanks."

"Okay." Layla knew there was no point in arguing. Tara was nothing if not determined. "I'll get your number off Joe and text you later, maybe tomorrow when you're more rested. Make sure you're feeling better. Is that okay?"

Tara looked touched that she had thought to do this. "That would be lovely."

Wincing again, Tara turned from her. Layla watched her retreat; the girl looked smaller than ever, as though somehow she had shrunk since coming back to Cornwall. Eventually, Layla turned away as well. It would be time to meet up with the others soon, see how their day had been.

chapter seventeen

Tara couldn't believe it. She had thrown up on Layla! All right, not on her exactly, but almost. She hadn't been able to help herself. She had started feeling ill just after breakfast, had taken some painkillers, but to no avail. The smell of the lasagna had made her feel even queasier. That's when the headache had got worse, alarmingly so, coming on like a freight train, relentless.

Hurrying up to her bedroom, glad both her parents were dozing in the living room, she quickly drew the curtains, tore back the covers of her bed, and burrowed herself into it. She wanted to obliterate all light, everything around her, in fact.

Nausea wasn't done with her yet, however. Another wave came crashing over her, as forceful as any Cornish wave slamming against granite rocks, wearing them away over time as she herself was being worn away. Throwing off the covers, she ran for the bathroom, stubbing her toe against the bedpost as she hurled herself out of her room, the pain registering, but infinitesimal compared to the pain in her head. She dropped to the ground beside the toilet pan, hung over it, and retched and retched and retched, only clear fluid coming up this time. She had barely eaten anything today, had no appetite. That story she had spun about breakfast to Layla was a lie. Her mother *had* wanted to cook for her, but she had said no, nibbling on a slice of toast instead, ignoring her mother's raised eyebrows.

The retching brought tears to her eyes, tears that started to gush as hard as her stomach previously had. The only thing she had to console her was the knowledge that she had done the right thing in leaving Lyons Bay.

God, but she missed Aiden. She hadn't known it was possible to miss another human being so much. That grin of his, the light in his eyes, she would give anything to see them both again. To hear his voice, feel his lips against hers, a perfect match, full and sensual. But she would not see him again. She knew that.

Gradually, she was able to push herself back up. Crawling across to the bath, she leaned against it, grateful for how cold its shell was. Again, sobs racked her. She couldn't stand the pain, she couldn't. The pain in her heart as well as her head. There was no way she'd be able to bear it. Why, oh why, had her world crashed and burned like this, especially when it had been so perfect? She had tried hard to live a good life, be respectful and kind to others as her parents had diligently taught her and her sister to be. She didn't deserve this. She didn't!

She hadn't realized her mother was standing at the door—looking absolutely aghast at the sight before her. Quickly the older woman rushed forward.

"Tara, darling, what on earth is the matter?" She knelt beside Tara, her arms immediately reaching out to enfold her daughter, offering mother love in abundance.

Now was the time. Now she should come clean, as soon as her mother released her, that is. Not that she wanted to be released. There was comfort in her arms—possibly the only real comfort Tara would find in this world again.

Eventually Lily did pull away, her face full of concern and worry. "Tell me what's wrong," she urged.

"I…It's just, erm."

"Yes, darling?"

Her mother's eyes, how she loved them. They were the eyes she had first looked into, the eyes that had burned so brightly for her throughout the years. She couldn't do it. She couldn't tell her. When, oh when, would she be brave enough?

"It's nothing. Nothing at all. I just don't feel well, that's all. A migraine."

"A migraine?" Lily's brows furrowed in confusion. "But you've never suffered from migraines before."

"I know, but that's what I think it is. A bad one too."

"Or the onset of flu, perhaps? You're shaking terribly. Whatever it is, we need to get you back into bed, and that's where you'll stay until you're better. Don't worry about a thing. I'll look after you."

"I know you will."

Lily had to hold on to the edge of the bath to stand up, breaking Tara's heart all over again. Her mother had been so strong once—a force of nature. To her children she had seemed indomitable. Time was running out on all of them.

"Mum, let me help you," Tara began.

"Nonsense." Lily brushed her hand away, but gently. "I'm perfectly capable. Now, come on. Back to bed." Looking at the toilet bowl, she added, "Have you been sick? Do you need a bucket?"

"Yes, please."

"And some water. I'll bring that too."

"Thanks, Mum."

Back in Tara's bedroom, Lily tucked her into bed, just as she used to do every night when she was a child. Tara relished her doing it, wanting to be that small child again when the life that lay ahead of her had seemed so exciting, the world and everything in it magnificent. To be fair, it was still magnificent. That hadn't changed.

Before Lily turned to fetch the water and bucket, she reached down to stroke her daughter's hair, again the way she had done when Tara was a child.

"I love you, darling girl. You know that, don't you?"

"Yes, of course I do. I love you too."

"And your father, we love you very much."

"I…I know."

"That's all I wanted to say," Lily finished, turning at last.

Watching her retreat, Tara had to bite down on her lip to stem the ever-ready flow of tears, stopping after a while because she was sure the metallic tang she could taste in her mouth was blood.

chapter eighteen

Bude was great—a town rather than a village, it was also home to another fabulous beach, Summerleaze. Such a romantic name, Penny thought. Upon arrival, she and Hannah went straight to it, discarding their shoes and relishing the feel of wet sand against bare skin, glad the weather was warm enough to allow such pleasures.

After their walk, they had hit the shops, Penny actually doing very well on the clothes-front, stocking up on a pair of summer heels, two pair of linen trousers—one pair white, one pair black—and three tops, one tie-dye. What was it about Cornwall that made you want to buy tie-dye, she wondered. In Brighton, she'd never wear it.

At lunchtime, Hannah suggested they eat in a small vegetarian restaurant, *Martha's Larder*, apparently something of an iconic hangout for Bude's young and hip crowd. Even though it was not the holiday season just yet, they had to wait for a table to be free, Hannah telling Penny to be patient, it would be worth it.

Neither girl was vegetarian, but both liked the look of the menu, written not on cardboard but in swirly script on a chalkboard over the counter. Hannah chose the vegetarian chili with nachos, and Penny opted for the Greek *mezze*. At last a table became free, and they quickly bagged it while their food was being prepared.

Sipping slowly at a glass of elderflower fizz, Penny cogitated as to whether she should tell Hannah what she had heard Joseph saying to Tara the previous night. If she had to keep it to herself any longer, she thought she might just burst.

The walk home with Joseph and Layla at the end of the evening had been awkward, although thankfully no one else had seemed to notice. She didn't want Hannah to feel awkward too once she imparted the news, but she couldn't keep it quiet either. She didn't know what Joseph and Tara had planned, but she was sure before long their rekindled passion would become blindingly obvious to everyone.

"Er, Hannah," she started, pushing her drink to one side. "I've got something to tell you. Something you're not going to want to hear."

"Oh?" Hannah cocked her head to one side. She really was very pretty, Penny thought, her features delicate, her demeanor enviably serene. Penny felt like a train wreck beside her. Who was she kidding? She *was* a train wreck beside her.

"Penny?" Hannah prompted. "What's bugging you?"

Penny took a deep breath. "Well, last night at the pub—you know, Tara's reunion—I popped outside briefly to phone Richard." She wouldn't bother mentioning the aborted attempt to smoke a ciggie. Hannah called them "devil sticks," so she was clearly not a fan. "It was quite loud in the pub, so I walked down the road a bit, to Joseph's workshop."

"The honey shop?"

"Yes, the honey shop as it is now. It looks good in there, doesn't it?"

"It is good. Their fudge is delicious. It's homemade."

Penny licked her lips. "I love fudge. So does Richard. I must get some to take home with me. Anyway, I was just passing the honey shop when I heard voices."

"Voices?" Hannah looked puzzled.

"Yeah, voices. Joseph's and Tara's, to be precise."

At this, Hannah leaned forward. "Go on," she urged.

Penny was about to continue when their food arrived, the waitress placing their respective plates down in front of them. After saying thanks, Penny continued. The food could wait; this was more important. She quickly related what she'd heard.

Hannah's face was a picture. "And you're sure that's what he said?"

"I'm positive. I can hear him now, saying exactly that." Pausing only briefly, Penny added, "Believe me, I wish I couldn't."

"'You can do this, you know. We can do this.'" Hannah repeated the words, trying them out for size. "'If you want me, I'm here for you, every step of the way.'" After a moment, she added, "Do what?"

"Exactly," said Penny, unable to resist popping a particularly plump green olive into her mouth.

Hannah leaned back in her chair. "That's just it. It could be anything."

Penny stopped chewing in disbelief. "But it's obvious what it is; they're planning to run away together. To leave poor Layla in the lurch."

"No." Hannah was emphatic. "I don't believe that."

"Not even though you've heard it from the horse's mouth?"

"I haven't, though, have I? I've heard it from your mouth. And whilst I believe you've translated their words perfectly, it's out of context. It could be innocent."

Penny pushed her plate away. "Hannah..."

"No, wait. Hear me out. I know Joseph, what he's like, and he's not dishonest. All the time we were together, he gave me no reason to distrust him...or his feelings for me." She lowered her head. "If anything, I'd say he's too honest for his own good."

Penny's frustration dissipated. Hannah was Joseph's ex too. And, although she didn't know much about their history together, she knew their breakup had been hard on Hannah. Apparently, Joseph hadn't felt as strongly for her as she had for him. It looked like he'd never tried to convince her otherwise, either.

"Aw, Hannah, all of this, it must be hard on you too."

"It's not." Hannah shook her head, a little too vigorously, perhaps? "Anyway, it's not my feelings we're talking about; it's Layla's. All I'm saying is, what he said, those words, you heard them in isolation. In context, they could mean something different."

Penny mulled this over, unable to resist polishing off the rest of the olives on her plate as she did so, as well as hummus mopped up with warm strips of pita bread.

"So, what do you think we should do about it?" she asked on her last mouthful.

"There's a saying: 'Fools rush in where angels fear to tread.' If we do rush in without the full set of facts, blow it up out of all proportion, we could do damage—real and lasting damage. Layla's feeling vulnerable at the moment, and little wonder, considering her history with Alex. If Joseph and Tara are up to something, we'll know about it sooner rather than later. Like I said, Joseph is too honest for his own good."

So, watch and wait was Hannah's advice. That was pretty much what she had decided to do last night. She was glad to have her instincts validated. But wait for how long? There was a time limit to be considered, but she, for one, wasn't going home until the matter had been resolved. Talking of which, she'd better phone Richard. She'd been putting it off, in all honesty, not feeling in the least little bit like groveling to him. Well, she wouldn't grovel. She'd just check on the baby—*Scarlett*—and then get back to what mattered right now—Layla.

When they reached home later that afternoon, Layla was already in residence, her feet up in front of the TV and a cup of tea beside her.

"Oh, hello, you two," she said, immediately switching off the TV. "How was Bude?"

"Yeah, good," Hannah said, plonking herself down beside her.

"Managed to buy quite a bit?" Layla continued, eyeing Penny's shopping bags.

"When do I not?" Penny said, smiling at her before dropping down too. Leaning forward, she asked, "So, how did it go? With Tara?"

Layla looked pleased. "It went well. She's nice, when you get to know her."

"So, she didn't do a big reveal or anything?"

Layla rolled her eyes. "No, Penny, she didn't."

Penny leaned back into the sofa, disappointed.

"There was one thing, though." Layla frowned slightly as she said it.

"Oh?" Penny sat upright again, her eyes briefly connecting with Hannah's as she did so.

"Yeah, she was sick. Violently sick, in fact, after we left the pub."

"Eww." Penny wrinkled her nose.

"Poor girl." Hannah, in contrast, was full of concern. "Why was she sick? Do you know?"

"Well, she'd hardly touched her food, so she obviously wasn't feeling that great. She put it down to a headache. She said it had been building all morning."

"But she still met you?" Hannah looked impressed, or maybe it was puzzled.

"She did, which was sweet. She could have just cried off, should probably have cried off. I would have understood. I tried to help her as much as I could, but she just needed to get home, lie in a darkened room."

"Some headache," commented Penny.

"She asked me not to tell her parents she'd been sick; they'd just worry."

"Makes sense," Hannah said, nodding.

"What's strange, though, is she asked me not to tell Joseph either. I don't know why. It's not as if it's anything to be ashamed of."

Again, Penny and Hannah exchanged glances. That *was* strange. It was clear from Hannah's furrowed eyebrows she thought so too.

Penny was about to quiz further when she heard movement. From the direction of the hallway, there was laughter and the rustle of bags—Jim and Joseph were home. Footsteps fast approaching, they burst into the living room, full of exuberance.

"Right, we've got the menu planned. Joe's cooking. I'm chopping. Who's opening the wine?"

Penny smiled. Jim was so full of fun. A fun rock god, it was a good combination, sexy. As he threw his leather jacket onto the sofa, the girls rose and followed him into the kitchen. Joseph was already in there, emptying carrier bags onto the counter. As soon as he saw Layla, his face lit up. If he was acting happy to see her, he was good at it. He grabbed her round the waist and pulled her close to him, kissing her on the cheek before announcing it was pasta he was cooking, with a chicken Florentine sauce, just in case Layla was feeling homesick.

"That'll be my second pasta dish of the day," Layla remarked good-naturedly. "But, hey, I'm not complaining."

"I should think not," he replied, kissing her again. "Good day?"

"Yeah, it was. I'll tell you about it later. Now, where's that wine?"

As the day had been warm, the evening was too. From Hannah's living room, French windows led onto a paved area and the garden beyond. On the paved area was a wooden slatted table surrounded by chairs. Suggesting they eat *al fresco*, Hannah and Penny laid the table as cooking aromas filled the air, making Penny's mouth water. Despite eating at lunchtime, she was starving, the sea air stimulating her appetite. There was laughter aplenty as food was prepared and wine was poured, the atmosphere relaxed and happy. Penny soaked it all up—it had been a long time since she'd felt like socializing. While pregnant, she had just wanted to curl up on the sofa, unable to believe the exhaustion involved in the growing of a child. After the baby, it felt like she hadn't even surfaced for air. For the first time and despite pissing Richard off royally—he'd been very distant on the phone earlier—she felt…what was it…normal? More like her old self again. Tonight, she was a person in her own right, not just a mother or a wife. She was Penny.

Welcome back, she thought almost nostalgically. *I've missed you.*

Joseph rushed past her with a big white bowl full of pasta. "Come on," he shouted over his shoulder. "It's ready."

Hmm, Penny thought again. *If he is planning to run off with Tara, you'd never guess.* Maybe Hannah was right. Maybe his words were innocent—when you put them in context, that is. She was glad she hadn't rushed into anything after all. Perhaps she should stop and consider more often, she mused.

The atmosphere around the table was lovely. Joseph and Jim kept everyone entertained with anecdotes of times they had spent together in the past—none including Tara, Penny was happy to note. Penny admired the relationship between the two boys. It was easy, relaxed. If she had to describe it further, she'd say guileless. She wished Richard was a bit more relaxed. Come to that, she wished she was too. When did they get so uptight? They certainly hadn't started off that way.

Suddenly she wanted Richard here, joining in the fun too. And the baby, fast asleep in a crib in the living room, slumbering peacefully. An ideal family—one that she'd imagined the three of them to be. One which, sadly, right now, they were not. Refusing to become morose, she concentrated on those around her instead. Dessert was more wine, after which they decamped to the kitchen for coffee—not the instant stuff, which she hated and evidently so did Jim, but proper coffee from a coffee machine, one Jim had bought with his first proper CD earnings. All of them except Hannah had their coffee black, Penny relishing the deep, earthy richness of the hot liquid inside the tiny white cup. Going in for seconds, she wasn't worried the caffeine would keep her awake. *Nothing* would keep her awake, not when she had so many sleepless nights to catch up on.

Thinking of bed brought on a longing for it.

"Okay, guys," she said, suppressing a yawn as she rose from the table. "It's way past midnight. I'm off. I'll see you all in the morning."

Minutes later, she returned to the kitchen.

"I give up. I can't work out that sofa bed. Can someone help me please?"

Jim and Hannah were washing up, and Layla was drying.

Hannah stopped what she was doing and started to dry her hands on a tea towel.

"No, it's all right, Han, I'll do it," said Joseph. "Come on, Pen."

Penny stiffened slightly and wondered if Joseph noticed. In a crowd, she could keep her feelings toward him under wraps; alone together, how transparent would she be?

"Thanks," she replied, stepping aside to let him pass and then following him reluctantly.

As he started removing cushions from the sofa, Penny stood by, staring at him, wondering if he really was going to let not just Layla down but all of them. He seemed like such a nice guy; she liked him a lot. Correction, *had* liked him a lot. It would hit them all hard if her suspicions proved correct.

Too late she realized Joseph was staring right back at her.

"What is it, Pen? Something on your mind?"

Was that a challenge or just an innocent question?

"Penny?"

"I'm fine," she said. "I just…I don't know. I'm glad it went well today with Layla and Tara. That's a relief, isn't it?"

Fishing, that's what she'd do, fish for clues instead.

To her surprise, Joseph sat down on the pull-out bed, but not before glancing at the door. *Why?* she wondered. To check that they were alone? That no one in particular was hovering outside—that no one being Layla?

He looked up at Penny next, his face slightly shadowed. "I don't know what happened yet. Layla's going to tell me later. But, yes, she seems happy enough with how the day went. I'm glad too."

"Strange situation for you, though, isn't it? Caught between two women."

Joseph looked a bit bemused by her comment. Bemused or annoyed? "I'm not *caught* between anyone."

"Aren't you?"

"No."

So quickly his guard had gone up. He was not going to say any more on the subject, she knew. Not unless she forced him to by revealing what she knew. Was this the time and place to do it? No. If they started arguing, the others would be here in a flash, demanding to know what was going on, and then it would be game over—for Joseph, for Layla, for her. She had to choose her moment more carefully than this.

Forcing brightness into her voice, she picked up the bedding that lay folded by the side of the sofa. "Come on. Let's finish sorting this out."

Joseph rose to his feet and helped her tuck the base sheet in.

"Strange, though, isn't it?" she commented as she worked.

"What is?"

"Tara being sick today."

Immediately, Joseph stopped what he was doing. "What did you say?"

Bugger! Too late she realized she shouldn't have said anything. Tara for some reason hadn't wanted him to know. But surely there was no harm in it?

Standing up straight, she repeated, "Tara, she was sick today. Layla was with her at the time. A migraine or something she had."

"You serious?"

"Er, yes." Why would she make something like that up?

"Oh, no. I've got to phone her."

She couldn't believe it. He looked ill all of a sudden too, his normal golden hue drained completely. He started patting at his pockets, trying to locate his mobile.

Edging round the bed, she drew closer to him, laying a hand on his arm. Why was he so panicked by Tara throwing up? Migraines could have that effect.

"Where the hell is my phone?" he muttered under his breath.

Quickly, she tried to reason with him. "Joseph, listen to me. It's late. It's nearly one in the morning. She's probably fast asleep by now. Especially if she was feeling unwell earlier. You can't phone her now; you'll wake her. Leave it until tomorrow."

Her words seemed to filter through.

Running an agitated hand through his hair, he replied, "You're right; it is too late. I'll do that. I'll check on her tomorrow. I wonder why Layla didn't mention it earlier."

She'd have to come clean now; she didn't want Layla getting into trouble. Wincing slightly, she confessed, "Actually, Tara asked Layla not to tell you—you or her parents. I shouldn't have mentioned it either. I'm sorry, I forgot."

"Tara told Layla not to tell me?"

"That's correct."

"Why?"

"I was hoping you could tell me."

Abruptly his head came up and his eyes met hers—blue against blue—both ice-cold shades, no warmth at all now.

"I'm afraid I can't tell *you* anything, Penny."

Oh, she was desperate now to call his bluff, to throw his traitorousness back at him. Her jaw was actually working to form words when Layla suddenly appeared.

"Haven't you two finished yet?" she said, flashing them both a big smile.

"Yeah, we've finished," Joseph said, still locked in a staring competition with her.

Would he tell Layla that he knew Tara had been sick? Somehow, she didn't think so. After what seemed like an eternity but in reality was mere seconds, he turned away and, taking Layla by the hand, left the room.

Penny sank down onto the bed, relieved to be shot of him. She had put her foot in it. Obviously Tara had wanted what had happened earlier kept quiet for a reason. But what reason? It was no big deal. And why such a strong reaction from Joseph? Switching off the lamp beside the sofa bed, she crawled under the covers and got herself comfy. Within seconds, she was sat upright again. Morning sickness? A bloody stupid name, considering it could strike at any time of day or night. Was that what was wrong with Tara? She herself had been sick a few times during pregnancy, but only during the first trimester; it had passed soon after that, thankfully. Despite her obvious slimness, could Tara be pregnant? Some girls took a while to show. If Tara was pregnant, who was the father? Not Joseph, surely? She hadn't been in Trecastle and, prior to that Florence, long enough…had she? In just a few seconds, her brain zoomed from zero to sixty. She knew, exhausted or not, there'd be no sleep for her tonight.

chapter nineteen

Layla's head felt heavy when she woke the next morning. She shouldn't have had that third glass of wine, or the fourth, or the fifth for that matter. As soon as she had hit the pillow last night, she'd been unconscious, but it had been a good night, the best she'd had in ages. Joseph had been on top form too, cooking up a storm for everyone. There was always a price to pay, though, for having fun, and it looked like she'd be paying it for a few hours to come.

Sunlight glinted through the curtains. And that was another thing. The weather they were having, it was beautiful, like the height of summer, all blue skies and warm temperatures. She hadn't checked on her mobile, but she was sure the weather in Florence wasn't as nice as it was here at the moment. Stretching out, she thought how lucky she was. Tara or no Tara, she was glad to be home, back with friends that felt more like family than family ever did. Although she hadn't been close to her mother while growing up, they had made amends the last time Layla was in Trecastle. During her "runaway year," Angelica had paid her a surprise visit, drawn back, as she herself had been, by the memories of the special times they had shared here while Layla was growing up, always staying in the same place, a cottage just outside of Trecastle that used to belong to a friend of a friend. She didn't know which friend; her mother had had an extraordinary number of them — although to be fair, Layla would call many of them acquaintances rather than friends. They surrounded Angelica every hour of the day, increasing the wedge that bereavement had already driven between them. But none of those so-called friends ever accompanied them to Trecastle. Holidays here were strictly their time, only to be spent with Hannah and her mother, Connie, but not every day. Some days, she remembered, they had hugged all to themselves.

When her mother had visited, the atmosphere between them had been awkward at first. But then they had talked, mother and daughter, really talked for the first time in so many years, perhaps the first time ever. Angelica had explained as best she could why she had pulled away from Layla after Greg had died, why she had immersed herself in friends, acquaintances, hangers-on instead. She had used them all to keep busy, to stop herself from having time to think, to keep afloat. Without them, she had explained to Layla, she would have sunk into a grief so deep she'd have been no use to anyone, least of all her daughter. It was hard to lose the love of your life, and in such a nonsensical way—in a car crash, the perpetrator of which had walked away without so much as a scratch on him. It was hard to lose your father too, Layla had wanted to respond, but she'd refrained. Instead she had done her utmost to see it from her mother's point of view, to understand, and, ultimately, to let it all go.

Angelica also lived in Italy, in Milan, with her partner Georgio, a merchant banker. Layla and Joseph had driven up to see them twice, and they had traveled south to return the visit. Angelica would never be the mother Layla had wanted so desperately throughout her childhood, someone homey like Tara's mother; there was no way she'd ever wear an apron or bake cakes. But she was grateful to have her in her life again. Trecastle had done that for them. It had bridged the gap.

Yawning, she stretched again, much wider this time. When her legs touched nothing but thin air, she frowned.

"Joseph? Where are you?" She hadn't heard him get up.

Turning swiftly, she saw his side of the bed was indeed empty. Sitting upright, her eyes searched the room—it was definitely devoid of his presence. She focused on the clock: 8:49, it read in big red numbers. Ooh, too early. No wonder she felt rough. She lay back down again, intending to get another hour's sleep at least. Closing her eyes, she tried to drift back off. But where had he gone so early? They were on holiday. He should be enjoying his lie-ins, taking advantage of them, of her too, if she were honest. The question rolled around in her head and seemed to bounce off the walls of her mind, the question mark that accompanied it becoming larger and larger, in the end too large to ignore. She started sniffing the air for smells of bacon—maybe he'd gone to whip up a big breakfast. Although whether breakfast at this hour would be appreciated by the other flatmates, she didn't know. Not that she should worry further on that score. There was no smell of bacon, so that theory was shot.

It took another twenty minutes before she gave up. Sleep was not on the cards for her again this morning. There was no point in lolling around any longer; she'd get up and go see where Joseph was.

Pulling on a dressing gown that Hannah had lent her, she quietly opened the door to her bedroom and sneaked into the hall. Soft snoring was coming from the direction of the living room; Penny was still flat out. From Hannah and Jim's bedroom, there was silence, so she continued sneaking into the kitchen. Empty. No coffee mug by the side of the sink or a plate with crumbs on it to indicate that Joseph had even been in the kitchen that morning. Maybe he'd popped to May's for supplies. She opened the fridge door. It was stuffed full of bread, butter, milk, and bacon. By the side, in a wired hen basket, were eggs aplenty—all purchased from a local farm up the road, as free range as it got. They didn't need supplies.

Layla searched for some pain killers, her head pounding. Swallowing down two pills with an entire pint of water, she decided she'd go out and look for Joseph instead. Maybe he couldn't sleep and had gone for a walk. Hopefully, she wouldn't have too much trouble finding him; they had promised themselves they'd spend today together. It was already Friday, and they hadn't yet done so. She was looking forward to it, especially as it was such a beautiful morning. Stooping slightly, she peered out of the window. There didn't appear to be a cloud in the sky.

Hurrying back into her bedroom, she pulled on her jeans, a T-shirt, and her black ankle-length boots. She brushed her teeth and splashed some water on her face, grimacing at the dark shadows under her eyes, more evidence of the heavy night before. After securing her hair in a ponytail, she grabbed her set of front door keys and headed into the sunshine, hoping the fresh Atlantic air might chase away her headache more effectively than the pills had done. The Defender was usually parked on the street behind Hannah's flat. She could walk round to see if it was gone, or she could continue down the high street. Deciding on the latter, she pressed forward. He was bound to be in the village.

As it was early, the high street hadn't fully come alive. Layla relished the silence; it was like having the entire village to herself, surreal somehow. As she reached May's, she saw someone leaning against the wall. It was Hilda, who worked full-time there. In her mid-fifties, she was short and round with obviously dyed reddish hair.

"Hello, love," she said, spying Layla. "Just popped outside for a cheeky fag."

"Lovely morning, isn't it?" Layla replied by way of greeting.

"Yes. I hope the weather continues for the Easter holidays. It's good for trade."

"I hope so." Layla smiled at her. "Erm, you haven't seen Joseph, have you?"

"Joseph? No, love. Mislaid him, have you?"

Layla laughed. "Something like that. He might be down at the beach. I'll head that way."

Hilda winked at her. "Good luck. I wouldn't go losing a fine young man like that if I were you."

I'm trying not to.

She was surprised such a negative thought had entered her head, especially when she had started to feel better about the situation she had found herself in. Ignoring it, she concentrated on the road ahead instead, squinting up in the sunshine at the silhouette of the castle as she drew nearer. Even when the sun was shining, it was dark and brooding, as though obsessing about all it had seen and experienced over the centuries, not wanting to share what it knew with anyone. *Like someone else I know.* Again, the thought had formed before she could stop it.

The beach was empty too, save for a lone man and his dog at the far end of the shore. She swung her head left and right, squinted again, but no, there was no Joseph to be found. As lovely as it was, the tide receding, the sands glistening, it felt lonely somehow. She'd make her way back; perhaps he was home now.

Outside Cake and Crumb was a signboard. Gail, who owned the café, must have just put it out; Layla certainly hadn't noticed it before. The sign was for Lavazza coffee, the thought of which made

Layla's mouth water. She'd love a cup. She glanced at her watch; it was coming up to eleven, still early. The others might still be in bed, and the wanderer was probably still wandering. She had time to treat herself.

A buzzer rang as she pushed open the door.

"Hello, love," Gail said from behind the counter, a beaming smile on her face. "I thought I saw you walk past the other day. How are you? Back for good?"

Nipping round the corner to give Gail a hug, Layla explained she was only here on a flying visit; they had the weekend to go, and then it was home on Monday.

"Florence," sighed Gail wistfully. "I went there in my twenties with a boyfriend. Wonderful weekend we had, sheer bliss. Now what can I get you?"

Gail insisted Layla sit down; she'd bring her cappuccino and blueberry muffin over to her. A young man was sitting at the table she would have chosen, in the café window, so she sat at the table next to him, wishing she'd brought her mobile phone with her so she could text Joseph. That was a daft thing to do, leaving it behind at the flat. She could have solved the mystery of his disappearance a lot quicker if she'd had her phone with her. Sighing, she blamed her hangover for the omission.

She was idly brushing imaginary crumbs off the white linen tablecloth when the man at the window table started speaking. It took a few moments to realize it was her he was addressing, the only other occupant besides Gail in the café.

"Sorry to interrupt you—and this is not a chat-up line, I promise. Are you from around here?"

He was a good-looking man, about the same age as her, she guessed. And he had an accent—Australian.

"Erm, well, yes and no. I lived here for a while, but right now I'm only visiting."

"Ah." He looked downcast all of a sudden. "It's a long-shot anyway."

"What is?" Layla asked, her curiosity piqued.

"Oh, it's nothing, I'm being silly. I...I'm sorry to bother you."

Gail arrived at the side of her table with coffee and cake in hand. "Can I get you anything else?" she said to the young man rather pointedly, her eyebrows arched.

"No thanks, I'm fine." As Gail walked away, he called out over his shoulder, "Great coffee, by the way."

Layla smiled at the exchange, taking a frothy sip, then wiping her top lip with a napkin in case she'd given herself a milk moustache.

"So, what about you?" she asked. "Are you on holiday in the UK?"

"Holiday? No, I'm on a mission."

"A mission?" She hadn't expected that. What was he? Some sort of James Bond-type character? Although not suavely dressed — he looked rather rumpled, in fact, in dark blue jeans and a navy T-shirt — there was something a little Sean Connery-like about him. His chest was broad and firm, his arms well-defined, and his eyes, well, she'd bet they could twinkle, although they weren't twinkling now.

Suddenly he smiled a smile that wiped away the melancholy from his face — almost. "I'm looking for someone. A girl." As if realizing how strange that might sound, he rushed on. "Not just any girl, a girl I used to know, not so long ago, in Australia. My girlfriend." Still tripping over his words, he continued. "She's not Australian; she's British. She comes from here. Well, not here, but just up the road, a place called Port Levine. I've been to her house just this morning, but there's no reply. It's her I'm looking for."

Layla almost fell off her chair. *Tara! He's looking for Tara!*

She immediately composed herself. "Look, do you mind if I join you?" she asked, picking up her coffee cup and plate and starting to rise.

"Not at all," he replied, clearly pleased he hadn't scared her off with his ramblings. Motioning to the chair opposite, he urged her to take a seat.

She introduced herself as she sat.

"And my name's Aiden. Aiden Taylor, from Lyons Bay, down under, as you may or may not have guessed."

Layla confessed she had. "Lyons Bay?" she queried. "Close to Sydney?"

"How did you know that?" He looked taken aback that she did. "Have you visited?"

"No, no," she quickly corrected him. "Just a lucky guess, I suppose."

"Very lucky," he replied, smiling at her. "It certainly is close to Sydney. About a two-hour drive, I'd say."

"Oh, right. Well, glad to meet you, Aiden." Layla held out her hand. Or was she? She didn't know yet.

"Do you…erm…have a picture of the girl you're looking for?"

"Yes, yes, I do, in my wallet." One hand retrieving it from his back pocket, he opened it to reveal a head and shoulder shot. It was Tara Mills, the one and only.

"You haven't seen her by any chance, hereabouts?"

Layla hesitated. How the hell was she going to answer that question? Of course she'd seen her; she'd been bloody *plagued* by her in recent days. Should she tell him the truth? That, yes, she knew her, his *girlfriend.*

"Layla?" Aiden prompted. Obviously, she had been cogitating too long.

"No, I haven't, sorry."

There was no way she could tell him, not without talking to Joseph first. Did he know about Aiden, the significant other Tara had denied? And he must be significant, coming all the way over from Australia to search for her. That was impressive. Yet another man prepared to move heaven and earth for this girl. She stared at her blueberry muffin before pushing it away, her appetite gone completely.

"If she's your girlfriend, surely you would know where she's gone," Layla tested.

Aiden hung his head. He certainly looked devastated. She almost covered his hand in hers—a universal gesture of sympathy—but hung back. There might be a good reason why Tara had left him. Underneath his pleasant exterior and seemingly gentle manner might lurk a monster of magnificent proportions.

"No, I don't. And I know that sounds weird, but it's true. I came home from work one day, and Tara—that's her name, by the way, Tara Mills—she was just gone. We worked as well as lived together, actually. I own a beach café in Lyons Bay, but she had the day off, said she was going into Sydney to do some shopping. I had no reason not to believe her; she hadn't lied to me before. But when I got back, most of her clothes were gone from the apartment we share, and on our bed was a letter."

"A letter?"

"Yeah, one of those *Dear John* ones." He sighed at the memory. "In a nutshell, it said 'I'm sorry it didn't work out between us. Please don't try and find me; it won't do you any good. Live life to the full.' That was it; it explained nothing."

Aiden's eyes glistened at the memory. He looked like he was in shock—still.

"When did this happen?"

"Just over four weeks ago."

Four weeks! Tara had left Australia a month ago? Layla had assumed it was a lot less than that. Where had she been all that time? In Florence? Had Joseph known? It was no use asking Aiden; he seemed as much in the dark as she was. Instead, she listened as he continued speaking, trying to make sense of the situation too.

"I was angry at first, bloody angry. She'd given no indication anything was wrong between us. Quite the contrary." He stopped for a moment. "And then…I don't know. It was like I was crippled with grief or something. For days I couldn't get out of bed. I mean, she'd agreed to marry me, for God's sake."

"Marry you?"

"Yes." There was so much anguish in that one word.

"And now?" Layla asked gently. "How do you feel now?"

"Now, I want answers. I need to know what I did wrong. I…I don't think I can rest until I do know." With a bit more fire in his voice, he added, "I think I have a right to know, actually. This was the girl I was going to spend the rest of my life with. The girl I *still* want to spend the rest of my life with. Why couldn't she just talk to me?"

Why indeed?

"Do you think she left because of someone?" she couldn't resist asking.

His head shot up in surprise. "Another man, you mean? No, Tara's not like that."

She admired his faith but couldn't help thinking him naïve too. "And you think she's come to England?"

"I'm not sure, not yet." His voice was soft again. "But I know her parents' address; she talked about this place all the time. I figure they must know where she is, and that maybe, just maybe, I can persuade them to tell me. Or at least give me a number I can contact her on. Her mobile, the number I do have, it's obsolete now."

Surprise, surprise.

"You've been to Port Levine already?"

"Yes, I landed in the early hours of this morning, hired a car, and drove straight there. I knocked on the door, but there was no reply. I went to the pub to enquire, but that was closed. So was the village store. I…I needed some coffee to keep me awake, so I drove until I found this village, grateful to see signs of life here, at least. But I'll be going back there in a while to try again."

Layla looked closely at him, his stubble, his eyes, how red-rimmed they were, the rings that lay just beneath them. "So, you haven't slept?"

He shook his head. "I haven't slept since she left me, not really."

Adopting a practical tone, she continued, "You need to sleep. You look exhausted. Why don't you book into a B&B? There's plenty here. Just for a few hours. The last thing you want to do is turn up on Tara's parents' doorstep looking wild eyed." Thinking further, she enquired, "I gather they're not expecting you?"

"No." He lifted one hand to feel at his chin as though to make sure the stubble she'd just hinted at was actually there. "If they knew I was coming, they might refuse to see me. Turning up unannounced, though, I might just stand a chance. Also, if Tara is here, if she has come home — and I can't for the life of me think where else she's gone — then I don't want her forewarned. If she is, she might run again." His voice broke at the prospect.

He wasn't a monster; she was sure of it. What he was, was in pain.

Aiden yawned and then smiled sheepishly, a sweet smile. "You're idea of a kip, it's a good one. To be honest, I can't even see straight, let alone think straight." Looking around, he said, "So, there are plenty of places I could rest my head?"

"Plenty. Gail, the lady who owns this café, runs a B&B too. Upstairs she has two or three en-suite rooms. I'll go and ask her if there are any free. Wait up."

Gail did indeed have a room for him. Although Layla had sensed she had seemed a bit suspicious of Aiden earlier, to the owner of Cake and Crumb, business was business. Layla imparted this information to him when she returned to their table.

"Ah, that's great. Thanks, Layla, thanks so much." Rubbing at his eyes, he added, "And for not denouncing me as a madman. Believe me, I know I sound dodgy."

To someone else, perhaps, thought Layla, *but not to me.*

"Look, can I take your number? If I do happen to catch sight of your girlfriend, I can let you know."

Aiden looked pleased and relieved. "I'd be grateful if you did."

From Gail, she procured a scrap of paper and a pen. Returning to the table, she scribbled down his contact details. "I hope it all works out for you, Aiden. Really I do."

And she did. He seemed like a nice guy. He didn't deserve this. To be fair, no one did. After saying good-bye, Layla hurried back to the flat. If she had been keen to see Joseph this morning, she was even more so now. This continuing secret of Tara's, it was beginning to wear thin—perilously so. Like Aiden, she too wanted answers. She had been right not to trust Tara, and she was going to make that crystal clear to Joseph. After all, if she had lied about Aiden, what else had she lied about?

chapter twenty

Tara hurried to the garden gate. Joseph would be here any minute now, and she didn't want her parents to see him. If they did, they would start asking questions, and she couldn't cope with that right now. She hadn't let on that Layla was his girlfriend, either, when she had come to visit yesterday. Instead she had said she was a friend she'd met in London who happened to be visiting family in Trecastle too. Her mother was suspicious, though; she was sure of it. She would want the full set of facts regarding why her daughter had come home, and she would want them soon.

"Why don't you come to Port Isaac with us this morning? We're meeting friends for coffee," Lily had asked her, after first checking she was better from the day before. She was — the blinding headache had eased — but in its place was an ache, dull right now but who knew when it would flare up again? All too soon, she'd bet.

After making her excuses, she had quickly gotten dressed. Joseph had texted her. He knew she had been sick yesterday — Layla must have told him, even though Tara had asked her not to — and he wanted to meet her. And she wanted to meet him. It would be nice to talk with someone, to be with someone from whom she had no secrets.

There he was, in his Defender, coming closer. Waiting outside for him reminded her of how she used to wait for him in another place, another time. In London, when she was younger, when *they* were younger, when they had their whole lives ahead of them. She had shared a flat with two other girls in Shepherd's Bush, a ground-floor Victorian flat with a chronic case of damp. She remembered mold actually growing on one wall of her bedroom, regularly wiped away but taking root again—and again, and again. The landlord had just shrugged his shoulders when she'd complained, telling her she could find another place to stay if she wanted, that there were plenty who'd move in there like a shot, mold or not.

It used to get her down. London life had gotten her down. It was too fast, too frenetic, and—she had to search for the right word—soulless. Everyone seemed to be in a hurry to get somewhere, their heads down, eyes on the pavement before them, walking hurriedly along roads, down escalators, in subways. Then walking back again the same way after the working day was over.

She guessed she was just a country girl at heart, and she was actually considering returning to Cornwall or maybe pushing on to Wales or Scotland. Their wide-open spaces, their wildness would suit her too, she was sure of it. And then she had met Joseph. She would wait outside for him excitedly before their dates. The reason? She loved to capture the sight of him roaring up on his motorbike—he looked bloody sexy in black leathers. When she had explained to him why she waited outside, he had laughed, creases appearing like dimples in his cheeks, his blue eyes dancing. Having borrowed a helmet from him, she would ride pillion, her arms and legs wrapped tight around him, her visor open as they sped through busy streets, all the while thinking London wasn't so bad after all.

Shortly after that, she had moved in with him. He had a flat in Hammersmith, small but decent, with no mold whatsoever. A Londoner born and bred, the city didn't scare Joseph; he was a part of it, confident in the crowds—a confidence that had rubbed off on her. Suddenly, London was full of soul, a glitzy and exciting metropolis. He showed her sweet pubs hidden down side streets where only residents drank, gorgeous restaurants full of atmosphere owned by real people, not big commercial chains, and markets where haggling for a bargain was a Sunday morning ritual. They went to gigs, since both of them loved music—rock, folk, indie, or a mixture of all three. Art shows, museums, exhibitions, London had it all. And in between, she'd take him back to Port Levine to sample life of another kind, a life that was a revelation to him also.

And now she was waiting for him again, unable to stop herself smiling as he drew closer. She noticed he was smiling too.

"Hey," he said, jumping out of the car once he had brought it to a standstill. "Impatient as ever, I see."

"To see you? Always," she joked back.

Standing in front of her, concern replaced his smile. "How are you?"

"Honestly, I'm better. It's another beautiful day; let's get some fresh air."

"Where do you want to go?"

Tara looked around her. "How long have you got?"

"As long as you want."

"Really? Layla doesn't mind?"

His face clouded, but only briefly. "No, she's fine. I'll text her later and explain. She was asleep when I left. She will be for ages, if I know her. Bit of a heavy night last night."

Motioning to the car, he continued. "Your chariot awaits, my lady. Where to first?"

Tara didn't need to think. "Rocky Valley. I haven't been there in years."

"Rocky Valley it is."

As she climbed into the front passenger seat, the darkening of his features earlier bothered her. Hopefully, Layla would be okay with them spending the morning together. She didn't want to cause trouble between them. She had caused enough. But the morning, that's all she needed him for. After that, she could let him go.

Rocky Valley. Tara used to think the name sounded like it belonged to an American high school, *Rocky Valley High*. She'd even written a few short stories about this fictional high school as a teen, strictly to amuse herself, not for the benefit of others—writing was not her *forte*. The real Rocky Valley was not a high school, however. It was one of the most mystical places in Cornwall and so named because of a cleft that ran between two cliffs, hollowed out over the centuries by the relentless Trevillet River, which ran from the hills behind to the sea below. And that river would never stop running, she wagered. Halfway to the ocean could be found the ruins of Trewethett Mill, opposite which, carved into a slab of granite, were two labyrinth petroglyphs, shrouded in mystery and intrigue. Experts couldn't decide if they dated back to the Early Bronze Age or were considerably more modern than that.

Tara followed the path of the labyrinth with her finger, as she had done so many times in the past. She knew what she believed — these were the real thing. In the trees above her, people had tied ribbons, a colorful assortment, some brand new, others weather-rotten, and to each was attached a wish. Above the carvings, people had etched their names or the names of loved ones deep into the rock. Since a local man had discovered the labyrinths in nineteen forty-eight, this had been a place of pilgrimage. For Tara, it had always been a place of peace.

Joseph crouched beside her too.

"I wonder if our names are still carved here," he said, running his hand over the wall above the labyrinth.

"I doubt it. It was such a long time ago we did that. Countless people have carved over our names since then, replaced us."

"*We* replaced us."

"Yes, I suppose we did."

Across from the mill was a rickety bridge, running from one side of the river to the other. Tara stood and walked over to it, positioning herself dead center on the wooden slats so she could stare down the valley, toward the ocean. She couldn't see the sea from this distance, but she could certainly hear it, waves crashing against rocks as though they had some perpetual ax to grind. Although many people beat a path here, locals as much as tourists, Rocky Valley remained determinedly unspoiled. In a place like this, the land held dominion, not the people.

"Let's take a picture," she called across to Joseph.

"Of us? There's no one around to take it."

"We don't need anyone to take it," Tara insisted. "Here, stand next to me."

Grabbing onto his arm, she pulled him into her, lifted the camera up high, and focused on their faces.

"Smile," she instructed before clicking the button on her phone. "And another. Make a face this time."

Joseph duly complied.

Recalling them back on screen, they both laughed at the one they'd pulled a face in.

"Handsome couple, aren't we?" Joseph remarked.

"We were," Tara contested. "Once."

Focusing on the valley below, he asked if she wanted to walk farther.

"No." Tara shook her head. "Let's go to St. Nectan's Glen."

Sacred places seemed to be calling her today, and in this part of the world, there were many to choose from. But of them all, St. Nectan's Glen was perhaps the most impressive. Reached via a wooded valley, steep in places and slippery too, the effort required to reach it was amply rewarded. On private land, you had to pay the couple who owned it a nominal sum for the privilege of viewing it, but Tara didn't mind. They were the guardians of this special place; she'd pay for its upkeep anytime. Passing through a white gate, she held on to Joseph as they climbed down to the valley floor once more. She looked around, pleased to note they had this to themselves too. The pilgrims were either busy elsewhere or enjoying a day off.

Walking over to the waterfall, she stood before it. Water cascaded from on high into a keeve—a big, round basin—and then down again, journeying onward. There was a ledge to one side of the basin, and years ago, people could jump from there into the keeve, which was deep enough to swim in. It was something she wished she'd done, swam in that frothing, steaming cauldron. She had always intended to, but the day had either been too cold, or she'd forgotten to bring a change of clothes. There was always some excuse. And now it was too late, but not just for her, for everyone. Health and Safety had put paid to such shenanigans a while ago.

She threw her head back. The coolness of the spray bouncing off the water and soaking her face and hair was delightful. Legend had it that King Arthur and his band of knights had stood on the very spot she was now occupying before going into battle, kneeling in supplication. Tara had the feeling a lot of people came here to do that, to pray before fighting battles of their own, personal usually. That was one of the reasons why she had come today, to tune in to something that couldn't be seen, only felt. Something good, something that was rooting for her to be the victor also.

All the while she stood there, Joseph remained beside her, not saying a word, just letting her *be*. She was grateful to him for that.

After St. Nectan's Glen, Tara felt famished—the first time she had in an age. Arm in arm, they made their way back through the valley to where the car was parked and headed for Boscastle, a popular village five miles from Trecastle. Harbour Lights, the café they chose, was located opposite the world-famous Witch Museum, a place full of macabre exhibits from the occult world, including pickled frogs in bottles and genuine handwritten spell books.

"Do you remember the first time I took you in there?" laughed Tara, nibbling at her cheese-filled baguette. "You thought us Cornish were a weird lot."

"And you think my opinion's changed?" He raised an eyebrow at her.

"Hey." She tapped playfully at his hand. "We're no weirder than you Londoners."

"Maybe," Joseph conceded.

After Boscastle, they returned to Port Levine.

"Joseph," Tara said tentatively while still in the car. "Can you spare another hour? It's just, I have a real hankering to go down to World's End, to see if the tide's out."

"Sure," he replied without even the slightest hesitation.

Not stopping in the village after all but driving right past it, they pulled off the main road about a mile or two outside of Port Levine and traveled down a much narrower road instead. At the beach, Joseph parked the car on a strip of grass verge so that other drivers, although they were few and far between, could pass unobstructed.

The tide was indeed out. Immediately, Tara slipped her shoes off and ran to the water's edge, licking at the salt on her lips as she did so, inhaling the briny smell that filled the air around her. After a while, she braved the surf, the coldness of the water causing a sharp intake of breath, the foam decorating her ankles prettily. Joseph caught up with her. He too had removed his shoes and rolled up his jeans.

"I hope you're not thinking of going in any farther," he commented, shivering.

"You mean skinny dipping like we used to? Do you remember?"

"Skinny dipping with you? I'm not likely to forget!"

She laughed out loud at the grin on his face. "Don't worry," she reassured him. "I won't go any farther."

It was hard to tell whether he was relieved or saddened by that.

Kicking the surf at one another, she knew that he, as much as she, was enjoying being in the moment, not worrying whether they were getting too wet or they might be cold later, just living for the moment, seizing the day and all that was good in it.

After a while, they retreated to an outcrop. The rocks, a mixture of granite and slate, were warm and dry. Only in one or two more worn-down areas had water collected, surrounded by barnacles that glistened like strings of pearls.

"I've missed this part of the world," Tara sighed, reveling in the view before her. "There's nowhere like it, nowhere at all."

"So, coming home, it was the right thing to do?"

Tara thought for a moment. "It was," she replied at last. "It's been brilliant seeing my parents again." Shyly she added, "And you."

He looked away, and she wondered why.

Taking a deep breath, she continued. "I'm telling them — my parents, I mean — this afternoon, when you take me back."

"If you think the time is right," he said, turning back to look at her again.

"It is. You know as well as I do, I can't keep putting it off. Besides which, you're going home soon, and I know you. You won't be happy doing that until I've told them."

"Florence can wait if it has to."

"It doesn't have to."

Each fell into silence, seabirds calling to one another above them. Tara listened intently. The sound was beautiful, more beautiful than she had ever realized.

"And Aiden, will you tell him?"

Tara started at the mention of his name. "No," she breathed.

"You know I think that's unfair, don't you?"

Tara cogitated for a few moments before trying to appease him. "I'll write him a letter," she said.

Joseph turned to face her fully now. She didn't want to listen to his next words; she wanted to listen only to the seabirds.

"A letter's too impersonal."

"Well, I can't exactly hop over on a plane, can I?" she protested.

"No, but you can phone him, let him hear your voice at least. Tara, Aiden loved you. Sorry, that's incorrect. He *loves* you. You were getting married."

A picture of the Coke ring Aiden had given her flashed up in Tara's mind—a vision that nearly undid her. She held firm, though, and made herself listen further.

"Not knowing why you suddenly upped and left will destroy him, or at least a part of him. You have to tell him, Tara. Maybe then he can get on with his own life, start again. I don't think he'll be able to do that until you've explained. He'll always wonder what he did that was so wrong. Not knowing will eat away at him."

Joseph was right. What she had done to Aiden, it was cruel. Perhaps it was even crueler than the truth. Aiden had really loved her; she had no doubt about that. It wasn't possible to feel the way she did about him and not have that feeling reciprocated. She hated to think how he had reacted to the letter she had left; she *hadn't* thought about it, in truth. Now she could imagine all too vividly his pain.

"Okay," she eventually conceded. "But my parents first."

"And then?" Joseph prompted.

"Then I'll call him, talk to him." After a moment, she added, "Say good-bye properly."

"No more secrets," he replied.

"No more secrets," she promised. Then she looked at her watch.

"We'll go back when you're ready," he said, noticing. "There's no rush."

"Thanks." She swallowed hard as she said it.

"One thing I must do, though, is text Layla. I should have done it earlier, really."

He stood and reached round to his back pocket. His eyebrows furrowed, he patted the other pocket instead.

"I must have left my phone in the car," he said, more to himself than Tara.

Immediately, she fished hers out of her jacket pocket. "Here, use mine."

Thanking her, Joseph took the phone and sent his text.

"Go ahead and tell Layla tonight, Joseph. That's long overdue too."

There was no mistaking the expression on his face; it was one of relief.

"Thanks," he replied.

"She's been incredible," Tara continued. "She really is one of a kind."

A smile crept across his face. He looked so proud. "I told you."

"Come on. I need to get back now, and so do you."

Joseph pulled her to her feet. "Good luck, Tara," he said. "With everything."

"Thanks. It'd be nice to think Lady Luck hasn't forgotten about me entirely."

No sooner had she said it than she was in his arms. He was holding her close, as close as he used to, close enough so she could feel how much he was trembling. He was sniffing slightly too. Realizing he was upset, she tried to comfort him.

"Hey, it's okay," she whispered. "It's okay."

But her voice cracked on the last word.

chapter twenty-one

"Is Joseph back yet?"

Despite how late it was in the day, Penny was still relishing being under the covers when Layla came flying into the room. After the suspicion that Tara was pregnant had hit like a thunderbolt, she had lain awake for ages, sleep finally claiming her, but not until a new dawn had broken. Even then, it had been a fitful sleep, one she had woken from many times. Only in the last hour or two had she managed a decent stretch, her mind exhausted with adding two and two together.

Bleary eyed, she forced herself into a sitting position. "Umm, I don't know. Has he gone out somewhere?"

Without answering, Layla ran out into the hallway, making her way to the kitchen, Penny guessed. While she did that, Penny supposed she'd better get up and check her phone to see if Richard had been trying to ring her. Grabbing it off the coffee table, she was surprised to see he hadn't. *Getting the hang of childcare, are you?* Still, even if he was, he would have phoned, surely, to gloat if nothing else. She had managed to speak to him late yesterday, but the conversation had been decidedly clipped, Richard still clearly fuming from her thoughtless words earlier on in the week. He was a sulker, was Richard. It was a trait of his that really got to her. She was more of a blow up, have a good scream, then forget all about it kind of girl. It irked her too that he hadn't checked in yet—it was noon, for heaven's sake. With the baby in the house, he'd have been up for hours. She dashed off a quick text to him instead, a curt *Is everything okay?* before heading to the kitchen too.

Layla was drumming her fingers on the Formica work-top. "Where is he?" she was mumbling. "Where the hell is he?"

"Have you tried his mobile?" Penny asked, shaking the kettle to check if there was water in it.

"I just did. He's not picking up. Story of my life, huh? I need to speak to him, and I need to speak to him now."

Trying to stifle a yawn, Penny pulled up a chair. "Can't you tell me instead?"

Layla stopped drumming. She looked at Penny intently instead. Too intently. Penny's breath caught in her throat. Had she guessed Tara was pregnant too?

Almost flinging herself in the chair beside Penny, Layla pushed the salt and pepper mills out of the way with a sweep of her hand. Once the coast was clear, she reached across to take Penny's hand in hers. Oh, crap. She did know.

"Tara's been lying to us," she announced, her eyes alight.

"I guessed as much," Penny replied, cringing.

"You guessed?" Layla was taken aback.

"Erm, sort of." This was going to hit hard. Who was she kidding? It *had* hit hard.

"How?"

"Well, I sort of…It's obvious, really."

"I know it is. Of course it is."

As Layla shook her head from side to side, Penny reached out a tentative hand. "Layla, I'm so sorry. How did you find out?"

"Because I've just met him, just now in the village."

Him? But she couldn't find Joseph; she'd just said as much. That's why she was trying to phone him. Poor girl, she really was in a state, unsurprisingly so.

Taking Layla's hand in both of hers, Penny urged her to calm down, to take plenty of deep breaths, in through her nose, out through her nose, the way she'd been taught in baby yoga classes. For good measure, she did the same.

After a few moments, Penny repeated her question. "How did you find out?"

Layla looked almost drunk on oxygen. "Find out what?"

"That she's pregnant."

"Who's pregnant?"

"Tara."

"Tara?" Layla's eyes widened so much, Penny feared they might pop out of their sockets altogether. "She's pregnant? How do you know?"

"Well, she was sick yesterday. Pregnancy tends to have that effect."

Layla shot to her feet and started pacing the floor. "Is that it? She's pregnant, and she didn't tell him."

Penny rose quickly too. Walking over to Layla, she gripped her firmly by her shoulders and forced her to stand still. "Do you really think he doesn't know?" she asked.

"Know what?" Layla's eyes looked wild.

"That Tara's pregnant."

Shaking her hair, golden strands in amongst the brown falling forward to temporarily cover her face, Layla replied, "I have no idea if he knows or not. If he does, he didn't let on. Is that the reason why she fled from him, do you think?"

"Fled from him? You mean *to* him, don't you?" Penny corrected.

Exasperation marked Layla's face. "No, I don't. I mean *from* him. Poor Aiden."

Penny was exasperated too. "Aiden? Who the hell is Aiden?"

"Her boyfriend." Layla was shouting now. "Her significant other, the one she denied having. I asked her outright, not once but twice. She denied him both times."

"Okay, okay, stop there. All this talk of denial, it's getting too biblical for my liking. Sit back down. I'll make us a nice cup of tea, and you can tell me exactly who Aiden is, and, more to the point, how you found out about him if not from Tara."

Thankfully the chamomile tea did seem to have a calming effect on her friend. Penny made her take several sips before allowing her to speak again. As Layla revealed who Aiden was, Penny could feel her own eyes widen too. At one point, her mouth dropped open, and she had to make a concerted effort to shut it.

"Her boyfriend? From Australia. He's come all the way over here to find her?" She said the words to herself as much as to Layla, trying to make sense of them.

"Yeah, and if she's pregnant, he gave no indication that he knew." After taking another sip of tea, she added, "And there's another thing."

"*Another* thing?" Penny was aghast. What else could there be?

"She was in Florence for an entire month before coming home to Cornwall."

An entire month? "I thought it had only been for a few days. No one said otherwise." Penny bit down on her lip—so it could be Joseph's baby. The time frames fit. "And where's he now?"

"Who?" Chamomile was clearly powerful stuff. Layla looked punch drunk.

"Aiden."

"He's at Gail's. She has holiday lodgings above the coffee shop. He's getting some rest. I insisted he did. He looks as if he hasn't slept much since she left him. Actually, that's what he said, pretty much."

"That's dramatic, isn't it, turning up on her doorstep? I mean, perhaps not if you live in the next village or town, but if you live thousands and thousands of miles away, it is. Actually it's bloody impressive when you think about it, traveling halfway across the globe." Aware that she was babbling, she forced herself to stop. Composed again, she asked, "And he doesn't know Tara's here? You didn't tell him?"

"No." Layla was adamant. "I thought I'd discuss it with Joseph first before I decide what to do."

"Good idea." Or was it? Penny couldn't tell. Again she calculated time frames, searching to give Joseph a way out, desperate to do so. The time frames were tight, admittedly, but not impossible, not impossible at all. And if the baby was Joseph's, is that what he had meant when he had said to Tara he'd be there for her "every step of the way"?

"Penny, what is it?"

Penny started at the mention of her name. "Nothing," she replied, her voice an octave or two higher than she'd have liked.

"Where's Hannah?" Layla asked suddenly. "Is she up yet?"

"I don't know. I'm not sure."

Layla got up, exited the kitchen, and knocked gently on Hannah's bedroom door. There was no reply. She pushed the door open, calling out to announce her presence. Penny came up behind her as she did so.

"They must have gone out too," Layla said, clearly disappointed.

Penny was too. Hannah was proving herself to be very level-headed in this whole Joseph-Tara and now Aiden situation. They could have done with her opinion.

"Where is he?" Layla muttered again. "I need to find him."

Penny wondered if she might start pacing the hallway this time, but she didn't. Instead, Layla swung around to face her.

"Do you think he's with her? With Tara?"

"Joseph or Aiden?"

"Joseph, of course. I've just told you, Aiden doesn't know she's even here."

"I…I don't know. Try his phone again."

Layla did. The call went straight to answer phone as it had done previously. "Bugger," she swore. "Where is he?"

Tea, thought Penny, panicking slightly. She'd make more tea, that panacea for all ills. Just as she did, Layla rushed out of the front door.

"Hey, where are you going?" Penny called after her.

"To check something. I won't be long."

Within minutes, Layla was back.

"As I thought. The Defender, it's not there. He *has* gone to Tara's. I know it." Slumping back down at the kitchen table, Layla let her head fall into her hands. "What's he doing there? And how early did he go? I was awake at eight forty-five."

Penny could voice why, but what if she was wrong? Although, she had to admit, Joseph had reacted strangely when she had let slip that Tara had been sick the previous day, very strangely indeed. Could it be something *had* happened between them during the month she'd been in Florence? That it had had repercussions? Perhaps Joseph had only suspected she was pregnant, but at the mention of her sickness, he knew it to be likely, rushing over there as soon as he could to confirm it. Or could the baby be Aiden's? Or possibly even someone else's, hence her running from Aiden. Ugh. The scenarios running round in her head, there were just too many.

"Sorry, Penny." Layla was rising again, tears in her eyes, her second cup of tea untouched. "Do you mind? I…I just need a bit of time on my own to try and work out what's going on. I'm so confused. I'll be in my bedroom if you need me."

Penny watched her go, hating to see how dejected she looked. Bloody Joseph, bloody Tara. What the hell were they up to? How could a man change so much and so quickly? Besotted with one woman one minute, falling over another the next. Were they all like Alex underneath, even Richard? Suddenly she felt like crying too.

Going through to the living room, she stripped the sofa bed, folded the linen, and then pushed the bed back into sofa mode. Sunlight streamed in through the French windows, but it did nothing to brighten her mood. She checked her phone again. Richard hadn't bothered to reply to her text. Let him sulk—she wasn't going to pander to him. Switching on the TV, she tried to concentrate on an episode of *Eastenders* that Hannah had previously recorded. The first episode finished, she started on another but fell asleep halfway through, her brain well and truly fried.

Sometime later, she was brought back once again to reality by an agitated Layla.

"Penny, wake up. I've found his phone. He left it in his jeans pocket. I heard it vibrating when I tried to ring it again." Layla thrust the phone into Penny's face as though she needed to verify her words.

"What time is it?"

"Time? Erm, it's nearly three. Why?"

Nearly three and still Richard hadn't phoned or texted. The phone wasn't on silent mode; she would have heard him if he had. A brief check proved her right.

Forcing herself out of the stupor she'd been in, she said, "At least that explains why he hasn't been in contact. I'd love to know what Richard's excuse is."

Layla wasn't listening. "Look, on the home screen, it lists all the calls missed from me, fifteen of them to be precise, and there's a message from Tara too. 'Text me five minutes before you arrive.'"

Just then Layla's phone beeped.

"Hang on," she said, looking from one hand, which held Joseph's phone to the other, which held hers.

"It's a text from Joseph, sent from Tara's phone."

"What does it say?" Penny leaned forward in anticipation.

"'It's Joseph,'" Layla read out. "'I've left my phone at home. I'm with Tara. I'll be back soon.'"

"Is that it?"

Layla nodded. "Short and sweet," she replied, her voice ladled with sarcasm.

"Well, I don't suppose he can wax lyrical on someone else's phone." Penny didn't know why she was bothering to defend him.

"So, he's been with her all day. From early this morning until now. Why?"

They've clearly got a lot to sort out, thought Penny, but she kept quiet.

Layla looked up then, her green eyes narrow. "I know his security code. I can check to see if there are other messages from her."

Penny bit her lip. "But do you think you should? I mean, it's a bit like looking at someone's diary, isn't it — looking at their phone?" There she was again, trying to protect him. But it shouldn't be him she was trying to protect; it should be Layla. Under the circumstances, perhaps Layla had every right to look at his private messages. It might help her to discover the truth. And although the truth was going to hurt, it couldn't be worse than living a lie…or with lies. Could it?

"Do it," she said at last.

Layla hesitated for just a few seconds more, but then she went ahead. While she was reading Joseph and Tara's text exchange, Penny kept her eyes on her, trying to gauge her reaction. Hoping against hope there'd be none.

Just when she was thinking it was going to be okay, that there was nothing on Joseph's phone to incriminate him, Layla's face crumpled.

Penny flew forward. "What is it? What have you found?"

"Look for yourself," was all Layla could manage to reply.

Taking the phone from her and feeling like a criminal for doing so, Penny read the text messages exchanged between Joseph and Tara.

Sorry to text so late, but I know you were sick today, when you were with Layla. Do you want me to come over? I can make an excuse here. ~J

No, it's fine. It's too late now anyway, and I'm still feeling rough. I don't want to alert my parents either. Come over in the morning, as soon as you can. ~T

Are you sure? It's not a problem. ~J

I'm sure. Now DON'T worry. I'll get cross if you do. ~T

The wrath of Tara? I'll try not to risk it. ~J

Lol! I love you Joseph—do you know that? I'll see you in the morning. ~T

See you in the morning. ~J

I'll be waiting outside. ~T

Like old times, huh? ~J

Penny felt the ground shift beneath her. *I love you Joseph—do you know that?* They did now. As for the wrath of Tara, it would be nothing compared to the wrath of Layla, Penny suspected.

Layla had her head in her hands, her whole body shaking.

"Layla, I'm so sorry," said Penny, shifting over so she could hug her friend.

"He asked me to trust him. I'm such a fool. I never learn."

"You're not the fool," Penny replied, impassioned. "He is, for running back to her."

"Penny, what am I going to do?"

As Layla sobbed in her arms, Penny agitated over whether she should tell Layla what she had heard Joseph say to Tara in the dark alley that ran beside the honey shop. Quickly, she decided against it. There was really no need to compound the facts further. Joseph had damned himself enough without any help from her.

Layla suddenly broke away. "Aiden," she sniffed. "I must tell Aiden."

"Don't worry about him," Penny started to say. Just worrying about herself was going to be challenging enough.

But Layla was insistent. "No, he needs to know."

Pushing away from her, Layla reached for her phone and dialed a number. "Aiden," she said. "I'm sorry to wake you if you were sleeping, but you need to know this, and you need to know now. Tara *is* here. She's at her parents."

Penny reached out to her, not sure whether what Layla was doing was a good thing or not. As she swiftly decided that it was, that Aiden *did* need to know, Layla spoke again.

"I know I didn't tell you before, but I'm telling you now. And Aiden? Joseph's involved, my current boyfriend, her ex. It's not good news I'm afraid—for either of us."

Closing the call, Layla started texting next.

"Who's that to?" Penny was confused. "Joseph's phone is here."

"It's not Joseph I'm texting; it's Tara. I'm letting her know." Betrayal had given Layla's voice an edge.

"Letting her know what?"

"That she's been rumbled."

chapter twenty-two

Layla sat at the kitchen table while Penny fussed over her. Her friend was trying to talk to her, force yet another cup of tea upon her, but it was no use. Walls seemed to have sprung up around her, ten foot high at least, and she was trapped inside them, she suspected trapped forever, nothing or nobody able to break them down again. Still Penny continued to chatter, the desperation in her voice evident, trying to get a reaction, to get something when she had nothing left to give—to anyone.

It had been an hour since she had sent that text to Tara, since she had tipped off Aiden. She hated storms, but she knew one was fast approaching.

She jumped as the front door opened. Joseph? She heard laughter. It wasn't Joseph; it was Hannah and Jim. She stiffened anyway. They would no doubt come straight through to the kitchen and sense something was wrong, start asking questions. And once they knew, they would feel sorry for her too, fuss around her as Penny was, make more tea. Her humiliation at Joseph's and Tara's hands complete.

Before they reached the kitchen, she sensed another presence, coming in hot on the heels of Hannah and Jim, an angry presence, pushing past the others in the hallway, heading straight through to the kitchen.

The wanderer had returned.

Taking a deep breath and ignoring the puzzled faces of Hannah and Jim, Layla pushed her chair back and rose to her feet, preparing to meet the storm head-on.

She opened her mouth, but Joseph cut across her.

"What do you think you're doing, sending that message to Tara?"

She took a step back. The swirling anger in his eyes had darkened them, made them fierce. They were practically black, not the blue she loved so much. He looked so different than the Joseph she knew, unrecognizable. Apt, really, as this person standing before her she realized she didn't know at all. Although she thought she had, better than anyone.

At last, she found the courage to speak. "Aiden has a right to know she's here, to know the truth. As do I."

"I'm not disputing that. But to spring his arrival on her so bluntly, that was brutal."

"Joe, mate." Jim came up behind Joseph, trying to calm him. "Is everything okay?"

Joseph swung round to face him. "No, it's not bloody okay, can't you see? It's far from okay."

As Layla had done a moment ago, Jim stepped back too.

Focusing his attention back on Layla, Joseph continued, "You should have talked to me first. We could have discussed what to do about it. Tara's in turmoil—again."

Tara was in turmoil? What about the turmoil she was in? That *they* had put her in?

"Is that all you're worried about?" Her voice rose with each word. "Your precious Tara?" She shook her head in disbelief. "What about me, Joseph? Since she's been back on the scene, you seem to have forgotten all about me!"

"Don't be so bloody stupid." Joseph looked exasperated as well as angry. "I haven't forgotten about you, but the world, it doesn't revolve around you, you know."

"I never said it did," she screamed, incensed at the unfairness of his words. "But Tara—your world seems to revolve around her now, to the exclusion of everything and everyone else. 'Trust me,' you said, 'I'll be able to tell you everything soon.' But guess what? I don't trust you anymore and with good reason."

Out of the corner of her eye, Layla could see Hannah coming toward her, bewilderment at the scene she had come home to written all over her face. She also saw Penny stay her with one hand, then quickly motion for them all to leave. They did, but only as far as the hallway, obviously too worried to leave the two warring factions alone entirely. In the kitchen, she and Joseph continued to stare at each other.

"What do you mean 'good reason'? I've given you no reason not to trust me." His voice was low now, even more menacing somehow than when he'd been shouting.

Breaking eye contact with him, she scrabbled around on the kitchen table instead. Locating his phone, she hurled it at him, not caring if it smashed to the floor and broke. Unfortunately, he caught it.

"You disappeared this morning without a word."

"You were sleeping. I didn't want to wake you."

"You went straight to her."

"I did," he admitted. "I had to."

"And I know *why* you had to. I read the texts you sent her; that she sent you—about how much she loves you."

"You read my texts?" He seemed surprised. "Texts addressed to me, not you?"

Layla refused to be diverted by morals. "She said she *loves* you, Joseph."

Hurling that heinous fact at him didn't have the effect she thought it would. There was no stuttering and spluttering of a strenuous denial. Instead he asked, "At any point during that text conversation did I say I loved her too?"

She didn't need to scour her memory. She wouldn't have forgotten if he had. "No."

"No," he repeated. "But I do love her, Layla."

"Whaa…" Her head snapped back. She felt like she'd been shot.

"I said I love her. I always have done; I always will do. But," he continued before she could react further, "I love her in a platonic sense, the same way she loves me. This may surprise you, but such a thing *is* possible between a man and a woman."

She hated the self-righteous tone that had crept into his voice. She didn't doubt it was possible, but not between two ex-lovers. He was not going to fool her anymore.

"You two, you're not just friends. And there's no way you accidentally bumped into each other, either. Besides finding out about Aiden, I found out something else. She left Australia over a month ago. She's been in Florence for weeks, not the days I presumed. Time enough for you to enjoy many rendezvous with her, for things to happen. She was sick yesterday, as you already seem to know, right in front of me. It couldn't have been lunch; she didn't touch it. But one thing it could be is morning sickness. Is she pregnant, Joseph? And if so, who's the father? Aiden or you?"

"Pregnant?" If she hadn't made him splutter before, she succeeded now. "What the hell are you talking about? I've only been back in contact with her for a matter of days. I'd have to be going some to get her pregnant."

"She left Australia weeks ago. Aiden said so. Don't even try and deny it."

"I'm not denying it. It's true. She did leave weeks ago. But she wasn't in Florence for that length of time. She had only been there a short while. I'm not even sure how long, to be honest. I never asked. Before that she'd been in Rome, and Venice too."

Layla shook her head vehemently. "You're lying—about everything. I bet you've been in contact for weeks, months, years. I bet you've never lost contact."

"What?" He looked truly stunned. "You really think I'm capable of that—of deceiving you for so long? That what we have between us isn't enough?"

"Yes, Joseph, I do." She was the one who sounded self-righteous now.

"You've got this all wrong."

Despite the warning tone in his voice, she was on a roll. She couldn't stop even if she wanted to. Every niggle, every doubt, every glaring concern she'd ever had since Tara had exploded onto the scene demanded voice. "The pregnancy—that's the big secret, isn't it? It makes sense, why you've both been so cagey, trying to decide on a plan of action, how to break the news to everyone—your infidelity made manifest. Poor Aiden." The thought of him wound her up even tighter. "She left him, just upped and walked away, leaving behind only a hand-scrawled note, a note that didn't explain a thing. He'd asked her to marry him, did you know that? And she had said yes. Then guess what? She decides, hey ho, it's not him she wants after all, it's you. And what do you do? Fall straight back into her clutches. Do you know how much it hurts to be left like that? Via a letter or nothing even so grand as a letter, by Post-it note, which is what Alex left me? To be used, then cast aside? How cruel it is? How cruel you both are? Aiden looked a mess; I'm a mess. But no, I don't think either of you do know or care, for that matter. You're welcome to each other. If Tara's the one you want, you know what? You go right ahead and have her."

In the face of her tirade, Joseph didn't even flinch. "Tell me, Layla," he replied coolly, "if Tara was pregnant with my child, why would we come back to Cornwall? Why wouldn't we go somewhere where no one knew us, where it would be just the two...no, sorry, the three of us, without any grief?"

Layla hadn't thought that far. "I don't know. Because it's easier to raise a baby on home ground?"

Even to her ears, that sounded lame.

"Next question," Joseph continued undaunted. "Why would we come back *with* you?"

That she couldn't answer.

"Is your opinion of me so low you think I'd do that? I'd torture you like that?"

Was it? Was it really?

Before she could contemplate further, before he could speak again and confuse her more, she demanded an answer to a question of her own.

"Just tell me, Joseph. What's the bloody secret?"

"She's ill."

"*Ill?*" That wasn't the answer she had expected. It brought her up short, slammed her straight into the brick wall she'd been so busy constructing before he had arrived. Unable to breathe, she waited for him to continue, a nagging voice within telling her that in the last few minutes, she'd made some very big mistakes.

"Yes, Layla, she's ill. She has a brain tumor. I don't know how long she has to live, and, more to the point, neither does she. But it's not long, or so it's been indicated—more tests are needed. That's why she was sick yesterday; because of the headaches she suffers, worse than any migraine could ever be. Each one, she says, feels like it's going to be the end for her. And in some ways, she wishes it would be, because the pain, it's that bad. So, no, Layla, she's not pregnant, by me or anyone else. There's no life involved. I wish there was, but there's only death."

Her legs buckled beneath her at the revelation. Quickly, she reached for the back of the chair to steady herself.

"Christ," she whispered. "I had no idea."

"No, I know you didn't. But I said this *secret* of hers, as you continued to call it, was serious. I also said I'd tell you as soon as I could. And I was going to do that tonight. Tara felt guilty, that you'd waited long enough. I thought so too. But, no, you'd jumped to your own conclusions already, that imagination of yours running riot."

Layla caught movement and turned her head. She could see Hannah, Jim, and Penny hovering, not in the hallway but just outside the kitchen door, drawn closer by Joseph's revelation. If they had looked shocked before, they looked even more so now, their horrified faces reflecting exactly what she felt inside. She groaned, a low, almost guttural sound. Why hadn't she held off? Waited just a little bit longer? As he'd said she'd been earlier, she felt brutal, hurling vile accusations at the man she was supposed to love, to *trust*. That imagination of hers, she damned it.

"When I met Tara in Florence," Joseph continued, "I told you she was in bits. I told you it took me a while to coax out of her what was wrong, that she didn't want to tell me. I told you I wanted to make sure she got home where she needed to be. I told you everything I could, but above all, I told you her secret had nothing to do with me, nothing at all."

"I know." Layla's voice was barely above a whisper. "It's just…It's been days…"

"It's been days because she couldn't bring herself to tell her parents straightaway. I thought she would, but she couldn't. But then, I suppose it's not easy to do, tell your mum and dad you're going to die. It's—" he seemed to struggle for the word, settling after a moment for "—unnatural. She wanted to enjoy a few days with them first, the way it used to be between them, before she went ahead and shattered their world." Shaking his head, almost in quiet contemplation, he added, "And I don't blame her."

"I don't either," Layla acquiesced. "I can understand that."

"You understand something at least." His scathing tone cut her to the quick. "When Penny let slip Tara had been sick yesterday, I was worried. There's every chance she might go downhill quickly. It's imperative she tell her parents sooner rather than later—not put it off anymore. I went over today to discuss that with her, but I didn't want to just come out with it. I wanted to build up to it, and I think she did too. We visited places she loved, places we used to visit together. We talked, not about her illness initially but about the way things used to be when life was so much simpler. At the beach, our last port of call, she brought the subject up before I could. She was ready at last. I'm sorry I didn't let you know earlier where I was. I'll admit that was a mistake on my part. And I hadn't forgotten we were supposed to spend the day together. But time just seemed to disappear, and to be honest, I probably wasn't thinking straight either. Tara and me, we're not in love with each other. It's not like that at all, but, yeah, we love each other. We've got history—more history than you and I, ironically. The fact that she's dying, I'm upset about it too."

Layla choked back a sob. He didn't just look upset; he looked devastated, grief, not deceit, clouding his eyes. Why hadn't she noticed that before? Standing up, she reached out to him, wanting to comfort him, but he backed away.

"How did you know about Aiden?" he asked.

"I...I met him in a coffee shop, Gail's coffee shop. He'd been to Tara's parents' this morning, but there was no one home. He didn't know if she was here or not, in England, I mean, but he thought they might know where she was. He thought by showing them how dedicated he was to finding her, traveling thousands of miles across continents and oceans in pursuit of her, they might take pity on him. Give him a contact number, at least. To be honest, I don't think he was thinking straight either."

"Why didn't you just wait, Layla, for me to come back?" His disappointment broke her further.

"I was going to," she hurried on, praying he'd believe her. "But then I...I found your phone, and I just reacted, I guess."

"Yeah, in the wrong way." She noticed a vein in his neck pulsating, evidence his anger had in no way abated. "Aiden's over there now. Her parents don't know what's going on, he doesn't know what's going on, that whole breaking the news to them gently, minimizing the stress involved, it's gone up in smoke, thanks to you."

Penny stepped forward then. "The pregnancy thing, that wasn't Layla, that was me," she admitted, her chin trembling. "I planted that stupid idea in her head. It's my fault entirely. I'm sorry."

Joseph looked from Penny to Layla. "You're both as bad as each other, then."

Layla grabbed at him, determined to make him hear her, to understand how sorry she was. But he threw her off, as though her touch seared him.

"Joseph..." she pleaded.

"Tell me," he said, staring at her, right through her, it felt. "As far as Tara was concerned, did you ever trust me?"

Layla bit down on her lip.

"Layla!" he shouted, making her jump.

She shook her head.

"So, you're the liar."

The truth of which pierced her.

He looked at her for a few seconds more, during which she could feel his contempt building.

"I can't stay here anymore," he said eventually.

"Where are you going?" Would he tell her? Did she even have a right to ask?

"I don't know. Somewhere. Mick's probably. I need space, some time to think."

"Joseph," she said again, no pleading in her voice this time, just absolute terror—not of him, but at the realization she was losing him.

He continued backing away from her. "Sorry, Layla. I don't trust you either, not now."

"That's not fair." It was Penny again, defending her when she didn't deserve defending. But still Penny persisted. "Joseph, Layla didn't *know* Tara was ill. You can't blame her for being suspicious. Anyone would have been."

Hannah stepped forward too. "Penny's right. You know what, Joseph? If you mess with minds, minds get messy."

"It wasn't my intention to mess with anyone," Joseph exploded again, "but Tara's secret, it wasn't mine to tell. She wanted her parents to be the ones to know next, not some—" he looked at Layla, sparks firing from his eyes, as terrifying to Layla as lightning "—some stranger. And I told you that too, that I had no choice. I *had* to keep quiet, at least for a short while. But still you wouldn't believe me—*trust* me. And if two people aren't prepared to trust each other, what's the point in carrying on?"

This time, Layla's legs did give way. She sank down onto the kitchen chair and let her head fall forward into her hands. He was right. She had taken what they had—something good, something honest and true—and she had turned it to dust.

Penny rushed to her side. So did Hannah. Joseph turned on his heel and walked away.

"Mate," Jim said, and Layla knew he'd try to make his friend stay.

"Leave it, Jim. Just leave it," Joseph replied before he disappeared down the hallway, leaving her to drown in shame and despair.

chapter twenty-three

"Aiden," Tara called out. "Please, don't go in there."

At the gate to her parents' cottage, Aiden swung round, an array of emotions fighting for dominion on his face. There was surprise, definitely, a touch of delight, but mainly pain and confusion. Tara was sure such emotions were playing out on her face too, in among them disbelief. Aiden was here, in Cornwall. He'd found her, and although he was standing just a few feet from her, she found it hard to trust her eyes.

"Tara." Aiden stepped forward but stopped, as though sensing how overwrought she was. Staring after the retreating car, he asked, "Is that Joseph?"

"Yes," she replied simply.

"Your ex Joseph?" he continued.

"My *friend* Joseph," she corrected.

The suspicion that darkened Aiden's face refused to retreat. What had Layla said to him, she wondered? How come he knew her, anyway? He knew nobody in England. She didn't think he was the type to cause a scene, but she didn't want to chance it, not here on her parents' doorstep. They'd been out for coffee this morning, but they'd definitely be home now, preparations underway for a late lunch.

"Do you have a car?"

Stupid question. How else would he have got here?

Aiden merely nodded in reply—too stricken to speak, she wondered? He motioned to a dark-green Ford parked a short distance away.

"Let's go, then," she said, turning from him and walking away. "Down the road, to World's End. It's not far." *World's End*—it had sounded so romantic once, but now it seemed…well, apt. What she was about to tell him would end both their worlds.

Sitting beside him in the car, she noticed how his hands, sturdy and strong, gripped the steering wheel, his knuckles practically white against the tan of his skin. She could also sense he was trembling, and her heart broke for the umpteenth time.

She couldn't control her dreams, but when awake, she had allowed herself only once or twice to imagine seeing him again—how they would hurl themselves into each other's arms, declare their love, and promise each other that nothing, absolutely nothing, could come between them again, that what they had could repel every damn hurdle life insisted on throwing at them. But reality was very different. And what they had, although powerful, was nowhere near powerful enough.

Tears blinded her vision as she motioned for him to stop in the same spot she had stopped with Joseph not even a couple of hours before.

"This is it," she said, amazed to find anger building up in her too. Why? She had nothing to be angry with Aiden for. Only herself—and this stupid illness that had struck from nowhere to seize her in its vice-like grip.

"Is it okay to leave the car here?" he asked.

"It's fine. Everyone does it."

"Are you sure? The road's quite narrow."

"Just leave it," she said, practically hissing at him.

Practicalities? Why the hell were they talking about practicalities? Who cared about the bloody car, where it was parked, or who it was blocking? No one came down here anyway. They wouldn't be inconveniencing anyone.

She followed the same path she had walked earlier, toward the ocean, the sun low in the sky now, the warmth of the day fading. Although they were side by side, there was a chasm between them, a void that could never be traversed. She wondered if he would reach out and take her hand, her arm, her shoulder. He didn't.

Still a distance from the waves lapping at the shore, she picked up pace, forcing him to hurry if he wanted to match her. Kicking off her shoes, she began to run as she had run with Joseph. But this was different. She wasn't running with someone; she was running away, again, not strong enough in the end to stand her ground.

Tears streamed down her face, and she made no effort to blink them back. She didn't think she'd be successful anyway; they were as relentless as the tumor growing in her head. Whereas before the coldness of the water had made her shriek, now she welcomed it. It numbed her, and that's what she wanted.

Plunging farther forward, she was suddenly pulled back.

"Tara," she heard someone shout. Aiden? Yes, of course, it was Aiden. There was no one else on the beach with them. "What are you doing?"

She struggled against him, tried to break free, but he held fast. She could hear loud screams and moans, terrible sounds, as though someone was being tortured. Wildly her head whipped from side to side. Who was making such a racket? Maybe they weren't alone after all.

"Tara," the man in front of her shouted again. "Tara, stop."

Stop what? What was he talking about?

"Tara, please."

That noise, was it coming from him?

Tara managed to focus on him, stared deep into his eyes. He was crying too, she could see that, but silently so. Realization hit her—the sounds she'd heard, they'd been coming from her. She'd been the one howling like a bear caught in a trap.

"Aiden." His name seemed to erupt from her as she collapsed against him.

Immediately, his arms came round her and held her tight. She clung to him too, as though he were a piece of salvage and she the drowning victim. She knew she had missed him, but she hadn't realized just how much until now. How agonizing it had been not to breathe the same air as him, to be so far apart.

Eventually, he released her, held her only slightly from him. "Tara, I've found you," he said, a kind of wonder in his eyes. Wonder that was again replaced with grief as he continued to speak. "Why did you leave me?"

She had wanted to save him from such grief, but she had failed. He seemed so much older than his thirty-one years when once he had seemed so young, so vital.

"I'm so sorry," she started.

"It is because of Joseph? Is that why? You love him, not me?"

"It's not because of Joseph." Again she shook her head. "It has nothing to do with Joseph. *You're* the one that I love. Being away from you, it's been torture."

"If you love me, why did you leave me?"

"Because...because I had to."

"Why did you have to?" He looked so confused. "Tara, I don't understand."

She reached a hand up to his face, her fingertips running over the bristles on his chin. Usually he was clean-shaven; rarely had she seen him this way. For a few precious moments, she allowed herself to bask in the shape of his mouth, his jaw line, his cheekbones, losing herself in a face that to her was the epitome of perfect.

"Come with me," she said, turning away. She had wanted to tell her parents next, but the best-laid plans didn't always work out—something she was acutely aware of. Somehow, though, she didn't think her parents would mind.

Leading him to a sheltered spot, she sat him down, clung onto both his hands, and told him everything.

Silence reigned, her last few words hanging like physical objects in the space between them. Aiden wasn't looking at her; he was looking beyond her, at the ocean, she presumed. Soon it would be glimmering in the moonlight instead of the sun. No matter. It would look just as beautiful. In contrast, Tara stared at him.

As if he had stopped breathing but was now gulping for air, words burst from him. "Why you? Why us? Why is life so fucking unfair?"

It was nothing she hadn't asked herself a million times already. So happy she had been, so blessed. She had lived a charmed existence: a wonderful mum and dad, wonderful friends, wonderful lovers, and wonderful places to live. Sometimes she had felt guilty about that. At least that was one thing; she didn't have to feel guilty anymore.

"Aiden," she said gently. "There is no 'us' anymore. No, don't look like that. Hear me out. It's not because I don't want there to be; it's because there can't be."

"What do you mean, there can't be? That's rubbish."

"Aiden—"

"No." He thrust her hands away from him. "Do you think I won't want you because of this? Do you think it's going to make me love you any less? It won't, Tara. In fact, do you know something? I've never loved you more than I do at this moment."

"Aiden." Tara stood firm. "I don't want you with me when I get worse, and I will get worse. Don't think I won't. I want you to remember me the way I was."

He stood, walked a couple of paces from her, and then swung back around. "And how come I didn't know you were ill? Before you left Australia? I would have known, surely? You seemed fine."

"I was getting headaches, more and more. It was odd because I've never been the type to suffer from headaches before, but suddenly my head hurt all the time. My vision suffered too, not greatly, but a bit. Things were blurry at times. I started feeling nauseous, even did a pregnancy test just to make sure that wasn't the reason. Ruling that out, I thought I'd caught a virus of some sort. I went to the doctor; he booked me in for a scan. I thought he was overreacting. He wasn't."

"Those headaches, I knew you were getting them, but I didn't think they were serious."

"Nor did I, but, Aiden, they are. They're as serious as it gets."

"How long?" he asked, his voice barely above a whisper.

"I don't know. They're getting worse, though, much worse."

He breathed deeply, as though trying to suck in her words, to bury them. "Have you seen a doctor? In England, I mean?"

"I'm due to, very soon."

"I'll come with you." He looked so determined, Tara thought, but desperate too. "And if he says there's nothing to be done, well, we'll go to another doctor and then another, until we find one who says, you know what, there's a ton of stuff we can do. I'll sell my café, Tara, my flat. We'll find the very best doctor there is."

She was torn between believing him and disbelieving. "Money can't solve this."

"No, but we can, Tara, if we believe. You read about it all the time. People beat disease and illness every day. And we're going to beat it too, Tara, I'm telling you. You're not dying. Not on my watch. I won't let you."

"Don't, please," she pleaded, seeing that he, like her, was torn too. That he believed and yet a part of him didn't.

Lunging forward, Aiden grabbed her roughly by the shoulders. "You are not leaving me, Tara," he repeated. "I've flown halfway round the world to find you. And I did, I found you. I'm not letting you go again. You're mine, do you hear? Mine!" Tears sprang from his eyes, chasing each other in mad rivulets down his cheeks. Stepping away, he wiped at his nose roughly with the back of his hand. "We belong together—you know that as well as me. Death will just have to wait."

Abruptly he stepped away.

"Aiden…" She flung herself forward, trying to reach him, the chasm she never thought they'd bridge starting to widen again. But it was no use; for the moment he was beyond reach.

Turning from her, he punched the air, not once, but over and over again, beating at the world with his bare fists.

"Shit, shit, shit," he screamed.

"Aiden," she tried again, daring to get close to him, despite the danger that one of his blows might graze her, knock her out cold. "Aiden, stop. Please."

He wouldn't listen; he carried on fighting, and then suddenly, as though he were a balloon someone had stuck a needle in, all fight left him. He fell to his knees, bending forward, his head in cupped hands, his body heaving with silent sobs.

Tara knelt beside him, covering his body with hers as best she could. "I'm so sorry," she whispered. "I'm so, so sorry."

He turned himself over to sit on the sand opposite her. She had seen pictures of him as a little boy, a cheeky little boy with a shock of black hair. He looked like that now, despite the fact his hair was short. He looked like he needed taking care of.

She sat down too, and moments passed between them. As they stared, that little boy began to fade, matured, not needing the span of years to do so. In his place was the strong young man she knew him to be, the man who would take care of her.

He shunted toward her, closing the gap once more. "Tara," he said, not in despair this time; his voice sounded remarkably steady. "Whatever happens, we'll face it together."

She knew there was no point in arguing with him anymore. The man in him had made up his mind; the man in him was immovable.

"Okay," she conceded, "but if at any point you want to bail out—"

"Stop right there." He pulled her closer to him, their legs wrapped tight round each other now. "It's you and me, babe, all the way, for better or for worse."

Tara laughed. There was both happiness and sadness in it.

"You don't have to say that. We're not married, you know."

"No, but we're going to be. You made me a promise back in Oz—I've got witnesses to prove it. You said you'd be my wife, and I'm going to hold you to it."

Tara shook her head vehemently. "I don't need you to marry me to prove you love me."

Reaching up to cup her chin, he stilled her. "You don't get it, do you? It's me who *needs* to marry you. Like I said, Tara, you're mine, forever, come what may."

Staring into his eyes, she thought the dark-brown of them seemed depthless, but it was his soul she was looking into, and that was what was depthless.

"Come what may," she whispered back, leaning closer, marveling at that ancient truth—that at the point of greatest darkness, the brightest light so often shines.

chapter twenty-four

As Hannah sat comforting Layla in the kitchen, Penny returned to the hallway with Jim.

"Brain tumor," he was saying, shaking his head at the revelation, trying, as they all were, to take in the sheer magnitude of it. "Tara?"

"I know, I can't believe it either," Penny replied just as solemnly. "She looks well, for God's sake. I don't know, it's...it's just too awful to even contemplate."

With a start, Penny realized she had never known anyone affected by a terminal illness before, and although she couldn't claim to know Tara, she certainly felt affected by it. Floored, to be precise. Her craving for Richard and Scarlett also intensified. She wanted them close to her; she wanted them here, in Trecastle, right now, this very minute, so she could keep them safe from what suddenly felt like a cruel world. The distance between her and her husband and daughter, it was too much.

"What are we going to do about Joe?" Jim broke into her thoughts.

"I don't know. I think I should go after him. Try and calm him down," Penny said. Looking into his eyes, she whispered, "It can't be over between them, surely?"

Jim didn't look convinced. "I've never seen him like that," he said. "In all the years I've known him."

Penny had never seen anyone like it, let alone Joseph. Angry didn't come close. The damage that had been done, she hoped it could be undone—some of it at least. There deserved to be some winners in this abysmal situation.

She was about to get her coat, but Jim stopped her. "No, it's okay, Penny. I'll go and see where he is. I don't know the ins and outs of what's gone on between you all, but I don't think he'd welcome you right now."

Penny felt tears prick at her eyes.

"Hey." Immediately Jim came forward and wrapped his arms around her. Bear hugs were a specialty of his. "It'll be all right."

"But what if it's not? What if he won't forgive Layla? All of this, it's my fault."

Releasing her, Jim took a step back. "It is not your fault. This thing, this illness, what's happened to Tara, it's no one's fault, it just… it just *is*. Joseph will be okay, you'll see."

Reaching out a hand to touch her cheek, he smiled down at her before heading to the front door. Alone in the hallway, Penny hugged herself, still in need of comfort. In the kitchen, Layla's sobbing had quieted. All Penny could hear was the low, calm voice of Hannah, murmuring, soothing. She went to go and join them but stopped. It felt too intrusive, somehow. As though her presence would only rile matters again.

Instead, she went into the living room and sank down on the sofa. In the space of a few short hours, the world had changed—again. Change wasn't something Penny particularly liked. Rather, she was a creature of habit; everyday routine comforted her. As wild as she tried to act on occasion, deep down she wasn't wild at all, something she blamed her astral sign for. She was a Virgo, a fixed sign. And Richard, he was Taurus—another earth sign, solid and dependable. And that was an apt description of him, she thought with surprising affection. As for Scarlett, she was Scorpio, a water sign—passionate with hidden depths. Penny had had the baby's star chart drawn up at birth. There was plenty of fire about her too—again very apt. Fiery was certainly one way to describe her. And scary. She could admit that now. Motherhood was the biggest change in her life, and it had scared her beyond witless. But she was also very lucky to have a baby, a family of her own. Tara never would have, by the sounds of it. A privilege denied.

Poor Tara, poor Joseph, poor Layla, and if she were going to be kind to herself for once instead of beating herself up for her myriad failings, poor her. If only she'd admitted she needed help, had talked to Richard, instead of being jealous of the easy relationship he had formed so rapidly, so *easily*, with his daughter—a relationship she was having such trouble getting the hang of. Rather than just accept that motherhood took some getting used to, she had gone on the defense instead, pushed Richard and the baby as far away as possible, despite occupying the same living space as them.

Rubbing at her temples with her hands, she had to admit it wasn't an easy thing to come clean about. She had gotten the impression from other women in prenatal and baby yoga classes that admittance of abject defeat would only be treated with the utmost disdain. Each and every one of the pregnant ladies she had met while she had been pregnant seemed almost serene with happiness, not exhausted beyond belief. And when their little bundles had been brought into the world, by water birth usually, that serenity for mother and baby seemed only to increase.

She recalled once meeting a group of new mothers at Treacle, a café in Hove. She, Beth, Lizzie, Jane, and Deryn had all had babies within days of each other. Once everybody could walk again—and she had barely been able to, thanks to an hour's worth of stitching post-baby—they had swooped with their prams on Treacle.

Only Penny seemed embarrassed that their parked prams effectively prevented anyone else from enjoying cake and coffee in the café too. There were a couple more empty tables, but you'd need to clamber over shiny new Bugaboos and Maclarens to get to them. The other mums either didn't seem to care or were oblivious. They were oblivious to everything except their babies, also shiny and new. And the babies themselves—Penny gritted her teeth at this particular memory—behaved beautifully. All except Scarlett, who had struggled and grumbled and groaned constantly. Penny had missed out on most of the conversation between the women, even though she'd been desperate to hear it, little anecdotes of how they coped. She'd been too busy pacing with Scarlett in what little space was available, jiggling her up and down in an attempt to soothe her but only succeeding in enraging her further. The end result? Prolonged bouts of deafening screams. When she could, though, she had listened in, wanting to be a part of the group, to be a part of something when she had felt so adrift.

"Darcy slept through the night, again. Can you believe it?" Deryn had cooed.

No wonder Deryn looked so bloody good; most people did if they'd slept.

"And breast-feeding, it feels so natural, doesn't it?" Beth had piped up.

Felt natural? It did not! She had tried it; it was nothing less than excruciating.

"It completes your life," Lizzie had sighed. "Having a baby."

Wrecked it, more like.

No, she was definitely the odd one out among them. When the next invite to coffee had come, she had politely declined. Far from making her feel part of something—the biggest club in the world—their raptures had made her feel even more isolated. Even so, she couldn't help but notice they hadn't persisted in inviting her. Clearly, whatever she had felt about them, they had felt about her too.

But surely, and this was something she'd thought a million times, not every mother in the world took to motherhood straightaway? Surely someone other than herself found the adjustment equally as hard. Often she fantasized about finding someone she could be honest with. Say things to like, "Changing nappies, it makes you heave, doesn't it?" or "I miss wild nights out. You know, dancing, drinking, staying up until the early hours." They could have laughed about it, consoled each other that such high dependency didn't last forever, that eventually you got your life back—or a semblance of it, at least. She yearned for someone who wasn't going to look at her as if she were Satan in a skirt for hinting that sometimes, just sometimes, it got boring looking after a baby day in, day out, that the mind disintegrated when your main vocabulary consisted of *mama, dada,* and *baba*. Richard could have been that someone. But, no, Richard had been as bad as the mothers. Sometimes more so.

Despite wishing they were here, Penny couldn't help thinking Richard and Scarlett were better off without her. They didn't need her in their lives. They had each other. That was enough. That was why she had left them in the first place—not because she wanted to, not really, not deep down. What she had *wanted* was to make it work between the three of them. What she didn't know was how to.

She tried not to cry. There'd been tears enough tonight.

"Bugger," she swore as tears fell regardless.

Blowing her nose hard, she heard a ringing sound. The doorbell! Joseph returning, realizing he'd been too harsh on Layla and desperate to make amends? Layla would be swift to apologize too. That mess cleared up at least.

She heard someone rush down the hallway. Layla, no doubt, thinking the same thing. She wouldn't investigate; she'd hang back, stay out of harm's way.

"Penny." It was Hannah's voice, not Layla's, calling. "It's for you."

For me? But who? The only people she knew in Trecastle had a key to this flat; there was no need to ring the doorbell.

Wiping at her nose again, she scrunched up the tissue and threw it into her bag; she'd dispose of it in the bathroom later. She then smoothed down her hair and her T-shirt before heading out of the living room, hoping she didn't look too frightful.

In the hallway, she almost fainted. There, as large as life, with a sheepish smile on his face and a struggling baby in his arms, stood Richard.

"Can I come in?" he asked, looking first at Hannah and then more beseechingly at Penny. "This baby lark, you're right, it's no picnic, is it?"

chapter twenty-five

When the doorbell had rung last night, Layla thought her heart might burst. *Please*, she remembered thinking, *let it be Joseph*. She was as shocked as Penny to see Richard and Scarlett there instead. Shocked and, she couldn't help it, disappointed too. Joseph wasn't coming back anytime soon; she knew that.

Hannah had settled the young family in the front room. The sofa bed was big enough for both Penny and Richard, and the baby could sleep in between them.

"Sleep? We should be so lucky," Richard had muttered. He looked exhausted, truly done in. To be fair, everyone around her did.

Layla had hung around only for as long as was polite. As soon as she could, she had made her excuses and escaped to her room, assuring both Hannah and Penny she'd be fine.

"Where's Joe?" Richard had asked, mystified.

Layla had left that to Penny to explain.

The night had seemed endless — and so lonely. Again and again she played Joseph's words over in her head, words like *tumor, brutal*, and *death* not causing her more pain as she thought they would but numbing her until she was hardly able to feel a thing. Like she had done when her father died, Layla packaged up emotions too hard to deal with and put them in a box, slamming the lid shut. It was a temporary measure, she knew. She'd have to revisit that box soon — in the morning, perhaps — but for the immediate hours ahead, she made the most of not feeling at all.

She must have dozed, because rays of sunlight woke her. But if she had, it was for moments only. With daylight, however, came resolve. She knew what she had to do. Rising, she made her way to the kitchen. In the drawer of the Welsh dresser, Hannah kept a notepad and pen. Retrieving them, she began to write.

Dear Tara

I know you probably don't want to hear from me. And if you tear this letter up without reading further, I don't blame you. But I want you to know, I'm sorry. I'm sorry for sending Aiden over without discussing it with you and Joseph first. I'm sorry for the way I felt toward you. I'm sorry I doubted you at all.

The strange thing is I actually liked you. I just wouldn't let myself believe it. When we had lunch together at The Admiral Inn, I thought you were just the kind of girl I'd like to hang out with. I wish I'd held on to that thought.

Joseph has told me about your condition, and I'm sorry about that too. My heart breaks for you—dramatic but true. I pray there's some way you can beat it.

I don't suppose we shall ever meet again, but the impact you've had on me is huge, and I don't mean in a negative sense. You've made me grow up. Quite frankly, it's about time.

Layla

She folded the letter neatly in half, found an envelope, sealed it tightly, and marked Tara's name on it. Returning to her bedroom, she left it on the side while she took a shower. As water splashed over her, she tried hard not to think about Joseph, about where he was and about how he was feeling too, upset about Tara and disappointed in his girlfriend. If she allowed herself to dwell on his feelings too much, what little resolve she had might break. As she dried her hair in front of the mirror, she found it hard to look at her reflection. When she did, she didn't like what she saw.

After pulling on some clothes, she returned to the kitchen and forced herself to have a glass of orange juice and a piece of buttered toast.

Penny came hurrying into the kitchen, looking tired but happy. As though she were ashamed of feeling that way, she adopted a more solemn face.

"Oh, Layla," she said, walking straight up to her and giving her a hug. "Did you manage any sleep at all?"

"A bit. What about you?"

"Strangely enough, we were fine. The baby settled peacefully—an all-time first."

"Maybe things are changing?" Layla suggested. "Getting easier."

"Maybe," Penny conceded.

"Penny, I'm sorry…"

"Hey, you've got nothing to be sorry about," Penny started to protest.

"I have," Layla rushed on. "So many things. I knew you were finding the baby hard to deal with. I saw how overwhelmed you were by her arrival when I came to stay. But I was so wrapped up in my life—my happy, perfect life—I put your feelings on the back burner. And then when you turn up in Trecastle without Scarlett, it's still my feelings I'm concerned with rather than yours. I never thought of myself as selfish, or jealous or vindictive, but I've proved to be all three. I'm sorry you felt so alone. I suspected you did, and I wasn't there for you. I'm sorry I'm such a bad friend."

Without a word, Penny drew her close again. Layla was not only relieved but grateful for the comfort she offered so unstintingly.

"You're my *best* friend," Penny said upon releasing her. "Never doubt that. And I don't blame you for anything. It wasn't your place to notice; it was Richard's. I was glad you were happy."

Her eyes resting on Layla's plate of half-eaten toast, she continued, "I'm going to cook you something. You'll feel so much better after you've eaten breakfast."

Layla stopped her. Half a piece of toast was all she could manage.

"Well, okay, if you're sure." With brightness in her voice that Layla knew was forced, Penny continued, "What shall we do today? Shall we go somewhere nice?"

"We?"

"Yes, you and me, I mean. Richard's okay. He's going to take the baby out sightseeing. We can go for a walk somewhere if you want. Get some lunch, talk."

A seven-month-old sightseeing? Layla had to smile at that.

"I take it from the look on your face that's a yes."

"Actually, Penny, it isn't. It's a no."

"Oh." Penny looked downcast. Grabbing the chair next to Layla, she lowered herself onto it. "What are you planning to do, then?"

"I'm going to see—"

"Joseph?" Penny interrupted.

"Tara," Layla corrected.

"Tara?" Penny looked horrified. "Do you think that's a good idea?"

"I'm not actually going to see her," Layla amended. "I've written her a letter, and I want to deliver it." Contemplating this for a few seconds, she added, "I would actually like to see her, you know, apologize to her too, but I doubt she'd want to see me."

"But what about Joseph?" Penny dared to ask.

"What about him?"

"Oh, come on, you know what I mean."

"I do, but right now, I can't think beyond Tara."

"I'll come with you," Penny declared, rising determinedly from the chair. "Give me ten minutes. I'll get showered and dressed too."

"Penny, stop."

Amazingly, Penny did as she was told.

"I appreciate your support, really I do, but this is something I need to do by myself. The Defender's still out back; I checked earlier. I'll take that."

"Oh, Layla." Penny reached across and covered Layla's hand with her own. "I'm the one who should be apologizing. I feel I'm as much to blame as you, more so even. Me and my stupid theories. I wish I'd kept my mouth shut."

"This is *not* your fault. It's me who made a mess of things, and me alone."

"Well, we're not going," stated Penny. "Me and Richard, I mean. We've agreed. We'll stick around for as long as you need us."

"Thanks, Penny, but don't worry. I still intend to leave on Monday."

"Go back to Florence?"

"Perhaps. I'm not sure yet. It depends on Joseph. But, if it is all over between us—" Her voice cracked on the word "over," and she had to stop to collect herself. "If it is all over," she continued, "yes, I'll fly back to Florence, pack what I need, and go and stay with Mum and Georgio in Milan for a while. I'll decide from there what happens next."

"It's *not* over. Joseph loves you. Good grief, it's embarrassing the way he looks at you sometimes. I'm like 'Get a room, will you?' He'll come round."

"I don't know, Penny." She was surprised to find some part of her actually felt resigned to this fact. "Sometimes there's no going back."

"I don't believe that. Joseph's feelings for you, they're a bit bruised at the moment, but underneath, they're as strong as ever. I know it."

"I hope you're right." Layla sighed deeply. "But right now, like I said, Tara is my priority. It's her forgiveness I want."

Leaving a bewildered Penny to stare after her, Layla collected the letter she had written earlier from her bedroom and the car keys and made her way to Port Levine.

Parking the car, Layla turned off the ignition, opened the car door, and ventured toward the purple front door. Her letter to Tara clutched in her right hand, she opened the letterbox with her left and pushed it through. Staring at the door for a few seconds, she then retraced her steps. Back in the driver's seat, she turned the engine over—at least, she tried to turn it over. Despite behaving perfectly en route, it was playing up now. Unable to believe it, she tried again. Nothing.

"What the hell…" she muttered under her breath. "This can't be happening."

But then she'd say that about a lot in her life right now. The sad fact was, it *was* happening. She was stranded—right outside Tara's house.

Letting her head fall against the steering wheel, she stayed that way for a short while before deciding to try again.

"I believe with an automatic, you need to put it into park first before you can turn the engine over."

Layla turned quickly to her left. Leaning against the half-open window of the passenger door was Tara, a soft smile on her face.

"I…" Layla looked down. The car was still in drive. No wonder it wouldn't start. There was nothing wrong with it after all. Only with her.

"Thanks," she whispered, feeling her cheeks burn.

"I got your letter," Tara continued, holding it aloft in her hand.

"That was quick." Layla tried to smile.

"I happened to be in the hallway when you posted it through."

"Have you read it?" she asked tentatively.

Tara nodded. "I've read it."

Struggling to breathe evenly, Layla lifted her eyes to meet Tara's. "I mean it, every word. I'm sorry."

"You look like hell," Tara replied.

Taken aback, Layla checked her face in the rearview mirror. Tara was right; she did.

She started to explain, but maybe because of sleep deprivation, her brain wouldn't play ball. No words came out, none that made sense anyway.

While she struggled, Tara swapped curbside for roadside.

"Scoot over," she said. "I'll drive."

Meekly, Layla did as she was told.

With Tara ensconced in the driver's seat, Layla managed to ask her if she'd be okay driving the Defender.

"Are you kidding?" Tara said cheerfully enough. "You should see what I drove in the Outback. This tank is a mini-tank, believe me."

As Tara started to pull away, Layla asked, "Where are we going?"

"Anywhere you like." Tara adjusted the seat and the mirror. "Where do you fancy?"

"I don't know. I…erm." Still she couldn't think.

"Okay." Tara made it easy for her. "North or south?"

North would take them back to Trecastle.

"South," Layla answered.

"South it is. I'll just keep driving until you want me to stop."

It took twenty minutes of rumbling down country roads before Layla felt composed enough to speak. "Anywhere here," she said. "Wherever's convenient."

"We're near Rock. There's a beautiful beach at Rock. It goes on for miles, right past St. Enodoc Church. That'll be a nice walk."

After Tara parked the car, Layla followed her toward the beach. A ferry had docked at one end of the bay, a handful of people climbing on board to travel the short distance to Padstow, famous for its seafood restaurant. She had been to Padstow once with Joseph, not to the restaurant, just to get an ice cream and walk around it. There were quite a few shops too, mostly selling holiday stuff. That was in the days when they had been friends, not even lovers, when she had first moved from Brighton. Happy, carefree days. Golden days, they seemed now.

"This way," said Tara, turning right, toward a golden stretch of sand. There were sand dunes and families with pre-school children making the most of the day.

"It's lovely here, isn't it?" Tara was watching the children too, a wistful look on her face. "My parents used to bring me and my sister, Leo, down here when we were kids. See that sand dune over there? Just to the left of those rocks. That was our favorite spot. My dad used to settle himself down on his fold-up chair; my mum would spread out the picnic blanket. Me and Leo, we'd start building sandcastles. After a while, I'd get bored and go swimming, but Leo hated getting wet. She'd just carry on, building sculptures all day, and quite happy she was, too."

It sounded idyllic. For a moment, Layla envied Tara, and then she clamped down hard on that thought. She had no right to envy anyone.

"Tara," she said, not knowing what to say but wanting to say something. "I..." But it was no use. Her brain still wasn't making sense; nothing made sense anymore.

As despair washed over her, Tara steered her toward the sand dune.

"Come on over here. Tell me all about it."

As Layla collapsed on the sand, words began pouring forth. At first they were garbled, but gradually they started stringing themselves together in the correct order to form semi-coherent sentences. She was able, at times haltingly, at other times in a rush, to tell Tara what had happened the previous day—meeting Aiden, the suspicions that prompted the text message, and Joseph's reaction.

Tara listened without interrupting. Sweetly, she held Layla's hand, something Layla was grateful for. If she truly hated her, she wouldn't be able to do that, surely?

When she finished, Tara did let go. Layla stiffened. She hated her after all, and who could blame her? But, instead of rising and walking angrily away, she inched up closer and placed an arm round Layla's shoulders.

"That Joseph," she said. "He's a hot-head at times. I remember that well."

"Really?" Layla's voice sounded so small, even to her.

"Yeah." Tara smiled. "He has what I call an overdeveloped sense of justice. When he feels something or someone hasn't followed absolutely the right path, he can get a bit hot under the collar. I used to tease him about it something rotten."

"But he's right. What I did was awful—you know, under the circumstances." She felt awkward even alluding to Tara's illness. "I acted out of spite, and that was wrong."

"But you didn't know the circumstances when you acted," Tara insisted, moving away slightly. "And besides, it could be argued, strongly, that what *I* did was wrong. My secret affected you as well as Joseph. I should have told you too. It's just…"

For the first time, Tara sounded uncertain. "My head was all over the place, to be honest. I know I told Joseph, but when he found me, I was desperate. I'd been wandering Italy aimlessly for weeks, in shock—I know that now—trying to come to terms with my diagnosis. When I met him, I was at breaking point, and he, well, he built me back up. But my parents, I wanted them to know next. I became fixated with it. They'd know what to do and say. They'd help. And I was right in that sense; they've been great. But I was wrong about you. You're Joseph's girlfriend. I should have told you. I know you would have kept my secret. I was the one unable to trust."

"Telling your parents next—I ruined that plan, didn't I, by sending Aiden over?"

"You didn't ruin anything." Tara looked as though she genuinely meant it. "Aiden was the next to know, and I wouldn't change that for the world. He's been incredible, Layla." Happiness lit up her face, erasing the signs of tiredness that had been there earlier. "He came with me back to my parents, and we told them together. His positivity—something I've always loved about him—well, I think my parents appreciated it too." She paused for a moment before adding, "In all honesty, I don't think I would have told them without him, despite what I had promised Joseph. I would have just kept putting it off until, well, until I couldn't put it off any longer, until it became too obvious."

"Tara, I'm sorry." Could she ever say it enough? "I'm so, so sorry."

Tara shook her head. "Please don't be. I consider myself lucky, you know, luckier than most. And who knows? I might even get lucky again. The treatment I need to have, there's a slim chance it might buy me more time, at least. Aiden's insisting it will, and I've made up my mind to believe him. The power of the mind, it's a wonderful thing. Now, enough about me. You and Joseph, you're going to go and talk to him, right? Make him see sense?"

"Actually, I'm not," Layla stated.

"You're not?" Tara looked confused. "Well, I'll speak to him, then."

"No! I don't want anyone to speak to him, not you, not Penny, not Hannah or Jim. I'm going to give him what he asked for, space. And to be honest, I need space too."

"But what if—" Tara began, then abruptly stopped.

"If he decides he doesn't want me? So be it. It's called consequences of actions."

Tara looked stunned. "Layla, you're being too hard on yourself."

"I need to be hard on myself, to understand."

"Understand what?"

"Why I did him a disservice, as well as myself, and why I was so quick to. It didn't take a week, it didn't even take hours; it took seconds to distrust him, the very first second he mentioned your name in fact." Before Tara could challenge her further, she continued, "You know when I met Aiden in the café, when we got talking?"

"Aha," Tara said, nodding.

"I asked him if he thought you'd left him because of another man. Do you know what he said?"

"What?" Tara looked genuinely intrigued.

"He said no, you weren't like that. He didn't even hesitate. I remember thinking how naïve he was, that nobody truly knows anyone. I was wrong. He knew you."

There was silence for a few moments as Tara seemed to ponder this. "Layla," she said finally, "have you ever been hurt?"

"Yes," Layla confessed. But hadn't everyone? She didn't want to go into detail, about Alex reeling her in and then spitting her out, about the father she had lost when young, her mother too, grief not uniting them but tearing them apart until so very recently. It would all just be excuses. But Tara, it seemed, didn't need detail.

"That's why," she replied.

Silence hung between them until Tara started speaking again.

"What about Florence? Your apartment there?"

"It's rented. If worse comes to worst, we'll give notice."

"You've both got jobs, though," Tara pointed out.

"I can't speak for Joseph, but I'll give notice on that too."

"To go where? Might you stay here?"

"I don't know yet. My mother lives in Milan. I might go there."

As Penny had been emphatic, so was Tara. "You're wrong, you know. This isn't the end for you and Joseph."

"It feels like it," replied Layla, remembering how Joseph had looked at her.

Tara leaned forward suddenly, excitement replacing concern. "Well, it's not. Besides which, you're going nowhere, not for the next few days. I need you."

Need her? What was she talking about? Layla would have thought she couldn't wait to see the back of her, despite how nice she was being.

"Yes, I need you, and I need Hannah too — she could have a word in Jim's ear — persuade him we need 96 Tears too. That would be awesome, having them play a set for us. Oh, and Penny. I like her style; she could be my advisor or something."

Penny — a style advisor? Layla almost choked. Now she really was confused.

Before she could ask why, Tara spoke again, a beaming smile on her face. "I'm getting married!"

"Married? To Aiden, you mean?" Immediately Layla berated herself. Of course it was to Aiden. Who else would it be?

"Yep, to Aiden," Tara confirmed. "Oh, but don't worry. It's not going to be a church wedding with me dressed up as a meringue or anything. We're going to get married on the beach—World's End. Mum's friend is a Humanist; he's doing the honors." Laughing, she continued. "I think Mum would prefer a big church do, to be honest, but, well, Aiden and I have different beliefs to her and Dad. Besides which, time is of the essence as they say, and it's not the legalities that count. It's the sentiment behind it."

"Oh, Tara, that's great. I'm so happy for you." And she was being honest; a part of her did feel happy. Tara's excitement was infectious.

"So, you'll help me? You'll stay?" Tara checked.

"Of course."

"And Penny too?"

"I'm sure she will."

"Fantastic." Hugging her knees to her chest again, Tara looked misty-eyed all of a sudden. "I want it to be the best wedding ever."

"It will be," Layla replied.

She, for one, would do her utmost to ensure it.

chapter twenty-six

Aiden was waiting for Tara when Layla dropped her home. Hurrying anxiously down the garden path toward her, he called, "Babe, where have you been? I was worried about you."

Tara giggled as he reached her, lifted her off the ground, and swung her around.

"Don't worry," she assured him. "The only place I'll ever run again is into your arms."

"I should bloody hope so," he said, burying his face into the space between her shoulder and her neck—the "sweet spot," as he liked to call it.

Reluctantly pulling away, she asked, "So, come on, spill. What clothes did you bring over with you from Oz? Anything smart?"

"Smart? Tara, I'm an Australian beach bum. I don't do smart." In mock dismay, he started singing Simply Red's "If You Don't Know Me by Now."

"I know you only too well," she replied, elbowing him playfully in the stomach. Taking his hand, she led him back toward the cottage. "We'll need to fit in a shopping trip, then, to Exeter, perhaps. It's not far, just over an hour's drive away. You are not coming to our wedding dressed in shorts and a T-shirt, believe me."

"Oh, Tara." He looked and sounded just like a little kid—a cute kid, though, she had to admit. "We're getting married on the beach. Why not?"

In the open doorway of her parents' house, she threw her arms around his neck. "Because I've seen how sexy you look in a suit, Aiden Taylor. That's why not."

"A suit? Me? When?"

"When you were best man at Landry's wedding, remember? It wasn't just me that was swooning at the sight of you. All the girls were."

"I know." Aiden pulled his sexy face. "Poor Landry. I didn't want to steal his thunder, but—"

"So, you'll do it? You'll wear a suit for me?"

"For you?" He rubbed his chin. "Hmm, I'm not sure. I'll have to think about it."

"Aiden!" She hit him playfully again.

"Ouch, stop that. I'll be black and blue by the time our wedding comes around at this rate." More seriously, he asked, "Actually, I wonder what day next week it is that I'll be making an honest woman of you?"

"Friday," her mother called from the living room.

"Oh, Friday," Aiden called back, winking at Tara as he did so. In a mock British accent, he added, "Thank you, Mrs. Mills. That's splendid news."

From the dark interior, Tara heard her mother chuckle.

"I can't believe it," Tara whispered.

"Believe what?" Aiden asked.

"I arrived here at the beginning of this week. If someone told me that, by the end of the second, I'd be getting married, there's no way I'd have believed them, no way."

Aiden bent down to kiss her lightly on the lips. "Well, you are getting married, Mrs. Soon-to-be-Taylor, and I'll make a deal with you. If you promise me mind-blowing, super-scintillating, extra scrumptious sex on our marital eve, I'll wear a suit."

"Extra scrumptious?" Tara's face colored at the thought.

"That bit has to be pinky promised," he answered, completely straight-faced.

Trying unsuccessfully to stifle her laughter, she shushed him in case her mother happened to be listening still. "I promise," she whispered, kissing him back as hard as was decent. Reluctantly breaking away, she ushered him into the kitchen.

"The thing is, Aiden," she continued, "we've got some putting right to do."

He leaned up against the kitchen counter to hear how so. If this was her house and they were alone in it, she'd swear she'd be the one up against that kitchen counter right now, with Aiden kneeling right in front of her. Banishing such naughty thoughts, she explained to him what had happened between Layla and Joseph.

"Bummer," he said after she had finished explaining.

"And that's why I'm getting them to help me. Not just Layla, but her friends too. I want them all in on the act. I want them to float along with us on bubbles of happiness—Joseph and Layla especially. I want what we have to rub off on them." She paused for a moment before adding, "They belong together, like we do."

"I'm glad you said that." Aiden closed the gap between them. "That he belongs with her and you belong with me. For a moment, down at the beach, I thought—"

"Joseph and I are good friends, nothing more."

"And Layla, she wouldn't accept that?"

"For a while. But she knows the truth now. I just wish I'd been clear with her sooner. If I had been, she and Joseph would still be together. Ironically, she's the one who feels guilty, when really it should be me. No, hang on, it *is* me."

"Hey, babe." Aiden took her face in his hands. "No regrets, huh? We said that, didn't we? What's done is done, but we'll make it better between them, don't worry."

Holding her close, he continued, "We'll make *everything* better, you'll see."

chapter twenty-seven

It was too good to last. The baby was crying again, screaming the living room down, in fact. Hannah, who had been rocking her at the time, hurriedly handed her back to Penny, mumbled some excuse about the dishes, and disappeared into the kitchen.

Scarlett's crying usually set every nerve ending in Penny's body on edge. In her opinion, it was the only sound worse than the slow drag of chalk on slate, but surprisingly, her nerve endings weren't suffering too badly today. Despite Scarlett's screams and protests, Penny felt happy, excited even. Although excited about what, she didn't know. Just then, Richard came back into the room, his hair still damp from the shower he had just taken. Oh, yes, that's what she was excited about—him.

Last night, when they were absolutely sure Scarlett was screaming in some dream world somewhere, scaring to death all the cutesy pink bunnies and fluffy black kittens that inhabited such realms, they had dared to move her from in between them to the travel cot. She was amazed Richard had thought to bring it, but then again, he had stuffed most of Scarlett's belongings into the car he had hired for the journey. How he had seen out of the back window, she didn't know. Amazingly, the baby hadn't stirred at all. Rubbing her hands together in barely suppressed glee, Penny had tiptoed back to bed and snuggled up against her husband—the first time in an age.

It had felt so good to hold him close again, to breathe in his familiar scent, to just be the two of them. Couple time, she was beginning to realize, was as essential as family time — if you wanted to maintain a healthy relationship, that is. He had immediately started kissing her, how much he'd been missing her making itself very evident.

Pulling briefly away, a frown had marked his face.

"Do you think we should do this? You know, with Scarlett in the room?"

"She's fast asleep, Richard. As long as we're quiet, we'll get away with it."

And she had to hand it to him; he had been impressively quiet, moving slowly but purposefully inside her, his breathing ragged, but softly ragged. Afterward, she had lain in his arms, sure their luck was about to run out, that Scarlett would wake at any minute. But she hadn't. She had made it, like them, right through to morning.

And now here he was again, standing in front of her, a lazy smile on his chiseled face.

"What's that for?" she asked, smiling too.

"What?" He was toying with her, she knew.

"That look?"

"I'm just thinking of the day ahead, that's all."

"Oh?" She raised an eyebrow at him.

"We're going to attempt another family day out, and this time we're taking a jar."

Penny and Richard had decided to spend the day around Trecastle, wander at leisure around the castle ruins and visit St. Michael's, also on the headland. The ancient parish church dated back to the eleventh century. The atmosphere inside was serene, and miraculously, it soothed the baby. She seemed to calm completely within the confines of its cold stone walls, and because she was calm, Penny was too.

Built in the shape of a cross, there was a stand with candles burning on the right-hand side. Handing the baby over to Richard, who was busy reading each and every epitaph, she made her way there. After a few moments, Richard ambled after her.

"What are you doing?" he asked as she tumbled some loose change into a pot that sat beside a box of tea lights.

"Lighting candles," she explained. "One for Tara and one for Layla. I think they could both use a bit of divine intervention right now."

Shifting Scarlett over to his left arm, Richard put his right around Penny and squeezed her tight. When Layla had gone to her room last night, Penny had caught him up on everything. His eyes had clouded over when she told him about Tara.

"Poor girl," he had said. "That's so unfair."

When she confessed how she had stupidly planted the idea of pregnancy into Layla's head, he had rolled his eyes.

"Penny." The admonishment was clear in his voice.

"Don't," she had begged. "You can't be any angrier with me than I am with myself at the moment."

"I'm not angry with you," he had assured her, kissing her instead.

But still, standing there, in the church, in front of the twinkling tea lights, she couldn't help but feel guilty because she was happy. She wanted everyone to be happy—Tara and Aiden, Layla and Joseph too. They deserved to be.

"Come on," said Richard, clearly sensing the change of mood in his wife. "Let's get out of here, go down to the beach instead."

On the glistening sands, they walked side by side, Penny contentedly pushing the pram, its all-terrain wheels gliding along. As the atmosphere in the church had calmed Scarlett, so the sea air tired her—she was fast asleep again. *Note to self,* Penny thought *Take her down to the beach in Brighton more often if it has this effect.*

Richard obviously hadn't noticed. "Stop a minute, Penny. I'll get her out, show her the sea."

"No," Penny said, tapping at his hand. "Scarlett's asleep. Leave her."

Richard stopped what he was doing and stared at her, aghast.

"What?" Penny queried.

"You called her Scarlett," Richard said, astonishment in his voice.

"Yes," she replied. "Because that's her name. Scarlett."

"I know that," he went on, "but I was beginning to think you didn't."

"What do you mean?" she asked. She had chosen it, insisted on it. He had wanted something traditional, like Edith—*Edith,* for God's sake!

"You know what I mean. You usually refer to her as 'the baby.' This is one of a handful of times." He stopped, inclined his head, and thought for a moment. "Do you know, it might even be the first time I've heard you say it."

"Oh, don't be so ridiculous," she started to say and then stopped. He was right, she knew it. There was no point denying it. Briefly, she wondered why she had found it so hard to call Scarlett by her name. Was it a way of distancing herself from her? It took a few moments to realize she was crying. Yes, that *was* the reason why.

"Hey, Penny." Immediately, Richard was holding her. "It's all right. I'm here."

"Thank God you are," she sobbed into his shoulder. How single parents coped, she didn't know. They were a breed apart. A breed she stood in awe of.

"I'm so sorry," she continued. The guilt she had felt up at the church expanded to include Scarlett too. She thought the weight of it might crush her completely. She was a dreadful mother to feel the way she did. She didn't deserve to be blessed. An injunction should be taken out against her as far as babies were concerned. With each troubled thought, her body shook harder.

"Penny, come on. We're okay. There's no need to cry."

"Oh, Richard," she managed in between sobs. "There's every need to cry."

He looked stricken all of a sudden. "Is it…is it because you don't love her?"

"No." Penny was horrified he could even think such a thing. "I do love Scarlett. I really love her. That's the trouble."

"That's the trouble?" Richard repeated.

"Yes…No…Oh, I don't know."

"Maybe you don't," Richard continued, this time a little more sure of himself, "but I think I might. If I say what I think, will you promise not to bite my head off?"

"Richard, I'm not that bad, for goodness sake," she protested.

"Penny, you are."

Curiosity won out over the need to retaliate. "Go on then," she said. "What's wrong with me?"

"Postnatal depression," he replied.

"Wha—"

"Hear me out," he pleaded. "When I went into the office to tell them I had to take emergency leave, Mr. Torrence…James asked me what was wrong, naturally."

"Naturally," Penny repeated, only slightly sarcastically.

"Well, we got talking. Thankfully, I'd thought to bring a bottle of milk to keep Scarlett quiet. I…Well, I told him how things were."

"How I was, you mean."

"Don't get defensive," Richard warned.

"I'm not," lied Penny. "Carry on."

"He and his wife's first child, she was a…you know…a difficult baby, right from the start. He was at work all day; she was alone with the baby, and she spiraled pretty quickly. She ended up having a sort of a breakdown, needed a stay in hospital. A short stay, but nonetheless she needed treatment."

"Poor thing." Penny was immediately sympathetic.

"Some of the symptoms of postnatal depression: mood swings, a lack of interest in the world around you, tiredness—and, yes, I know you've been tired for a good reason. Scarlett does seem to hold a bit of a grudge against sleeping—well, they're some of the symptoms that I've noticed in you. Maybe, you know…"

"I might have it," Penny finished for him. "Yes, Richard, I think I might. I've got something, anyway, something I'd rather not have. Mrs. Torrence, what happened?"

"She got counseling, support as well, from her husband and her local health visitor, who was fantastic, apparently, and is now a good friend. Basically, she pulled through. They went on to have two more kids, and they might even have more."

So, it didn't last forever. That was a relief.

"Penny, I know I've been remiss. But that talk with James, it hit home. I'd have been better off spending my time researching depression than baby-led weaning."

"Amen to that," Penny replied, but she was smiling as she said it.

"I'm sorry. I should have been most astute. I should have noticed."

"And I should have been more up front, more honest with you about how I felt. But some things, you know, they're not easy to say."

She was going to say more, but the look on his face stopped her.

"What is it, Richard? What's so funny?"

Richard looked on the point of convulsions. "You," he spluttered. "I never thought I'd hear the words 'some things aren't easy to say' coming from your mouth."

Affronted, she was about to point out she hadn't let slip what she'd heard between Joseph and Tara on that evening beside the honey shop when she remembered what she had let slip: Tara being sick and the possibility she might be pregnant, causing Layla to buy a one-way ticket on the wrong flight of fancy. He had a point, she conceded. Keeping schtum wasn't something she was renowned for.

Thankfully, it didn't take long for Richard to gain control of himself. "Look, dry your eyes, and we'll go for a cup of tea. We can talk more."

"Tea?" Penny almost spat the word back at him. "A glass of wine, more like."

"Penny!" Shock replaced the mirth on Richard's face. "Not in front of the baby."

"That's what you said last night," she reminded him, "when we were in bed. Didn't stop you, though, did it? Come on; follow me. We're going to the pub."

Hannah was working a shift at the bar. "Hi, guys," she greeted them as they entered. "What are you having? It's on the house."

Richard ordered while Penny settled them at a table closest to the window. Miraculously, Scarlett was still sleeping, snoring even, and emitting little snuffling noises. Despite feeling raw, Penny smiled at the sound.

"That's better," said Richard, returning with a glass of wine for her, large she was glad to note, and a pint of Tribute for him. "That's more like the Penny I know."

Taking her drink from him, she drank half of it down in one go before setting it on the table, ignoring Richard's raised eyebrow as she did so. Through the door, some local people she recognized came in and were greeted warmly by Hannah also.

She took a deep breath and picked up where they had left off on the beach. "It's just, I find it all so frightening at times, you know?"

"Find what frightening?" Richard was about to take a sip of his beer but paused.

"Being responsible for a whole new life. The enormity of it, it's…
it's incredible."

Richard placed his pint back on the table untouched. Looking
over to where Scarlett lay slumbering, he narrowed his eyes.

Oh, great, thought Penny, *here we go. He's going to start banging
on about how there's nothing scary about it, that having a kid is great,
blah, blah, blah.*

She nearly fell off her chair when he shrugged his shoulders and
sighed heavily before replying, "Yeah, yeah, it is."

"It is?"

"Look, Penny, I'm not a fool, despite what you may think. That
chat with James, these past few days without you, they've opened
my eyes. When you left me alone with Scarlett, you know what I
did? The very first thing? I panicked. Without you to fall back on, I
started spiraling too. It can get a bit intense at times with Scarlett."

"A bit?" That was putting it mildly.

"But you know what?" he continued. "I think she gets that off of
us. No, hang on, don't interrupt. Let me explain. You're tense around
her, and you and me, we're tense around each other. I don't know;
we're just whipping up so much damn tension between the three of
us, we don't stand a chance."

What he was saying, not only did it make sense, it was something
her sleep-deprived brain had suspected—that they all plugged into
one other. It didn't excuse the fact that she was crap at this mothering
business, though, and she said as much.

"Rubbish." Richard actually looked quite angry that she could
even suggest it. "You are not a crap mum, Penny. You're great. No,
I'm going to go the whole hog here. You're brilliant. All right, okay,
it's fair to say you're not your typical Earth Mother. You hate cooking,
and you don't knit, but you've got your own way, and that's good
enough. Besides which," he added, "Earth Mothers wear dungarees,
don't they? I don't think I'd fancy you in dungarees."

"You think I'm brilliant?" she whispered, again having to double check.

"Yes, I do. And don't worry, there's nothing wrong with your
hearing." He smiled at her, his eyes twinkling now. "But, I do recognize we've had a few…teething problems," he continued, clearly

proud of his play on words. "I need to be more supportive; I know that. I'll do a few night shifts if you like. Well, one or two anyway."

"Oh, Richard, if you could, that would be great," Penny felt lighter all of a sudden. "Maybe take over at the weekend or something when you don't have to get up so early in the morning. If I can get a good night's sleep once in a while, it would make all the difference, I'm sure."

"Yep, no worries."

"And bath times? Perhaps you can take over that particular ritual too."

"But she hates bath time." Richard looked horrified. "She always makes such a fuss."

"Exactly."

"Okay, okay," he relented. "I can do that too."

Reaching for his pint, he was the one who gulped it now, the liquid disappearing from the glass at an impressive rate. Wiping his mouth afterward, he looked relaxed again.

"Feeling better?" he asked.

"Much better." She smiled, draining her glass. "I'm so glad you came, both of you."

"Me too," he replied, and then, leaning forward and winking at her in a suggestive manner, he whispered, "And hopefully the little lady will leave us to get on with a few nocturnal activities of our own again tonight."

Penny frowned. "Actually, she won't sleep at all tonight if I don't wake her up now. She's been out for the count for ages."

Slipping swiftly back into mother mode, Penny stood. She was just about to bend over the pram to retrieve Scarlett when she caught movement at the door. Joseph had walked in with Mick.

Immediately, his eyes locked on to hers then looked around to see whose company she was keeping. He hesitated before coming over. "Hi, Penny," he said, rather curtly, she thought. To Richard, he was a little friendlier. "Hey, Richard, good to see you back in Trecastle."

Richard got up. "You too, mate. How have you been?"

Penny rolled her eyes. Why did he have to ask that? He knew perfectly well how Joseph had been.

"Yeah, fine," Joseph mumbled.

But he looked far from fine. His face was unshaven, his eyes dull.

"Anyway, have fun whatever you're doing," Joseph continued, backing away.

Penny looked from Joseph to Richard, then back again.

"Joseph, wait," she said, going after him.

"What is it, Penny?" he said, an edge back in his voice.

"Layla, you know she really is sorry about what happened. I am too."

"Where is she?" he asked.

"Layla? I…She…Well, she went to see Tara, actually."

He started visibly. That wasn't the answer he had expected.

"I'm sure she'll come and see you soon, though," she added in appeasement.

"I don't think so."

"Why not?" Penny was taken aback by his absolute conviction.

"If she was going to come and see me, she would have done so by now."

"Joseph! That's not fair. It was only yesterday all this happened."

"Life isn't fair, though, is it? We've learned that lately."

"She loves you," Penny insisted.

"But she doesn't trust me."

"Joseph —"

"Penny, please, enough. I've changed my flight. I'm going back to Florence tomorrow. I expect Layla will be going back on Monday as planned. If she is, tell her not to worry; she won't bump into me. I'll collect what I need from the apartment and go and stay at Paolo's while we decide what we're doing."

"Tomorrow? Sunday? You — you can't."

"I can, and I am."

And with that, he extracted himself from her and went to join Mick at the bar. Desperately, she racked her brain for a way to make him stay. He had to stay — he had to. And so did Layla. Sort themselves out on British shores. But how she'd pull something effective out of the bag in the time she had, she didn't have a clue.

chapter twenty-eight

After dropping Tara back home, Layla returned to Trecastle.

"Hello," she called as she let herself into Hannah and Jim's flat.

Silence greeted her. Layla went through to the living room, which seemed to have turned into a crèche overnight. There was a travel cot, toys galore, nappies, baby wipes, baby clothes in abundance, and a selection of jars containing rather lurid-looking contents. Grimacing, she went into her bedroom next to check for signs that Joseph might have returned in her absence—to do what, she didn't know. Grab some clothes, perhaps? He'd need them if he was staying at Mick's. Then again, Mick was about the same size as him, so perhaps he'd borrow some.

She sighed, and the sound seemed so loud. It was quiet in here, too quiet. She needed company, someone to share the news with about Tara's wedding. She'd head to the pub instead. Hannah, she knew, was working a shift there.

All the way along the high street, she wondered if she'd bump into Joseph. Part of her wanted to, but another part recoiled at the thought. It was too soon; she didn't feel ready. They'd see each other at Tara and Aiden's wedding anyway, which was to be held in a few days, although which day she didn't know yet. Tara was going to let her know. Surely, once he'd been told, he'd stay also, he of all people.

Whether she was ready or not, as she pushed open the door to the Trecastle Inn, she came face to face with Joseph. Mick stood just a short distance behind him. As she was entering, they were on their way out. Struggling to control what surely must be a look of shock on her face, she also searched for something to say.

"Hi," was all she could manage.

Joseph looked slightly aghast. Clearly he was expecting something more. Of course he was expecting something more! "Sorry" for a start. Had she even said that yet? Thinking back to the night of their fallout, she honestly couldn't remember. Before her lips could form the word, however, he continued on. She had hesitated too long. Mick also passed by, a sympathetic smile on his face as he did so.

As though through a veil of fog, she heard someone call her name. It was Penny.

"Layla! Layla, over here."

Although it felt akin to wading through quicksand, she forced one foot in front of the other, sitting down on the bench beside Penny and staring blindly at the door.

"Sorry about that." Penny looked mortified. "I didn't know you were coming to the pub. If I had, I would have texted to warn you Joseph was here."

Layla shook her head. "There's no need to warn me. It's fine. Anyway, let's not worry about that right now. I've got some news I want to share."

Hannah had left the bar and come hurrying over, obviously concerned for her friend too.

"Hun, are you okay?" she said, reaching out to touch her arm.

"I'm fine," Layla said, surprised that she felt annoyed with Hannah, that she wanted to shrug her off. Because she wasn't able to sympathize with herself, it seemed she couldn't accept sympathy from others. "Sit down. I've got something to tell you."

"You're not leaving, are you?" Penny gasped in horror. "Not you too."

"Me too?" Layla queried.

"Oh, nothing," Penny quickly corrected herself. "I meant not yet."

"No, not yet." Layla attempted a smile. "Not until after the wedding."

"What wedding?" It was Hannah this time.

"What…? Joseph…?" Penny started.

"No," Layla almost shouted, eager to stop Penny from pursuing that particular train of thought. "I'm talking about Tara and Aiden. They're getting married, next week."

"Next week?" Hannah seemed surprised. More solemnly, she added, "Actually, considering the circumstances, I suppose it makes sense."

"And," Layla continued, looking at Penny and then Hannah in turn, "she wants us involved, you two as well as me. She wants us to help her organize it."

"Us?" Penny looked stumped. "Why us?"

"Why not?" Layla replied. Focusing entirely on Hannah, she said, "Could you talk to Jim? Tara would love it if 96 Tears could play a set at her wedding."

Hannah didn't hesitate. "He's got that gig in Exeter on Friday, but if the dates clash, I know which one will take priority."

"Thanks, Hannah."

"And what about me?" asked Penny. "What's my role in all of this?"

"Style advisor, apparently." Layla couldn't quite keep the sarcasm out of her voice.

"Style advisor?" Clearly Penny was thrilled. "She likes my style?" Looking at Richard, she continued, "Wow! Someone thinks I've got great dress sense."

Richard shrugged his shoulders. "I've told you, as long as you don't go wearing dungarees, you look great to me."

"Dungarees?" Hannah frowned at the remark.

"A private joke," Penny explained.

"Penny," Layla said, "I know you and Richard have to get back home because of work, but are you able to either hang on for the wedding or come back for it? I know Tara would love it, obviously, but…in truth, so would I."

"I've told you," Penny leaned across but thankfully—and intuitively for her—didn't touch her arm. "I can't speak for Richard, but I'm not going anywhere until you're sorted."

"I've accrued quite a bit of holiday anyway," Richard contributed. He looked at Penny and smiled. "And you know what? I bloody feel like taking it."

Layla was about to thank her when Penny piped up again. "A wedding. Oh my goodness, that's just about the best news ever." She wrapped her arms tightly round herself. "It couldn't have come at a better time."

It *was* good news, but even Hannah looked confused as to why Penny was quite so ecstatic about it.

Standing suddenly, Penny declared, "I've got to dash out. Erm… formula. I need formula."

"But we've got loads of formula back at the flat." Richard looked bemused now. "I must have brought about a ton of it down with me."

"A new bottle, then," Penny shot him a withering glance before continuing. "We need a new bottle. The old one, the teat's worn or… or something. I shan't be long."

And with that, she was out the door, faster than a bolt of lightning.

Tara rang to let Layla and the others know what day the wedding would be the following week: Friday. Everyone was staying for it, even Joseph apparently, although he and Layla had kept their distance from each other during the days following the announcement. If she couldn't face him, well, it seemed he couldn't face her either. They were at stalemate. Completely.

On Wednesday, Layla, Penny, Hannah, and Tara piled into Hannah's car and drove to Exeter in Devon. A shopping spree was on the cards. Layla felt a slight unease at leaving Cornwall behind her, as though the dividing line between two counties brought into sharper relief the division between her and Joseph. Despite the fact she hadn't seen Joseph since their encounter in the pub, he remained close by, at least, which gave her a crumb of comfort. Jim had been to visit him several times, taken some of his clothes over. When she had asked him how Joseph was, he had done his utmost to answer positively.

"He's fine, doing really well. Why don't you go over and see him?"

Why? She'd have thought it was obvious why. It was at the wedding she'd see him, and at least preparations for it were keeping her busy beforehand. They'd have to go back to Florence soon after, though, the pair of them, ending the stalemate. Would they go back together or apart? She hoped it was the former, that the wedding, bound to be a magical affair, would lend them some magic too. They'd fall back into the life they had, although, if she were honest, her former life seemed far from real right now. It seemed like a dream, a sweet dream she thought she'd never wake up from. But woken she had, to a reality that was nothing less than stark.

She reminded herself to focus on Tara and Tara only—she was whom the wedding was all about. Layla wanted her to have the most beautiful day possible; she *deserved* the most beautiful day possible. Her dream realized, at least.

Arriving in Exeter, they parked in a multi-story car park.

"Look, there's a Topshop!" Penny squealed once they had climbed down from on high and reached the city center. Clearly, she had been parted from decent shops for too long.

Tara, however, was enjoying Penny's enthusiasm. "I don't mind going in and having a look," she said, "but really I'm after something a little less mainstream."

"Of course, of course," Penny said, linking arms with her. "There's bound to be plenty of really good boutiques here too. I'll sniff them out. Don't you worry."

Hannah and Layla fell into step behind Tara and Penny, Hannah chuckling as she did so. "They get on well, those two, don't they?" she remarked.

"They do," Layla replied, thinking of the previous evening when the three of them had gone over to Tara's parents' house to draw up a list of wedding guests. Then, instead of practicing their calligraphic skills on gilt-edged invites, they had texted everyone to let them know instead. Both Penny *and* Tara were squealing then, marveling at how quickly people were replying and how many friends could make it at such short notice.

"This is such a brilliant way to do wedding invites," Penny had said almost in a state of wonder. "So modern, so cost-effective."

Aiden and Tara's parents had looked on in amused silence.

"Any idea what you're going to wear?" Hannah asked Layla, bringing her back to the present.

The last thing Layla felt like doing was dolling herself up, but she had to make the effort—something bright and light, in complete contrast to the way she felt.

"I'm sure I'll find something appropriate today. Are you buying anything?"

"You seriously have to ask?" Hannah looked amazed. "I'm going to a wedding. Of course I'm buying a new outfit. I might even treat myself to a hat as well."

As they trailed around the shops, Layla did her best to match their frivolity. The others were so upbeat, she felt mean for not matching them smile for smile. And she did want to look good—she wanted to look knockout, in Joseph's eyes anyway.

It was in a little boutique called Luna that both she and Hannah found what they were looking for. Hannah chose a dress that was ruby in color, had bell sleeves, and fell just above the knees. She looked beautiful in it—a pocket princess. Layla opted for a wrap-around dress in sage green, this time on the knee rather than above it. Everyone agreed it suited her coloring perfectly, especially her eyes.

In contrast, Tara and Penny couldn't find anything they liked. Over frothy coffees in a local café, Penny's enthusiasm was dented.

"There's not an awe-inspiring selection here, is there?" she complained.

"There is compared to anywhere I've been in a long while," Hannah defended.

"But it's not comparable to London, is it? That's where the glitz and glamour is."

"We don't have time to go to London," Layla reminded her. "But we're not done yet. There's plenty more shops on the horizon."

Penny refused to be convinced, while Tara just shrugged and smiled, taking it all in her stride.

They hunted for Aiden's suit next. Tara had originally intended to go shopping with him, she explained, but really, Aiden and retail establishments didn't mix too well. Instead, she had taken his measurements, popped into Next, and chosen a dark-blue linen suit off the shelf, casual in style rather than formal, the trousers cool and loose. She also bought a white linen shirt to go with it and black ankle boots too.

"That's him done and dusted," she said, pleased with herself.

"How about something funky for his tie?" Penny suggested, her eyes lighting up again. "Red, perhaps, as a contrast to the blue? Or this yellow? It's practically neon."

Tara and Penny decided on the yellow tie, Tara giggling that Aiden was going to be so unimpressed with what she had bought for him.

"It might be a casual suit, but he's still going to hate it," she confided.

"Good." Penny winked. "He'll be even more eager to get it off when the day's over."

After another hour traipsing, Penny found the outfit she wanted, a fifties-style dress with a white-and-blue floral pattern. It suited perfectly her hourglass figure.

"Had I known I was going to a wedding," she whined, despite the great fit, "I might have dieted first. Got a size twelve instead of a fourteen."

"You look fabulous." Layla shoved her. "Stop moaning."

Penny grinned. She knew Layla was right.

It was in a vintage shop that Tara found her dress—they had almost walked right past Bygones because in the windows either side of the door, only costume jewelry was displayed. It was Penny who had spotted the "Vintage Clothes Upstairs" sign, despite the fact several chiffon scarves had been draped over it. After she had herded them in, they had oohed and ahhed at the sparkling brooches, necklaces, and rings downstairs first as well as a huge variety of vintage handbags, one in crocodile leather that Layla actually found quite disturbing, especially when Penny, who had been looking at it too at the time, held it up to her face and shouted, "Snap!" She had jumped, despite suspecting Penny was going to do such a thing.

Upstairs, it smelled quite musty, but investigating further, they found some real gems on the rails, not especially suitable for Tara. Many of the dresses were too long for her petite frame; they would swamp her. The assistant asked what the occasion was, and Layla explained.

The woman sized Tara up carefully before saying, "Hang on, I might just have something."

Disappearing into a room at the back of the shop, she reappeared only moments later. In her hands was a calf-length dress in gold satin.

"It's pale-gold silk satin, to be precise," the woman replied when Tara asked her what the material was. "And it's from the nineteen thirties. Lovely, isn't it? Try it on."

The dress looked beautiful on Tara, as though it were made for her.

"I think it would be rather nice to leave the neckline bare," the assistant continued, "but what about this bracelet? It matches perfectly."

The silver-toned diamante bracelet with its ornate filigree design was indeed the ideal accompaniment.

"Ah, you look really…Hollywood," Penny said with a sigh, misty eyed.

Swinging around, Tara told the assistant she'd take the lot. "Any shoes to match?" she asked hopefully.

"Shoes? Oh, God, shoes," shrieked Penny upon hearing the S-word. "What sort of a style advisor am I? I nearly forgot."

The shoes, thankfully, weren't as painful as the clothes to find. Tara chose heels in nude to make her look taller—a fashion tip she said she had picked up from Angelina Jolie—but did confess she'd probably only wear them as far as the beach. Heels didn't tend to work too well on sand, she pointed out.

Bearing this in mind, Hannah, Layla, and Penny opted for ballet shoes in the softest leather, but they too doubted they'd be wearing them. Barefoot was probably going to be *de rigueur* for pretty much everyone on the day. Soon the girls were on their way back to Trecastle, intent on a drink at the pub before Aiden came to pick Tara up.

As she crossed the border back into Cornwall, Layla felt herself relax. It had been a great day, and soon she'd be in the same airspace as Joseph—although the old adage "so near and yet so far" had never seemed so pertinent.

She noticed immediately the Trecastle Inn was devoid of Joseph, or Jim, or Mick, or any of the gang for that matter. There had been no more "bumping" into each other, which in a village this size was quite an achievement. Where was he? What was he doing? This yearning for him, it hurt so bad and only seemed to increase in pain rather than lessen. But Friday, she reminded herself. She'd see him on Friday. Everyone kept telling her it would be all right; he'd come round—he'd want her again. By then tempers would have simmered, *his* temper that is. She could only hope.

Settling around a table, Hannah went over to the fridge behind the bar and brought back a bottle of Moët and Chandon.

"I think after such a successful shopping trip, a few bubbles are in order, don't you agree, girls?"

They did, heartily, clinking glasses and cheering Tara.

After talk of what they'd bought that day and how they were going to wear their hair and makeup, Penny piped up, "This wedding you're having, this humanist approach, is it legally binding?"

"Not legally, no."

"In which case, will Aiden be allowed to stay on until…you know…until…"

"Penny." Layla frowned at her. Discretion had never been her strong point.

"It's all right." Tara looked amused, not offended. "Although Aiden was born in Australia, both his parents are English, so he won't have a problem on that score."

"Gosh, that's a relief," Penny said, before adding, "Sorry."

"Do you know if I ever hear the word 'sorry' again, it'll be too soon? No one's got anything to be sorry for." Looking specifically at Layla, Tara repeated, "No one."

Layla looked away.

After they had finished the bottle, Layla nipped to the bathroom. When she came back, she saw Hannah had been collared by Gail from Cake and Crumb. Penny and Tara, meanwhile, were standing at the bar, engrossed in conversation too.

Going to join them, she stopped when she heard Joseph's name mentioned, staying out of sight but within earshot of their conversation.

"So, Joseph was just going to leave, without saying a word?"

"He had changed his flight; he was going home on the Sunday instead of the Monday." Sighing, she continued, "Your wedding, you know it couldn't have come at a better time, and not just for you either. If he had just upped and left, without even saying a word to Layla beforehand, it would have finished her, I'm sure. At least now, they'll have an opportunity to sort this mess out."

"And Layla doesn't have a clue?"

"Nope, she doesn't suspect at all. But surely when he sees how well you two get on together now, how much she's helped you with all your wedding prep, not to mention how gorgeous she looks in that dress of hers, he'll fall at her feet again."

"Fingers crossed."

"Mind you," Penny continued, "they're both as stubborn as each other. She wants to give him space. That's why she hasn't gone round to see him. But if that were me, I'd be blazing a trail to his door, banging it down. I can't understand her."

"They're both playing it cool," Tara agreed.

"Too cool, if you ask me."

After a quick peek around the corner, Layla noticed they were about to turn. She shrunk back, glad there was a pillar she could hide behind.

Joseph had intended to leave Trecastle? Fly back to Florence without telling her? Only the fact Tara and Aiden were getting married had stopped him. She knew what she was guilty of, but was she to be condemned forever because of it? As for playing it cool, she wasn't. She was burning up inside. Shudders coursed through her, but she refused to let them take hold. Tara's wedding was less than forty-eight hours away; she had to hold it together until then. But if she was hoping that the happiness of the day might guide her and Joseph back toward each other, she now knew she had been deluding herself. She would smile her way through the day certainly, clap and cheer for the bride and bridegroom enthusiastically, but from Joseph she would continue to keep her distance. She was his ex now. He had decided that for both of them.

chapter twenty-nine

T ara opened her eyes. It was here — her wedding day. She could hardly believe it. Despite Aiden's protests, she had made him sleep downstairs last night in the living room, on an old camper bed her dad had retrieved from the attic.

"But, babe," he had protested. "We're not doing that whole traditional wedding thing. We're doing it our way. Let me sleep with you up here."

"No." She had stood firm. "Some things remain sacred."

Her mother would have given him Leo's room, but her sister had come home for the wedding. Previously, Tara had agreed with her parents to tell Leo about her illness after the wedding. She wanted her day and everyone who attended it to be happy — to feel the way she did, not weighted down by sorrow and sympathy. She *needed* their happiness to make her believe in happy ever after too. The only people, as far as she knew, with sorrow in their hearts would be Layla and Joseph. And it was because of her and the secret she had made him keep. She was the rift that had come between them, and somehow she would have to make amends.

Besides her mother and father and Aiden, the few people who knew about her illness had been sworn to secrecy too. She knew they wouldn't let her down. She hadn't seen Joseph since Aiden's return — he was intent on keeping himself to himself — but she had texted him their plans. He had replied, saying how pleased he was for them and that of course he would attend their marriage; he wouldn't miss it for the world. When she had sent a tentative "Are you all right?" he had bounced back one word: "Fine." That was the Joseph she knew of old, private, incredibly so.

Their sudden wedding had been greeted with bemusement by her friends and extended family members.

"That's typical of Tara," she had heard her sister comment to her mum last night but not without affection. "She doesn't do anything by halves."

No, she didn't, and she was glad she'd been made that way. Life was too short not to give everything and *everyone* your full attention.

Thinking of Leo seemed to materialize her. The door flew open, and she came bounding in, her younger sister, almost a carbon copy of her but with longer hair.

"Come on, lazy bones. We haven't got time to waste. We've got to get you looking beautiful."

"Cheers," murmured Tara, not sure whether to be pleased by her remark or offended.

"I've run a bath for you, put some nice scent in it too. It's one we sell in my shop, amber and patchouli. I brought it especially. Go and soak yourself while I lay out your outfit."

"What about Aiden?" Tara asked, rising onto her elbows.

"He's downstairs tucking into a full English breakfast Mum's made him."

"A full English?"

"Yep, the works."

"Does he look nervous at all?" she asked in slight trepidation.

"Nervous? Aiden? Not a bit of it. He looks far too chipper to be the bridegroom, if you ask me. And boy, he's got an appetite, hasn't he? He even asked for an extra sausage. Mum's as pleased as punch."

Relieved, Tara levered herself off the bed and lowered her feet to the floor.

"Oh, look," enthused Leo, throwing open the curtains. "You've got the luck of the devil, Tara. The sun is blazing today."

As daylight poured into the room, Tara winced. She could feel the stirrings of a headache.

No, not today, she thought, cold fear making her spine tingle.

As she reached for the door, she stumbled.

"Tara," Leo called out, all concern now. "Are you okay?"

"Yeah, I'm fine." Quickly, Tara tried to make light of it. "Aiden might not be nervous, but I am. Would you...would you mind helping me to the bathroom?"

"Of course not," Leo replied, rushing to her side.

The perfumed air in the bathroom made her feel nauseated. Leo's thoughtfulness had been very sweet, and she appreciated it, but how she was going to languish in that smell, she didn't know. For a while now, strong scents had upset her.

Plastering a smile on her face, she turned to Leo and said, "Thanks for helping me, but I'll be fine now."

"Are you sure?" Leo didn't look convinced. She looked downright suspicious.

"I'm sure."

As soon as Leo left her alone, Tara closed the door, not locking it just in case she should pass out, something that had happened only once before. Thankfully she had been alone at the time—Aiden had remained none the wiser. Also she had been thankful when she came round to find she hadn't done herself any damage in falling. It was perhaps the only time she'd been grateful that Aiden had left his clothes in a pile on the floor—they'd made for a soft landing. Quickly, she let the scented water out of the bath. Next she opened the window wide, breathing in deep the fresh air.

Refilling the bath with plain water, she sank into it, the nausea slowly subsiding.

If she lay still, perfectly still, the headache might pass—that, too, she knew from experience, was possible. Rare, but it had happened once before. Unfortunately, the headache showed no sign of passing. It persisted, the pain in her head starting to blind her almost. Although she screwed her eyes shut, tears still managed to squeeze themselves out. She could feel them, hot and angry on her cheeks.

Not today, she thought again, digging the nails she'd had perfectly manicured yesterday into the palms of her hand. *Please, not today. Whatever universal forces are out there—tomorrow is fine, but leave me alone today. Please, please, please.*

She could feel her body sink lower and lower into the bath — perhaps if she sank below the water…If she stayed there, it might be for the best. The thought of being able to end this pain was a tempting one. The water came up to her chin, covering her lips as she pursed them together. Soon her nose would be under water too. It seemed such a peaceful way to go, not frightening at all. As she sank lower, she heard a sound like a thunderclap. Had Aiden burst into the room? Had Leo gone downstairs and said Tara wasn't quite looking herself and he had cottoned on?

She sat bolt upright, water splashing around her as she did so, some of it escaping over the side. There was no one in the bathroom but her. The sound had been in her head. But what was it? The tumor? Immediately, her mind conjured up a lurid image of a huge boil exploding, the contents seeping out, infecting her further. In sheer panic, she clutched on to the sides of the bath, her knuckles white with pressure. It took a full minute, perhaps even longer, for the panic to subside and the realization to hit that her head no longer ached; the pain had subsided.

At that moment, the door did indeed open. Leo had gone downstairs and said something about her not being quite right after all.

"Are you okay?" a breathless Aiden said, throwing himself down beside her.

"I'm fine," she replied, grinning. "Absolutely fine."

After shooing Aiden back downstairs, Tara grabbed a towel, wrapped it round her, and rushed to her bedroom. It was true, she *did* feel fine, her headache non-existent. A reprieve granted, if only for the day. A prayer answered, for now, at least.

"Thank you," she whispered, although who it was she was thanking, she didn't know. Still, she repeated the sentence a dozen times before she felt able to stop.

Leo came back into the room. "Who are you talking to?" she asked.

Who indeed? She couldn't explain. Instead, she suggested they start doing their hair and makeup. She glanced at her watch; it was just after ten.

"Yikes, we haven't got long."

She and Aiden were due to exchange vows on the beach at noon. Then, in true Aussie-style, there would be a barbecue, music, and dancing. Somewhere around sunset, she imagined guests would start departing for home. Layla, Hannah, and Penny had offered to go down to the beach early this morning to set everything up. She had gratefully accepted. She looked forward to seeing their handiwork.

The sisters set to work, giggling like the schoolgirls they had once been as they messed about with colors, with brushes, different looks and textures.

"Hey, not too much," Tara said. "You look better *au natural.*"

Leo looked at her, her head to one side. "You know, you do too," she said.

Without further comment, they quickly removed the war paint they had slapped on and started again, this time in not such a heavy-handed fashion.

"Much nicer," Leo decided after Tara had applied just some gold eye shadow and brown kohl around her eyes and a tawny-colored lipstick.

Reaching across for the bronzer, she dabbed just a bit of it on Tara's cheeks, chin, and nose, declaring both her and her handiwork "perfect."

Tara's hair was next. Leo stood behind her, teasing her bleached-blond strands into spikes. Funky was the look she was going for—funky but chic. In contrast, Leo's hair was like spun silk, her curls shimmering whenever the light caught them.

The dress fit perfectly, and the shoes gave Tara the height she craved. Putting on the bracelet last, she stepped back and asked her sister what she thought.

"There's something missing."

"Really? What?"

Without answering, Leo rushed off to her room and returned only moments later.

"This," she said, holding a pale blue garter triumphantly aloft. "Something blue…and sexy."

Taking it from her, Tara tried it on for size. Once it was in place, she pulled a face. "There's still something missing," Tara said, repeating her sister's words.

"What?" Leo looked aghast.

"A sixpence for my shoe."

"A sixpence?"

"*Something old, something new, something borrowed, something blue. And a silver sixpence in her shoe.* That's the rhyme, Leo. My dress is old — well, vintage — and my shoes are new. I've borrowed Mum's citrine ring, and now I've got something blue. But that silver sixpence, I don't know what I'm going to do about it."

Leo appeared to be thinking hard. "I know," she said after a few moments, her eyes, blue like Tara's, lighting up. "Perhaps Mrs. O'Brien's got one stashed away somewhere. You know, the old lady who lives next door to the village store? It's feasible. She's about a hundred years old. I'll go there right now and see."

Tara burst out laughing. "I'm only teasing, sis. I've got everything I need." Stepping forward, she hugged Leo before adding, "And *everyone.*"

"Oh, Tara." Leo's voice cracked. "You look stunning." Pulling away slightly, she continued, "And you're definitely okay? I wasn't sure earlier. You looked really peaky all of a sudden, as if you were going to pass out or something."

"I told you, just last-minute nerves getting the better of me," Tara assured her. "Now, come on. Let's go and show Mum and Dad how pretty we can be when we try."

chapter thirty

Aiden had already gone to the beach to wait for Tara—Joseph had agreed to drive him there. Outside her parents' cottage, she hugged her father and then her mother.

"Hey, no tears. We agreed that," Tara said.

"Oh, don't mind me, dear." Her mother waved a conciliatory hand in the air. "Happy tears—they're allowed, surely?"

Leo rushed out—she had been busy adjusting her hair in the hallway mirror—and all four of them squeezed into her father's Vauxhall and drove toward World's End.

On arrival, it wasn't just Tara who gasped at the sight before her; her parents and sister did too. Whatever she had expected, it had been surpassed. The girls, along with Joseph, Jim, and Mick, had erected a cream-colored gazebo just out of reach of the tide. Under it stood tables heaped with food ready to be barbecued and three different gas stoves—one for carnivores, one for pescetarians, and one for vegetarians. There were tall-stemmed glasses too, rows and rows of them, bottles of champagne on ice as well as plenty of soft drinks for those who were driving. Band instruments were set up to the right of the gazebo—an acoustic set—Jim, Ryan, and Curtis in position. As soon as Tara had stepped out of the car, they had started playing "Here Comes the Bride"—not part of their usual repertoire, she was sure.

When she saw two elaborately decorated porta-potties, Tara had to do a double-take—the blue boxes, one for the girls and one for the boys, had been made much of as well. Bunting had been festooned over the top of them, and in front, someone had erected a wooden signpost with the words "The Watering Hole" marked in black. From the signpost hung corks on strings—a nod to the Antipodean amongst them. When Tara had announced she wanted her wedding on the beach, all that had concerned her had been the romance of it. Certain practicalities hadn't crossed her mind. Thankfully, they had crossed someone's—a lot of people were going to be very grateful for that.

At the sight of Tara and her family, those sitting on brightly-colored picnic rugs rose to join those who were already standing to clap and cheer their arrival. There were even a few whoops and wolf whistles. She knew who'd be responsible for those—Crazy-Boy et al. As well as his usual exuberant self, there was Del, Murray, Nico, and Alice, and her mother's sister Jean and her family. Other faces too, friends she had grown up with and then grown apart from, together again despite the silent years. Layla stood with Hannah, Penny, Richard, and the baby to one side of the group. Mick and Joseph, she noticed, stood on the side farthest from them. She homed in on Layla and Joseph. Although they were smiling, the strain they had both endured in the last few days was clear. Hopefully, Plan A would be enough to thaw the arctic temperatures between them. If not, she'd have to be more aggressive.

At the forefront of all the people who made up her world, past and present, stood Aiden. Love and pride seemed to ooze from him; she could almost see both emotions forming a halo around him, shimmering in the sun. She briefly wondered if she had indeed passed into another realm; he seemed too heavenly to be true.

As she drew closer, she felt like she was falling again, but this time further in love. A part of her was amazed that such a thing was possible. If Aiden was awed by the sight of her, she was awed by him. As she had predicted, he looked edible in his linen suit.

Layla, Penny, and Hannah asked everyone to form an avenue that Tara, on the arm of her father, could walk down. Everyone shuffled into place, except Nico, who busied herself scattering rose petals for Tara to walk on—red, the color of passion, but also of anger, a color that suited a few moods here today.

Standing at the head of the aisle, her father beside her, Tara surreptitiously pinched herself to make sure she wasn't dreaming any of this; it was so surreal. *Everything*—her friends, the weather, the tide, her headache subsiding—seemed to have conspired to bring her the perfect day. She had never felt so…well…so *alive*.

The silence was almost reverential as she started walking forward, her nude shoes, as she had told the girls they would be, long since discarded. Instead, her toes connected with sand the same color as the silk dress she wore.

Coming to a standstill beside Aiden, she smiled across at him. "You look lovely," she said. "You'd look better naked, though."

"Cheeky." He grinned, leaning across to steal a quick kiss from her.

David, who was going to read the words they had written to each other, coughed. Like children caught messing about during a lesson, they stood to attention.

Before David could get into his stride, however, Aiden leaned across once more.

"I just want you to know, Mrs. Soon-To-Be-Taylor," he whispered, producing a Coke can ring from his pocket—the ring that meant more to her than diamonds ever could, "that as far as you're concerned, I totally do."

After more clapping, cheering, and hugging, 96 Tears struck up on the guitar and drums, Jim's sexy, gravelly voice suiting the song she had chosen well. She and Aiden had listened to Savage Garden a lot. Their song "Truly Madly Deeply" summed up their love if ever words could. As the first notes rolled out, Aiden, who hadn't known the song she had chosen for their first dance, nodded in recognition—it was the tune he had played in the background when he had asked her to marry him. Stepping dramatically in front of Tara, like some Spanish Matador, he held out his hand to her. Giggling, she accepted it, only to be thrown backward in his arms for a long and lingering kiss. Releasing her lips, he then swirled her round and round, Aiden the Showman coming to the fore.

She had only asked Jim on Thursday morning if they could play this song for them, kicking herself she hadn't thought about it the day before, at least. If she had, it would have given him, Ryan, and Curtis more time to learn it. He had been a sweetheart about it, though.

"No worries at all," he had said, patting his more uncertain-looking band mates heartily on the back. "Come on, boys, back to the studio. We've got work to do."

Halfway through the dance, Aiden dramatically stripped his jacket and tie off and threw both items into the crowd, people almost as excited about catching them as they would be about her bouquet later. Then he grabbed Tara again and, molding her to his body this time, swayed with her from side to side. The crowd loved it, and eventually, at Tara and Aiden's behest, joined in the fun.

Jim's band continued to play, this time songs from *Jagged Shore*—all except the title song, which she had asked him to hold back on. Meanwhile, those in charge of cooking hurried over to their respective stations to get the coals burning. Mick had bagged the fish grill and brought with him practically a day's catch by the looks of it, all kept fresh in iceboxes. Mick chuckled as Aiden and Tara marveled at his haul.

"Thanks so much for doing this." Aiden grabbed his hand and shook it warmly.

"My pleasure." Mick looked truly chuffed to be involved. "Do you know, if I wasn't a fisherman, I'd be a chef? Maybe I'll combine both occupations one day."

"Hey, we can't have this." It was Hannah, coming up behind them.

Wondering what was wrong, Tara turned swiftly around.

"You haven't got a glass of champagne, neither of you. Come on, take these." Hannah pressed two flutes filled to the brim with bubbles into their hands.

Much to their bemusement, Hannah produced a whistle and blew it to get everyone's attention. When people had quietened, she raised her voice.

"To the new Mr. and Mrs. Taylor," she roared.

Both Tara and Aiden held their glasses aloft, followed swiftly by everybody else. The applause was almost deafening this time. Tara had to cover one ear with her free hand, but she laughed as she did so.

Before Hannah could disappear back into the crowd, Tara reached out for her.

"How's it going between Layla and Joseph?"

Hannah pulled a face. "Honestly? It isn't. Even when they're standing right in front of each other, they're looking through each other."

Tara sighed. *Okay,* she thought. *Plan A, let's roll you out.*

Although guests were happy enough to sit on picnic rugs to eat or stand around in groups, for Aiden, Tara, and her parents as well as a few of the more elderly guests, a long table had been erected. Around it were placed an odd assortment of chairs, some brought from the pub, Tara knew, and others simple fold-up chairs borrowed from friends' houses. The table was also makeshift. Richard had explained to Tara earlier that he and Joseph had asked permission from the man who rented Joseph's cottage if they could rummage around in the shed at the bottom of the garden. When he had left for Florence, Joseph had stored a lot of his carpentry tools in there. The tenant, an easy-going guy, was only too happy to let them. They had grabbed several sheets of plywood, a few carpenter trestles, and *voilà*—a table was born, right here on the beach. To cover up its roughness, the girls had artfully arranged crisp white tablecloths on top, strewn with more flower petals—not just red this time but softened with pink and cream. No paper plates for the guests of honor; white chinaware and silver cutlery had been perfectly laid out instead.

Happiness seemed to make everyone ravenous. Chatter and laughter quieted as everyone concentrated on their food instead. Tara's appetite hadn't been right for a long time, but today she managed to eat a decent plateful, steering clear of the meat and concentrating on Mick's fish and a side of fresh green salad.

After everyone had eaten and returned their plates to the gazebo, they settled themselves in front of the head table.

"Oh, right, yeah, the bridegroom's speech," said Aiden, looking tentative for the first time.

"You're not losing it now, are you?" Tara playfully jibed.

"Lose?" he replied, holding her gaze. "I don't intend to lose anything."

Rising to his feet, he took an empty wine glass and banged a silver spoon against it. As is tradition, he made a show of clearing his throat before speaking.

"Thank you so much to everybody for coming to our wedding. I realize it was a little impromptu, but you know what?" He looked at Tara and winked. "That's just the way we roll. And guys, particularly Layla, Hannah, Penny, Richard, Joseph, Jim, Curtis, and Ryan—shoot me if I've missed anyone—we will never be able to thank you enough for what you've done for us. This day is perfect. It's beyond perfect, and you've helped make it that way, every one of you." Looking again at Tara, he continued, "I know I speak for both of us when I say we feel truly blessed."

Although she was sure no one else in the crowd could, she detected a slight tremor in Aiden's voice. Now was as good a time as any to intervene, to say what she had to say—use words as weapons, but this time in the kindest sense.

Rising too, she took hold of Aiden's hands, looked into his eyes, and said, "We *are* blessed—to have each other, our family, and our friends. I love you, sweetheart. Long may blessings continue to rain down on us."

Yes, Aiden was definitely starting to crack. Leaning over to him, she whispered, "Rest your laurels, hun. I'll take it from here."

As he returned gratefully to his seat, she turned to face her audience. Some of them had caught on to his emotional mood and were dabbing at their eyes with napkins, others were sniffing, and others still sat there with beatific smiles on their faces, reveling in the splendor of the day. Sticking out like sore thumbs were Joseph and Layla, both of them at opposite ends to each other still, both of them in almost identical poses, gazing not at the bride and groom as everyone else was but at the ground, as though sand were suddenly the most fascinating thing in the world.

She cleared her throat too before she spoke. "Like Aiden, I want to thank you also—not just for creating paradise on a Cornish beach but for turning up to celebrate with us at such short notice. I know you all lead busy lives, and we're grateful that you could fit us in. I promise when we renew our vows, years from now, on this same beach, we'll give you a bit more notice."

The crowd laughed, as did Aiden. Well, a girl could dream, Tara thought.

Turning her attention to Aiden, she continued, "And you, my gorgeous Ozzie beach bum, I want to thank you too—for your love, for your courage, your humor, and your belief. At a time when I lacked three of those qualities, you stood firm, and in doing so, you strengthened me. What I never lacked, though, was love. The love I have for you will last through time and space, through the ages, because love doesn't die. It's the one thing that's eternal." Hearing her own voice catch slightly, she turned to her parents. "And that goes for you too. I love you, Mum and Dad. Thanks for giving Leo and me the best childhood two kids could have. And, Dad, do you remember what you used to say to us when we were younger? 'You have wings; don't be afraid to use them.' I want to thank you also for encouraging us to fly."

Pushing her chair back, she went to her mother and father and gave them each a hug and Leo too — "my playmate, my best friend."

Returning to the spot in front of her chair, she took a deep breath. "But as wonderful as love is, I don't think there's one amongst us who'd disagree with me when I say it's not for the fainthearted. So easily it can take a wrong turn, and when it does, it can hurt — like a wrecking ball aimed straight at the heart. Belief and trust are essential ingredients in any relationship, but sometimes they're tested and often in the strangest of ways. If you're thrown a curve ball, the best thing to do is catch it."

There, that had got Layla and Joseph's attention. She also noticed Penny look up sharply, and Hannah too. Hmm, what were their stories?

"We all make mistakes; the trick is not to let those mistakes own you. Or tear you apart. Love is about forgiveness; it's about giving second chances when second chances are deserved. It's also about forgiving yourself." Looking at Aiden, she continued. "My belief and my trust were tested — not in Aiden, but in myself. But I was given another chance. I won't let them waiver again." As he smiled at her, she looked away, sought out Joseph once more. He was looking directly at her now, but there was a reticence in his eyes. Even with the distance between them, she could tell that. Briefly, she glanced at Layla. If she had to find a word to describe how she looked right now, she'd choose beaten.

"That curve ball I was talking about, sometimes we drop it, sometimes we run. That's the only option open to us, or so we think. But guess what? It doesn't solve a thing. I've run from two people in my life — two amazing people. When I think how amazing they are…" Tara faltered slightly. Before continuing, she swallowed hard. "But the good news is, miracles do happen. I've got them both back, one as a friend and one as my husband. Running sucks — especially when it's cross country."

Again, some people laughed, but mostly people sat or stood in silence. She'd bet that if someone dropped a hatpin right now, she'd hear it.

"I know enough about love to recognize when it's real between two people. And when it's real, it's incredible. And by incredible, I mean it's a gift. Damn it, I'm telling you, if waves are coming at you — big waves, crazy waves, waves that seem insurmountable — ride them. Weather the storm, because in between blue skies, they're going to keep on coming. Stand together, stand strong, and you'll survive."

The crowd rose almost simultaneously to their feet. There was clapping, stamping, and yelling. Thank goodness the couple that resided in the house overlooking the beach had long since moved out; they'd probably call the police again at such a commotion, thought Tara. It was even more deafening than before. She also noticed some people throwing their arms around their partners if they had one, and if not a partner, a friend. She seemed to have struck a chord in everyone. Almost everyone.

Aiden stood too and put his arms around her.

"Nice one, babe. Do you think that hit the spot?"

When she didn't reply, his eyes followed her line of sight, straight to Layla and Joseph — as far apart as they had ever been.

chapter thirty-one

"Ah, crap, they're still not talking." Penny sidled up to Tara in the queue for the loos to give her the latest report.

"I know," Tara sighed. "I didn't want to do what I'm going to have to do. Joseph is such a private person, but if the mountain won't come to Mohammad—"

"We take Mohammad to the mountain," Penny finished.

"Exactly."

Penny was just about to ask her what she had in mind exactly when Hannah came over to join them, looking more than a little flustered.

"Leo and Jim, they're getting on well, aren't they?"

Both Penny and Tara looked over to where Hannah's eyes seemed to be fixated. She was right; they were. Leo's laugh was loud and uproarious, slightly affected, perhaps? Jim didn't seem to mind. He seemed to be enjoying the attention.

"Oh, she's always had a crush on him," Tara commented, almost absent-mindedly. "She used to follow him round like a puppy dog when she was younger."

Hannah stiffened even more.

"Shall we go over and say hi?" Penny said, sensing Hannah was champing at the bit to do just that, and not because she wanted to make a new friend.

Hannah made a short, sharp movement with her head—a yes, then.

To Tara, Penny said, "I'll catch you later."

"Not too much later." Tara winked back. "We've got Plan B to implement."

"Plan B?" said Hannah.

"Erm, yeah, come on," said Penny, hurrying her along.

"Hi, Jim. Hi, Leo. Mind if we join you?" she said, shoving Hannah at Jim.

Hannah glared at Penny but wasted no time in linking her arm through his, again not for reasons of affection, but to highlight to a certain someone this particular band singer was very much taken. Penny snuck a glance at Leo. Disappointment was evident in her face, but she had the good grace to quickly cover it.

"Hey." Jim extracted his arm from Hannah, and a tense moment ensued—surely he wasn't going to brush her off? To Penny's relief, and she was sure to Hannah's also, it was only to place his arm round her shoulders instead. "This is Hannah, my girlfriend, and Penny, my friend. This is Leo, Tara's sister. We grew up together."

"Pleased to meet you." Penny smiled, extending her hand. Hannah, however, kept hers firmly plastered by her side, affording Leo only the faintest of smiles.

"I was just saying," Leo said, addressing her words solely to Hannah, "how talented 96 Tears are. No wonder they're doing well. World domination calls, I think."

"They're great, yeah," Hannah mumbled back. "I've said so right from the start."

The word "start" she emphasized. Clearly, she wanted Leo to know she wasn't the only one who had history with Jim.

"Loads of gigs on the cards, then?" Leo questioned further, but not Jim, Hannah still.

"Yeah, quite a few." Hannah looked puzzled now. Penny knew Hannah was wondering why the questions were aimed at her, not Jim.

Jim meanwhile continued to look amused.

"That's going to be hard," Leo said, playing nonchalantly with her curls.

"What is?" Hannah's eyebrows had furrowed.

"Fighting off the groupies. You've landed yourself one hot man."

Hannah looked amazed Leo could be so bold, but then she looked worried, as if the idea hadn't occurred to her before. Very worried, in fact.

"Good job he adores you, isn't it?" Leo finished off. "We were saying that as well."

And with that she turned and disappeared into the crowd, but not before Penny saw the smirk on her face. Hannah looked up at Jim, not half as amused as he was.

"What's the matter, Hannah?" he asked, raising an eyebrow. "Jealous?"

Hannah rolled her eyes in a show of disgust. And then she smiled. "I might be," she answered, tightening her grip on him further.

"The only groupie I want is you," he assured her, leaning in for a kiss.

Her work here done, Penny left them to smooch and went in search of Layla. If Tara's words hadn't had an obvious effect on Joseph, they must have had on her.

As Penny weaved her way through the crowds, Richard caught her attention. He was pointing somewhat frantically to Scarlett, who was arching her back in the Bugaboo, trying to fight her way free. "Help?" he mouthed hopefully.

She held up both hands and wriggled her fingers.

"Give me ten," she mouthed back, trying not to laugh at how demoralized he looked at the prospect of ten more minutes of continued sole childcare.

Where was Layla anyway? She hadn't seen her in the last hour. Penny stopped short. *Oh no, she hasn't done a runner, has she?* Slipped away unnoticed?

To her relief, the crowd in front of her dispersed, and there Layla was, gathering paper plates and taking them back to the gazebo to throw in bin bags. She seemed thoroughly absorbed in what she was doing, even though the task was so mundane.

Penny quickly caught up with her. "Hey, Layla, don't worry about clearing up yet. We'll get stuck into that later. I've got an army of people willing to pitch in. It won't take long."

"It's okay," Layla insisted, carrying on tidying. "I'm happy to make a start."

Penny caught at her arm this time. "Layla, listen to me. Stop. You've got more important things to be doing than this."

To her surprise, Layla shrugged her off. "No, Penny, I haven't."

Hesitating, but only for a second, Penny proceeded to take the empty plates from her friend's hands and placed them down on the table in front of her.

"Layla, let's not beat about the bush. You should be talking to Joseph, not bloody clearing up."

"This is not the time or the place," Layla said, her eyes averted.

"It couldn't get any more perfect than right here, right now, on this beach." Risking being brushed off again, she reached out to hold Layla's hands. "Look at me. Didn't you listen to a word Tara said, her speech? It was about you, you and Joseph." She faltered slightly. "Well, apart from the stuff about Aiden and her family, that is."

"He's flying back to Florence tomorrow. Did you know that?"

Penny was taken aback. She did know, but she didn't think Layla did. "I...erm. He told you?"

"Hannah told me. She thought it only right I should know. She said she'd had enough of people keeping secrets round here," Layla finished pointedly.

Penny considered this for a moment. "When did she tell you?"

"Yesterday."

"And you didn't tell me?"

"You knew already, by the looks of it."

Following in Hannah's footsteps, Penny decided to come clean. Hannah was right; secrets led to trouble, which in turn led to disaster—or so it seemed.

"Tara told me," Penny confessed.

"Oh." Layla's shoulders slumped in defeat.

"When are you going back?" Penny asked.

"To Florence? I've decided not to. I'm going to Milan instead."

"To your mum's?"

Layla nodded. "For a while anyway."

"Does Joseph know?"

A cynical smile made Layla look even more tragic. "He hasn't asked, so, no, he doesn't know."

"But what about your job, your clothes, your stuff?"

"Penny, I don't care about *stuff* right now, okay?"

"Okay, okay." Penny let go of Layla's hands and held her own up in appeasement.

"It can all be sorted out later. Stefania's a good friend. She'll understand."

"Yeah, no, I'm sure. Oh, Layla…" Penny wanted to hug her.

As if sensing this, Layla took a step back. "I'm busy, Penny. Let me go."

Balking at Layla's choice of words, Penny could only watch as she turned away and began engrossing herself once again in the business of plates.

So frustrated she thought she might explode, she went in search of Joseph next. Again, she bypassed Richard.

"How long now?" It was not a question; it was a definite plea. Scarlett was in his arms by now and not looking particularly happy about that either.

"Another five minutes," Penny promised, hurrying past.

Thankfully, Richard was deterred from protesting further as a group of young women appeared out of nowhere and surrounded him, cooing and pointing at the less-than-impressed bundle in his arms. The babe, it seemed, was a babe magnet.

Joseph was talking to a man Penny hadn't seen before.

She went marching up to them and without pause took hold of Joseph's arm and said, "We need to speak."

His partner in conversation looked taken aback, but, Penny reasoned, explanations could be given later.

"What is it?" Joseph said, hastily disentangling his arm from hers.

"Like you don't know," Penny retorted.

Repeating almost exactly the same words as Layla, he said, "Penny, this is not the time or the place."

"What are you? Cosmic twins?" she replied, shaking her head in disbelief.

"Cosmic what?"

"Oh, never mind. We have to talk now. You're leaving tomorrow."

"Because I have to work," Joseph reminded her.

"And that takes precedence over everything else, does it? *Everyone* else."

"Yes," he responded simply. "It does."

"You're making a mistake."

"I told you; I don't want to talk about it right now."

She continued as if he hadn't spoken. "The biggest mistake of your life—"

"Penny…"

"—if you walk away, if you get on that plane."

"It's none of your business."

None of her business? She could swipe him! "You're a coward."

His jaw tightened. "And how do you make that out?"

"Because you're blaming Layla entirely for what's happened. You won't accept that you were unreasonable too. What you asked of her, it was too much."

"To trust me?" he replied, still stone-faced.

Penny held firm. "Under the circumstances, yes."

"Maybe for some people, but I thought better of her."

"Well, now you know. You shouldn't put people on pedestals. Layla, she's human; she gets it wrong, just like me, just like Richard, oh…and, guess what, just like you."

He faltered. Was she getting through to him?

"I thought we had more than we did," he said at last.

"What you have is more than enough."

Again he hesitated. Seizing the moment, she begged. "Talk to her, please. Sort this mess out."

"Penny." She had to concede, he sounded as frustrated as she felt. "I've been here all day, since early morning, the same as her. She hasn't even looked at me."

"Stop making excuses," she growled.

"I'm not," he said. "I've made no secret of where I'm staying either, at Mick's."

Penny was the one to falter now. He was right. Layla had known his whereabouts at all times.

"You told her to stay away," she replied, determined to carry on the defense.

"I didn't."

Seriously? She thought back to the night they had argued—he *had* told her to stay away. He must have done. But there were so many words that night, being flung like tennis balls, she had to admit she didn't know for sure. She had just presumed.

Still she persisted. "You should fight for her."

He seemed to consider this, the sadness that drowned out the light in his eyes almost unbearable. Finally he replied. "And maybe she should fight for me."

His reply nearly sent her over the edge. She could scream! How could they do this to each other? How could two people so obviously in love let go so easily? But the sad fact was it happened all the time. It had nearly happened to her and Richard, and not just the once, either. She was about to say more, but as Layla had done earlier, he turned his back on her and walked away, disappearing within seconds.

Sighing heavily, she made her way back to Tara, avoiding Richard astutely this time. Coming up beside her, Penny gestured she needed a word. Quickly, Tara made her excuses, and together they found a quiet space beside the wedding table.

"I've just spoken to both Joseph and Layla," Penny confided.

"And?" Tara said eagerly.

"Words aren't enough. This Plan B of yours, what's it all about?"

Her comrade in arms leaned forward and whispered in her ear.

As Tara spoke, Penny smiled. "I see what you mean now about Mohammed and the mountain," she said. "When do we implement it?"

Tara looked at her watch.

"Wait just a bit longer—the sun will be setting soon. We'll do it then."

"Going for maximum romantic impact?"

"Pulling out all the stops," Tara agreed.

Holding up her wrist, Penny said, "Okay, let's synchronize watches."

As they did so, Tara reiterated, "In half an hour, I'll make the announcement."

"But what if Plan B isn't enough either? What then?"

Tara looked away briefly as though she were busy contemplating. As she did so, Penny could hardly catch her breath. This *had* to work. Time was running out. They had no more aces to play. When Tara looked back at her, Penny was amazed to note she didn't look troubled at all by the prospect of failure.

"Penny," she said, flashing that thousand-watt smile of hers. "Have a little faith."

chapter thirty-two

A few people, those who had far to travel, had already said their good-byes to Tara and Aiden. It was getting late, and the sun would be setting soon, bringing the party to a natural end. Discreetly, Layla, as well as several others, continued to clear away debris as well as filling boots of cars with plates, cutlery, bottles, and glasses that were no longer needed. The gazebo would be taken down at the last minute and the porta-potties collected in the morning by the supplier. The beach would belong to no one but itself again.

As she continued to work diligently, Layla thought back to the last truly happy day she'd had—the morning before Joseph had come home to tell her he had met Tara again. She had made him late for work, but he hadn't minded one bit, their bodies melding and their minds too. She had never been happier. She had perhaps never been so blind either to the needs of those around her. Everything that had happened since, perhaps she deserved it.

She shivered. The April skies had been bright, but as the sun faded, so did its warmth. Crazy-Boy and Del had taken it upon themselves to build a bonfire, collecting bits of driftwood from all around and piling them high. After several attempts, the fire had caught light, and clusters of people were huddled around it, suffused in a golden glow. There'd be fireworks later too, the final celebration.

How she wished she'd brought a jacket. If she was with Joseph, she would have borrowed his and wrapped it round her. Heck, she would have wrapped *him* round her. That would have kept her warm, guaranteed. Again, she wondered where he had gotten the suit he was wearing today. She knew he hadn't brought it with him. Most likely he had borrowed it from Jim—it was a charcoal-gray linen suit, and he had worn it with an open-necked white shirt. He had never looked so handsome.

She had to stop what she was doing momentarily and collect herself. All day she had coped by chasing thoughts of him from her mind, by not even making eye contact. Even so, she had felt his close proximity acutely, known where he was with every minute that had passed. How was that possible, against a backdrop of so many people? A beautiful day for everyone, it had been torture for her. She only hoped she had hidden it well. Tonight, in no time at all, he would be leaving for Mick's, and in the morning for Florence. When she might see him again, she didn't know. Panic seized her, but she batted it away.

She checked her watch. The day would be over soon—not long now until she could find sanctuary in Hannah's spare bedroom, give rein, albeit silent rein, to the feelings crashing about inside her, until she could stop pretending to be happy.

The high-pitched squeal of a whistle interrupted her thoughts. Momentarily confused, she looked around. It was Tara, obviously about to make an announcement. She must have borrowed the whistle from Hannah, who had been using it at pivotal moments all day—to herald the toast, the speech, when the food was ready. It was certainly an effective attention-grabber. Stopping what she was doing, she stepped forward along with others to hear what Tara was about to say.

"Ladies and gents, I want to say thank you all again so much for coming today. *You* are what's made our day special, every one of you."

Someone piped up, "No, Tara, thank *you*. It's been magical." Strong murmurs of agreement rippled through the crowd.

"It *has* been magical," Tara replied. "And I want the magic to continue. No…" She shook her head and laughed as a few double entendres were thrown her way. "I don't mean just for me and Aiden; I mean for all of us. I don't want anyone to go away with a sad heart today. I want your hearts to be like ours, bursting with love."

Impossible, thought Layla, her expression deliberately sanguine.

"I know some guests have had to leave already, but those of you who are still here, please bear with me for a bit longer. I can't let you go just yet. You see, we've had the first dance, but to round the day off, there has to be a last dance too."

Mystified looks and queries were exchanged. The Last Dance—what was that?

"But we're not going to be the ones to see you out," Tara continued. "Aiden and I—we need to save our energy for later." And this time she did wink lasciviously, to everyone's delight. "Instead, I'd like two of our friends to do the honors for us."

People started looking round—who could she possibly mean?

"Penny..." Tara started, and Layla felt relief rush through her. It was Penny and Richard who would take the last dance, a good choice. "...could you get everyone to form a circle?"

What?

"Jim..."

Oh, okay, it was to be Jim and Hannah. Just as good.

"Take up position, please, with Curtis and Ryan."

Take up position?

Mystified, Layla watched as all three band members shuffled back toward their instruments. She then looked around her. Who else did Tara have in mind?

The guitars started up first and then the drums. Layla recognized the tune straightaway. It was the first few chords to 96 Tears' most popular song, "Jagged Shore." She had wondered earlier why they hadn't played it, had meant to ask.

Tara started to speak again.

"Joseph..."

Joseph? What the hell?

"Layla..."

No, she wouldn't. She knew the situation, what had happened between them.

"Take it away."

At the mention of both their names, Layla's heart stopped beating; she was absolutely certain of it. At the same time, she felt hot and cold wash over her in alternate waves. Her stomach heaved; she was going to be sick, right here and now, in front of everyone. How awful! She mustn't be sick; she must stay in control. But how? Her arms, her legs, her entire body started shaking like a pneumatic drill.

Where was he? Where was Joseph? When the crowd had formed a circle, she had temporarily lost sight of him. Frantically, her eyes sought him out. There he was, being pushed forward by Penny—a *smug*-looking Penny, if she wasn't mistaken, smug as well as something else. Determined. Layla's eyes locked with his, just for a moment before she had to look away again, but it was time enough to register the effect the Last Dance was having on him. He was as horror-struck as she was.

Jim started singing the first verse—soft, sweet words about finding love and then losing it. Ryan was playing the harmonica too, such a haunting sound. She had loved this song from the minute she had first heard it—it had been her favorite on the album—but not once did she think she would be able to apply its sentiment so keenly to herself. His voice, those words, seemed to bounce off the granite rocks surrounding them and fly straight back at her, increasing in amplification as they did so, taunting her—although Jim, she knew, would never taunt anyone. In contrast, the crowd had hushed entirely. She was the center of attention now, she and Joseph.

If it wasn't for Tara, she would have turned and walked away. She knew without a doubt that Joseph would have done the same. As excruciating as this was for her, it must be even more so for him. He liked to keep his private life exactly that, private. Tara was well aware what he was like, so why had she done this? Humiliate them both so publicly, compound their pain? Why take the knife and drive it farther in?

She couldn't move forward; she just couldn't.

"Guys," nudged Tara.

But she had to. She couldn't refuse the bride on her wedding day. Neither could Joseph. Her wish was quite literally their command. She had to be brave enough to enter the space between them—a space as forbidding as no man's land.

Forcing one foot in front of the other, it seemed Joseph mirrored her actions—slow, measured, and reluctant—until gradually the distance between them lessened. The lyrics that accompanied such movement were beautiful and poignant, sung with a plaintive edge, a pleading almost. Such a shame that plea would fall on deaf ears.

There was barely even a foot between them now. What should she do? This was supposed to be a dance; she couldn't just stand there. She had to reach out to him, hold him in some way. That's what you did when you danced with someone; you held them. Tentatively, she raised both hands and placed them on either side of his waist, cringing as she did so, expecting him to brush her off and to do so none too gently either. Thankfully he didn't. Like her, he seemed resigned to continuing this ridiculous charade and placed both his hands on her hips.

As her own body had felt strange to her earlier, now his did too. How was that so? They knew every inch of each other, had taken time to explore at leisure. She knew his smell—subtle, male, and addictive. She knew his taste—divine. He shouldn't feel like a stranger.

She attempted to sway—she couldn't just stand there—but her movements were imperceptible, she knew. In contrast, he didn't move at all, but she could feel his eyes bore into her, although she wasn't brave enough to lift her head, to meet his gaze.

Jim had reached the chorus.

Drift back to shore,
This jagged shore.
Don't leave me standing here alone,
Baby, come back to me.

It was sound advice to follow, perhaps, if the shore was in sight. But in such a short space of time, she seemed to have lost sight of everything, of what had even anchored her in the first place. And still she drifted, from the friends who surrounded her, the bride and the groom, the beach itself. They faded to nothing around her. She thought she was drifting alone—she fully expected to be—and was surprised to find she wasn't. With a start, she realized Joseph was drifting beside her, the two of them together, his hands still on her hips, hers still about his waist. This feeling, of being the only two in the universe, she had experienced it before—on the first night of her runaway year.

Should she allow herself to remember it? It seemed she had no choice. Joseph had walked her home after she had spent the evening with him and Hannah and Jim at the Trecastle Inn. She remembered she had been slightly tipsy, fumbling for the key to the door of her new home—The Outlook. Finally locating it, she had swung round to say good-bye to the man waiting patiently behind her. And that's when it had happened, when the world had melted like butter around them.

The first time they had made love, the world had stopped too. She hadn't intended to bed him on that long-ago night. They had been friends—good friends—and he had come over for dinner, not an unusual occurrence. He lived next door, and they regularly ate together. But on that spring evening, with the promise of summer in the air, desire had hit from nowhere and consumed her—consumed him too. He had moved not just inside her body but in her soul, because that's what he was—her soul mate, and she was his. How could she have doubted that when it was clear he never had? Instead, she had allowed past hurts to destroy her future and readily so.

There was no way she could suppress anymore the emotions she'd been suppressing all week—the despair, the disappointment, in herself, not him, the shame and self-loathing that had kept her from his door—from begging for a forgiveness she felt she didn't deserve. Every single feeling surged to the surface, but in among such bleakness was something else, something stronger, more determined. This couldn't be their Last Dance. There had to be a way back, no matter how tenuous. This man in front of her, she could live without him if she had to; she had lived alone before. But it would be an empty life, a scarred one, a life in which she'd only ever go through the motions, depthless. She welcomed the new emotion, let it take hold, become the most powerful of them all.

"Joseph…" she started, determined to make him understand that she loved him, would spend her lifetime loving him if he would let her, and not only that, but *trusting* him, because that's what he deserved, nothing less. And in her head, she was explaining, her words delivered in a neat and orderly fashion, packing quite a punch, actually. So, how come she could hear no sound other than Jim and his band?

"Joseph…" she tried again. What was wrong with her? This was no time for the power of speech to up and leave. Tara had said it was important to forgive—not just others but yourself. But if she let him go, she'd never forgive herself that.

All too quickly, the band wrapped up the final notes of the song. How she wanted them to play on and on. It was too quiet now—*expectant*. Still she tried to force words from her mouth. What she had to say wasn't a secret; let everyone hear what was in her heart. But the silence continued, growing heavier. She could damn herself well enough with words, it seemed, but save herself? That was proving harder.

Get a grip, Layla. Get a grip. She *would* save this relationship. She would not let him walk away. And if he did, she'd follow him.

But if he doesn't love you…

Could love die that quickly? Of course not. Why was she still doubting, still so flawed? And if he couldn't forgive her, was he flawed too or justified? The trouble was, she couldn't decide.

Tears of frustration started to fall, and she was powerless to stop them. Quickly, she removed her hands from his waist and covered her face. He would hate that she was making such an exhibition of herself and, by proxy, him. She had tried so hard to fight, but she had failed. All she had succeeded in doing was embarrassing them both.

Fervently, she hoped Penny or Hannah would come to her rescue, but the seconds dragged on, each one an intolerable length. Where were they when she needed them? Couldn't they see the state she was in? What were they doing?

And then she was in someone's arms, but they were not soft and feminine. They were hard and strong. Whose arms was she in? Had Jim rushed over? Richard?

She looked up. No, it was not Jim or Richard. It was Joseph who had his arms around her, tears in his eyes too. One had even escaped, leaving a trail down his cheek. She was momentarily stunned. She had never seen him cry before.

"I'm sorry," he said, his words not a whisper but loud and clear, discernible to all.

Still incredulous, she looked at him. He *was* sorry. And it was right that he was. She couldn't shoulder the guilt alone anymore. It was too much. She needed him to share the load. Before she could echo him, however, whisper her own apology, his lips were on hers, one hand cradling the back of her head, the other holding her lower half so hard against him, she didn't know where she ended and he began. Countless times he had kissed her in the past, but not like this, not so deeply.

As Layla came back to the world and all who were in it, fireworks started exploding around them. Everyone's attention was drawn from them to the skies above—everyone's except Tara's. Her eyes sought Layla's and caused her again to gasp in wonder. What shone in them no firework could match.

After waving a beaming Tara and Aiden off in her father's car—they were going to spend their wedding night at The Trecastle Hotel, where the bridal suite was all ready for them—Joseph and Layla found themselves the only two people left on the beach. Since the kiss, she hadn't stopped clinging to him, nor had he to her.

Penny and Hannah had swiftly disappeared, not even saying good-bye, just leaving them to it, she supposed. There was still a lot of making-up to do.

Joseph grabbed a picnic rug and a cushion, took her by the arm, and said, "Come this way."

Like a child being led, she followed him farther down the cove. The tide had gone out again and would stay that way for some time.

Joseph laid out the rug and threw down the cushion. Still holding on to her hand, he pulled her down. He then took his jacket and wrapped it round her, leaning over to kiss her briefly on the lips as he did so.

"So," he mused, breaking away. "Jim. Do you think he's got some sort of sixth sense? That song of his, who'd have thought it'd be about us?"

"Well, you know what they say about Cornish people," Layla replied. "They're fey."

Joseph laughed, a sound she'd never be able to get enough of.

"Joseph, I—" she began. Surely she had to say something, explain?

"Don't. There's no need to go over and over it."

"But I have to say it. I haven't yet. I'm sorry."

His reply was equally somber. "It's a sorry situation, and we both made a hash of it. But we can learn. We can move forward, look ahead, not behind us."

He was right. They could learn. They *would* learn. And the here and now, their future, was all that mattered. Because at least they were lucky enough to have one. No longer would she let the past influence her. It was over; it was done with. Finally.

"What about Florence?" she couldn't resist asking. "Are you still going back tomorrow?"

"No," he replied.

"No?"

"Mine was the last seat; you won't be able to get on the plane."

"I could follow a day or so later," she suggested.

Joseph shook his head. "We'll go when we can go together."

For a few minutes, they sat in silence, content to listen only to the ebb and flow of the distant tide. Eventually, Joseph spoke again. "Layla, how would you feel if we didn't go back—permanently, I mean?"

"To Florence? Are you serious? Where would we go instead?"

"That's just it. We'd stay right here, in Trecastle, where home really is. Where our friends are, where we might be needed."

"But Stefania, Paolo..."

"We'll have to work out our notice for sure, but Paolo, he has plenty of carpenters and restorers champing at the bit to help him in the workshop, eager to learn from him. And I know you like working with Stefania, but, Layla, you should be concentrating on writing. That's what you love doing, what you're good at."

"But it doesn't rake in the money, does it? Not yet, anyway. How would we manage?"

He didn't look fazed at all. "We've still got the rent coming in for my cottage. There's a bit left over each month. We can use that to rent too—a flat in the village, or on the outskirts, at least. I'll open up another workshop. I made it work last time; I'll make it work again."

"Stay here?" Layla double-checked, a grin spreading across her face.

"Yes. You and me, where we kick-started."

She'd love it; she knew she would. Florence might be stunning, but it was this part of the world that truly inspired her, that she felt she belonged to as she belonged to him. Had perhaps always belonged to, her entire lifetime.

"Layla..." he prompted. "What do you think?" There was anxiousness in his voice.

"I'll start looking for accommodation straight away."

He smiled at her, that slow-burn smile of his, before grabbing at the cushion and laying it behind her. Pushing her down onto it, he started murmuring in her ear.

"And that reunion scene..."

"What reunion scene?"

"The one in your book."

She pulled away slightly. "I told you, there is no reunion scene..." And then she stopped. "Oh, the *reunion* scene," she said instead. "What about it?"

"I've thought of a way to improve it."

"Improve it?" she questioned.

"To make it mind-blowing, in fact."

She shrugged. "Well, what are you waiting for? Let's put it into action."

As he leaned in to kiss her again, she closed her eyes, but not before noting how bright the stars were up above. It wasn't her imagination. In a Cornish sky, they were so much more dazzling, shining not just for her but for all of them—always.

the end

acknowledgments

Once again, thank you to my trusty band of beta readers for all the feedback, all the suggested changes, and for all your unstinting support and encouragement. Thank you also to the fabulous Omnific Publishing, working with you is always such a pleasure. And thank you too to the readers, I hope you enjoy another rollercoaster ride.

about the author

One of those rare creatures—a true Brightonian—Shani was born and bred in the sunny seaside town of Brighton on the UK's south-coast. One of the first literary conundrums she had to deal with was her own name: Shani can be pronounced in a variety of ways, but in this instance, it's Shay-nee not Shar-ney or Shan-ni, although she does indeed know a Shanni—just to confuse matters further! Hobbies include reading, writing, eating, and drinking—all four of which keep her busy enough. After graduating from Sussex University with a degree in English and American Literature, Shani landed a job at a well-known holiday company. Although employed as a Brochure Production Executive, she promptly reinvented herself as a copywriter, a new position they were happy (if a tad bewildered) to concede to. At twenty-four, Shani became a freelance copywriter and has been one ever since, in between writing novels, that is. Her first book, *The Runaway Year,* is set between Brighton and North Cornwall, the latter a home-from-home for Shani, her husband, and three lovely kids. She also has a penchant for Glastonbury, another magical place, and don't even get her started on Scotland—we'd be here all day!

New Adult Romance

Three Daves by Nicki Elson
Streamline by Jennifer Lane
The Shades series: *Shades of Atlantis* & *Shades of Avalon* by Carol Oates
The Heart series: *Beside Your Heart, Disclosure of the Heart* & *Forever Your Heart*
by Mary Whitney
Romancing the Bookworm by Kate Evangelista
Flirting with Chaos by Kenya Wright
The Vice, Virtue & Video series: *Revealed, Captured, Desired* & *Devoted*
by Bianca Giovanni
Granton University series: *Loving Lies* by Linda Kage

Paranormal Romance

The Light series: *Seers of Light, Whisper of Light* & *Circle of Light* by Jennifer DeLucy
The Hanaford Park series: *Eve of Samhain* & *Pleasures Untold* by Lisa Sanchez
Immortal Awakening by KC Randall
The Seraphim series: *Crushed Seraphim* & *Bittersweet Seraphim* by Debra Anastasia
The Guardian's Wild Child by Feather Stone
Grave Refrain by Sarah M. Glover
The Divinity series: *Divinity* & *Entity* by Patricia Leever
The Blood Vine series: *Blood Vine, Blood Entangled* & *Blood Reunited*
by Amber Belldene
Divine Temptation by Nicki Elson
The Dead Rapture series: *Love in the Time of the Dead* & *Love at the End of Days*
by Tera Shanley
The Hidden Races series: *Incandescent* (book 1) by M.V. Freeman

Romantic Suspense

Whirlwind by Robin DeJarnett
The CONduct series: *With Good Behavior, Bad Behavior* & *On Best Behavior*
by Jennifer Lane
Indivisible by Jessica McQuinn
Between the Lies by Alison Oburia
Blind Man's Bargain by Tracy Winegar

Erotic Romance

The Keyhole series: *Becoming sage* (book 1) by Kasi Alexander
The Keyhole series: *Saving sunni* (book 2) by Kasi & Reggie Alexander
The Winemaker's Dinner: *Appetizers* & *Entrée* by Dr. Ivan Rusilko & Everly Drummond
The Winemaker's Dinner: *Dessert* by Dr. Ivan Rusilko
Client N° 5 by Joy Fulcher

Historical Romance

Cat O' Nine Tails by Patricia Leever
Burning Embers by Hannah Fielding
Seven for a Secret by Rumer Haven

Anthologies

A Valentine Anthology including short stories by
Alice Clayton ("With a Double Oven"),
Jennifer DeLucy ("Magnus of Pfelt, Conquering Viking Lord"),
Nicki Elson ("I Don't Do Valentine's Day"),
Jessica McQuinn ("Better Than One Dead Rose and a Monkey Card"),
Victoria Michaels ("Home to Jackson"), and
Alison Oburia ("The Bridge")

Taking Liberties including an introduction by Tiffany Reisz and short stories by
Mina Vaughn ("John Hancock-Blocked"),
Linda Cunningham ("A Boston Marriage"),
Joy Fulcher ("Tea for Two"),
KC Holly ("The British Are Coming!"),
Kimberly Jensen & Scott Stark ("E. Pluribus Threesome"), and
Vivian Rider ("M'Lady's Secret Service")

Sets

The Heart Series Box Set (*Beside Your Heart, Disclosure of the Heart* &
Forever Your Heart) by Mary Whitney
The CONduct Series Box Set (*With Good Behavior, Bad Behavior* &
On Best Behavior) by Jennifer Lane
The Light Series Box Set (*Seers of Light, Whisper of Light, Circle of Light* &
Glimpse of Light) by Jennifer DeLucy
The Blood Vine Series Box Set (*Blood Vine, Blood Entangled, Blood Reunited* &
Blood Eternal) by Amber Belldene

Singles, Novellas & Special Editions

It's Only Kinky the First Time (A Keyhole series single) by Kasi Alexander
Learning the Ropes (A Keyhole series single) by Kasi & Reggie Alexander
The Winemaker's Dinner: RSVP by Dr. Ivan Rusilko
The Winemaker's Dinner: No Reservations by Everly Drummond
Big Guns by Jessica McQuinn
Concessions by Robin DeJarnett
Starstruck by Lisa Sanchez
New Flame by BJ Thornton

Shackled by Debra Anastasia
Swim Recruit by Jennifer Lane
Sway by Nicki Elson
Full Speed Ahead by Susan Kaye Quinn
The Second Sunrise by Hannah Downing
The Summer Prince by Carol Oates
Whatever it Takes by Sarah M. Glover
Clarity (A *Divinity* prequel single) by Patricia Leever
A Christmas Wish (A *Cocktails & Dreams* single) by Autumn Markus
Late Night with Andres by Debra Anastasia
Poughkeepsie (enhanced iPad app collector's edition) by Debra Anastasia
Poughkeepsie (audio book edition) by Debra Anastasia
Blood Eternal (A Blood Vine series single, epilogue to series) by Amber Belldene
Carnaval de Amor (*The Winemaker's Dinner*, Spanish edition)
by Dr. Ivan Rusilko & Everly Drummond

coming soon from
OMNIFIC PUBLISHING

The Forever series: *Forever Autumn* (book 1) by Christopher Scott Wagner
Something Wicked by Carol Oates
Going the Distance by Julianna Keyes
The Enclave series: *Closer and Closer* (book 1) by Jenna Barton
The Dead Rapture series: *Love Starts with Z* (book 3) by Tera Shanley
The Hidden Races series: *Illumination* (book 2) by M.V. Freeman
Missing Pieces by Meredith Tate